WASHOE COUNTY LIBRARY

3 1235 03762 1443

D0762272

DAWN OF THE DEB

CHAPTER ONE

Trust your gut.

As the owner of the Debutante Detective Agency, and the on-again, off-again girlfriend of a Fort Worth police detective, if there's one thing I've learned the hard way, it's questioning my sixth sense. So on a beautiful winter's day when the sun shone like a big orange thumbprint, melting the snowflakes on my blue-haired grandmother's front porch like slushy doilies, who would've thought I'd live to regret opening the front door?

Gran's chiming doorbell should've been a non-event and shouldn't have made an impression on me at all—except that Gran lives in a multimillion-dollar Dallas mansion with a formidable wrought iron gate that can only be accessed by a computer-chipped key—and nobody had buzzed the intercom asking to be let in. That's when the hair on the back of my neck stood up.

Even though Gran's ultra-exclusive neighborhood tended to be safe, that didn't mean we hadn't had our scary share of trouble since she allowed me to move in last year. Shortly afterward, my soon-to-be-single, undiagnosed alcoholic, out-of-touch father unceremoniously cut me off financially, and then presented me a bill for $1,996,854.78 "for having to raise your spoiled, pampered ass." Then my twenty-one-year-old sister, Teensy, who attracts all sorts of unsavory characters, moved in to recuperate after a bloody, near-death experience in Mexico.

During the previous nine weeks, I'd been cheated on, stalked, kidnapped, held at gunpoint, shot at, bid-on by human traffickers, and generally made to feel unwelcome rattling around in my petite-framed, blue-eyed, blond-haired, alabaster-skinned body. By opening Gran's door, I had no reason to believe I wouldn't be staring down the barrel of a gun held by marauders who'd come to finish me off. This kind of stuff didn't happen to most twenty-three-year-olds, but in addition to owning the Debutante Detective Agency, I'm a substitute anchor who mostly does grunt-work reporting for WBFD-TV, Channel Eighteen, in Fort Worth, Dallas, and the rest of the Metroplex. Now that I'm on TV, I get all kinds of unwelcome attention, mainly from people I'd just as soon forget.

I pretended to ignore the doorbell and moved, inconspicuously, toward the library.

Gran, who happened to be in the kitchen baking sticky buns for no good reason, projected her warbly, birdlike voice. "Teensy, get the door."

Wide awake, Teensy Prescott had a pulse and apparently hadn't won any large sums of money at the Indian casino in Oklahoma over the weekend, so I figured she ought to earn her keep by looking through the peephole instead of trying to duck up the winding staircase in the rotunda to avoid being seen.

Teensy, who I've been on the outs with ever since I rescued her with a yawing crevice in her skull, put there by robbers driving a gypsy cab in the filthy murder capital of Ciudad Juárez, Mexico, projected her voice, too. "Dainty's closer."

"Fine. Dainty—get the door," Gran called out.

I balled my fist and shook it at Teensy as she lurked from the second-story landing. Her mouth opened into a wide grin, as if she'd been waiting to ruin my day since breakfast.

Whenever we stay at Gran's, you can pretty much count on bizarre occurrences happening; we just don't know what it'll be until it sneaks up from behind and clobbers us. You figure you might get screwed over, but you never imagine the black cloud hanging over your head might actually be there because people are trying to kill you.

I slogged my way to the door, unable to see through the peephole because Gran's drop-in company had a finger pressed over it. And that's how we might've left it, with me slinking to safety, had the caller not pressed the doorbell until the Westminster chimes sounded more like Morse code. I torqued my jaw and swung the door open to reveal the face of Gran's visitor. Thrilled that I wasn't murdered where I stood on the intricate Hamadan, relief turned into a serpent of nausea coiling in my stomach.

Avery Marshall, one of Fort Worth's richest oil barons, and one of Daddy's contemporaries, stood on the welcome mat. By way of explanation, the so-called welcome mat didn't mean you were actually welcome at Gran's Preston Hollow estate. It meant if you made it as far as the front door, you'd better wipe your feet before stepping into the marble rotunda.

I blinked in dismay.

I last saw Avery Marshall at The Rubanbleu debutante ball over two months ago, when Teensy made her debut into Fort Worth society. Although I'd already experienced a harrowing day at the hands of a crazed hostage-taker, I dressed in my beautiful ball gown and made an appearance to lend moral support—especially since Daddy didn't bother showing up to present her to the doyennes of The Rubanbleu. Daddy's absence later became a forgivable offense since it turned out he'd been poisoned by my wicked stepmother, Nerissa. Avery'd seen me on the six o'clock news earlier that same evening, when the news reporter introduced *moi*, Dainty Prescott, as the owner-operator of the Debutante Detective Agency, and the heroine of the night's breaking news. The night of the debutante ball, Avery expressed an interest in hiring me for a job. Although he

11

didn't say what he wanted me to investigate, he sent me a big fat retainer check.

The men in the Marshall family had been perfecting ways to break women's hearts for generations. Falling victim to the tall and imposing Avery, with his easy smile, good graces, and a headful of dark hair that had silvered at the temples—but also a man whose twinkly-yet-ruthless gray eyes said, *I can snap your neck and enjoy it*—I did what any well-bred, broke fashionista would do. I fell under the hypnotic spell of his money, and spent it.

It dawned on me why Gran made a big deal out of making cinnamon buns from scratch. She knew Avery Marshall was coming to the estate, and she knew why he'd shown up. Once I saw his frumpy stepdaughter, I wanted to throw up everything but my childhood memories.

The lackluster girl looked out of place next to Avery in his custom Italian suit. With wild, sandy blond hair spiking out of her head, she only needed a pitchfork, a bale of hay, and a couple of crows on each shoulder to pull her drab brown ensemble together. I hadn't seen her in a while, but I heard she'd shaved her head in support of her best friend who'd had cancer. Even so, she wasn't altogether unattractive with short hair, but on the rare times she blew up on our radar, Teensy always referred to her as a "confused transgender."

"Dainty, it's great to see you." Avery extended his hand for me to shake. Even though his stepdaughter and I met five or six years ago, he reintroduced her anyway. "I'd like you to meet Dawn." He said this in the same impassive way that someone comments on your shoelaces or toenail clippings. Which translated to: *That retainer has everything to do with her, and now that you cashed my check, you can't say no, and there's nothing you can do about it.*

Nodding mechanically, I sensed my beaming smile mutating

into a crazed snarl that abruptly angled up the left side of my face. With a *Won't you please come in?* that would've fooled all but the people from my inner circle, I did the polite thing and invited them in out of the cold. Letting them inside was like waiving a toy gun at a cop. Either way, the ending was going to be bad.

My breathing quickened. "What brings you here?"

Avery skewered me with a look. The night of the ball, I didn't know why he wanted to hire me, and we didn't get a chance to discuss it because I boarded an airliner for El Paso the next morning to get my sister out of the first of many jams. Once I saved Teensy from certain death, I returned from Mexico to find Avery's check in the mail and spent every crying dime of it.

Nothing had gone right since the Mexico debacle except for my new car, a custom-pink Porsche with DBUTNT license plates. But the only reason I got a new car is because my jackal of a father conspired with Gran, and the two decided I'd never make it back from Mexico with a two-million-dollar bounty on my head. They sold my silver Porsche because, in Gran's words, "We thought it'd be easier than going through probate." Lesson learned. Don't go to Mexico if you expect to find anything in your driveway—or closet—when you return home.

Avery's eyes slewed over to the stairs where Teensy still waited on the second-story landing. "Hmmm," he said noncommittally, leaving me to wonder if Teensy should thank him or feel insulted.

Since the night my sister made her celebrated debut, rumors swirled like toxic fumes. Socialites love scandals, especially when it concerns one of their own. Of all the annoying douchebags, hypocrites are the worst, and Avery had no doubt turned on the news in time to see a live report about crime being on the upswing in Fort Worth, wherein my glassy-eyed drunk of a sister appeared behind the news reporter, buck naked and dancing.

13

Or maybe he'd heard the talk about Teensy recently waking up in a ditch. In a different state from where we live. *Allegedly.* Bluebloods—while charming and well bred—tend to be notorious gossips while looking down their perfectly slanted noses at those less fortunate.

Avery fixed Teensy with a smile that seemed less of a smile and more of a gnashing of teeth. "Glad to see you up and around, my dear."

"Don't judge me." Teensy protectively hugged herself. Then she pivoted on one foot and flounced off the landing and into her bedroom, slamming the door behind her. I heard the snick of the toggle bolt. For no good reason, breaking news stories about women who had their faces ripped off by chimpanzees, or those zoo visitors who had limbs ripped from their sockets after straying too close to the tiger cage, flashed into mind.

Thanks a heap, Teensy, you coward.

I motioned Avery Marshall and his stepdaughter toward a camelback sofa in the parlor. "Won't you have a seat while I get Gran?"

Before they could answer, I glided toward the kitchen in my tropical wool camel-hair slacks and cream-colored silk shirt and found my grandmother loosening the sticky buns with a spatula. My eyes flickered to five plates, stacked next to the cookie sheet.

"Avery Marshall and his stepdaughter, Medusa, are here, and I'm not going to entertain her."

"Of course you are," Gran said sweetly. "Because you took money from Avery, and now you have to do what he says or pay the money back."

I cringed. It wasn't as if I could return the retainer. It flat didn't exist anymore because I needed things that one could only buy at Harkman Beemis, the poshest department store in the DFW Metroplex.

After returning to the parlor with plates of sticky buns balanced in my hands, I made small talk while waiting for Gran to bring coffee. The caramel scent of doughy deliciousness even lured Teensy back downstairs. But my carefully orchestrated conversation, designed to put Gran's guests at ease, soon tanked when Dawn implied that Teensy looked like roadkill—which was the same as accusing me of looking like road kill, since Teensy and I are both blue-eyed blonds with beautiful bee-stung lips, flawless pale skin, faces like those Grecian statues that are carved out of marble, and our height is proportionate to our weight. Teensy implied that Dawn probably needed to be bludgeoned with a tire tool by gypsy cab drivers down in Mexico.

"Oops, my bad," Dawn said unconvincingly. "Apparently, I made a huge *fox paws.*"

"*Faux pas* is not pronounced 'fox paws.' " My brittle smile put her in her place.

Avery seemed oblivious to the increasing tension. By the time he chased his sticky bun down with black coffee, the visit with his stepdaughter distilled down to this: Dawn's mother wanted her to make her debut in the fall, and who better to show her the ropes to poise, perfection, and personality than *moi*, Dainty Prescott—the ultimate debutante. Despite a litany of excuses—too busy with my reporter-and-substitute-anchor job at WBFD-TV; too exhausted from dogging Teensy to ensure she didn't make front-page headlines for getting duct-taped, naked, to a stop sign in Deep Ellum again; too busy starting up my fledgling detective agency—the conversation came full circle.

Avery's age and experience equipped him with a *je ne se quois* radar that helped him cut to the chase. He reminded me I'd cashed his check. The entire time, Dawn sat smugly on Gran's antique jacquard-weave sofa, guiding pastries down her throat like a human wood chipper—an image I tried to blink from my mind, but nope . . . still there.

15

I didn't like this girl. Neither did Teensy. We knew her from prep school, when Avery and her mother transferred her out of public high school because of bullying. A boy nicknamed her "Candida" after the Tony Orlando and Dawn song when he found out candida was a yeast infection. The label stuck. Girls treated her like she was invisible. She became the token Goth at the school, and when classmates passed her in the halls, they avoided eye contact to discourage her from casting evil spells, or putting voodoo curses on them. With white makeup, black lipstick, and black eyeliner, she resembled a Kiss roadie. It's said that you can't fix stupid, but I say you can fix stupid easier than you can fix a girl with no fashion sense. Unfortunately, Dawn had two strikes.

After she enrolled in our school, the student body pretty much treated Dawn the same way bullies from public school treated her, only this time, Avery and his wife paid tuition for the privilege. I imagined her high school years turned out like *Carrie,* only without a bestseller or deaths. Although, in retrospect, a couple of Dawn's fiercest tormentors died in separate incidents. Uneasy with the memories, I studied the sheep-killing dog in Gran's parlor and wondered how to make a graceful exit.

Finally, I stood and made my apologies for having to leave. "Well, then, I'll look forward to seeing you soon"—*head down, avoid eye contact*—"and thank you, Avery, for thinking of me, and for having confidence in me to prepare Dawn for the debutante ball."

Avery laughed without humor. I'd always liked Avery but, at the moment, his mouth inclined at a disdainful tilt. The visit went from merely souring, to complete decay when I assumed they'd take my cue and leave. They apparently assumed I'd entertain Dawn because she hopped up from the sofa and headed for the door, with Teensy skulking behind her like a criminal behind a defense attorney, looking both clueless and borderline sinister. Within a few minutes, Dawn returned, winded, from hauling in a vintage piece of hot pink molded Samsonite, and its matching-but-jaunty little hard-shelled train case. Decals from places like Booger Hole, West Virginia, and Bloody Dick, Montana, served as an indictment on her as a world-class traveler.

While Dawn looked on, Bambi-eyed, I stood, slack-jawed, as Avery told me how the cow ate the cabbage: He'd paid for me to take Dawn and Teensy to his friend's lodge in west Texas for a spa weekend so we could groom Dawn on the finer points of etiquette. If he'd called it boot camp, I would've run away screaming. But since he described it as a resort, my prevailing thought was to just get it over with.

I immediately excused myself from the room and darted across the rotunda and into the kitchen, where I picked up the aqua princess phone Gran kept by the pantry. I called one of my two best friends, dark-haired, jasper-eyed Venice Hanover, since she'd finally returned from Africa the previous evening, and I couldn't wait to see her.

I said, "You won't believe who's in the next room," and she was all, "Who is this?" and I was like, "I'm not kidding, Avery Marshall's stepdaughter is standing in Gran's rotunda. Seriously."

After Venice stopped banging her head against the wall, she pointed out that I hadn't learned from her advice not to make fun of Dawn's lack of fashion sense back in prep school. "I'm afraid that bitch Karma has come home to roost, and now you have to pay."

Her reminder left me largely unfazed. In "misery loves company" spirit, I invited Venice and my other best friend and recovering sorority sister, Salem Quincy, to join us on our free luxury weekend in west Texas. Knowing that the words "west

Texas" and "luxury" didn't belong in the same sentence, I shoved aside the nagging image of a half-star motel since the word "free" had also been used.

Since our estrogen-driven, designer-luggage-toting group had swelled to five, Salem used the power of her fiery red hair and big aquamarine doe eyes to coax her father into letting us borrow his Suburban. Lured by Avery's description of a spa, sauna, and heated pool, not to mention him peeling a wad of hundred-dollar bills off a fat roll of currency—and because I was young and impressionable and broke—I called shotgun to avoid being sandwiched between Dawn and Teensy. How could I have known that heading out to a fly-speck town where God lost His left shoe would turn out to be one of the worst decisions of my life?

Five hours into the gut-wrenching ride to Suck Dog, Texas, my eyes drifted to the passenger-side mirror. The driver of a black SUV neither accelerated nor lagged too far behind us. At first, it didn't alarm me. But as time went on and the driver didn't pass the Suburban out of sheer boredom, being followed took on sinister tones. When I mentioned this to the group, I only got heavy eye rolls.

"Really, Dainty, you're such a drama queen." Salem tossed back her springy red curls and focused on the highway.

"Yeah, Dainty, do you think everyone on the road is after you?" Still loopy from jet lag, Venice giggled. "They'll probably turn off at the next big town. Chill."

"It's a public road. Where does it say you own it?" Teensy dug her phone out and started texting.

Dawn wanted to stop and take pictures at each historical marker, ghost town, and every dead cotton patch along the way. As we inched closer to the destination near Alpine, I saw a lot of beautiful, camera-worthy scenery, but let's face it—that's not what I like to photograph and I think we all know it.

18

Hours into the drive, we crested the railroad tracks, exited the highway at the first truck stop we'd seen in the last fifty miles, and pulled beneath a metal awning overhanging several full-service fuel pumps. The black SUV shot past us and kept on going.

Salem rifled through her handbag for a credit card. "Since when did they start charging more to put air in your tires? It used to cost a quarter."

"Inflation," I deadpanned. People who laugh at their own jokes annoy me, so I bit the inside of my mouth to avoid becoming a cliché.

Dawn said, "I'm hungry," and acted all gung-ho about the greasy spoon across the road. She whipped out the wad of bills Avery had given her and offered to treat, so we finished refueling and drove across the highway to the dusty parking lot of the Rockin' Roll diner. The place looked as old and weather-beaten as the countryside surrounding it. Since I'd picked up a few tricks of the detective trade from my boyfriend, Jim Bruckman, we selected a corner table where I could watch the front door and read the blackboard specials while we waited for our server.

We were given sticky menus that crackled when we opened them, and made our food selections to a background of redneck country music that blared so loud through the speakers of an old Whirlitzer that it made the rough-hewn plank floors vibrate. We took advantage of the lunch specials and stuck with chicken-fried steak, mashed potatoes and gravy that probably came out of a box, and waxy green beans that almost certainly came out of a can. Our gum-smacking waitress wrote the order on a guest ticket before sticking the pencil back into her box-dyed, lacquered hair and gliding off. After she returned with five sweet teas and clean utensils rolled in paper napkins, she told us to raise our hands if we wanted dinner rolls with our meals. What she neglected to tell us was that, the moment we raised our hands, the fry cook would pelt us with dinner rolls through the pass-through. When we all got hit in the head—except for Dawn, whose Sphinx-like smile suggested she already knew the routine, not to mention that she ducked—I decided to add this place to my "Don't Go There" list.

Dawn glanced around at the taxidermied wildlife positioned around a central fireplace built of stone, and got a faraway look in her eyes. "Know anything about bobcats?" None of us answered. "I had a Siamese cat. When nobody else understood me, he did. And I loved him, too. One day, he Marine-crawled toward me, sick with bobcat fever he'd picked up out in the wild. I rushed him to the vet, but the vet said nobody'd developed a cure for bobcat fever. I guess the Aggies were too busy working on their football game to work on saving my cat."

I shot Venice a withering glance. She was a big Texas A&M University fan, but starting a feud with our insufferable travel companion would ruin the entire weekend even worse than I'd imagined. I decided Dawn had just edged out the competition—which is to say, the rest of the world—as the most boring person I knew. Since I held the contest in my head, I also crowned her with an invisible black tiara for being the most negative, socially inept person I knew.

Lunch conversation was like tiptoeing through land mines. The waitress dropped off our tab at the same time she brought our food. I'm pretty sure it was because we scared people with our inappropriately loud laughter, and she wanted us gone.

By the time we ended up in Condemned Flats, I'd lapsed into paranoia again. A vehicle similar to the black SUV that had caused me alarm earlier had fallen in behind us, and I imagined, once more, that we were being tailed. Because of the darkness, I couldn't be certain it was the same vehicle, but I began to pay attention to the mile markers along our route in the event we needed to call for help. Besides worrying, I'd added Dawn to my ever-growing list of "People who annoy the hell out of me." Oddly enough, Dawn seemed no less enchanted with us.

Suddenly, the parched flat land in west Texas gave way to the sight of denuded trees. Branches reached skyward like gnarled fingers clawing their way out of a graveyard. Following the GPS route, we took the turnoff for the Rocky Road Resort, and listened as the tires on the Suburban crunched pea gravel. From a distance, the architecturally significant ranch resort with its lush landscaping looked stunningly beautiful. Unfortunately, the positives ended there. Up close, the place looked more like a house of cards.

The thought that I might be going crazy was confirmed when we bailed out of the big SUV and took stock of the place. The only other car in the parking lot—a battered old truck covered in so many bumper stickers that it would've probably fallen apart if they'd been removed—made us feel collectively and unimaginably stupid. Clearly betrayed over getting swindled out of the luxurious vacation they'd been promised, the mouths of Salem and Venice rounded into "O"s. Anyone witnessing our horror might've thought we comically exaggerated the point, but deep down, we all knew . . .

I admit it. I felt dizzy.

A june bug landed on me, reminding me of the time our cat tried to take down the neighbor's Great Dane by jumping on its back. I swear I had moves like Jagger and planned to mark the experience down as exercise.

I drew a bracing breath. "Teensy—look alive. Here comes a buzzard." Then I expelled a resigned sigh. "Avery hates us."

My gut feeling stemmed more from the idea that these property owners were hoodwinking the clientele than from my own frustration. I know, aren't I nice? But I'd gone two meals without dessert and was about to lose it. I needed some trans-fat Danish wedding cookies or a gooey pastry, and one look told me this place just wouldn't be offering that.

Salem and Venice took a bit longer to absorb the horror that came with such a dilapidated place. Then I cut my eyes to Teensy, looking lost and wringing her hands, and I sensed the potential deathtrap might send my sister into one of her patented depressive spirals. Instead, she asked, for the third time in as many weeks, if we could have a pet raccoon. I told Teensy she wasn't allowed to speak anymore.

Dawn's reaction poured out in one long, astonished breath. "Cool."

While the rest of us found the place disgusting, Dawn thought it was horrifically awesome. I'd always considered Dawn to be socially awkward, but labeling the place *cool* convinced me that she must be a psychopath.

From here on out, I figured any story describing our bucolic weekend would start with, "It was a dark and stormy night," and end with, "Dainty Prescott then turned the gun on herself."

"Bonjour," I said to the desk clerk in a daring French accent, prompting him to ask if we had a reservation. *Really?* The place looked like a ghost town. "Yes. Yes, we do."

Full-scale bickering erupted behind me. Venice and Salem insisted on rooming together, while Teensy—upon seeing her odds dwindle—furrowed her brow in undisguised panic and demanded to stay on a rollaway in the room with my friends rather than get stuck in a room with Dawn.

An elderly man with thinning gray-brown hair and a receding hairline, who looked like an older version of the desk clerk in facial features and body size, moseyed up to a computer behind the front counter and took charge, effectively sidelining the younger guy. While he processed us in as guests, the younger man got into a loud, one-sided argument with a black-and-silver striped tabby cat.

As the old man fumbled through a drawer for room keys, he turned his focus to me. "We don't get many city gals like you out here. Too rustic and not high-falutin' enough, I reckon, but we'll bend over backwards to make sure you enjoy your stay. Say, didn't I see you on the Miss Texas pageant?"

I get that a lot. With a practiced look of coyness that I'd learned from watching old film clips of the late Princess Diana, I demurred, casting my eyes downward.

Then he said, "You're the prettiest little filly I ever laid eyes on."

"You should get out more," Teensy responded, unimaginatively rude.

He pushed a log book across the counter and winked creepily at me. I backed away and left it to one of the others to sign.

Really, if you plan to stalk me and are over the age of seventy, be sure to install fresh tennis balls on your walker's front legs. That scraping sound annoys me, and I resent having to walk so slowly.

While the old-timer finalized our accommodations, I stared out the huge expanse of plate glass windows that overlooked the swimming pool, and ran the length of the back side of the lodge. Beyond the metal fence surrounding the pool, leafless trees and scrub brush seemed to extend clear to the horizon.

Teensy sheared my thoughts with a mean-spirited suggestion. "You should room with Dawn; after all, you're supposed to be teaching her how to act. How can she copy you if she's not around you?"

From the moment we arrived, I'd been waiting for my sister to blurt out something inappropriate to fill the awkward silence. To be sure, many have tried to imitate me; precious few have succeeded. Except maybe Teensy, who looks so much like me that people have often mistaken us for twins. Peeved by Teensy's saucy ignorance, I suggested Dawn get a room all to herself. But I was thinking she should stay down the hall from us. Or in a different part of the lodge. Maybe even at a different resort.

I spoke with the elegance of a southern belle. "I think Dawn would be more comfortable in her own room, don't you?" Feeling the need to defend myself, I glared at Teensy to back off, because *In case you hadn't noticed, Teensy, I'm trying to salvage our weekend, you little jerk.*

The old desk clerk, who should've been looking me in the eye while he spoke to me, not staring at and making conversation with my breasts, finally booked us into rooms. After this, he should probably get his priorities straight, like, get us a chocolate meringue pie from the nearest bakery.

Venice, who'd looked forward to experiencing the creature comforts of life after spending the last six weeks in Africa, said, "I just want to know one thing—is the pool heated?"

According to the old desk clerk, it was. He handed us each a key to our suites, along with a brown paper bag tied with a jute bow. "For your time at the resort," he said, giving me a knowing look.

And what were those items? A Taser and pepper spray. At first, I thought our welcome gift was a joke. As the evening wore on, I should've insisted that we take turns driving and head back to Fort Worth. But we were young and shrugged off danger, not realizing that the Rocky Road Resort was exactly the kind of location film crews sought out to shoot video for slasher movies.

Unable to curb my irritation, gentility and impeccable manners obliged me to at least try to mask it, so I gave Dawn a frosty smile. "I can't tell you how happy I am to be here with you."

"How do you think I feel?" she shot back, keying in on my sarcasm. "I walked into what I thought was going to be a surprise birthday party for me. I didn't know Avery staged an intervention over my upcoming debut." She took stock of our surprise'd faces. "Yeah, that's right. Today's my birthday."

"Well, that went well, don't you think?" I pivoted on one foot and headed for the room, dragging my suitcase-on-wheels behind me like a tail.

While my uneasiness mutated into anxiety, Venice and Salem began the process of learning how incredibly difficult it is to spend more than a few hours with people who are mentally unstable—that would be Dawn and Teensy—as well as a suite-mate who's perpetually OCD and locks the door to a strange room ten times just to make sure she barricaded herself in— that would be me.

Salem and Venice occupied one-half of the suite; Teensy and I took over the other half, while Dawn got a room to herself across the hall from us. We tried to play this off as a good thing, making a big deal about how she deserved her own accom-modations since Avery'd been so generous with us.

My room was colder than ice. It turned out the door had been left open, and whenever someone left the door open, the heat switched off as a money-saving feature. Note: This was the start of a trend. Then I figured out that the heater wasn't designed to actually warm the room as much as it functioned to blow cold air . . . another cost-cutting measure.

The first thing I did was peek behind the shower curtain. Then I went into the connecting suite and peered behind Venice and Salem's shower curtain. Next, I glanced under the beds. True, such OCD-ism didn't prepare me for what to do if I confronted an ax murderer, but after that awful trip to Mexico, it became *de rigueur*. My friends gave me funny looks like they were double-dog-daring me to explain my overreaction to our surroundings, so I ticked off a list of safety concerns before we ventured out to see what kind of nightlife the town had to offer.

Then Dawn smarted off. "The entire time you recited this information, I watched a drug deal go down in the courtyard, and you never even noticed." She sighed at me in disappointment.

While everyone else showered and put on fresh clothes before dinner, I went into the bedroom intending to take a little catnap. As I sat on the bed and kicked off my shoes, I watched a trail of ants trying to shove a dead roach into a power socket. I picked up the phone and dialed the front desk. The entire time I talked to the desk clerk, I watched the ants stuffing that roach into the socket. And yet the old man refused to admit they had a pest infestation. He also said the maintenance man had left for the day, but after sufficient whining, he sent in what appeared to be a homeless Mexican who only spoke broken English, and looked like they'd snatched him off the streets. He said he'd get right on it, and then left. I drifted off to sleep waiting for him to come back with ant spray and never saw him again.

I woke up, hyperventilating, from the worst nightmare of my life.

I dreamed Avery Marshall asked me to take his stepdaughter under my wing and teach her how to be a debutante.

Oh, wait. That really happened.

Teensy waltzed in, wrapped in a bathrobe, while toweling off her hair. "You need to do something about that chatterbox."

I was still half asleep and scrunched my face to indicate I had no idea who she was talking about.

"Your friend Venice," she said with a scowl. "She's monopolized every conversation with stories about her trip to Africa ever since we left Fort Worth. It's enough to make you zone out. Seriously. I had to look at the clock to see if I'd had an epileptic seizure and lost two hours."

I had no plans to tell Venice to button it—she and Salem had done me a favor by accompanying us so that I wouldn't have to spend the entire weekend shotgun-married to Dawn.

The five of us gathered in the common area of our suite.

Everyone but Dawn had dressed in fashionable clothes, especially Venice, whose career goal is to become a couture designer in the garment district of New York City. Dawn, on the other hand, dressed in a long, dowdy gray dress, and looked more like a Sister Wife than a potential debutante.

"A dress . . . that's nice," I said in a calmer voice than I would've expected.

"Amazing for vintage clothing, don't you think?" she said in the same way someone might remark that a hail storm could ding the paint on your car, or that snakes couldn't bite underwater. Then she mimed a big fat smiley-face for the group and gave us what I assumed was her best version of jazz hands.

The highlight of the evening came when we returned from dinner and changed into our swimsuits. Except for Dawn, who cocooned herself in a blanket at one of the bistro tables next to the pool and muttered snide remarks about us all being crazy since it was practically freezing outside. But I had a new waterproof camera to try out, and Venice wanted to swim after spending six weeks on a continent where water's in short supply. Salem and Teensy called dibs on the spa. I took a seat on the diving board and watched Venice test the water with her toe before lowering herself into the shallow end of the pool.

While focusing my camera, I felt a disturbance in The Force.

My peripheral vision alerted me to movement. Urgency gripped me. From my place on the diving board, I watched, helplessly, as men in black clothing and black ski masks fanned out through the lodge—four, maybe five. Too many, moving too fast. My mind must've played a trick on me. I pulled the camera back up to my face and snapped a succession of frames. I don't recall getting up, or moving hurriedly across the concrete pool surround, or the camera dangling below my chest by its leather strap. It was as if I'd levitated myself to my feet with one prevailing thought: *run*.

CHAPTER TWO

Shock paralyzed me. My friends in the shallow end of the pool, and in the spa, drew my gaze. My heart raced like a hunted animal. A sense of great peril snared me in its trap. Not knowing where to turn on the outside lights, and not caring enough to contact the desk clerk to ask him to do it, had turned out to be a blessing in disguise. But these girls had a tendency to bark out laughter at the slightest provocation, and doing so could get us killed.

"Venice. Salem. Teensy," I hissed. When they turned their attention to me, I patted the air in a downward motion. "Robbery. Lie low." Instead, they riveted their gazes to the chaos beyond the veranda.

Eerie stillness cast a pall over us. A four-foot iron gate nearest the spa opened onto a footpath leading down to the trees. I crept past Dawn, who attached herself to me. When we reached Venice, who'd snagged her towel and looked ready to bolt, Dawn ripped it from her grasp. Before Venice could protest, Dawn handed over the blanket, and Venice cloaked herself in its warmth. In seconds, I understood—a white towel in the darkness could've alerted the men inside to our presence.

The assailants failed to look in our direction, but that could change in an eyeblink. We collected Teensy and Salem at the spa and moved outside the gate.

I surveyed the veranda, the glassy stillness of the swimming pool, and the woods beyond the lodge. By way of documentation, I took several more pictures before leading my friends deeper into the thick foliage, beyond the park-like area behind the resort. As we receded deeper into scrub brush, birds erupted from the trees, batting their wings to take flight from the mayhem.

Then I heard a noise. My inner voice told me to keep moving, but I defied it and turned to look.

Movement beyond the blazing fireplace drew my attention to the center of the lobby. Flames reflected off of the thick varnish of the open-beam ceiling, as if the devil's yellow tongue licked the rafters. The dead air surrounding us felt thick and oppressive in the quickly darkening twilight.

We sneaked glimpses of the terror taking place inside, taking great care to avoid becoming backlit by any glow or slice of moonlight that could make us easy targets. I had no doubt these psychopaths had come here to harm us, and that the desk clerk and the remaining staff might use our whereabouts as a bartering chip to secure their own freedom.

With most of us crouched and barefoot, we chimp-walked past the scrub brush and into the stand of trees, keeping as close to the ground as we could to mask our visibility in the pale, eerie glow of the moon. And while I'm five-feet-four and physically fit, I had no delusions that I could outrun or outmaneuver these crazies. Even if I could, abandoning the others just wasn't my style.

Venice hunkered over and slipped her right shoe onto her foot. As she slipped on the left shoe, Salem thumbed the button on a small metal flashlight and lit the way.

Dawn surged ahead and snatched it from Salem's grasp. "Have you lost your mind? You want them to find us?" Her voice had changed. It seemed deeper and huskier, and I wrote it off to carnal panic.

Beyond the ambient glow cast off by the lodge's interior

lights, something grazed the nape of my neck—tree branches that threatened to put out an eye. The area where we huddled was pitch black and so full of darkness that I got the opportunity to taste a live spider when I walked into its web. I remembered the last time I'd been this afraid—in Mexico, running from unknown subjects who wanted me dead, and who'd placed a two-million-dollar bounty on my head to make sure I didn't get back home. But was an invisible enemy in a foreign country more frightening than the ones we could see lurking beyond the grove of trees? In many ways, these ninja-dressed assassins—criminals in my own country, operating with impunity—were worse.

Dawn took the lead, and we reluctantly let her. With more opportunity to take pictures of the goings-on inside, the masochistic need-to-know part of my personality hijacked my common sense. Snapping away, the sheer gravity of the situation didn't fully resonate until we heard the first crack of gunfire.

People were positioned near the fireplace, on their knees, with their hands finger-laced together on top of their heads. Then the old desk clerk pitched forward, face-first, onto the terra cotta tile floor.

A cold serpent of nausea writhed in my gut.

Salem grabbed my hand and squeezed. I felt her trembling presence beside me as Venice—so quiet that she seemed like the living dead—stood still, barely breathing. Clouds peeled back, revealing dark pockets within the trees, triggering distortions to my eyesight, my surveillance, and my terror.

"God help us." My voice broke.

I worried that Teensy, in her fragile state, would hyperventilate, or make hysterical mewling sounds that could cause us to be discovered, but I never thought abject craziness—enough to get us murdered—would come from Avery Marshall's step-daughter.

Dawn gave my shoulder a light tap. I turned and saw that her face had changed.

"I'm going for help." Before I could voice my "safety in numbers" theory, she added, "Hey—I know what you're thinking, and that's what eight out of nine student nurses thought when Richard Speck led his victims, one by one, into a room and murdered them. Those girls believed him when he said he wouldn't hurt them, because nobody made a move to run. Like sheep." She practically spat the word.

I felt my face contort with horror. "What?"

"Did you ever watch *Born in East L.A.*? Cool flick. They all rushed the border at the same time."

"You're not going anywhere. You don't even know where we are. Or where the closest house is." But she'd already slipped farther into the darkness and disappeared like a phantom, taking the only light we had with her.

Teensy bounced at the knees to keep warm. She gave a full-body shudder, and then stood perfectly still. "Are we going to die?"

My friends shifted their collective gazes toward me.

"No." The sharp edge in my voice was meant to calm her.

"Oh. Okay." Then, "Promise?"

I shushed her. "Stop talking, Teensy. The quieter, the better our chances."

We needed to get back to the SUV but our purses were inside our rooms. So were our cell phones. I wondered how long it would take these intruders with their covered faces to come outside and search for us, once they realized the resort had guests staying there—guests who belonged with the silver Suburban parked out in front.

A second shot exploded. Our attention riveted on the activity inside the lodge. After a few seconds of hang time, shards of glass from one of the plate glass windows rained down onto the

31

veranda in crazed chunks. In the time it took me to refocus, another body sprawled, face-down, onto the tile floor.

The owner's wife was missing from the lineup.

Horrified, I turned away. Unable to overcome the pull of the macabre, I looked back through the plate glass windows running along the veranda. For a second, my eyes played a trick on me. Did I really glimpse a hand and part of an arm pop out from behind one of the walls? I blinked. Instead of four men in black, I counted only three. The killer nearest the wall had disappeared from view. Had he come for us?

After giving myself a headshake vigorous enough to rattle my eyeballs, a blazing inferno instantly eclipsed my *What just happened?* moment.

Flames that had previously been confined to the masonry fire box now plumed from the cowhide sofa and rustic, loose-weave drapes. Beyond a cowl of thick smoke, I witnessed even more of man's capacity for cruelty.

Less than a month ago, I'd witnessed similar cruelty in Mexico, when I crossed the border to find my sister and bring her back home. I saw similar inhumanity, again, when I returned to capture my father's fugitive second wife, Nerissa, and haul her white-trash ass across the border to be prosecuted for murdering my mother and attempting to murder my father. Shaking off the flashback, I inwardly beat myself up for not being mentally and emotionally prepared for an event so lethal that my friends, my sister, and I might have our lives abruptly snuffed out at the hands of madmen.

Dread consumed me. Clearly, the assailants intended to torch the place to cover their tracks. With the owners dead or mortally wounded, only the younger desk clerk and a handful of staff remained. Even if the owners felt an obligation to keep their guests safe, the staff had no loyalty to us. Clinging to hope, I fleetingly wondered if the workers overheard our conversations, and what impressions we'd left on them. Most likely, they viewed us as spoiled, pampered, and entitled.

"One of the pamphlets at the front desk showed a picture of a man-made lake beyond these trees. We have to get to the lake. Maybe there's a boat." My idea invited instant rebellion from the others.

"Snakes." Salem rooted her feet firmly in the moist earth. "No."

Venice turned to me with undisguised terror. "No snakes. Scared of snakes."

Then Teensy spoke in a voice that seemed calmer and more capable than I'd ever imagined she could be. "I'll go. I'll go look for a boat."

Because of her closed-head injury, my sister could barely tie her own shoelaces. If she left our group, we'd need tracking dogs to find her.

Above the pop and crackle of burning wood, another gunshot erupted inside the resort. At least I thought it was gunfire. I couldn't really be certain that I'd heard actual gunfire until I saw the aftermath. The younger desk clerk, the one I assumed to be the owners' son, pitched, face-first, onto the floor.

Coherent speech eluded me. When I looked back at my friends, Teensy had already left.

And then there were three.

But inside the resort, I counted only two masked gunmen. Where'd the others gone? I experienced a skin-crawling a-ha moment: They must've been sent to look for us. Were they ransacking our rooms? Would they find our IDs and learn where we lived? Blood whooshed between my ears. My heart beat so loud I could feel the pulse throbbing in my neck and throat.

My sense of time had been temporarily short-circuited.

The old Mexican man who'd been sent to pacify me with ant killer made a break for the door. He made it as far as the blazing cowhide sofa before the *ping* of a ricocheting bullet took him down.

In the distance, a car ignition fired up and we heard the crunch of gravel against tires. I wondered if Dawn had made it to the road, or if someone else managed to slip away from what had quickly turned into a massacre.

Inside the lodge, all faces inclined toward the front drive. No headlight beacons lit the way out. We stood, petrified, with our guts sinking, fearing that a secondary gang of intruders might have arrived.

Another shot exploded, and a robust Mexican woman wearing a kitchen apron flew into hysterics. She clasped her hands in prayer, but worse, her mouth moved with alarming animation. And even though it was the groundskeeper beside her who'd toppled over, I knew she was about to give us up. Probably because I asked her if she knew how to cook Mediterranean dishes instead of just keeping my mouth shut and settling for Mexican street tacos off the menu.

Fate may have turned my friends and me into unwilling participants by drop-kicking us into this sinister tragedy, but we were not victims. Not yet. And if I had my way, we wouldn't be. The niggling feeling that Nerissa had masterminded the attack to keep Teensy and me from testifying against her continued to eat away at me. I never expected such a murderous fury to erupt inside me, or to manifest itself in the surge of adrenaline that motivated me. Animal instinct prevailed. It filled me with such visceral determination to take the lodge by storm that my only hesitation to do so came from the lack of a suitable weapon, and the gauzy cloud cover that threatened to tear away and expose the looming moon.

Shivering and slipping into shock, Venice said, "Dainty, are we going to die?"

"Don't even think that . . . Salem? Listen carefully. Where are the keys to the Suburban?"

Salem gave me a blank look. Cotton candy clouds thinned and disappeared. Moonlight filtered through shadows, bluing her pale face. I grabbed her wrist and tightened my hand around it painfully. She didn't even wince.

I reached up and grabbed her face to focus her. When she tried to pull free, I knew I'd broken her trance. "Salem. The keys. Where are the keys?"

"In the room." She experienced an epiphany. "There's a spare set in the SUV."

"We need to get to the truck." I turned to Venice. "Can I count on you?" She nodded dully. "Okay, I'll lead. Everybody hold hands. Nobody let go. We're in this together." I took the first step farther into the trees. Twigs snapped underfoot.

Venice whispered, "Dainty—wait. Do you know who's behind this?"

I glanced back over my shoulder. After penetrating the lodge so effectively, the murderous men remained animated behind the plate glass windows. I gave a reluctant nod. "I might have an idea."

"Is it Dawn's fault?"

"No." Consumed with guilt, I urged my friends to keep moving. Our lives depended on it.

It was only a matter of time before one of the captives pointed those men out to the pool. Upon seeing the white bath towels we'd brought from our rooms, our absence would be enough for them to fan out into the woods. If they found us, I had no doubt we'd meet the same grisly end as the mom-and-pop owners and their employees. Until I ran short of ideas, we had to escape this deathtrap before revealing ourselves to another human being.

"There's plenty of time to assess blame later." I omitted the obvious—the part where assessing blame could only take place if we made it out alive.

Salem, who's sweet-natured and gullible and loves everyone, spoke an uncharacteristic thought. "I hate Dawn. I wish she'd never come here."

Venice agreed. "This is all her fault."

Salem delivered a low-level rant. "She just left us out here to die. I swear, if we survive this, I'm blackballing her from making her debut at The Rubanbleu ball."

For no reason I could pinpoint, I became suddenly fearful of leaving a spot I believed to be a place that offered reasonable protection.

Should've trusted my gut and never opened Gran's front door. But since I did, I couldn't blame Dawn for running for her life. I'd like to think everyone, when put to the test, is brave. But they're not. Survival instinct nearly always trumps courage.

"It's my fault, not hers." Then I encouraged my friends to recede further into the shadows.

CHAPTER THREE

All the preparation in the world can't ensure safety. And apparently the resort's owners knew it, or why else would we be issued a Taser and pepper spray for the duration of our stay? I wondered, briefly, if the men on this killing spree had a beef with the owners. I rather hoped they did, so Teensy and I wouldn't turn out to be the goats in this tragedy.

Dense smoke kept us from seeing through the lodge's picture windows, but the flames that shot out from the big vaulted ceiling lit up the night. Crackles and pops added to the terror.

Footfalls pounded the concrete walkway surrounding the pool.

"C'mon, hurry." My heart tried to beat right out of my chest.

What sounded like the plodding of a grizzly bear trounced the deadfall beyond the woods. Venice dropped to the ground and defensively shielded her head with her hands. She'd given up.

A tiny circle of light bounced in the distance, and then faded like a firefly, only to reappear as a larger beacon a few seconds later. Without warning, Teensy crashed through the foliage, breathless. The beam from the little flashlight diffused. Then it died out.

"There's a manmade lake about a quarter of a mile from here. I found a boat, and this flashlight, and a first-aid kit. And some dude's lunch box. Let's go." Her attention shifted to Venice, curled up on the ground, wrapped like a won-ton in Dawn's blanket. "What's with her?"

I dropped to one knee and prodded my friend. "Teensy found a boat. We're getting out of here." I had no idea where this boat would take us, but it'd put a lot more real estate between us and those horrible men, and that was a good thing.

"Go without me."

"We're not leaving you, Ven. Get up."

Then Teensy, the voice of reality, said, "We don't have time for this. Leave her."

Footsteps on the veranda turned into footfalls on the concrete pool-surround. Flashlight beacons sliced through the night.

"They're coming for us." I spoke with such urgency that the three of us made a concerted effort to rally around Venice and pull her to her feet.

With Teensy in the lead, we followed along until Venice panicked and broke from the trees.

A gunshot rang out. The bullet zinged past Salem. She let out a yip and did a face-plant into the deadfall. Once I realized she'd fallen about twenty feet behind me, I jackknifed to the left and went back for her. I didn't hear the next gunshots, but I heard wood splintering all around me.

Teensy panted, "Leave her—we'll come back for her." But Venice, seeing that I wouldn't abandon our friend, whipped around and came back to grab Salem's arm.

Salem gasped. "I'm hurt."

"Well, crap." Teensy returned to grab Salem's ankles.

I don't know why I suddenly worried that we'd get kicked out of The Rubanbleu over Teensy's trash mouth when we'd probably end up dead for turning back.

The scream of distant sirens filled the night. Footfalls that had terrorized us suddenly retreated in the opposite direction, fading into a deadly silence that was even more horrifying. Then we heard a car engine turn over, followed by tires crunching gravel. A few seconds later, we were left with only the slithering sounds of unseen wildlife, and the howl of coyotes calling out in the night.

By the time we worked our way through the brambles and trees, and back to the front of what was left of the lodge, I saw Dawn standing beside a fire truck, and a TV reporter and his photographer making a beeline toward her for an interview. Barrier tape that read *Crime Scene—Do Not Cross* had been strung from the parking lot and tied off at the tree line. An officer lifted the Day-Glo yellow tape and I sprinted toward Dawn, speechless with gratitude.

It wasn't an altogether altruistic move on my part. This was the kind of news story that went national. Even with exigent circumstances, no good could come of her blabbing to the world that she'd hotwired a car in order to go get help. Not that the viewing audience wouldn't forgive her, but the very act that saved us would open up a can of worms with the ladies of The Rubanbleu, ninety-nine percent of whom didn't know how to boost a car—a number I came up with, out of the ether, because I actually did know how to boost a car, so sorry-sorry-sorry I didn't think of doing that myself.

And how'd I acquired such a skill?

Let's just say I watched my cockgoblin of an ex-boyfriend, Strayer Drexel Truett III, Drex-for-short, when we were in the eighth grade, and he wanted to take me for a spin in his father's Bentley.

A tall, commanding figure of a lawman strode up to us. Steeped in tradition, he wore the boots, pistol belt, and western-style white hat of his predecessors and had a swagger to his walk. When he came within a few feet of us, I saw the badge pinned to his shirt. The super-distinctive round shield had a star within a circle and cutouts unique to the Texas Rangers.

Even in the ambient light of the fire truck's headlights, the Ranger had eyes so shockingly green that they seemed to jump right out of his head. With a strong jaw and a no-nonsense mouth, he struck me as the kind of man who possessed the know-how to kill using an instrument as simple as a bottle cap; yet his very presence instilled a sense of calm in me.

By way of a polite greeting, he touched the felt brim of his silver-belly Resistol and pinned me with his eyes. "Ma'am, I need you to come with me."

Standing in awe of him, listening to the silky baritone of his smooth southern drawl, I almost forgot that I had a boyfriend. And because no law enforcement agency anywhere exhibited the history and romance of the American West like the Texas Rangers, I followed him without hesitation.

While an ambulance ferried Salem to the nearest hospital, the Ranger removed the rest of us from the crime scene and transported us to the nearest Department of Public Safety office. At the DPS, we were met by State Troopers, who split us up and took our statements, but Ranger Duvall "Dusty" Hill separated me from the rest of my pack with the precision of a cutting horse, and kept me all to himself. It should've been pretty obvious that I was a little more than slightly unhinged when he took me into an interview room. With adrenaline still coursing through my veins, I probably wouldn't sleep for days, and would look like the raccoon Teensy kept asking for by the time I did. From my seat at the gunmetal government-issue table, I noticed the mirrored glass and knew it was two-way. Then I wondered who might be lurking on the other side watching us.

Catching sight of myself, I didn't like my reflection: grim-faced and drained of color; forehead dampened with sweat; cheeks smudged with dirt and eyes hollowed with lack of sleep; bee-stung lips, pale and in need of lip gloss; mouth slightly agape; and a small crimson scratch on one side of my jaw. My eyes, usually bright blue and swimming with intelligence, especially disturbed me. I no longer saw myself in them, but rather the person I'd been reduced to during the terror-filled night.

Hours later, when the interview finally ended and Ranger Hill collected my camera as evidence, he called the ER to check on Salem. Hospital personnel told him she'd be fine—a bullet had merely grazed her thigh. He not only relayed that information to us, but offered the four of us a ride to the hospital so we could see for ourselves.

Knowing Salem only received a flesh wound, I thanked him and declined. Since it appeared that the firemen contained the blaze before it reached the guest quarters, I wanted to retrieve our belongings and make sure those men hadn't ransacked our rooms. "If you could just give us a ride back to the lodge so we can gather up our stuff, we'll drive Salem's car to the hospital." *So we can get the hell out of this godforsaken swill pit.* That part remained unsaid.

Flinty green eyes pierced me with a look. He seemed to read my thoughts. "I don't recommend that." No-nonsense lips suddenly cracked a smile. "After all, how else can I get you to stick around long enough to have lunch with me?"

CHAPTER FOUR

"I learned a lot about myself tonight," I said over a cup of hot chocolate at a downtown café called the Retro Diner.

"Well that ought to make our trip worthwhile." This, from the sarcastic mouth of Teensy.

"I just meant I never realized I could get so riled up that I'd want to commit a homicide." Cupping my hands around the mug, I took small sips while letting the coiling steam snake up my nostrils.

"Not me," Teensy said, slurping a cherry phosphate through a straw. "I want to commit murder lots of times, especially when you touch my stuff."

"*Me*—touch *your* stuff? You're the one who messes with mine." I raised my voice to be heard above the din of customers chatting away at nearby tables.

Venice moved whipped cream around on her hot fudge sundae until it covered the cherry. She remained quiet as Teensy and I continued our tiff, probably because bickering was the norm for the Prescott sisters, and, at the moment, the one thing we desperately needed was a sense of normality.

Word had already gotten out about the fire at the lodge, and the deaths of the owners, their son, and a hired hand. The fourth victim was still in surgery at the same hospital where ambulance drivers took Salem, and the small-town locals were already putting in their two cents' worth as to the identities of those responsible for the slaughter. Men at the next table speculated,

It's the cartel, come to town, and launched into a deep discussion about the drug trade disrupting life in their otherwise peaceful community.

Others made noise about a personal beef where the owners "rubbed somebody the wrong way." I hoped we wouldn't overhear any conjecture about *Those city girls come to town,* because I didn't want to start a war. As a debutante of The Rubanbleu, violence tended to be off limits, but I'd been through so much the previous night that my ability to come across as a genteel southern lady remained sketchy.

For the longest time, Dawn said nothing and went through the motions of eating her breakfast without enjoying or even tasting it. Fine by me. Inwardly, I *did* blame her—and Avery—for making us part of this terrible tragedy.

Teensy pulled her phone out of her purse. She tapped her thumbs against the digital display with lightning speed, the way she did when she composed a text message.

"What're you doing?" I said.

"Isn't it obvious?" Teensy's eyes remained glued to the digital display screen. "There. I have a breakfast, lunch, and dinner date."

"Really? You must be going to jail to get all three meals."

"Duct tape comes in a variety of colors." She did a little head-tilt, smirk combination. "You should get a roll."

"You're such a cow." But I was thinking, *Thank God we're all still alive.*

A lady at the next table inched her chair farther away from us. At the same time, Venice put a finger to her lips, warning me that I'd gotten too loud.

Of all the people in our group, I worried about Venice the most. She'd remained conspicuously silent and withdrawn since the ambulance had taken Salem away. I barely dared to look at her.

"It's okay, Venizzia." I used the pet name I'd heard her parents call her when they were feeling particularly adoring and playful—which I was not—but the look that had settled onto her face scared me. I never wanted to see that look again. "Salem's in good hands and we're safe now."

My eyes cut to Teensy, who continued to text. "What'd you tell the trooper who questioned you?"

Without looking up, she gave me a one-shoulder shrug. "I said I didn't know anything. Except that you'd had a stalker before, and that didn't turn out well. And that you were on TV so you probably had a lot of people out to get you. Oh"—she lifted her gaze—"and Nerissa wanted all of us dead."

While I realized the importance of focusing on Nerissa, I zeroed in on the part where my sister thought people were out to get me. "Why would you make an idiotic statement like that?"

"It's true." She kept her eyes on her cell phone and went back to texting. "You can be annoying."

"*J'accuse*. You're annoying." I heard a faraway feminine laugh that caused me to turn in its direction, and saw our waitress talking to someone beyond my line of sight. "You're *more* annoying."

"You don't know that for sure. Annoyance is subjective." Teensy smirked.

"Hey—I'm not the one who makes a new enemy every time she turns around." Then I reminded my raving psycho of a sister about the lowrider filled with a pack of dangerous Latina 'hood rats that showed up at Gran's estate shortly after Thanksgiving. They came to beat Teensy into a pink stain because she posted inflammatory comments about illegal immigration on a public forum website, and was stupid enough to furnish her real name and address when she challenged anyone who didn't agree with her post to "Come shut me up if you think you're ballsy enough."

"They needed to hear that," Teensy said, looking up from her phone.

Privately, I knew we were talking about everything under the sun to keep from reliving the bloody carnage at the resort. I was about to give Teensy a big piece of my mind when the waitress approached and discreetly cleared her throat.

"Yes?" I flashed my beauty pageant smile as if she'd shoved a microphone in front of me so I could answer the Miss Texas interview question: *World peace—if I could have anything, I'd wish for world peace.* "May we help you?"

"There's an officer at the door who wants to speak to you."

"Stay put. I'll go see what he wants." In an uncharacteristically charitable mood, Teensy pushed her chair back from the table, scraping the feet of the chair legs against the rough-hewn plank floor.

When she reached the halfway point to the door, Venice spoke. "You're both annoying."

I knew Venice so well that her tone told me exactly what expression shaped her face: dark eyebrows slammed together and jasper-colored eyes, all-knowing and thinned into slits, as if she'd cracked the code hidden in the folds of a conversation between siblings.

Dawn and I collectively twisted in our seats to face her. Even though she refused to make eye contact with either of us, hearing her speak was a good sign.

"What'd you tell the trooper?" I asked.

She stared into her cup as if she were reading tea leaves and was about to inform us that we were in deep trouble—which we already knew.

"Hello?" I sarcastically waved my hand in front of her face.

Zombiefied, she lifted her gaze. I braced myself for the worst.

"What's to tell? I got back from Africa night before last and you bullied me into coming on this trip—the hell, Dainty? I didn't even have time to repack. Just grabbed my textile bag and off we went."

"So you're mad at me, and you're holding me responsible for what happened?"

"Not mad. Not holding you responsible. But you have to admit that you have a propensity to get into trouble wherever you go."

"Me?" This dumbfounded me.

"Yes. Teensy, too. You don't have to agree with me, Dainty, but it is what it is. I had nothing to do with this." Suddenly clear-eyed, she got her second wind. She squinted in calculation and fixed me in her electrified, cat-eye gaze. "And I'll tell you something else . . . I survived waking up to a snake in my tent on the one day I decided to try something fun, and by that I mean, go out on safari. But let me come home to Texas, where it's safe, and . . . again, I ask you, *What the hell?* What if they come back?"

Rather than lie, I said, "We'll be long gone."

Venice's dark hair, which was normally shiny and had a lot of bounce, had dampened with sweat and tacked itself to her neck and forehead. Her eyes took on a speculative gleam. "No—what if they were after the three of us?"

Dawn looked up from playing with her food, but I knew the "us" Venice was talking about meant Venice, Salem, and me. Hard experiences over the past two months supported what she said, but I'd already worked through those encounters and didn't want to relive the recent terror that the three of us suffered through when a holdover tenant held us hostage in the condo we'd just rented.

"They weren't after us," I insisted, infusing false bravado into my claim. I scanned the early dawn beyond the plate glass windows, half expecting to see those men lying in wait for us in a panel truck or beat-up old van; but dawn broke and I doubted

46

that they'd stuck around now that the sheriff and his posse and our larger-than-life Texas Ranger were out looking for them. "Why would they be after us?" I sniffed at the thought. "They're not after us."

They're after Teensy and me.

I injected a chipper lilt. "Okay, we'll come back to you, Venice." My attention shifted to Dawn. "What'd you tell the trooper who interviewed you?"

"Nothing."

My eyelids fell to half-mast. Avery's stepdaughter annoyed the hell out of me. "Of course you said *something.* What'd you tell them?" I asked sweetly as I slapped her across the face five times—but only in my head.

"Nothing." She rested her fork on the plate. "I called Avery when we first got to the station. He told me to button it. Next thing I knew, a west Texas shyster Avery hired to represent me showed up."

Bad vibes landed like darts.

"Why would you need an attorney?"

Venice's cell phone rang. Saying nothing, she thumbed it on and waited. Her face drained of color. I know Venice so well that no matter how much she wanted to terminate the phone call, astonishment and horror, tinged with morbid curiosity, compelled her to keep listening. Different scenarios—both real and imaginary—ricocheted through my mind:

Salem took a turn for the worse.

We were seen on TV and now we're getting kicked out of The Rubanbleu.

Somebody died.

Venice thumbed off her phone. I badgered her until she related a one-sided conversation that would escalate the terror.

"He said a lot of people are going to end up dead. And that

47

we should just tell them where to find it. I don't even know what *it* is."

The waitress sashayed by, looking for half-empty cups to splash coffee into, and I snagged her attention with an upraised hand and a request to move to a corner table.

One without windows or shades.

Near a back exit.

That couldn't be seen from the street.

CHAPTER FIVE

Outdoors, dust whipped up around me. The tan landscape of west Texas reminded me of the three-D craquelure of a crumbling Old Master.

I found my sister loitering next to the entrance like a common vagrant, still texting. I held open the door and motioned her back inside but Teensy said, "Wait—I have to finish this." She continued to send text messages on her cell phone while the wasteland around us sucked the air out of the diner.

"Come on, Teensy, this is ridiculous. You can finish that inside."

"Don't be stupid. Can't you read the sign?"

The café, with its eclectic menu of American, Mexican, and simple Asian stir-fry dishes, had a "No MSG" sign posted on the window. My idiot sister—the one my parents hoped would become a lawyer to settle family feuds that kept cropping up— thought it meant "No Messages."

I shook my head in disgust. "What'd that officer want?"

"Oh, that. Ranger Hill stopped by to return your camera." Without fanfare, Teensy handed it over. "He kept your memory card, though. But he said he'd make you a copy of the pictures you took and send them to you on a disk." She touched a finger to her lip and gave me a pensive look. "I sure hope you didn't take any photos of yourself with whipped cream boobs and maraschino cherries for nipples."

"Have you lost your mind?" One never knew what would

come out of Teensy's mouth.

"Wow." She paused long enough to take in the vista. "This part of the state really sucks. But I'm glad we came. Know why? I'll tell you. Because the next time I get an invitation to visit the Wild West, I'll know to say no." She took a cleansing breath and scanned the panorama again. "I'll admit I prayed to God for different scenery because I'm really sick of living at Gran's. But I didn't ask Him to send the devil from hell to flick his dandruff here on earth."

A beige Tahoe in the parking space next to the door became the focus of her close scrutiny. And just like that, Teensy made a new enemy when she walked over to the dirty Tahoe and wrote, *Also comes in white* across the dirt and the dust and the grime.

Teensy, you're on a steep trajectory to hell.

My cell phone rang and I heard Salem on the other end. She'd been discharged from the hospital and wanted us to come get her. She couldn't wait to get home, and the rest of us felt the same way.

After stopping at the ER, I drove Mr. Quincy's Suburban back to Fort Worth with Dawn calling shotgun, while Venice and Teensy sat in the back and kept an eye on Salem. We drove straight through, with only one stop to refuel, and nobody had much to say except for Teensy.

Getting Teensy off the Ranger Hill bandwagon was like trying to get a mule out of a cabbage patch. *Not gonna happen.*

"He has nice eyes. Don't you think he has nice eyes?" she announced to the SUV at large.

"For the love of God, Teensy, would you just zip it? None of us want to think about anything that happened during the last twenty-four hours."

Upon our late-night return to Fort Worth, we picked up our respective cars at Salem's house and pretty much scattered in all directions. Everyone blamed Dawn and me for getting us into such an untenable situation in the first place. Once Dawn and Venice left the Quincy residence, Teensy and I headed for Daddy's house in Rivercrest. When we bounced into the drive, I noticed a *For Sale* sign in the yard. I didn't pay much attention to it because I was exhausted and wanted to fill Daddy in on what happened in west Texas in order to take extra precautions setting the security alarm and keeping the doors locked at all times.

"So what'd these intruders look like?" Daddy asked.

"Like Cirque du Soliel meets Teenage Mutant Ninja Turtles—really, Daddy—what do you think they looked like? They looked like men dressed in black, with black knit caps with eye holes pulled down over their faces, and huge black guns."

No surprise—when I suggested Nerissa organized the brutal storming of the resort, he echoed my sentiments. By the time I finished the details, he seemed more convinced than ever.

"We all talked to law enforcement officials—except for Dawn. Avery called her a lawyer. I wanted to call her an ambulance."

"Avery's just looking out for his own interests."

"In what way?"

"That girl's an embarrassment. Who knows what she would've said?"

"Daddy—she *should've* said exactly what *we* all said. She should've told what happened." Then I experienced a moment of clarity and turned the topic of conversation to the *For Sale* sign in the front yard. "You can't sell our house." I looked to Teensy for moral support.

"To be clear, it's not *your* house, it's *my* house. I only let you freeload off me for the first eighteen years because public policy dictated that I feed, clothe, and provide shelter for you until you turned into adults." His eyes cut to Teensy. "Except for you. You never really grew up. You just learned how to act in public."

"Again"—I redirected the conversation—"this is our home."

He appeared indifferent to our plight. With Nerissa in jail and their divorce nearly finalized, Teensy and I had hoped we could move out of Gran's place and back into our old rooms. "You can't sell the house we grew up in."

"I can, and I will. It has too many bad memories and requires too much upkeep for one person. I'm rattling around in here." Even as Daddy said this, my eyes darted around, assessing vulnerable areas on the first level of our two-story mansion.

I wondered if he'd left any doors unlocked when I realized he'd stopped talking. "But that's where you're wrong. I can cook for you." With Nerissa gone, the thought of my new role as lady of the manor excited me.

Teensy, looking alive and campaigning for the vacant position of chief tattletale, said, "Who're you kidding? Your idea of cooking means a trip to the market, buying precooked bacon from the salad bar, and throwing it on top of a bag of lettuce. *Voilà*— salad. Have you ever even operated a stove?"

When Teensy trashed my cooking skills, I volunteered her as the new housekeeper. She shot me an ice-pick glare, and I felt the need to defend myself, *because in case you hadn't noticed, Teensy, I'm trying to keep Daddy from selling our house, you little twit.*

Daddy said, "Two couples are coming over in the morning to see the house." He looked from me to Teensy, and back to me. "I can't be here. I have an important meeting, and then Avery and I are having lunch at the Petroleum Club. I'll get to the bottom of what happened out at the lodge."

My sister and I blinked.

"My point is . . . you'll need to show people around."

"You expect us to give them a tour of the house?" This flabbergasted me. Why not just hand me a knife and tell me to slit my own throat?

"One couple should be here at nine, and the other couple's

coming by at ten. Make sure you're up and dressed, and don't junk up the bathrooms with your makeup and do-dads while you're staying here. I just had the house cleaned."

Staying here? "In case you've forgotten, we're living at Gran's."

He snapped his finger close to his ear. "About that. You're grandmother's going on a cruise with Old Man Spencer, and she doesn't want the two of you staying there without a chaperone." Seeing the reactions on our faces, he added, "It's just for two weeks."

"Why can't we stay there?" Teensy asked. "I finally got all of my stuff moved in."

"She doesn't trust you not to throw parties in her absence. And she doesn't want her home trashed by a bunch of lawless cretins."

I challenged him. "We have nice friends." True. Actually, not true. Most of Teensy's childhood friends should've been paddled with a three-hole board. I traced this maladaptive behavior back to when Teensy and her friends' third-grade teacher asked them each to tell the class how they felt when they found out Santa Claus wasn't real. On the other hand, most of my friends attended church, held good-paying jobs, and didn't imbibe more than a couple of alcoholic drinks at a sitting. Unlike Teensy, who, out of partying reflex, downed communion wine like a vodka shot the last time we went to church.

Daddy turned to Teensy. "While under my roof, you're not to drag in late. Or half-clothed. The next guy you bring home for me to meet, I'm swabbing his mouth for DNA and taking his fingerprints." Then he issued us a warning. "And don't be running over to the strip center for lottery tickets, thinking you'll win enough money to buy the house. Pipe dream."

I don't run. And if anyone ever sees me running, then they should run too, because someone's probably after me. Tears welled. "Why're you doing this?"

"Again"—he ticked off the reasons on his fingers, one, two, three—"bad memories, too expensive, too much house for one person. Pick one, or dream one up on your own." His attention shifted to Teensy. "First thing in the morning, you're mowing the front lawn. Curb appeal."

"I don't know how to mow grass," Teensy whined.

"Nothing to it. It's a self-propelled mower so all you have to do is start it and hold the bale down to make it go." He angled off toward his bedroom and left us standing in the living room with our mouths agape. "And Dainty," he called over his shoulder, "don't forget to take down all the photos in the den and stick them in a drawer. I hear buyers don't want to see other people's family pictures on display. They want to envision their own family photos."

The idea of removing our photos drew my gaze to the bookcase. Daddy had pictures of all the important family members displayed throughout the house, with one glaring exception: me. Now, he only had one photograph of me when I was little, standing next to my horse, with my back to the camera.

"Daddy, wait," I called out, "how come there's only one picture of me?"

"I only keep pictures from when I liked you."

"I don't get it. This bookcase used to be crammed with my photos. What happened to them?"

"Every time you disappointed me, I burned one." He disappeared in the direction of his bedroom.

I motioned Teensy to follow me. Once inside the kitchen, I handed her a can of ant spray and told her to get to work. If Daddy really planned to sell this house out from under us, then he needed to get top dollar for it, and ants beneath the kitchen cabinets make a bad impression.

She gave the baseboards a liberal dousing and then burst into tears. Upon realizing how hard she'd taken the news of the house sale, I felt a twinge of guilt for not showing more compassion. "Aw, you're sad because Daddy's getting rid of all of our wonderful memories here, aren't you?"

"No, I'm sad because, on this battlefield of ant corpses, there's still one surviving ant that's cradling a dead ant in its arms. I'm pretty sure I've just become the villain in this tragic ant disaster, and I can't bear to tear another ant family apart." Then she drew the back of her hand across her eyes and said snootily, "Of course I'm sad. Daddy's wiping out our history like we never even lived here."

I'd had my fill of Teensy for one night and checked the kitchen door to make sure it was locked before moving through the rest of the house to ensure the other doors were locked and dead-bolted. Between Teensy texting her friends and erecting booby traps by stacking empty soda cans near the doors, my sister had turned into a raving psycho. But, hey—good news—we seemed to share simultaneous thoughts: Backlit by the glow of the living room light, we made easy targets. She abandoned her cell phone long enough to draw the silk drapes, while I left her standing next to the liquor cabinet and headed down the hall to what used to be my bedroom.

Because Nerissa had hired a Fung Shui master to walk around the house with a compass, moving furniture to help improve the "energy flow," I no longer had a bed to sleep in. All that was left of my Barbie-pink bedroom was a lamp, several yoga mats, and buttery yellow walls.

I took a look around and dreamed of what used to be, then snuffed out the light and moved to the window, parting the curtain enough to look out and take stock of the outdoors. I distrusted the darkness beyond the window as much as Teensy did. My return home had turned into a nightmare. I kept hearing weird sounds in the room, and when I got out my camera and tried taking pictures, the face-recognition feature kept coming on . . . but only in my bedroom. That did it.

I ended up in one of the upstairs guest rooms, in a beautiful mahogany Lincoln bed that Nerissa hadn't managed to get rid of. I didn't even bother to change into pajamas, just stripped down to my lingerie and crawled between Egyptian cotton sheets that smelled of my mother's perfume.

The room was pitch black. I should've been able to see shadows, but . . . no. The luminescent indicator bar on the alarm system keypad should've glowed as green as toxic waste, or as red as a taillight, but it didn't shine at all. I feared that the power had been cut and that the psychopaths who killed the people at the lodge had arrived to take us out. I wanted a gun. *The hell?*— even my blue-haired grandmother owned one. If she wasn't afraid to shoot in self-defense, then why should I be?

I flipped on the bedside lamp and stepped lightly into the hall to the alarm keypad. The digital display spelled out BAT LOW, so I opened the fall-front desk beneath it and found fresh batteries. After I popped them in, ZONES NORMAL flashed on, along with a random time from a third-world country. I pressed ALARM STAY and the countdown began. If Daddy left the house, then he could reset it.

Early morning, a rosy dawn broke to the sound of Daddy's big diesel-guzzling penis-truck roaring out of the driveway. Electric numbers on the digital clock pulsed 6:30. When I tried to incorporate the bleating alarm into my dream, it just got louder. The truth is, I'm in love with this bed. We're perfect for each other, but the alarm clock didn't want us to be together— *the jealous whore.* Then I remembered why I set it to go off. I'd heard that baking chocolate chip cookies embedded a sense of home into the subconscious minds of prospective buyers. Like staging, only for the nose instead of the eyes. I threw back the covers, grabbed my shirt, and padded downstairs to Teensy's room.

Using my knuckle to flip on the light switch, I fried her eyeballs with a sixty-watt bulb. To my shock and awe, I found her cowering in a corner, hugging a bag of potato chips and sobbing hysterically, while the robotic vacuum cleaner gently bumped into her.

I caught a whiff and nearly gagged.

She reeked of alcohol and smelled like the devil's toenails, not to mention her red nose and bloodshot eyes made her look like hell served cold. The longer she poured out her problems, the more I wanted to beat my head against the wall. I'm used to her over-dramatizing things, which is fine for reality TV, but I don't get how it's not an excuse to keep from serving a lengthy prison sentence. To hear her tell it, she'd apparently polished off a bottle of booze and was having second thoughts about uploading pictures on her camera phone. According to her, she'd just figured out that the search engine she used had automatically uploaded her pictures, and so far, her friends had seen photos of her left boob, her ex-boyfriend's penis, and numerous other things too horrible to imagine.

"What's that awful smell?" I whiffed the air several more times and did a little face scrunch.

She pulled at her sleeve and sniffed an armpit. "I guess it's me."

"Ya think?" Said sarcastically. "Maybe you could transfer some of the passion you have for Daddy's liquor cabinet into making yourself presentable."

"Quit hounding me. I'll change before the people get here."

I nodded "yes" mechanically.

Then I shook my head "no" mechanically. Sinister thoughts germinated in my brain. Just because Daddy wanted to sell the house didn't mean the house would actually sell. After all, I grew up in a gazillion-dollar neighborhood, and not that many people could afford to spend that much on a house like ours. To unleash my diabolical plan, I'd need Teensy's help. And Teensy could barely brush her hair.

"What if . . . ?" I waited for my sister to focus. "What if we could make that odor appear all throughout the house?" I moved to the edge of her bed and took a seat on one corner.

"What're you talking about?" Nonplused, she sniffled. "Why would we do that?"

"Did you do your laundry last night?" When she shook her head, I said, "What if you took your dirty laundry and hid it around the house so the house smelled really bad?"

Teensy recoiled. "Why would I do that?" Followed by a sobering realization that brightened her face. "So you're saying . . . ?" I nodded. "And it's disgusting?" I nodded again. "Wow. That's pretty conniving. But I don't have enough dirty clothes."

Excitement rippled through me. "There are other things we can do to turn off prospective buyers. Hurry up and get dressed and meet me in the kitchen."

Instead of exploring my theory with me, Teensy ran for the bathroom. I could hear her throwing up the liquor she binge-drank. Since we were a family of sympathy pukers, there was no getting around those sounds coming from behind the door. I ran for the hall bathroom.

I barely managed to keep down the roiling in my stomach. When I returned to Teensy's room, she was standing at the vanity splashing water over her face.

I said, "You're disgusting. You go mow the front lawn and I'll burn a skillet of eggs."

While Teensy staggered to the back of the property like a reeling, drunken sailor, and brought out the self-propelled lawnmower from the gardener's house, I pulled up the *For Sale by Owner* sign and hid it behind the front hedges. Maybe if Daddy's prospective buyers didn't have the address and were looking for a sign, they'd keep going. Then I went back inside and watched my sister through the kitchen window.

Teensy may have a great scholastic mind, but she's lazy as all get-out and lacks common sense. She tied the bale to the hand bar so she wouldn't have to push the mower. While considering other ways to facilitate my devious plan, Teensy painted her nails while the lawnmower blasted across the estate.

I had no intention of removing the sterling-silver-framed snapshots of us from the bookcases in the den. Not that Daddy was big into photographs. At my debutante ball the year before Teensy made her debut, he took a picture of a blond doing the Texas Dip on stage and tried to pass it off as me.

That's why I quit asking him to take photos to commemorate events.

The pictures stayed.

I burned a couple of eggs and threw them in the trash. Then I relaxed on the French chaise lounge in the formal living room, near the front door, and flipped through an outdated fashion magazine addressed to Nerissa.

A horrific crash rocked my serenity.

Tossing aside the magazine, I dashed outside to find Teensy standing by the next-door neighbor's fence, slowly fanning her hand through the breeze in order to air-dry her newly polished fingernails. She looked at me, slack-jawed, and then back over at the jagged fence boards.

What. The. Hell.

Stunned speechless, I actually only formed this un-Rubanbleu question in my mind since I could already tell by the gigantic lawnmower-shaped hole in the pickets that it had crashed through the neighbors' fence. I ran straight to the splintered fence panels and saw that the lawnmower had sunk to the bottom of their swimming pool. Turning away, I walked back over to Teensy.

"Hi. Whatcha doin'?" I spoke in a sing-song, *oopsie-daisy* sort of way.

"Thought I'd try my hand at landscaping."

"You're not very good at it."

"Really? Hey—I have an idea. Why don't you go inside and cook us some breakfast? Oh, wait—you're not really good at it." Said nastily.

"Okay, let's try this . . ." I swished my hand back-and-forth through the air between us. "Hocus-pocus . . . no, you're still a bitch."

Since saving my sister's life down in Mexico, I've put a lot of thought into it, and I don't think being an adult is going to work for Teensy.

When our very horrified neighbor ambled out in his bulldog boxer shorts, with his face turning beet red and a cell phone pressed to his ear, I slunk toward our house and left Teensy to fend for herself.

Teensy yelled, "Where do you think you're going?"

"To make a phone call." Molding my hand into the shape of a telephone, I held it to my ear. "I'm pretty sure we're going to need the fire department to put out the little coil of smoke spiraling up from the top of his bald head."

The first buyer-couple showed up a few minutes after nine. Teensy had already retreated to the house and gotten herself cleaned up and had come into the living room to greet them. As luck would have it, the police arrived at the house next door a few minutes later. I watched the animated neighbor through the living room window, gesturing toward our house, and was pretty sure he mouthed the name "Teensy Prescott" so they'd know whom to arrest.

As we welcomed Daddy's buyers inside, I spun my index

finger around one ear in the universal "cuckoo" gesture. "Crazy neighbor. It'll be nice to get away from those people. I mean— look at that god-awful fence-turned-to-rubble. Who'd want to live next door to that eyesore?"

Not to be outdone, Teensy said, "I think we're supposed to disclose anything that might cause you to not want the house." The lady, a pert, petite blond with a short bob hairdo and twinkling peridot eyes, arched an eyebrow. "Daddy's selling because of the bloody massacre. That was a few years ago."

My eyes bulged in their sockets. This was not part of the plan.

"The police took their sweet time releasing the crime scene," Teensy went on. "The construction crew painted the walls but the dried blood spatter kept seeping through, so they pulled out all the drywall and started over. Personally, I thought the brain matter could pass for texturing, but . . ." Big sigh. One-shoulder shrug. "It took a long time to fix everything back the way it was, and that's why the house hasn't come on the market until now."

The hell, Teensy?

Even I wouldn't have taken it that far.

With the polished presentation of a museum docent, my sister led them into her flooded bedroom. My jaw dropped. Thanks to Teensy, stuffing toilet paper down the commode clogged the plumbing and swamped the room. The only thing lacking was a tiger for me to reenact *Life of Pi.*

"Sorry." Teensy tiptoed across the sopping wet floor. "C'mon in. Don't be afraid, it's not too deep today."

The lady gave a sniff of unsuitability. The man made noises like he was swallowing his tongue.

"Happens a lot," Teensy said with a cavalier flick of the wrist. "But don't worry about the smell. You get used to it. It's old plumbing." She looked over at me. Hand to mouth, with a look of practiced innocence, she said, "Oh, was I not supposed to tell that? Boy, am I going to get in trouble . . ."

Whenever I found Teensy to be the most mystifying, it was because she showed me a side of her I didn't expect to see. This particular facet turned out to be *très, très* destructive. Of the two of us, she clearly wanted to foil Daddy's attempt to sell our childhood home more than I did. My heart swelled with so much pride, I thought my chest would explode. I gave the people staring at us a weak smile.

We repeated our performance with the second couple, who spent even less time with us than the first prospective buyers. I remembered to stick the sale sign back into the ground before Daddy returned, but when the wind blew it over, I just left it, face down, on the lawn, and reasoned that God didn't want Daddy selling our childhood home either.

When Daddy rolled up in the driveway, Teensy was spraying air freshener in the kitchen to mask the revolting odor of burned eggs while I ground up the evidence in the garbage disposal. Since he ran the truck up to the kitchen door and left the engine idling, I figured he'd be going out again, leaving Teensy and me to refine our plan to keep additional prospects from falling in love with our home. We also needed to discuss why Gran booked a cruise with Old Man Spencer without telling us, and to talk about whether to get our stuff out of the house before she locked us out for the next two weeks.

While I discreetly pulled back the curtain and watched Daddy through the window, Teensy took inventory in the refrigerator.

She pulled out a small box of coconut water, scrutinized the container, and then wagged it at me. "This yours?" When I shook my head, she said, "I'll bet it belongs to that woman at Tranquility Villas. What's her name—Jillian Wicklow? You think Daddy's still dating her?" Then she slit open the carton of coconut water with a fingernail. "Wonder what it tastes like."

"I tried it once. If you like that taste in your mouth after you vomit, you might enjoy it."

Teensy rejected the box and exchanged it for a carton of milk. She took a swig directly from the carton and, in her gluttony, ended up spilling it all over her face. I clapped to show my appreciation just as Daddy stuck his house key in the lock and flung the door open.

He took one step and stopped dead in his tracks. For about ten seconds, he stared at Teensy in stunned silence, watching milk dribble down her chin. Then he strolled across the threshold, huffed out a sigh like he was deflating, and said, "I don't even want to know . . ." He turned to me for a report. "How'd the house-showing go?"

"I can't tell you what a great showing we had." Since I honestly couldn't tell him it was great without lying, I told the truth. Literally. Not my fault if he took my enthusiastic head bob the wrong way.

"Well, come on—out with it. Did they say anything about the house?"

"Not to me." We'd probably get spit-roasted in hell for torpedoing these potential sales, and yet I gave a lackadaisical shoulder shrug and cut my eyes to Teensy. "What about you?"

"Not that I can recall." If not for the influence of our late mother, Teensy was just one chromosome away from being a criminal. But her angelic expression, perfected over a twenty-one-year period, seemed to be working.

Confounded, Daddy gave a derisive grunt. His eyes cut from one of us to the other, as he sized us up. Then he strode out of the house and slammed the door shut on the way back out to his truck.

"Well, that went well, don't you think?" Teensy high-fived me on the way out of the room.

Apparently Daddy couldn't appreciate the entertainment value of two grown children who didn't want their childhood home sold out from under them. As his offspring, he should've known we wouldn't go down without a fight. Not our fault he put us in charge. So . . . *ha.*

CHAPTER SIX

With the Baccarat chandelier dialed down low, Teensy and I sat at the dining room table discussing our next move when the doorbell rang. Daddy didn't say anything about anyone else wanting to see the house, so I had no idea what sort of rude, ill-mannered person would drop in unannounced.

Avery's stepdaughter, that's who.

Holding a change of clothes. On a coat hanger looped over her finger.

I stood with the door barely ajar, with my body wedged against the small slit I'd created, and effectively barred her entry.

"Dawn." Said with fake enthusiasm. "I'm so sorry, did we have an appointment?" Translation: *not sorry, and, of course we didn't.*

She took a step toward me and I naturally backed away. Which created a bigger gap for her to bulldoze her way inside without invitation.

What the hell are you doing? What. The hell. Are you doing?

Teensy's uproarious laughter filtered in from the kitchen. She sauntered into the living room with her cell phone pressed against one ear and her even white teeth displayed in dazzling rows.

We exchanged eye-encrypted looks that suggested we really should be more cautious about who we let into our house.

Hoping to bail out of this fix, I addressed Avery's stepdaughter

65

with the utmost gentility. "Dawn, it's not that I don't want to work with you"—*big fat lie*—"I just think we shouldn't hang out together after what happened at the lodge. For safety reasons. I'm sure you understand." To further illustrate the point, I parted the living room curtains enough to eye the front lawn with suspicion.

"I'm okay with it." Dawn looked around the living room and surveyed our digs.

Clearly, I needed to be more firm. "It's just that we don't know who was behind the shootings. For all we know, they were after Teensy and me." Which I truly believed, and felt a moral obligation to warn her. "You might not be safe."

"That's true," Teensy chimed in, and offered up an anecdote about the umbilical cord being wrapped around my neck when I was born. "That was God's first attempt to kill her off. She may not be so lucky next time."

Dawn gave a subtle head bob and a resounding, "I'll take my chances."

And that's when I almost wished those men had killed me, because I couldn't think of anything worse than having to spend another day with this annoying, dowdy, exceedingly boring ex-schoolmate. But the most cringe-worthy thought occurred to me that other young ladies who made their debut with me might see us together and actually think she was part of my social circle.

With renewed vigor, I tried to nip the visit in the bud. "You do realize that I have to work."

"Yes, and since you're a superstar, and so important, I'd like to accompany you to your job to see how you interact with other people."

Disregard; let's not pull at that thread.

On the one hand, my ego screamed, *Finally, someone noticed that I deserve a tiara.* I fought the inclination to buy into her

66

shameless flattery and did the lesser of the evils. "You can't come to the TV station." Then I crumbled like a fifty-year-old cookie. "Fine. *Entrez.* I can spare a few hours."

"Not a few hours, Dainty; you'll have to attend a debutante party with me this afternoon."

Arguing with Dawn was like playing chess with a pigeon. You may be good at chess, but the pigeon is just going to knock down all the pieces, drop its "calling cards" all over the chessboard, and strut around, victorious.

I took her into the yoga room that used to be my bedroom and we sat on the floor mats.

First, I examined her party dress, made of pale blue silk with eyelet lace around cap sleeves . . . quite stylish—*sixty years ago.* "You can't wear this to a party. It's the dead of winter and this screams spring, circa 1950. You'll be laughed out of the country club."

Dawn squared her shoulders. "It's all I had. I'm not much into dresses, and it belonged to my grandmother. I think it's pretty."

"It is pretty—pretty awful. We'll have to go see Venice. She's the best clothing designer I know. Maybe she can whip something up for you on the spot. If not, you'll have to call the hostess and tell her you've come down with the flu and don't want to spread it."

She blinked back the tears beading along the rims of her eyes.

"It's the only way, Dawn. If I'm really going to help you, I can't let you wear this to a deb party."

In a way, it was too bad that Dawn was several sizes bigger than Teensy and me. We would've sacrificed the proper clothing just to get her out of the house.

I put in a call to Venice, who grudgingly agreed we could drop by in an hour. While we waited, I decided to test Dawn's

Rubanbleu acumen. "You're going to a garden party in the afternoon, but you don't have the proper shoes to go with your dress. What do you do?"

She gazed thoughtfully into the distance before experiencing a light bulb moment. "Pick a pair of shoes in a neutral color and wear those?"

"No," I practically yelled. "You go to Harkman Beemis, take your dress with you, and buy a new pair of shoes. Jeez—it's like I'm talking to a brick wall. Give me your purse."

I searched her handbag and ran across a condom. "I doubt you'll ever need that." Words slipped out like they'd gotten a fresh shot of lubricant.

"I don't even know how that got there. Somebody must've put it in my bag. Are you making fun of me because I don't have a boyfriend? Because I already explained to my cat why I'm single."

"Think about what you just said. I'm pretty sure that's why."

I used to think you were weird, Dawn. Now, I think you're a mental patient in sheep's clothing.

I handed her purse back to her. "This handbag makes you look like a shoplifter. Look—all you really need is a purse big enough to carry a small compact that has a mirror so you can take the shine off your nose; lipstick, or lip balm, which you can also use to put color on your cheeks if the need arises; a small aerosol can of hurricane-resistant hair spray; and a tiny brush in case your hair falls flat." Reflexively, I refluffed my hair and pointed to myself. "You don't want to give people the idea that you have to work hard to look like this."

"Hairspray, hmmm?" Dawn let my words soak in. "The last time I flew to Atlanta, a can of hairspray detonated in my suitcase. I don't have a clue why that happened. It didn't have anything to do with me. But I'm on a list at the airport and I can't travel by commercial airline for six months."

Whaaaaaa?

My jaw dropped. I blinked. Then I projected my voice. "Teensy, bring me a rubber band."

In a voice dripping sarcasm, Teensy called out from the direction of her bedroom. "Please?"

My jaw tensed. I addressed her with mock politeness. "Teensy, if you're not doing anything at the moment, like, oh, say—getting plastered, or destroying the neighbor's property— would you please be so kind as to bring me a rubber band? Thank you so much. You're the best." I turned to Dawn. "Did you see how I did that? A debutante always remembers to say please and thank-you."

Teensy trotted in with a rubber band and handed it over.

"Thank you, Teensy. You're excused."

My stubborn sister stood rooted in place. "The hell, Dainty. I'm not going anywhere."

"Fine. Please have a seat. And feel free to play the 'Quiet Game.'" I mimed a smile, but secretly wanted to hold her head underwater until the bubbles stopped coming up.

"Why, thank you for asking, Dainty. I would love to." She sat cross-legged on my yoga mat.

I wanted to order her out of my former room, but I'd already wrestled her to the floor and punched her in the face five times in my mind, so that'd have to do. I held out my hand and when Dawn clasped it, I slipped the rubber band onto her wrist.

"What's this for?"

"Hush. Learn from the best. Have you had elocution lessons?"

"No, we didn't get to do any kind of electrical stuff when I was growing up."

My sister guffawed. You ask me, Teensy's all of Gran's bad parts amplified.

"For the love of God, do you even know what that means?" I

yelled. "Wait—of course you don't. Fine. Let me ask you a series of questions. First question: Do you say y'all or you all, or you plural?"

She put some thought into that one. "You all."

"No. Y'all is the correct answer. You're in the South. Act like it." I reached out and snapped the rubber band. She mouthed the word "Ow" and jerked her hand away. "Second question: How often do you need to go to the tanning salon?"

"I'm guessing . . . couple of times a week?"

"No!" This time, I practically screamed. "You'll ruin your skin. Don't you know that magnolia blossom skin is the new tan?" I snapped the rubber band hard enough to make her eyes water.

She looked at her calves, cross-legged on the mat. "What I know is that brown bacon looks a lot better than raw bacon."

Teensy leaned in conspiratorially. "Dawn told me about her last relationship. Back in high school, she did have a boyfriend. He told her he'd broken up with his girlfriend because she was 'too smart' for him, and that he felt better being with 'a girl who didn't have too many lights on upstairs'—if you know what I mean."

"I asked you not to repeat that, Teensy."

If Avery's stepdaughter was any dumber, she'd have to be watered once a week. I said, "Dawn, you do realize he was calling you dumb, right?"

"Oh, sure."

My mind cast back to high school, back when the girl all the boys called "Candida" had a locker near mine at the gym, and I once overheard her ask a guy out.

"Honestly? I'd rather smash my balls with a mallet—no offense."

Well, none taken, I'm sure.

Dawn was a last resort, even for weirdos. And yet, for some strange reason, I felt the need to defend her. "You can't let

70

people talk to you that way, especially men."

She shrugged it off. "That's okay. I told him I broke up with my last boyfriend because his dick was too big and I wanted to settle for something smaller—like in the Vienna sausage category."

I reached out and snapped the rubber band again.

"Ow. That hurt." Her eyes widened like plates. "I thought that was a great comeback."

"It was super-great."

"Then why'd you snap the rubber band?"

"Because prospective debutantes shouldn't mention penises in polite company."

Turns out I'd wasted a lot of time and trouble trying to rectify Dawn's social awkwardness, when I could've streamlined the process by quoting Cee Lo Green songs and giving her moral support.

After rummaging through Teensy's closet and selecting several pieces of clothing that I thought Venice could make use of to try to remake Dawn's pitiful dress, I did a visual check of our surroundings before driving Dawn over to the Hanovers' house. I also scanned the area for assailants once we arrived. Her mother let us inside and I navigated the way across the huge expanse of house to Venice's sewing room.

She stopped sewing and looked up from her machine. Flashing a broad smile, she seemed happy to see me until Dawn trailed me in. Her smile turned into a scowl.

"Hi. Whatcha doin'?" I said playfully.

"Making a straightjacket. For me."

"Aw, I'm sorry. Do you need a hug?"

"No, a gun. Again, for me."

Seeing no way to put a good spin on my predicament, I huffed out a sigh. "I need a huge favor. Dawn has to be at a debutante tea in a few hours and this is all she has to wear." I thumbed at the dress as Dawn peeled off the dry cleaner's protective plastic.

Venice took one look at Dawn's frock and her head almost rolled off her neck in disappointment. "That's hideous. What you really need to do is sprinkle holy water on it and give it a nice service."

"Here's the deal," I said. "I hoped you could whip something up for her like you did for me to wear to the debutante ball. A *Venice Creation*. I brought things from Teensy's closet that you can cut up and incorporate into this dress however you see fit."

We had two-and-a-half hours for Venice to work her magic. As an amazing couture designer, she wanted all of the rich Westsiders to hire her, so I thought she'd jump at the opportunity to redesign a vintage dress, since Dawn could showcase the finished product to these prospective debutantes and their Westside mothers. Instead, Venice treated the whole ordeal like it was a rock in her shoe.

My plan was to leave Dawn with Venice in case Venice needed to fit the dress to her and wander around the house until I found Dr. Hanover, Venice's mom. But no matter how hard I tried to shake Dawn, she stuck with me—like a piece of toilet paper caught in the back of your waistband, or a bad case of HPV. *I can only assume.*

For no good reason, Dawn confided in me. "I have a copy of your debutante picture on my dresser at home. Avery snapped a picture of you when you took your bow and had it framed for me."

I realized that I'd just stumbled into "I want to staple your face to my face" territory, but part of me thought: *Who among my peers wouldn't want to emulate* moi, *the most beautiful, graceful debutante in Fort Worth?*

Screeeeeeeeech! Reality check. I'm not in the Make-Me-

Pretty business, especially when I don't even like the person. I wanted to ask whether she'd heard the story of the miserable little pig that tried to be a show dog and lost every competition it ever entered, until a friend convinced it that it was a beautiful pig with pretty pink skin and lovely beady pig eyes, and then talked it into entering the pig category at the county fair—and it won the blue ribbon. Not that I'd compare Avery's stepdaughter to a pig—but she should find another way to make herself stand out by being exceptional at one thing. As for Dawn and her hero-worship, I decided to be gracious about it, since she kept shamelessly promoting me to my face.

Back in the sewing room, Venice refused to be rushed. "This is an art piece. If you don't have an appreciation for my art, then go buy something at Waldo World." Her eyes narrowed into slits. "Dawn, I'm not going to give you the dress back—I'm not even going to let you try it on—if you don't go wash those clown spots of rouge off your face. Who taught you to do your makeup?"

Dawn stood rooted in place. With a brow furrowed with worry, she cut her eyes to me.

"Venice is probably worried that you'll get makeup on it," I said helpfully.

"No, I'm not. Those red dots on her cheeks look ridiculous. No wonder people make fun of you." She shook out the dress and held it up to inspect. "Go on—go. Scrub that face clean."

Dawn blinked back tears. I suddenly felt a twinge of compassion for her. When she closed the bathroom door behind her and turned on the faucet, I whipped around to Venice. "You don't have to be so mean about it."

Venice gave a little headshake. "Sorry. I picked up some kind of nasty virus in Africa. My doctor just put me on a new medication that's making me hallucinate." She pushed her sleeve halfway up and showed me a bruise shaped like the United

States. "I told the nurse she got one shot at hitting my vein. She said no problem, that if she didn't get it in the first time that she'd call Dee-Dee to do it. I asked her to go ahead and call Dee-Dee now. When she ripped off my tourniquet and left the room, I knew she was pissed off. But when she came back to report that Dee-Dee was busy and to suck it up, I smiled and blinked back tears as she savaged the vein in my arm . . . wait—can I tell you something funny? In my delirium, I thought you brought Dawn to my house and she had clown spots of rouge on her face."

"Yes. Not a hallucination." Neither was Dawn, exiting the bathroom with bloodshot eyes and blotchy skin. I felt horrible.

Venice thrust the dress at her. "Try this on."

While Dawn retreated to the bathroom, I implied that Venice was largely ungrateful for all the things I'd done for her, while she implied that I should be repeatedly smacked across the face for forcing Dawn and Dawn's fashion problems on her.

Then Dawn came out of the bathroom wearing the dress. I gasped.

Stunning. Except that it had Dawn as a human coat hanger. She wasn't wearing the dress so much as the dress was wearing her.

"Oh, thank goodness," I blurted out. Dawn shot me an odd look, probably because she didn't understand how appreciative I was that she had a dress to wear to a party that was clearly out of her league.

"I know," Dawn enthused. "It's gorgeous."

And it was. Not surprisingly, the reconstructed frock had something of an African flair that popped with winter colors. Venice had incorporated so many fabrics into Dawn's dress that the original garment seemed to vanish where the geometric designs took over.

"How'd you do this?" Dawn studied her reflection in Venice's mirror, touching the darts that shaped what had previously been an almost nonexistent bustline. Then she smoothed her hand along the waistline, and finally pressed her hands against fabric that conformed to her hips.

The whole thing fit like spandex on King Kong. I couldn't imagine Venice getting that dress to hug Dawn's curves any better without making the dress look vulgar.

"It's perfect." I looked her over. People Gran's age would approve of her hemline, and people our age would feel smugly self-satisfied that they didn't have to wear such an *avant garde* outfit, so Venice had pretty much hit all the demographics remaking the party dress.

"Yes, it's perfect." Venice gave Dawn a strained smile. "Thank you." Relief melted the tension in Venice's face. She let out a deep sigh, and I decided to just smile mindlessly and nod in agreement to whatever either of them said.

Then a panic-stricken expression on Dawn's part cast a pall over the moment. "I don't have the right shoes."

"I have shoe samples in my closet," said Venice. "They're last year's fashion, but maybe we can find a pair that work." She pushed back from the sewing machine. Soon we heard her rummaging around in an adjacent room. When she returned, she had three pairs of shoes. "What size do you wear?"

"Eight."

"I have an eight, a seven-and-a-half, and an eight-and-a-half."

The smallest shoe looked best with the dress, but Dawn walked around, hunched over and hobbling, to the extent that she seemed to be going the wrong way on the *Homo erectus* scale of evolution.

"These pinch my feet."

"Beauty knows no pain," Venice said and handed Dawn the larger pair. "I have footpads if you need them to help the shoes fit better." Without waiting for an answer, Venice retrieved a set

75

of spongy insoles from a nearby drawer and handed them over. "You have to return the shoes but . . . enjoy the dress." To me, she said, "You absolutely must take her to Harkman Beemis and get them to do her makeup. If you don't, she'll get laughed out of the country club."

Venice was right. Dawn took the pads and pushed them into the shoes, and I told her to wait in the car for me. When she'd left the room, I turned to Venice.

"Want to hang out later?"

She gave me a non-committal shrug. "Last night, the satellite to our television went out and the Internet went down. I was forced to spend time with my family. They seem like good people. I think I'll do it again tonight."

A shrill whistle from the other room caused my head to rivet in the direction of the Hanovers' kitchen.

"Argo fuck yourself. Hook 'em Horns. Kiss my nut."

I took a backward step. "What the . . . ?"

"That's Bob." Venice's entire body seemed to wilt. A serene smile appeared on her face, the kind that said *I'm a victim of other people's cruelty.* "I had an African Grey Parrot sent home for myself. When I returned from abroad, my brother had taught him to say stuff to upset me. I think it's actually supposed to be saying, 'Kiss my butt,' but my bird may have a speech impediment."

"Nice." *Not so nice.* "What do I owe you for the tailoring?"

"I'm not a damned seamstress, Dainty, I designed a dress," she bit out.

It was almost as if her reaction had nothing to do with the dress and everything to do with *moi.* As in, *Don't mind me, I'm a little high strung and I just polished off five donuts, but you ate the other seven.*

"Fine. What do I owe you for designing Dawn's dress?"

"I don't know. This will cost you. I'm still pretty furious at you for almost getting us killed."

And I was like, "What are you—a psychic? Do you have ESP? You don't know that for sure. What kind of psycho accusation is that?" But I said it in my mind, or possibly using my indoor voice, because I was still trying to keep my dignity and maintain my professional focus, since, *Hello—the investigation is still ongoing and they haven't gathered enough evidence to prove that I'm the reason those people died, Venice.*

And all the while Dawn was probably headed out the door thinking, "This is so über-cool. Finally, I'm going to be friends with Dainty Prescott."

CHAPTER SEVEN

After swinging by the Harkman Beemis cosmetic counter for a quick makeover, the cosmetician pronounced the results of her work "exceptional," but made a veiled remark about the unsuitability of Dawn's hair. True, it looked like it'd lost a fight to Teensy's lawnmower. She'd definitely need an appointment with my celebrity hairstylist to fix that in the coming week.

Instead of accompanying Dawn to the party—which I wouldn't dream of without an invitation; not to mention I didn't want to be seen with an outcast—I drove her there myself. On the ride over, I listed topics she shouldn't discuss, which, in retrospect, was like subconsciously encouraging her to choose those exact prohibited subjects I didn't want her to talk about.

"Don't say anything that makes you come across as weird. After you left yesterday, Teensy and I were talking about the creepy guy you hung out with back in high school. Don't talk about him." That alone would be enough to make people at the party back away from her to join any other conversation. I had no doubt the other debutantes would treat Dawn with courtesy, but only because of her legacy status. "And for heaven's sake— and your own—don't mention that you have a cousin serving time in the pen for insider trading."

Hand-to-mouth, she reared her head back like I'd sentenced him there myself.

"Don't look so shocked. Everybody knows. It's not like telling your kids their sick basset went to live on a big farm where he could play with lots of animals . . ." That really happened.

"My cousin was set up," Dawn said unconvincingly, with her eyes downcast.

Ha. Even the debutantes my age knew about it after overhearing their parents discuss it at the dinner table.

Then I felt a tug of affection for her dilemma because my blue-blood, blue-haired grandmother had recently become such a topic of conversation:

"Did you hear about Eugenia Prescott?"

"What about her—I adore Eugenia, her manners are impeccable—is everything okay?"

"Scandalous. I heard her son Beau took her out to a swanky restaurant over in Dallas for her birthday and she created a public spectacle."

"Oh, my stars." Hand to mouth. *"What on earth did she do?"*

"Well, in a very loud voice, Eugenia asked the Mexican waiter how he planned to celebrate Cesar Chavez Day—pick a melon, go on strike, tag a building, work on his car, or stage a drive-by at a quinceañera. Can you believe it? I swan."

"That's just terrible, making a scene. She shouldn't have said it where everybody could overhear. Where'd you hear such a thing?"

"Well, you know what they say, 'If you don't have anything nice to say' come sit by me!*"*

That actually happened when Gran tried Ambien for the first time. After the birthday dinner, she had to call Old Man Spencer to apologize for emailing him to see if he'd be interested in getting together for a game of naked Twister.

Gran's like . . . eighty-five or something.

Ugh. Naked Twister. Ugly visual.

After dropping Dawn off at the poshest, most exclusive country club in Fort Worth—*head down, don't make eye contact*—I arrived back at the Rivercrest estate and found Teensy in the kitchen, surveying the shelves in the pantry.

"What're you doing?"

"Looking for the baking chocolate."

"What for?"

"Daddy's paying me to bake chocolate chip cookies. Apparently *somebody* hid it." She shot me an accusatory look. "Just so you know, I found the location of Gran's 'special hiding spot' "—she made air quotes by crooking her fingers—"where I'd 'never find' the baking chocolate. Well, I actually did find that spot when I preheated the oven to bake a batch of cookies. But I can't find where the chocolate's been moved to in this house."

I gave her a pensive nod and feigned concern. My special hiding spot is my stomach. Nobody ever finds my chocolate.

"If you want chocolate chip cookies why don't you just go buy a dozen?"

"Because, one"—she ticked off reasons—"I don't have any money and, two, people are coming over to look at the house today, and Daddy's supposed to be here."

"Sellout." I sighed.

"Don't call me a sellout. I'm not a sellout."

"Traitor."

"I'm not a traitor either. I just know when to cut my losses. In order for our plan to work, one of us would have to be present at all times."

"I can't take this anymore. You're on your own. I'm going to Gran's to pick up a few things before she leaves on her cruise." Knowing Gran, she probably already changed the door locks.

I left Teensy in the kitchen, and an hour later, I arrived at Gran's. I decided to endear myself to her by stopping at the wrought-iron security gate in front of her estate to pick up a couple of pieces of trash that had blown out of the neighbors' garbage and into the gutter. As I cleaned up the litter, Old Man

Spencer, a withered, stooped, and wrinkled geezer, wearing a snappy cranberry-colored driving cap, skulked down the street and demanded to know who I worked for.

"Oh, hi there, Mr. Spencer." I flashed my pageant smile. "I'm just doing a bit of community service on my own in order to give back."

"You're a piece of shit whore." He spit on me. "When you finish, you'd better get over to my house and clean up my driveway." Then he turned and loped off down the street.

I guess he didn't recognize me as Gran's granddaughter.

Old Man Spencer is a conspiracy theorist and believes the government—or "guv-mit"—is out to kill him. At Halloween, someone got the bright idea to shine a laser light into his window. He burst out the front door and ploughed under most of the trick-or-treaters whose parents had driven them into the neighborhood to their grandparents' homes.

When I finally entered Gran's house, I went upstairs to tell her about Old Man Spencer's erratic behavior and found her standing at the entrance to her bathroom with her back to me. As I got closer, I saw that her eyes were closed and she had her hands beneath her chin in the prayer position.

"Give it up, Gran. Faith healing doesn't work on plumbing. I should know." Then she turned and I saw flesh-toned Band-Aids all over her face. "What's with the polka dots?"

"I'm never going back to that dermatologist. He has no bedside manner. I showed him a few spots I thought were melanomas and he told me they were just barnacles—that old people get them when they've been out at sea too long."

I shifted my eyes to the far corner of the room, to the set of Louis Vuitton luggage bursting at the seams. "Daddy said you're going on a cruise." When she gave me a vacant stare, I knew that getting answers to my questions would be like pulling teeth. "Who are you going with?"

"I really don't think that's any of your business."

"Are you and Mr. Spencer sharing the same quarters?" Lord only knew how many times I'd endured her lectures on propriety.

"I find it unimaginatively rude of you to ask such a personal question," she said with an aristocratic sniff.

"Well you should be aware he spit on me." She arched an eyebrow like she didn't believe me, so I cut to the chase. "Daddy says Teensy and I can't stay here while you're gone. Is that true?"

"It's time you girls went home. You're putting a damper on my social life."

"Please let Teensy and me stay here while you're gone."

"Not a chance. I don't want my eighteenth-century chairs wallowed on. Or my other antiques torn up. Or the two of you throwing wild parties in my absence. Besides, your sister doesn't have the sense God gave her, and you'll need your father's help watching out for her to make sure she doesn't pull any more dumb stunts like the time she made the ten o'clock news."

"Did you know Daddy's selling our house?" Her guilty expression made my head snap back. "He doesn't even want us there."

"At least he's not using you as a human shield. Quit complaining."

And that's how we would've left it, with me picking up my belongings and her giving me a brusque kiss good-bye at the kitchen door, had she not noticed a scorpion on the back terrace. Instead of getting a shoe or rolling up a newspaper, she went upstairs to her bedroom and got her .38 and shot it. I wasn't sure if I should count this as an epic win, or be worried that, one of these days, my entire family would hold family reunions in a mental facility.

Either way, she wasn't letting Teensy and me move back in

until she returned from her cruise. Not to mention she fleeced me of my house key to make doubly sure it didn't happen.

Nice to know she thinks we're both a couple of brain-dead, gullible dimwits.

Also nice to know that her gun is somewhere in her bedroom in case I ever need it.

On the drive back to Fort Worth, I felt the first pangs of hunger, pulled into the Speedy Mart parking lot, and went inside to see how much junk food the last two dollars in my wallet would buy. Salivating, I stood at the hot dog aquarium, mesmerized by the wieners turning in their greasy casings. I considered this to be a metaphor for my life—always moving forward yet never getting anywhere.

I saw a box by the condiments and slipped one of those thin plastic gloves over my hand, pulled a bun from the steamer drawer, and reached for the tongs to get my quarter-pounder wiener, which is even less glamorous than it sounds. The tiny bell overhanging the double glass doors tinkled and a shift of incoming air moved past me. Not that I cared. The chili dispenser sputtered out little farting sounds each time I pushed the button and I didn't want anyone to think those noises were coming from me.

I quickly wrapped it up and walked over to the chip display when a man shouted, "Nobody move." The commanding voice came from behind my shoulder and to the right.

Those two words were the actual sound of my heart collapsing in on itself and shriveling into a prune. Trapped in the presence of pure evil, I wasn't even aware that I'd dropped the chili dog on the tile floor until it splattered on my shoe.

As I shielded myself behind the chip display, I glimpsed a young stocker holding a swinging metal "Employees Only" door ajar. Peering through eyes wide with horror, he jutted his chin to motion me inside. For no good reason, I glanced back at the front door, where two men dressed in black, wearing black ski masks, menaced the customers. Halfway to hyperventilating, I did what any terrorized shopper would do: ran for my life. Only it was more like skulking for my life, since sudden movement might've called unwanted attention to myself.

They waved their semi-automatics at the two young men working the cash registers behind the counter. "Where is she?"

"Who?" Said the two cashiers in stereo.

"The blond."

I didn't need to hear any more; it was enough to know they'd come for me.

Once I cleared the swinging metal door, the stocker, who couldn't have been more than a teen, eased it shut. He led me through a maze of boxed inventory and quietly pushed the safety bar on the back exit. We took off running toward a steep embankment, sticking together tighter than barnacles on a Galveston shrimper. I made a split decision to head for the strip center nearby and veered off. He grabbed my wrist and redirected me, pulling me along until we were standing at the precipice of a gully filled with runoff water from the recent rain.

"Why'd you do that?"

"Too far to run if they come out the back," he said, winded. "You can't outrun a bullet."

I wasn't sure I trusted an acne-faced teenager to make life decisions for me, but he'd gotten me this far, and what he said made a lot of sense—until I realized what he had in mind.

I gave him a vehement headshake. "No. Don't."

"There's no other way out."

Apparently, I believed him because my next move entailed sliding down the embankment with my skirt peeled up around my waist. When we stopped inches from the brackish water, he stared intently at my purse.

"Do you have a phone?" Brown eyes, wide with fear, fixed me in their gaze. "My friends are still back inside. We have to call the police."

A great sense of urgency propelled me into movement. I pulled out my cell phone and dialed 9-1-1.

The young stocker said, "Who are those men?" I shook my head. He must've thought I was still waiting to make a connection because he asked, "What do they want with you?"

The phone purred twice before the police dispatcher came on the line. "9-1-1; state your emergency."

"Two masked men are holding up the Speedy Mart at . . ." I looked to the stocker to provide the address, and then relayed the information to the calm, capable police operator. Who, incidentally, seemed a little too calm and laid-back compared to the hysterical screaming going on in my head.

"What do they look like?"

I found the question jarring. Sarcasm kicked in. "Well, they're wearing ski masks. Black ski masks. Their clothes are black. They want to kill us, so if you could please send help . . ."

At that moment, a soft beep sounded in my ear. I pulled the cell phone away long enough to see Venice's cell phone number pop up on the phone's digital display screen.

The dispatcher redirected my attention and Venice's call routed to voicemail.

"Do they have weapons?"

"Yes," I practically shrieked. The stocker boy pressed his hands against the air in a downward motion, and I resorted to my inside voice. "Yes," I whispered. "Black guns, maybe Glocks. They looked plastic-y to me. I really couldn't tell, *because I was running for my life.*"

"Stay calm. You say they're dressed all in black?"

Frustration set in. "Once again—men dressed in black. Black ski masks. Black guns. I already told you. As soon as I saw them, I ran out the back. But people are still inside. Please, please send help. There are two of them. Send the SWAT team. I don't care, just get your law dogs out here to stop them."

"How tall are they?"

"Lady, I'm five-feet-four. Everyone looks tall to me."

I pulled the phone away from my ear and stared at it. I also gave the back of the storefront a quick eye scan. I didn't want to go into cold dirty water in the dead of winter, but I would if it'd save my life.

"What is your name, caller?"

"What?" My patience had worn thin. If they didn't get somebody out here quick, crime-scene detectives could take my personal information off my driver's license.

"What is your name and a callback number?"

Sirens screamed in the distance. I knew she could see my cell phone number on the display screen at the dispatch console. I'd had enough, secure in the knowledge that help was only seconds away. I thumbed off the phone and trudged up the embankment.

When I was inches from the top, the back door of the Speedy Mart flung open and the two armed men burst out. My knees nearly buckled. The essence of their murderous spree still tormented me.

The stocker grabbed my wrist for a second time and pulled me back. I watched, helpless, as the men yanked off their ski masks and wrangled out of their dark clothing. With a second set of clothes underneath, they ditched their black clothes in the outside dumpster and calmly ambled toward the strip center next door.

It took only seconds to brand their faces in my mind. I didn't recognize either of them, but felt pretty certain I could identify them in a photo or police lineup.

Working with a sketch artist for the next two hours at the

Dallas Police Department depleted the last of my energy. He had to erase the drawing so many times that I finally badgered him into pulling out an old Identi-kit and letting me assemble my own rendition of the men. The Identi-kit—a tool detectives used to put together a composite sketch of criminals or persons of interest—contained transparencies of eye shapes, hairstyles, noses, chins, and other facial features that could be overlaid to recreate a face. Because I wasn't that close in proximity to the men when they blasted out the back door, I got the red hair down pat on one of them and the shapes of their faces. I told the detective about the murders at the lodge, but I also told him I suspected Nerissa and asked him to interview her at the Tarrant County Jail.

While I worked with the Identi-kit, two more phone calls came in from Venice. Both cycled to voicemail. By the time I left the station, another missed call came in, this one from Dawn. Instead of listening to the messages, I texted Venice. Tapping out messages with a Beverly Hills manicure is like trying to get frisky in a Fiat. My cell phone's autocorrect kicked in and sent her a profane message that I then had to apologize for by way of a subsequent text message. My smartphone made me look stupid. I texted: Call me.

Seconds later, the ringtone assigned to Venice shattered the quiet. I immediately launched into an apology for the sleazy autocorrect message.

"Dainty, stop talking. Listen carefully." The drama in Venice's voice quickly phased into icy despair. "After you left, a couple of men came to the house and rang the doorbell. I saw them through the peephole. They had on black clothes and ski masks on top of their heads. It was them. I didn't know if they had more people at the back door so I ran upstairs and climbed up into the attic and hid—"

"Did you call the police?"

"*Don't talk.* I had my cell phone with me and called 9-1-1. When the police got here, the men fled." Silence stretched between us. "Aren't you going to say anything?"

"What. The. Hell?" was all I managed to bite out before she completely broke down. I'd been so certain this had been about Teensy and me. Now I wondered if I'd been followed to Venice's house.

She launched into full panic mode. "Dainty, my mom's due home any minute. If these men come back, my whole family could be slaughtered."

My stomach churned as if a swirling vat of battery acid had been emptied into my gut. My abdomen made noises like Chewbacca trying to get out. A soft beep sounded in my ear and I told Venice to hold on while I got rid of the incoming caller. When I pulled the phone away long enough to tap the button to switch over, Dawn's name appeared on the digital display. She likely needed a ride home from the party since she was so weird nobody would volunteer to take her.

I bristled at the intrusion. My stomach clenched. "Dawn, I can't talk to you right now. Something bad happened."

Her voice shrilled. "How could you possibly know what happened to me? I mean—it just freaking happened."

"I'm talking about Venice. What're you talking about?"

"I got one of the other debs to give me a ride home, just like you said. Only halfway there, I realized we were being followed."

"Hold on. Don't hang up." My "safety in numbers" theory kicked in. Survival instinct told me to gather everyone together.

I got back on the call with Venice. "Take a cab to my house," I said, trying to keep the hysteria out of my voice as the Dallas detective escorted me out to my car—my undercover custom-painted Barbie-pink Porsche with the DBUTNT license plates on it. "Whatever you do, don't drive your own car."

CHAPTER EIGHT

After convincing Dawn and Venice to meet me at the Rivercrest estate, I called Salem on my cell phone. She didn't answer, but I spoke to Mrs. Quincy and got my ass handed to me on Interstate-30 for being "a bad influence on Salem." She warned me to keep my distance from her daughter until the Texas Rangers figured out who the architect of the plan was for the massacre at the lodge. It was all I could do to keep her on the line long enough to tell her about the two men who'd tracked me to Dallas, and the men who'd gone to Venice's house. I made her promise to be careful, and to take care of Salem.

"All the more reason to keep your distance, Dainty," said Mrs. Quincy.

That's when I started to feel like a leper.

My phone gave off a series of beeps notifying me that I had an incoming text from Teensy. I'm on a perpetual diet, and she sent me a vivid enough photo of her steak and lobster dinner to make me want to lick my phone. Teensy's evil.

I called her. When she gave her location, I told her I'd swing by the restaurant to pick her up, despite the fact that she claimed to be out with a friend. The restaurant wasn't far from the Rivercrest mansion, and since I was almost home, I pulled into the parking lot and went inside to get her. She sat across the table from a man roughly our father's age. Obeying instinct, I apologized for having a family emergency and stole her away.

When I had her buckled into the passenger seat, I quizzed

her. "Are you so desperate that you've decided to date homeless men?"

That's when I found out that Teensy, idiot that she is, forgot to lock the side door leading into the kitchen. A drunk man apparently walked into the house, calling out, "Honey, I'm home." He'd gotten the wrong house, but—cheer up—it looked like we'd finally met the tenant living in our carriage house.

"Who is he?"

Teensy shrugged. "I think he's Daddy's AA sponsor."

In light of recent events, I remained wary. We had enough problems with one recovering alcoholic on the property, and by that I meant Daddy. Now we had two. Maybe even three if Teensy didn't stop boozing it up. I'm only basing my soon-to-be-recovering-alcoholic theory on the last time she went out, unsupervised, and woke up naked, duct-taped to an exterior wall at a local brewery with no memory of the night before.

She said, "What's so important that you had to make sure I didn't finish the first decent meal I've had all week?"

Teensy's gotten pretty eccentric over the past several months, so I wasn't fazed when she opened her purse and slipped on a pair of sunglasses. When I stopped talking, I noticed her head against the headrest, her slack-jawed mouth, and she was snoring.

I admit it. I smacked her arm. This latest stunt served as an indictment on her as a good judge of character.

Ensconced in the den with the television volume down low and tuned to the news station, Venice and Dawn joined us within minutes of each other. As I drew the curtains closed, we took turns swapping stories.

Dawn went first. "I think we were followed when you drove me to the country club."

Venice tuned up like a howler-monkey. "I knew this was your fault, Dainty, you led them to me."

I ignored her. "Just tell us what happened, Dawn."

"I convinced Melody Ritchey to give me a lift home because my mom was too busy to pick me up and Avery couldn't be bothered."

Thirty seconds into the conversation, I'd lost patience and, let's face it, I was scared for us. I twirled my finger to hurry her along. "Get to the point."

"When the valet brought Melody's car, two men pulled in behind us. They didn't get out, so they weren't there for any legitimate reason because the only events going on that afternoon were for ladies."

The air between us thickened.

"As soon as I realized these might be the men from the lodge, I told Melody to drive straight to the police station and let me out. She thinks I'm crazy, but at least she did it. I went inside and slipped into the restroom. They saw me get out of the car wearing my Venice Creation—and, *Oh-Em-Gee,* Venice, my dress was such a hit. I collected cards from ladies who want you to create clothes for them."

I barked at her to stop rummaging through her purse. "Finish the story."

"I knew those men would be waiting for me. So I found the ladies' room and redressed with my Venice Creation turned inside-out. Then I called a cab, walked out behind a couple of cops, and got in the taxi."

My jaw dropped. Impressive. I turned to Venice. "Tell them what happened after Dawn and I left for the country club."

Venice obliged. Words spilled out in nervous torrents. I shuddered as she became increasingly agitated retelling a story that left me terrified for the four of us, and everyone else we loved. Much later, I wished we'd fully grasped the darker implications of her words.

I got up from my place on the sofa and moved to the window,

then moved the curtain slightly until I could see outside. Shadows from the mercury vapor light across the street danced in the darkness. I let go of the fabric. While pacing, I told them about the men in black clothing and ski masks storming the convenience store in search of me.

"We need to get out of here." Venice choked on her words. "We're not safe."

I nodded in agreement. "But not tonight. Tonight we stick together. After tonight, anyone wanting to go her separate way can do so."

CHAPTER NINE

We spent a restless night under blankets on the living room floor while tiny shards of sleet pecked at the window panes like they wanted to be let inside. When a hazy blue dawn broke, a thick sheet of impassable ice blanketed the city. It glimmered with such intensity that the room brightened when the curtains were drawn back a smidge. I peeked outside. No unfamiliar vehicles had parked down the street. Nobody ventured out of their house to check the weather. No one's children clamored to play outdoors.

I noticed Dawn seemed particularly despondent so I asked why she had such a hang-dog look on her face. Then I pointed out that if her frown froze, she wouldn't make a pretty debutante.

The tension in her forehead relaxed. "Last night, after y'all went to sleep, I texted someone I met recently, and fell hard for. Looks like that relationship turned out to be an epic fail. Absence is supposed to make the heart grow fonder." Dawn's eyes rimmed red. "I guess it did—for someone else."

Teensy goaded her. "Aw, you got dumped? Well, suck it up. Debutantes don't cry over guys."

Dawn said, "We're never getting back together. Ever."

"Gonna write a song about it, Taylor Swift?" Teensy challenged.

I intervened. "Dawn's our guest—for now—and there's safety in numbers." But what worried me was having one more person to keep track of, or drag us down if we needed to bolt.

"I'm bored," Teensy said. "I think I'll bake chocolate chip cookies."

"Great idea." I turned to Dawn. "Teensy's right. Debutantes don't display their emotions for the world to see. Debutantes are elegant and even stoic when the need arises. Instead of brooding over a guy, you should count your lucky stars that you're free to do what you want."

Venice, who'd covered her head with a blanket, sat, bolt-upright, like a pop-up target.

"I need my sewing machine and my fabric. Didn't your mother own a sewing machine?"

"Yes, but it's in the attic." I pointed upward.

"Can we bring it down?"

"It's not portable so we can't take it with us once we're able to leave."

"I don't care. I need to do something with my hands or I'll go stark raving mad."

I wanted to tell her she could start by strangling Teensy and Dawn, but Teensy was already spooning store-bought cookie dough onto a sheet pan, and I wanted some; and Dawn was—well, Dawn had turned into an emotional wreck—so I told her I understood, patted her back, *There-there,* and got her to follow me to the attic to see if we could get my late mother's sewing machine as far as the second floor.

We set it up in one of the upstairs guest rooms. I chose the one with corner windows that overlooked two sections of the cobblestone driveway and asked Venice to keep a lookout for anything unusual. I also found a box of fabric with Vogue patterns stored away in an old steamer trunk and we brought that down for Venice to paw through. By the time we got the sewing machine set up, the sweet scent of chocolate chip cookies wafted upstairs. I suggested we claim our share before Teensy scarfed them all down.

We ate our cookies and, once Venice got squared away with her sketch pad, Dawn and I sat around the table hammering out a plan while Teensy tidied up the kitchen. In the middle of our discussion, Teensy dropped something in the walk-in pantry. It sounded expensive.

I excused myself from the table to investigate. Sure enough, when I walked in, Teensy was squatting on the floor, picking up broken ketchup packets that Nerissa had rat-holed from Whataburger. *I can only assume.* She's the only pack rat we know of with a predisposition to hoard. Probably dated back to living in poverty, before she scoped out a rich Westsider to seduce and kill off. *Again, I can only assume.*

The pantry floor looked like a crime scene full of blood spatter cast-off.

To my shock and amazement, Daddy's big pickup rolled up next to the kitchen door.

"You'd better get that cleaned up." I left her to tend to the mess.

Booted feet crunched the ice as Daddy stomped a footprint into the frost, then carefully planted each footstep to test its stability before putting all of his weight down. I met him at the back door, truly thrilled to see him. We needed a handgun, and Daddy owned plenty. After all, this was Texas and that's what we do. I just didn't know where he kept them locked up.

He wiped his feet on the doormat, stepped inside, and took one look at Dawn. Then he gave Teensy and me the visual onceover. Steely eyes said *Have you looked in the mirror lately?* but his mouth said, "No way." He turned around to leave again.

I followed him outside to have a conversation. He didn't seem to be paying attention to me, and I needed to catch him up on everything that'd happened in his absence. Despite what I said, he continued to navigate his way back to the truck, with me following behind in the footprints he made.

"Daddy, *listen* to me." Frustration built. Tears welled. With his back still to me, his arms rose in surrender. I took it to mean that my words were registering with him, but I needed more. "No, Daddy, listen to me with your *eyes.*"

He turned to face me. "Did you let the Ranger know what's happening around here?" He said this in the same impassive way someone comments on the tag poking out of your shirt.

"No. What can he do from way out there?"

Heavy eye roll. "Dainty, he's in charge of the case. Don't you want to know where the investigation stands?"

"I already know where it stands because those men are here in Fort Worth. They targeted each of us, except maybe Salem. But if they found us, they can find her, too. We're not safe."

He heaved a sigh so heavy that the vapor trail from his breath shot out a good two feet. "I suppose there's no choice." I held my breath in anticipation until he finished his thought. "Take these morons to your grandmother's." He dug into his pocket, pulled out a key ring, and extracted one of the keys. "Here."

"They're not morons, Daddy." Sulking, I defended them. At the same time, I wanted to shout, "Nailed it!"

"Isn't that Avery's stepdaughter sitting at the table?"

I'd left the kitchen door ajar, and the girls were inside watching us. "Yeah. Dawn."

"Moron." He pointed an accusatory finger. Then the finger shifted to my sister. "Teensy—moron." Then he stuck the finger inches from my face. "You—moron."

When labeling us, he'd conveniently left Venice out. "I suppose Venice is a moron, too?"

"Especially her. Why're you looking at me like that? The moron went to Africa thinking she'd gotten a raise and found out she'd negotiated her salary in two different currencies. She barely scraped up enough money to buy a plane ticket back home. Moron."

It already felt like I'd been cooped up in the house with these people for seven straight days. A thick sheet of ice prevented us from venturing outdoors, and the roads all around us were treacherous, but—good news—inclement weather made it less likely that four ninja-assassins would show up here unannounced. Teensy'd spent all morning baking cookies and eating them, while I spent all morning thinking about the Whataburger a mile away that I couldn't seem to get to; as well as good Mexican food down the street that I couldn't seem to get to; and *The Shining*. I'd been thinking about that, too.

"Could you loan us one of your guns?"

"No. But I can loan you a broom. You'd better make sure this house is spic-and-span before you head over to your grandmother's fortress, because I have a shit-slew of buyers coming in to see this place as soon as the roads are cleared. In the meantime, open the cabinet doors under the sinks and let the water faucets drip so the pipes don't freeze."

"Where will you be?"

He wagged his finger in the direction of the kitchen table. "Anyplace this outfit can't find me."

Being iced in made me realize that I know exactly what to do in a Zombie Apocalypse.

After Teensy polished off the last cookie, Venice went back upstairs to get creative with my late mother's steamer trunkful of fabrics. Dawn thought it'd be a great time for us to hang out and resume debutante orientation. I thought it'd be an even better time to lock myself in my room and beat my head against the wall.

"How sweet," I gushed. *Not sweet.* "I have calls to make. Why don't you watch TV?"

"Because I'm not accustomed to watching mindless adventures. Can't I just sit here with you? I'll just watch and listen. I won't talk." She made the invisible zipped-mouth gesture, then turned the invisible key in the invisible lock and tossed the key over her shoulder. For a second, I could've sworn I heard it clink hitting the floor, but that was just Teensy dropping utensils in the kitchen.

"I'm sorry." *Not sorry.* "But one of these is a business call. I have to phone the TV station to find out when Gordon wants me to come in to work." I flashed a smile.

"What—that'll take about a minute, right?"

"I have other calls." I said this with an edge. Since Daddy thought I should call Ranger Hill to let him know the assailants from the lodge had followed us back to Cowtown, I put him on the notification list. And then there was the more pressing matter of on-again, off-again Jim Bruckman. I'd make that call in private.

The last time I saw Jim Bruckman, we agreed to take a two-week break from each other. Clearly, I'd been off the grid for a few days, so he knew nothing of the threat on our lives. Since I'd been through a handful of harrowing ordeals lately, and probably shouldn't have lived through any of them, I decided it might be a good time to tell him about the shootout at the lodge. Teensy's convinced that I have a guardian angel, but if I do, this latest disaster made me think he'd either taken the day off or been fired. Bruckman's convinced that I'm "conflict habituated" and, therefore, way too much trouble to keep as a girlfriend.

Locking myself in my bedroom, I broke our agreement and made the call. I sensed his cornflower blue eyes crinkling at the corners and his charming grin at the other end of the line.

"How are you enjoying the weather being shut in with a bunch of estrogen-driven females?"

"I'm sick of these people. I've had it up to there with these people." Although he couldn't see me, I measured over the top of my head to show how fed up I was. "Wait—how'd you know about the girls?"

"I got a text chock-full of profanity from your sister. I asked her who taught her to curse like that. She wrote: 'Dainty's other boyfriend.' "

"Why're you talking to my sister?"

"She calls sometimes to chat."

"Are you sure she's not a mole in my operation?" Instead of answering my question, he mentioned that a lot of people in the city had no power, and asked if I was staying warm at the Rivercrest mansion. "Yes." I parted one of the curtains a sliver and scanned the street for cars that didn't fit the neighborhood. "But looking out the window, I think it'd be safe to say the squirrels' nuts are frozen."

He let out a roguish chuckle, and it almost felt like he'd forgiven me for all the dumb stunts I pulled over the past five weeks. So I asked if he'd supply me with guns. Which I instantly realized made me sound like a gun-runner, distributing arms to nefarious people. People such as myself.

"Yeah, because I want to spend half a day giving a statement to Internal Affairs about how come the ballistics in a homicide matched a gun registered to me."

"Well, can you at least drive over and pick me up and take me to buy one?"

"Absolutely not."

That's when the conversation went downhill.

My next phone call went to Ranger Hill. Since he didn't answer, I left a voicemail catching him up and asking him to return my call at his earliest convenience. Then I put in a call to Salem. She asked how I was doing and mentioned her mother was standing right beside her. That dried up the conversation.

A few minutes before three o'clock, when I was in mid-dial

to Ranger Hill again, Venice let out a blood-clotting scream. I dropped the phone and ran to the stairs by way of the fireplace. I grabbed a brass poker and took the steps in twos. I'd almost reached the landing when Venice ran past me, sending me halfway down a flight of steps, screaming bloody murder as if someone tried to slice her throat.

"He climbed the wall." She spoke in breathless, abbreviated strokes. "Thought it was a bird. Crashing into the glass. Turned around. Saw his face. Soulless eyes looking at me."

Teensy and Dawn grabbed her protectively and pulled her beyond my field of vision.

I knew this man couldn't get inside without breaking a window, and I hadn't heard glass shatter. I entered the room brandishing the fireplace poker while a man dressed in black, with a ski mask pulled down over his face, framed his head in the window.

With all of the force I could muster, I reared back and swung, shattering the pane and catching him in the middle of the forehead. He let out a noise that sounded like the *woof* of a gas stove burner coming on. Then he dropped out of sight. The sickening thud of dead weight hitting the ground compelled me to stick my face through the hole I'd made in the window. Near his head, frozen snow turned crimson.

Sluggish footfalls caused me to lift my gaze. Daddy's tenant in the carriage house took cautious steps toward our house as he broke the ice with a rock buster.

He hollered, "Call the police," but I stood anchored in place and made no attempt to do anything of the sort. After a quick eye scan of the back half of our property, and seeing no other ninja-assassins, I ran downstairs and pulled Teensy aside from the others.

"We have to talk to your boozer friend."

Teensy said, "Did you kill that man?"

"Don't know. But we have to get out of here, now. The others could be waiting nearby. I'm not going to stick around and let them pick us off like they did those poor people at the lodge. Now, go get the others and grab your things. Move."

I left through the kitchen door with purpose in my step, crunching through a thick layer of ice on my way to the rear of the house.

Daddy's tenant had almost come even with the bleeding man on the ground.

"Is he dead?" My voice shook. So did my knees. I hadn't dressed for temperatures in the teens and my body shivered from the cold as well as the shock of having a man scale my house in the middle of the afternoon. And let's face it, my teeth chattered from pure fear because I'd probably killed him.

"I don't know." Daddy's renter kept his gaze fixed on the body. "Do you know this guy?"

"No. Are you kidding?" Flabbergasted, I noticed a couple of tools and a suction cup embedded in the ice. This led me to believe he intended to enter the house by cutting the glass and removing it in such a way that it'd be too late by the time we discovered our intruder. "We have to get out of here. *Right now.* Do you have a car?"

"An SUV. Where do you want to go?"

"I'm not sure. Maybe Dallas. Will you take us?"

Without taking his eyes off the man in black, he nodded.

I'd become so focused that I hadn't heard anyone else until I sensed Teensy beside me.

She lifted a limp hand and extended her pointer finger. "Did you kill him?"

"Go get the others. Your friend, Mister . . ." I paused in mid-sentence and waited for one of them to supply his name.

"Green," he said. "Herb Green."

"Your friend, Mr. Green, is getting us out of here. Now go

lock the house."

"What about him?" Teensy pointed again.

I whipped around to face her. "What. About. Him?"

"Are we just going to leave him here?"

Part of me wanted to ask if she'd like to take him with us. The other part wanted to shake her until her teeth rattled. "First, we're getting out of here. Then we'll call the police."

While Herb Green hiked back to the carriage house, I wielded the fireplace poker above my head and stood guard over the man, watching a river of blood oozing across the clean, white snow. I couldn't see myself pulling off his mask. I couldn't see myself getting close enough to check his pulse, only to have him grab me with his hands and apply a cello stroke to my neck with a box cutter like the villains who won't die in those gratuitously violent slasher movies.

Teensy broke my concentration. "Holy guacamole—look what I found." She bent down, picked up a 9mm Glock, and held it aloft.

Venice and Dawn plunged out the back door, making their way across the ice by using the footpath we'd created.

When they came within a few feet of us, Venice called out in a voice that sent a serpent-like vapor coiling up from her mouth, "We heard a noise. I think someone's inside the house."

CHAPTER TEN

Through the back windshield of Herb Green's SUV, we had a view of Teensy's and my childhood home—our sanctuary. We played there, celebrated birthdays and holidays there, planted thirty-foot windmill palms in memory of my grandfather, and grew into a tight and loyal family there. But as the sprawling Rivercrest estate shrank beyond the glass, I wondered if we'd live to see it again.

The very idea left me cloaked in profound sadness, but even I knew that our best interests wouldn't be served by remaining at our estate. If my suspicions were correct, and Nerissa orchestrated these vicious attacks, then our home was far from impenetrable at the hands of skilled, diabolical criminals. Nerissa knew every inch of the place, including the alarm code, which meant these calculating, controlling hit men knew the same details—and their brazenness continued to evolve.

Until I could figure out what to do, I sat with the 9mm Glock beneath my thigh and gave Herb Green directions to WBFD. I chose the TV station because it had a gated entrance and a high cinder-block wall that surrounded it. The architect of that barricade had put some thought into safety by embedding broken glass bottles into the mortar at the top to keep the creepy neighbors on the other side out, as well as anyone who thought they could scale it and overtake the station and its occupants.

I studied Venice in the failing light. She'd become quiet and withdrawn, but at least I didn't have to talk her down off a ledge. As for Dawn, she sat stoically next to Venice, occasionally patting Venice's knee and whispering that everything would be all right "now that Dainty's in charge." Venice only looked up long enough to glare at me once, which I interpreted as *Dainty's the reason we're in this fix.*

The ensuing silence was anything but comforting.

When we pulled up to the gate, I hung far enough out the window to swipe the key pad with my electronic card. The sodium vapor street lamps had come on, casting an orange glow that made the station's parking lot look like we'd rolled onto the world's largest Dreamsicle. A thick sheet of ice obscured the lines to the parking spaces—not that it mattered because there were fewer than ten cars in the entire parking lot, and it would've been like sliding across glass if we'd tried to walk it.

"Would you mind letting us out at the front door, please, Mr. Green?" I asked sweetly, as if I hadn't just killed a man and left him to bleed out in the snow. Knowing that the same man and his friends wouldn't have given it a second thought had our roles been reversed helped me move beyond the guilt.

Mr. Green pulled up to the steps and waited while we got out and carefully navigated our way up to the glass doors. Ice that had thawed out earlier froze over once the sun went down, but judging by the tiny transparent rocks scattered about, it looked as if the Korean janitor had gotten around to casting out rock salt or sand to melt it. I swiped the electronic lock and the three girls went inside. From my place at the front door, I studied Mr. Green in the shadows of the SUV and mentally retracted every rotten impression I'd formed about him. He saw me coming back down the steps and hit the electric button to slide the passenger window halfway down. His face was easier to see under the light of the portico—long nose with a bump on the bridge of it, large ears, thin, gaunt facial features, and a receding hairline. His skin appeared slightly leathery and a bit unhealthy, as one might expect after years as a hard drinker.

"Thank you." Shivering, I reached through the open window to shake his hand.

"My pleasure."

"I'll call the police. They'll send a unit by, and maybe the M.E.'s Office. I won't say you were there." I took a breath. "I'll need you to tell Daddy about the broken window."

"I'm not going straight home but I'll let your father know."

I didn't blame Mr. Green for not wanting to talk to the cops. I didn't relish the thought of talking to them, either. And I needed to let Dusty Hill know what happened. Not that he could do anything now that the die had been cast, but the old saying went "One riot, one Ranger," and I figured I needed him on my side when it came down to the nut-cutting.

After I entered the building, I ushered the girls to my postage stamp–size office and struck out to find Rochelle. Rochelle is J. Gordon Pfeiffer's right-hand woman, and J. Gordon Pfeiffer is the station manager, and my boss. We have kind of a host–parasite relationship and, believe it or not, I'm not always the parasite. As owner-proprietor of the Debutante Detective Agency, I'm often the host, especially since Gordon hired me to pull his bacon out of the frying pan on several occasions.

Rochelle even hired me once, to find out if Aspen Wicklow, our popular red-haired anchor, needed to be worried as to whether her boyfriend, the Johnson County Sheriff, might be carousing with another woman. He wasn't, and now they're getting married. So there's that.

The menopausal Rochelle wasn't at her desk, but her jacket had been fitted over the back of her chair. I caught sight of the bedraggled plant I'd given her for Christmas and did a slow burn. I spent good money on that orchid and devoted a lot of time picking it out, obsessing over whether it was too big, too small, too whatever. The last time I'd been at the station, the plant looked robust and hardy.

I found Rochelle in the break room, hunkered over a Styrofoam container filled with what smelled like hot-and-sour soup from the Asian diner down the street. She'd spread little condiment packets of soy sauce, duck sauce, and hot mustard across the little bistro tabletop like the winning poker hand, and was spelling out swear words by drizzling a packet into her soup bowl. When she looked up, her gray eyes glittered like ice cubes. Immaculately dressed, with flawless alabaster skin and glossy dark hair strained back from her face in a French twist, she didn't look so much like Gordon's elegant, ball-busting assistant as much as a human vessel to channel the presence of the Evil Queen.

She leveled a shotgun gaze at me. "What." This seemed less of a question than a demand.

I did an over-the-shoulder thumb gesture toward her desk. "Looks like your plant froze."

"That's like saying the *Titanic* took on a bit of water." She let out a sigh that sounded like she'd punctured a lung. "I thought the roads were impassable. How'd you get here?"

"A friend with a four-wheel-drive dropped us off. He took it slow. Like forever."

Rochelle, who drove a red Nissan "Z", became even paler, if that were possible. She reacted as if I'd put her on a train bound for a death camp instead of merely reaffirming that the roads were treacherous. Then she smiled, dazzling me with rows of even white teeth, and pulled herself together like a crazy woman with the ability to present well for about five seconds. "Why? Why are you here? You're not supposed to be back until next week."

"I brought my friends—"

"This isn't the country club, it's a business."

106

"It was the only place I could think of to go where it'd be safe."

She put the empty condiment pack on the table and picked up one filled with hot mustard. Drizzling new letters—F-U-C—she reached for another mustard packet to finish her word.

"What have you done?"

"I . . . we . . ." Still unconvinced that Teensy and I were the catalysts for the bad stuff that had happened, I included my confederates when I voiced what might just become my confession.

"Spit it out, Dainty. It's been a dismal day, we're operating on a skeleton crew, these new SMU interns are blithering idiots, and I have to run outside every half hour just to keep my turbo-charged hot flashes in check." She pushed back from the table a few inches and twisted in her chair to face me full-on. Her face grew taut with irritation. "Know what I've been doing all day? Of course you don't. I've been interviewing applicants for the vacant position in Production. The job fell to me because Gordon wasn't around. Would you like to know what kind of applicants we've been getting?"

I had the good sense to shake my head, because no, I seriously did not want to know.

"Of course you do. So far, none of them are qualified for the job. Except maybe the last guy who walked in here about an hour before you arrived. But then we'll never know, will we? Because he stumbled in out of the cold with little shards of ice clinging to his beard, wanting to know what he needed to do to pick up an application."

My palms went clammy and my throbbing pulse picked up its pace. Anxiety had fully kicked in, drawing me to the conclusion that I should probably consider getting on some sort of medication regimen. And Rochelle wasn't even the most insane person I had to deal with at the station.

"Know what I told him would get him an application?" Rochelle inclined her head to the right. "Of course you don't."

Unwilling to guess, I shrugged.

" 'Pants,' " She announced this with authority. "That's what I told him. 'Two forms of identification and putting on a pair of pants will get you an application.' "

Her reaction probably seemed confusing to the applicant— who'd shown up naked from the waist down—*who was just trying to get a job, and get off the government dole, Rochelle.*

The Evil Queen continued her rant. "Now you have a peek into what my day's been like until you showed up. Your sudden appearance here can't possibly be the harbinger of good news for me, since I don't see a rotisserie chicken with cornbread dressing in your hands to replace my shitty bowl of soup." Her eyes went wide, as if she'd experienced a light bulb moment. "Oh, goody—thought of another word."

She snatched a condiment package from the bunch, and tore off the end with her teeth.

Watching her drizzle an "S" above the bowl, I stared, fascinated, as she added an "H."

Okay, now I'm really scared.

"So, why?" Rochelle finished the word, put down the empty packet, and braced her arms across her chest. "Why are you and your entourage here?"

"I may have killed a man."

Eerie, translucent eyes lit up like slanted little cat eye–shaped headlights. "Well, why didn't you say so?" She opened her wallet, pulled out a business card, and thrust it at me. "Call this guy. He's the one who got me off when I shot that rapist who bludgeoned my best friend's daughter. Tell him I sent you. I keep him on retainer." She eyed me up. "Come to think of it, you probably should, too." Then she handed it over. "Go ahead, take it. He'll give you a good price."

And I was all, "Exactly," and "I can't tell you how long I've waited for this moment," even though I didn't really mean it, because I still secretly held out hope that I hadn't killed anyone; or that I wouldn't have to spend three days in front of a grand jury; or that I wouldn't need a lawyer to keep me out of jail. I *cannot* do jail. Jail would get me kicked out of The Rubanbleu, and being a member of the most exclusive ladies' social group is all Teensy and I had going for us at the moment.

I dropped into a bistro chair and recounted the west Texas shootout, and described the four mass murderers who'd followed us back to the Metroplex.

For once, I managed to ding the carnival bell on Rochelle's emotional strongman attraction. Gordon's right-hand woman looked suitably impressed.

She said, "Will you be staying long enough to do the ten o'clock news? Steve Lenox claims he's iced in and can't get here. Personally, I think he's a liar and a sociopath."

I briefly considered it. For one thing, I'm like the biggest ham ever. And you never know when important people will see one of your broadcasts and—*voilà*—Yours Truly gets her own talk show in the national market. But as desirable as the opportunity sounded, I couldn't risk being seen on television until those men were caught and dealt with. Vestiges of their murderous spree still overwhelmed me. If I thought about it more than a few seconds, my mind would replay those executions and I'd relive the sounds of agonizing screams, and actually visualize the victims pitching forward in slow motion.

In an uncharacteristic move, I shied away from the camera. "I think I just need to talk to Gordon."

Talking to Gordon had gotten easier now that my investigation—or, rather, the Debutante Detective Agency's investigation—into his wife's so-called murder actually cleared him as a suspect. To date, there'd been no arrests, and police still considered it to be an open investigation, but I suspected it wouldn't be long before the cops made an arrest. In a word, he owed me.

"Gordon isn't here. But if you want me to tell him you won't be in for a while, I will."

I was thinking she'd probably start with something like, *Guess what that Dainty Prescott got herself into this time,* and end with telling all of her friends that she'd known me way before I got sentenced to life in prison. Rochelle can be fickle that way.

"Tell him people are out to get me and I'm in hiding. He'll understand." In my head, I could almost hear Rochelle's interpretation, *That Dainty Prescott killed a guy and now she's on the lam.*

But he *would* understand. I'd recently been the target of a stalker who'd seen me on TV, and Gordon became way more involved than he meant to when my stalker sent threatening letters and severed blond Barbie heads to me at the TV station. He wanted his employees to be safe, but there were also things Gordon didn't want: like wearing jewelry on-air unless a sponsor sent it; or females wearing anything but solid, gem-tone colors while delivering the news; or lawsuits—or for employees of the station to come under the cold scrutiny of the judicial system.

"Where will you go?"

"I'm not sure."

I didn't want to disclose our new location. Rochelle and I had a tenuous relationship, and it was fair to say I didn't fully trust her. But lately she'd been nicer to me, and, in the event the cops investigated me, I'd like to think she'd *have* my back rather than *stab* me in it.

"One more thing, Rochelle. We need a ride." I mentally considered a handful of other employees and ruled them out as fast as their names sprang to mind. Tig Welder, the senior investigative reporter and resident snake-in-the-grass, wasn't an option. I didn't have the nerve to ask Aspen Wicklow, who still held it against me for inadvertently getting her kidnapped by a psychopath, and was probably scared shitless she'd end up being my stepsister because Daddy went on a few dates with her mother. Stinger Baldwin, the station's junior investigative reporter, was out on location in the station's electronic news-gathering van, better known as the ENG van. The two photographers, Reggie and Max, would've been willing to take us to Gran's, but one or both were out on location with Stinger.

That left Chopper Deke.

Chopper Deke scared the hell out of me. Before meeting the station's helicopter pilot, I'd never before seen anyone with the whites of their eyes exposed all the way around such dazzling, pale blue irises. Even though he looked like a mental patient, Chopper Deke was probably the bravest person I'd ever met. I was on my way to find him when I caught Gordon coming out of his office dressed in faded athletic sweats and carrying his rumpled brown suit and a tan shirt folded over his arm.

Figuring that Rochelle hadn't out-and-out lied to me, as much as she'd run interference for Gordon by telling me he wasn't at the station, I momentarily forgot about Chopper Deke and stepped into the boss's path. Using his middle finger, our portly, balding station manager pushed the wire-rimmed eyeglasses with Coke-bottle lenses back up the bridge of his nose. I wasn't at all certain this was an innocent gesture on his part, or if he was suggesting that I keep my distance and refrain from annoying him.

I seized the moment to let him know I'd be going off the grid for a few days. Maybe longer. "I need to talk to you about taking more time off, Mr. Pfeiffer."

"Gordon," he corrected me.

His breath, a weapon of mass destruction, drifted over to me.

He'd been boozing it up again. Apparently, he didn't know whether to head for the gym and get to work on that overhanging paunch, or have happy hour in his office, behind closed doors. He should probably work on a business plan to open a workout place called Gym and Tonic. That way, he could either work out, or have a drink, or both.

"Is this because of your grandmother?" he said.

"My grandmother?" True, she was old—he probably thought she'd gotten sick and needed me to care for her. "My grandmother's fine. She's not sick or anything." I grinned. "She's on a cruise—can you believe it? With Old Man Spencer from down the street. It's all on the up-and-up," I quickly added. "His son's along to chaperone. You never know what kind of mischief old people can get into, right?"

"You didn't watch tonight's newscast?" His expectant face fell. "Oh, damn." He snared me in his nickel-plated gaze. "Nobody came to your house? No police?"

Police? They already know I killed a man? Confused, my mouth hung open. I blinked.

"When's the last time you saw your old man?"

"I saw my father a few hours ago." My voice broke on *my father*. "What's this about?"

"It's not my place to be having this conversation with you. Just tune in to the news, kid."

After Gordon gave me a sympathetic pat on the shoulder and hurried off to find Rochelle, Teensy bolted from my office. The ghastly look on her face told me our problems just got worse. She mouthed the word "look" and pointed to the television mounted in the station's foyer. The "Breaking News" ribbon flashed across the bottom of the screen. Then Aspen Wicklow, our station's most trusted anchor, cried as she broke the tragic news about an oceanliner that sank off the coast of Cancun.

The same ship that Gran and Old Man Spencer boarded.

It seemed that the universe had just called my note and demanded a lump-sum payment on my Karmic debt.

CHAPTER ELEVEN

Precious little of the ride to Gran's estate stuck with me. I do recall Chopper Deke popping his head into my office, rattling the keys to Tig Welder's Hummer, telling us to bundle up, and leading us out into the freezing parking lot in a full-on death trance. I pretty much remained numb as we rolled past smears of colored lights and neon signs that advertised motels, businesses, and restaurants along the way. A huge orange moon hung low in the sky, playing peekaboo with the buildings that made up the city's skyline. Fearing that the chills running up and down my spine would never go away, I sat silently in the front seat with Chopper Deke while Teensy sandwiched herself in the back seat between Venice and Dawn.

When I glanced over my shoulder, Teensy's eyes glistened with unshed tears. Like Teensy falling forward into my arms in the typical grief response that no one ever wants to witness; or like Aspen Wicklow reporting breaking news through sobs, I could've broken down into a sniveling mess, too, but I kept my dignity. Being a Prescott, as well as a debutante of The Rubanbleu, gave me two good reasons not to pull a dying swan act where others could see.

Truthfully, other than a profound sense of loss that snared me in its grip and threatened to suffocate me, I didn't know what to feel. After our mother died—*pardonez moi*, after Nerissa *murdered* our mother—Daddy pretty much ignored Teensy and me. On some level, we understood that he needed to come to terms with his own grief; but his apathy toward us left no one to shepherd us through our own horrible ordeal—that is, until Gran took us on as her project. For a socialite whose life revolved around day trips with her cronies, Wednesday afternoon bridge games at the country club, shopping at Harkman Beemis, luncheons with her friends at Michelin-starred restaurants, and The Rubanbleu, her involvement with us had only been one of convenience. After all, Teensy and I were co-eds at different universities. But once Daddy started dating Nerissa, Gran dropped everything to take us under her wing and insulate us from "white trash."

That's when membership in The Rubanbleu and my debut into Fort Worth society, followed by Teensy's debut a year later, became the rebar in the infrastructure of our miserable existence.

Thoughts of my grandmother's last moments consumed me. *Did Gran suffer? Was she asleep when the ship ran aground and capsized? Did she fight for her life in the ocean's black abyss?*

A violent twist in my chest wrung the air from my lungs. I got a gut-wrenching visual of Gran, struggling against the undertow, desperate and freezing and afraid. My heart hurt. My eyes burned from holding back tears. I drew in shallow breaths until I got my wind back, but the pain didn't abate. I regretted our past squabbles and wished only to see her alive once more, so I could express my appreciation for everything she'd done for me back when Daddy decided he didn't love us anymore.

Although Chopper Deke frequently cut his eyes in my direction, he allowed me the "alone time" I needed to wrestle with my thoughts.

For no good reason, my mind cast back almost two weeks ago, after Bruckman and I decided to take a break from our on-again, off-again relationship. Mostly it was Bruckman's brilliant idea. My separation anxiety had gotten so intense that I found myself sniffing his T-shirt that I'd promised to launder. Without making a sound, Gran crept up to the attic where I have my own room and caught me surrendering to raw emotions. Instead of acting like the Village Scold, she studied my reflection in the dresser mirror until I became aware of my audience and abruptly pulled myself together.

For as long as I'd known her, Gran had been a huge believer in the "what doesn't kill you makes you stronger" theory. But instead of berating me for being so emotionally caught up in a man who didn't reciprocate my feelings to the same degree, she delivered a totally unexpected response. Elegant in her silk kimono, enveloped in a fragrance that hinted of chocolate, oranges, and vanilla, she cracked a sad smile.

"I used to do that too, after your grandfather died."

In that moment, I experienced a densely complicated emotion. For all of my difficulties with Gran—like the time we both donated blood and regained consciousness on the floor holding half-eaten cookies; or critiquing her bad driving habits; and especially the time she and Daddy sold my Porsche because they didn't think I'd return from Mexico with a two-million-dollar bounty on my head—I believed, in that shared moment, she understood me.

Inhuman sounds released me from my trance.

Teensy whimpered in the back seat. I should've been sitting beside her, holding her hand and being the big sister, while comforting her with platitudes, and yet I couldn't help her. Watching her repress her tears, the best I could do for her was to force a reassuring smile.

A terrifying childhood memory flashed into mind. While flying a major airline, the cabin pressure suddenly changed. Without warning, the oxygen masks dropped out of their compartments. Spellbound, I watched my parents put their masks on first before sliding mine over my face. The sight of those masks popping out like jack-in-the-boxes convinced me we were about to die. Our plane landed safely, but the experience of helplessness that rushed back to me was every bit as disheartening as learning of my grandmother's death.

Chopper Deke seemed to read my thoughts. Still, he said nothing.

I lifted my finger and pointed to the off-ramp. As we drove through the intersection a mile down the frontage road, I pointed again. Before long, we ended up at the end of the cul-de-sac, in front of Gran's house. I robotically dug into my wallet for the electronic key to the intimidating wrought iron gate and passed it to Chopper Deke. Without a word, he swiped the key pad and handed it back to me as the gate yawned open.

When he came to a stop in front of Gran's red-brick Georgian manor, I barely met his spooky, blue gaze. "Thanks. Please don't tell anyone where you took us."

Chopper Deke handed me his business card. I flipped it over and saw a phone number scripted in penmanship that looked so psychotic you'd have thought he'd written it in Arabic. I assumed this was the number to his cell phone and nodded understanding: *If I needed anything, I had permission to call.*

I glanced past my headrest and into the back seat. Sobbing softly, Teensy had buried her face in Venice's neck. Dawn looked like she'd rather be anywhere but with my sister and me at our dead grandmother's estate, so I handed her Gran's house key and told her to help Teensy and Venice inside. When the security alarm didn't go off, I assumed that Teensy had the wherewithal to disconnect it. As soon as the front door closed behind them, I shifted in my seat and faced Chopper Deke.

"I . . . I . . . I . . ." Thoughts hung in my head, but I couldn't seem to get them out.

"You need my help."

"No. I mean, yes. Well, maybe."

"What's the problem, toots?"

"Besides what happened to my grandmother?" When he nodded, I drew a bracing breath. As objectionable and slimy as Chopper Deke could be with his leering, demeaning, and chauvinistic ways, he'd helped Teensy and me out before. Would he do so again? And at what cost? The last time I ended up owing Chopper Deke, he knew I couldn't come up with the thousands of dollars it'd taken to fly into Mexico at his own peril just to medevac Teensy out, so he agreed to forgive the debt in exchange for ten seconds of playing grab-ass, which I finally negotiated down to a simple "thank you" and a thirty-second kiss. I'd imagined that kissing Chopper Deke—with his wild eyes and a body enveloped in two packs' worth of cigarette smoke—would be disgustingly awful, and that I'd end up projectile-vomiting the moment the stop-watch reached the thirty-first second. But the kiss was soft and tender, and cinnamon-y, and didn't turn out anything like I'd expected; ten seconds into it, I almost forgot those sensuous lips belonged to Chopper Deke.

"A few nights ago, my friends and I witnessed a massacre out in west Texas." Oddly enough, he didn't seem particularly surprised. Like Rochelle, I could almost hear him saying, *Well, you ask me, that Dainty Prescott sure seems to attract violence.* But he listened, without comment, so I gave him the rundown on how two of the gunmen found me at a convenience store in Dallas, but I'd given them the slip. And how they followed Dawn to the country club, but she'd shaken them off, too. Then I told him about Venice's encounter, and how she hid in her attic and called 9-1-1 on her cell phone.

Finally, I said, "One came to my house. I'm pretty sure I killed him."

His expression remained unchanged. I supposed that was to be expected from a man who'd been held as a POW in Vietnam for a year. Chopper Deke was a hard man to rattle.

"That's why I came to the station—to buy time so we could figure out a plan."

"Why would armed men be after y'all?"

"When they killed those people at the lodge, I wanted to believe we had nothing to do with it. That it was a dispute someone had with the owner and his wife. Or a drug deal gone bad. Then I thought maybe they planned to murder all of the guests—*Dead men tell no tales*. But when they followed us to the Metroplex, I realized my stepmother might be behind everything. That she hired hit men to do away with Teensy and me so we couldn't testify at her trial. Now I'm not so sure, because *why would they come after our friends?*"

"Collateral damage." When I arched an eyebrow in confusion, he said, "Maybe what happened to the people at the lodge had nothing to do with you. But maybe they had to take out all the witnesses to make sure there'd be nobody left to testify against them if they got caught."

After a long pause, I realized I'd been chewing my lower lip. "Any advice?"

"I'll sleep on it."

A normal person might've read complete disinterest into his comment. Not me.

"Well . . . thanks for the ride. I guess I should go tend to my sister." Teensy and I were drunk on grief, but I hoped we could put on stoic faces in the presence of Venice and Dawn.

I had one leg out of the Hummer and was trying to plant my foot firmly on the ice when Chopper Deke said, "You need disposable phones with prepaid minutes."

"What?"

"Disposable phones. In case they're tracking you. Could be the GPS feature on your cell phones, so turn them off unless you absolutely have to use them. And don't charge the disposable phones to your credit card. Pay cash to keep from leaving a paper trail." Great idea, coming from a man most people thought of as a menacing bully. "And don't drive that pink rocket of yours. Lock it in the garage and leave it there. Don't drive your sister's car either."

I thanked him. "There's an underground sensor that'll activate the gate when you leave. Whatever you do, don't back up once you clear the pole that houses the electronics. If you do, let's just say that Tig won't be getting his Hummer back in the same condition it was in when he loaned it out."

"Who says he loaned it out?" Chopper Deke winked.

I gave a little snort of disapproval, tucked the business card into my wallet hoping I'd never have to use it, and braved thirty feet of icy conditions just to navigate my way inside Gran's house without a nasty fall.

After programming the security alarm to the "Stay" mode, I found the girls in the kitchen and warned them not to open any of the doors or windows. Teensy had already pulled out a mixing bowl from under the counter and was searching the pantry for parchment paper.

"What're you doing?" I cut my eyes to Venice and Dawn, who regarded me with awkward expressions.

Teensy said, "I decided to make divinity to take down to Old Man Spencer's."

My eyelids fell to half-mast. Just like that, I recalled the time he intercepted me as I jogged past his house, insisting that we communicate with each other by making animal noises so we could build up a secret language. I chuckled, then sighed a sorrowful sigh—the Spencers had lost their loved one, too.

"Why don't you wait a few days? His family may not know yet. Besides, I doubt anyone's home."

"You're not the boss of me."

"Fine. You asked for it. Here's the real reason: Your divinity isn't tasty, and it looks like pigeon droppings. If you're going to bake something, pick something you're good at. Like mac-'n-cheese. Out of a box. Only this time, read the directions. And don't add anything to it. Or take anything away from it."

Personally, I try not to eat anything Teensy bakes. It's just a rule I have. In my defense, I did try to forewarn Venice and Dawn with a cello-stroke to the throat when Teensy turned her back.

By the time Teensy finished whipping up her concoction, the kitchen looked like a marshmallow bomb exploded, leaving a crime scene of white spatter coating several large appliances.

"You'd better clean this up before Gran sees this mess." I clapped my hand over my mouth but the words had already tumbled out. Seeing Teensy's stricken face, I fell apart. "I'm sorry. I don't know why . . . for a few seconds it felt like it wasn't true. Excuse me." I got up from the table. "I'll be in my room. Teensy, show them to the guest rooms and make sure they have clean linens."

I've learned the hard way that when my sister threatens to embarrass me in public, the wrong response is to say, "Yeah, I dare you." But this time, it was me who'd embarrassed myself in front of Venice and Dawn.

Up in my bedroom, I peeked out my window and developed cabin fever again. Outside, landscape lights illuminated the trees and blued the beds of pink tulips the gardener planted around the grounds. I'd barely nodded off to sleep when I heard a noise. For all I knew, the sound of Gran's cruise ship slamming into the coral reef startled me awake. The very thought made me shudder, and I knew there was no way I could drift back to sleep with that jarring image weighing heavy on my mind.

I shrugged into my silk robe and padded downstairs to the

second floor, past Teensy's room and the two guest bedrooms. For no good reason, I halted in my tracks. I have no conscious memory how I ended up at the opposite end of the hall in front of Gran's bedroom door, but when I put my hand on the crystal doorknob and looked over my shoulder, Teensy's room and the two guest bedrooms lay behind me.

Reverently, I stepped inside and closed the door. Blue light filtered in through spun-silk curtains. For a few seconds, as I inhaled the chocolaty-orange fragrance that still lingered in her room, I took in the shapes and shadows of my grandmother's sanctuary: the ornately carved four-poster with Irish linens covering the bed; French nightstands in carved walnut on either side with rose marble tops; a small working fireplace flanked by two silk-upholstered chairs; and craftsman-carved crown molding abutting the tall ceiling.

So many family values were formed at the dining table downstairs. But many more were shaped in this very room, at the foot of Gran's bed, as she put down whatever book she was reading to weigh in on my problems.

My stomach roiled. When I was little, my mother used to refer to it as a "nervous stomach." I worried constantly that I wouldn't live to be eighteen. Now there's a name for what I had: paranoia. I couldn't help but believe my preoccupation with death could be traced back to a single event, when my grandfather passed away unexpectedly. I realized it could happen to me. Each night thereafter, I fought off sleep, fretting I'd be next. Every day, I'd awaken exhausted.

I noticed the neon red numbers on Gran's bedside clock and saw there was still time to catch the end of the news. I slid onto the French settee at the foot of Gran's bed and picked up the remote control off the marble coffee table. Once I clicked on the TV, the anchors for Channel Eighteen were still delivering the news. Which boggled my mind—not that the news was still on, but that Gran actually watched Channel Eighteen. Everyone in the family knew I worked at the worst TV station in the Metroplex. True, we'd climbed to number three in the ratings after the previous "sweeps," but prior to that, WBFD came in dead last. My face cracked into a smile. The only reason Gran would've lowered her standards and tuned in to WBFD would've been to watch me.

A tear leaked out. I drew the back of my hand across my cheek to wipe it away. God love her. She would've died rather than let me know. Ironic.

Aspen Wicklow was the on-air talent for the "News at Ten" broadcast. With her bright red hair, shocking emerald eyes, pale skin, and features that looked like they'd been carved out of wax, she reported a news piece on the feral cat population along the Trinity River. Video of cats and ducks played out. Then she stared directly into the camera and delivered the news about Gran's cruise ship.

I heard "coral reef" and "capsized" and "huge gash in the hull" but my mind refused to process information having to do with the sunken ship. I heard "skipper under house arrest" and "manslaughter charges" and "thirty-six people unaccounted for." I couldn't fathom that everyone got off alive except for my grandmother, Old Man Spencer, and thirty-four others. My mind shut down and went off to play somewhere else because I'd reached my saturation point and couldn't bear to hear anymore.

Video of the wrecked cruise liner ended, and Aspen looked, red-eyed, into the camera and wished the viewers a good night. As the musical trailer ended, the intro to late-night programming began.

From the comfort of Gran's settee, I picked up the house phone and dialed Daddy's number. When he didn't answer, I left him an urgent message to phone me back.

I spent a few more minutes alone in Gran's haven before heading downstairs to the kitchen to raid the refrigerator. When I walked into the dark room and flipped the light switch, I found Teensy sitting with her elbows on the table. She rested her head in the palms of her hands. When she lifted her face, I saw that her eyes were rimmed red, and her nose shined bright pink.

"Hi. Whatcha doin'?" I sing-songed, in what turned out to be a wary, world-weary voice.

"I keep replaying all these stories about Gran."

"They're not stories. They're repressed memories." I opened the pantry and knuckled on the light switch. Teensy had staked her claims on boxes of food using yellow sticky-notes.

I poked my head out past the door frame. "What are you—like twelve?"

"Don't touch any of my food."

"To be exact, it's not your food. It's Gran's."

"Don't know if you've heard," she said sarcastically, "but Gran's not around anymore so the food I called dibs on is mine."

"And the horse you rode in on." I said, "Gran has two grand-daughters, and I'm first."

"Means nothing. Don't touch that brownie mix."

The way to get to Teensy is to talk about her weight. We're about the same size, and neither of us is overweight. If anything, we're perfect. But Teensy's self-esteem is crap so I decided to go for it.

"I wasn't taking your brownie mix. I don't care if you get so big you block out the sun."

Teensy sucked air. "How dare you. Fine. Keep the brownie mix."

Don't mind if I do.

I strolled out to the screened-in porch, where Gran allowed me to store my treadmill and exercycle until I got my own place. I stepped on the treadmill to do my walk and burn off energy, and hopefully exhaust me to a point where I could fall back to sleep. The thing I enjoyed most about the treadmill was walking past it. The whole time I did my pitiful walk, I couldn't stop thinking about baking brownies. By the time the treadmill showed that I'd walked a mile, I'd already made that pan of brownies five times in my mind.

The additional light filtering into the screened-in porch from the kitchen abruptly dimmed, and I knew that Teensy'd gone on to bed. Her absence gave me unfettered access to the pantry. *Screw it,* I thought, and took out a bowl and hand mixer and set them on the kitchen counter. Next, I retrieved the brownie box from the pantry and read the directions. Preheated the oven. Got the measuring cups out of the drawer. Water . . . check. Oil . . . check. Egg . . . uh-oh. That meant opening the refrigerator.

Next to Teensy, that little "open door" bell on the refrigerator is the worst tattletale I've ever encountered. Try sneaking a midnight snack when your grandmother can hear a pin drop a mile away. Gran's hearing aids didn't help with conversations, but the fridge, she could hear. But I'm older now and know where the wire cutters are; and *I'll get you if I ever find you, you little bastard.*

I took my chances and baked the brownies. I *had* to. Otherwise, the box mix would expire in February 2018. I didn't want the expiration date to creep up on me. Safety first. As in, *Thank God you got right on that, Dainty.* In thirty minutes— *presto*—I donned Gran's red oven mitts that looked like lobster claws and took a pan of brownies off the oven rack.

The "Law of Being Watched" is directly proportionate to the stupidity of your act, or, the bigger the secret is that you're trying to keep. With a fork halfway to my lips, I looked up from my place at the table and made eye contact with one irritated houseguest.

Dawn stood in the doorway with her arms braced across her chest. "Share."

I pulled the brownie pan closer to me.

"Is this Rubanbleu-worthy, Dainty, sitting in the dark without a plate, diving in with a fork?"

I sighed in exasperation. "Fine. Fork yourself." I thumbed at the appropriate drawer and she plucked out a utensil.

"Want to know a secret?" she said, pulling up a chair to join me at the breakfast table.

Maybe I did. Maybe I didn't. So . . . whoa—loaded question.

Without a preamble, Dawn swallowed her first bite. Lowering her voice, she spoke in a confidential whisper. "People are watching me."

"What people?"

She gave a non-committal shrug. "They were watching me earlier."

I'd grown pretty tired of Dawn, and my frayed nerves got the better of me. "What—do you think you're that English princess? Nobody's looking in the windows at you. Those yard guys were busy getting their work done. And quit yelling snark at the TV. It can't hear you—unlike the rest of us."

"I see dead people."

My jaw dropped open.

"And spirits. It's true." She said this with conviction, possibly because my face had contorted into a ghastly mask of fear. "Don't look at me that way—like I'm crazy. I'm not crazy. You're the one who's crazy if you don't believe me."

"Are you serious?" And then I realized she was absolutely serious.

"By the way, you have a large black Doberman following you everywhere you go."

That particular idea resonated with me. We could use a big ugly canine with powerful jaws and a threatening bark to protect us. To let us know the bad men were out there before they got the jump on us.

"This Doberman—is he here with me now?"

"Of course."

"I see." I *didn't* see. Because only one of us at a time could be crazy around here, and, for sure, this time it wasn't me. "Is he playing dead?"

"Of course not."

"Then we need to get rid of him because he's a lousy watchdog and he's not doing anything to protect me."

"He's not here to protect you. The devil sent him."

That torpedoed the conversation. I sent Dawn off to bed, but stayed in the kitchen long enough to clean up the crime scene. After washing remnants of brownie batter out of the bowl, running hot water over the mixer's batter-caked beaters, and storing the brownie pan with the rest of the evidence in the dishwasher, I wrapped the leftover brownies in foil and stuck a Post-It on top for Teensy's eyes that read: *Rat bait. Poison. Do Not Eat.*

Before heading back up to my room in the attic, I OCD-checked all of the doors at least five times and reset the alarm, just to make sure that it took the first time. And the second . . .

CHAPTER TWELVE

For no good reason, I awakened in the night to the smell of cigarette smoke. I sat, bolt-upright, and sniffed again but the odor was gone, replaced by the scent of my grandmother's chocolaty-orange fragrance. While lying in bed, trying to get back to sleep, I heard a strange grating noise coming from outside. After recovering from my initial assumption that an evil spirit had come to steal my eyes and cut out my kidneys, I eased back the covers, threw my legs over the side of the bed, and scooted my feet into a pair of fuzzy house slippers.

Terrified by what I might see, my mind cast back three months, when scandalous gossip made the rounds that I attributed to one of the cotton-headed SMU interns at the TV station. The ditzy little cutthroat spread a rumor that I was seeing a married guy who worked in Production. As a debutante of The Rubanbleu, I would *nevah-evah* date a married man. When I confronted him, he also thought we were seeing each other. I guess he didn't know that lurking outside my window at night didn't qualify as dating. So while Gran believed in the "what doesn't kill you makes you stronger" theory, I preferred the "what doesn't kill you gets you fired" theory. Apparently so did Gordon.

I removed the Glock that belonged to the intruder I killed at our Rivercrest estate from its hiding place inside my Capodimonte jewelry box. Stepping over to the window, I took a deep breath, pointed the gun, and ripped back the curtain, fully prepared to kill again. Instead of coming face to face with a madman scaling the side of Gran's mansion, I noticed a tiny wren nesting outside my window in the howling wind. When my heart stopped racing, I picked up the phone and punched in Daddy's number.

As soon as I heard his voice, a sense of relief flooded over me. "Hi, Daddy, how've you been?"

"Wrong number," he scoffed and hung up on me.

It's a sad commentary when your own father doesn't want to talk to you. But after losing our mother, I took a philosophical approach and considered Daddy's abrupt disinterest in us to be less of a lack of caring, and more of him distancing himself to protect his emotions. If he emotionally disconnected with his daughters, maybe it wouldn't hurt as much if, like Momma, something bad happened to one of us. At least that's how I worked it out in my head.

His indifference reminded me of what happened a few months ago when Teensy couldn't return to her university to finish her coursework at the end of that semester. After the near-death experience in Mexico, doctors put her in physical rehabilitation and forbade her to travel. As part of one final exam, Teensy's professor faxed her a questionnaire for Daddy to complete. The sentence read: *I would like to see my son/daughter* . . . followed by a blank to be filled in. Daddy completed the sentence by printing "as little as possible."

In the wee hours of the morning, I left my room and padded down to the second floor, only to have Teensy intercept me in the hall on my way to the bathroom. The way it works at Gran's is that there's a bathroom in Gran's room that's strictly off-limits, and one off the second-floor hallway. When Teensy's here, I have to share because there isn't a bathroom in the attic. There's a Jack-and-Jill bathroom that connects the two guest bedrooms, too, but I knew if I tried going in there, I'd wake up

Venice or Dawn, or both—and I, for sure, couldn't deal with Dawn.

Teensy said, "Hey—Nancy Drew—you left the front door unlocked."

My breath caught in my chest. "Did not."

"Did too."

At first, I thought she was messing with me, but her panicky retelling of how she thought she heard movement in the house and went to double-check, convinced me otherwise. The very idea that I'd failed to keep us safe for even a few minutes, much less an hour, sent a lance of fear through my core. Turns out I might have accidentally unlocked the front door when trying to lock it for the last time. This was a perfect example of why I have OCD when it comes to security.

Because of my mistake, I let her use the bathroom first. But what I really wanted was to ask her if I could stay in her room for the rest of the night. I didn't ask, of course. Teensy's less of a problem if she fears me, and I didn't want her to perceive me as weak.

Later that morning, after the sun popped up like a big tangerine, I walked into the sulphur-smoke of hell's kitchen to find Teensy puttering around by the stove, while her pampered minions sat at the breakfast table waiting to be fed. She'd turned Gran's immaculately kept kitchen into a wasteland, and by wasteland, I meant it wasn't far off from needing a back hoe and a front-end loader. In fact, I thought I heard one idling in the background. The huge mess triggered a rant.

"Teensy, you're such a slob. Who uses five pans and three bowls to cook a damned egg?" I checked my speech. Dawn was soaking up the drama like a *ShamWow!* while I was supposed to be teaching her good manners. I changed to a more playful tone—and ladled out my passive-aggression in a Rubanbleu-worthy voice. "And what about the towels in the upstairs bathrooms? They don't just jump off the towel racks and slide down the laundry chute and do themselves, you know."

By way of a response, she gave me a dedicated eyeblink.

That did it. My influence on Dawn be damned, I continued my rant. "You're so selfish and self-centered, you probably make out with yourself." I regained my composure and addressed Venice and Dawn with saccharine sweetness. "Ladies, as long as we're under one roof, I would appreciate it if you'd pick up after yourselves, please." I returned my attention to Teensy. "And where'd you get the idea you could cook? Just stop it already."

I figured Teensy was trying to masquerade as a self-ordained chef in order to fit in better with these helpless, hungry, and privileged houseguests. I wasn't even angry that my sister had turned into a brain-dead conformist, but this time she'd set fire to the eggs and almost burned down the house.

And then I was like, "What kind of freaking fiasco have you created this time?" But I just said it in my mind, or possibility using an indoor voice, because I was still trying to teach Dawn the kind of impeccable manners that would serve her well at her Rubanbleu debut.

Everyone in the room fell silent, probably because they were busy thinking that, yeah, Teensy sucked as a cook and probably shouldn't be allowed to use a stove unsupervised. Or they'd clammed up because I'd walked in on them while they were talking about me. Or because they were talking about me and wanted me to leave so they could finish talking about me.

Through the stench of a burned omelet, I whiffed the lingering odor of cigarette smoke. Other than my late grandfather, who occasionally lit a pipe tamped with a sweet-and-fruity scented tobacco in his office filled with safari trophies, nobody smoked in this house—nobody.

"There's someone in our attic," I shrieked.

Reactions unfolded in slow motion. Mouths gaped. Eyes widened. Venice clutched her throat and pointed to something sinister over my shoulder. Dawn swung her legs around to bolt out the back door.

I didn't need to be told of an intruder behind me. I grabbed the hot cast iron skillet and swung hard. It connected with a man's head. In my heightened state of awareness, the watermelon thump lingered in the air for several seconds. The intruder's mouth went slack. Blue-gray eyes were wide open and fixed. He dropped to his knees and lingered long enough for me to swing again. I grooved his skull and he pitched over, face-first, onto the floor.

My stomach flipped.

Teensy, Venice, and Dawn stampeded for the door, converging at the exit leading out onto the terrace, while I stood there like a super-hero holding a frying pan. Poised to strike again, I reached for the aqua princess phone Gran kept in the kitchen so I could rotary-dial 9-1-1. As my trembling hand closed around the receiver, the telephone rang.

"Hello?" I planned to tell the caller I couldn't talk, but Daddy's voice came across the line.

"Just so you kids realize I'm not completely insensitive to your predicament, I've been out of pocket the last—"

Quaking in my tracks, I kept my eye on the home invader sprawled out across Gran's linoleum, fully prepared to crack the iron skillet over his head a third time if he so much as twitched. Words tumbled out in shallow breaths. "Can't talk. Have to call the police. Call you back."

"The police? What the hell? What's going on?"

Wait. What? Something very wrong here. What kind of intruder wears a suit and tie?

I tabled the urgency to dial 9-1-1 and considered the need for medical attention.

132

"Answer me," Daddy thundered. Distracted, I forgot he'd asked me a question.

"Nothing. Never mind. What were you saying?"

"I'm saying I'm not the hands-off, uncaring son of a bitch you girls think I am. I've been interviewing bodyguards the past few days and I hired one. Name's Robert Roquefort. Like the cheese. I let him in last night, but you girls had already gone to bed. Told him to keep a low profile. I texted you this information. Didn't you see it on your phone?"

"Roquefort?"

"Yeah. Like the cheese. Short guy. Ear bud sticking out of his ear. Feeds into a handheld talk set that allows him to communicate with his office."

The man lay splayed out on the floor like a three-dimensional subject from a Botero canvas. The only thing missing to complete the look was a bowler hat and a Granny Smith apple.

"Wearing a dark suit and rep tie?" I studied the form on the floor. "Maybe ten pounds shy of a Sumo wrestler? With a face that looks like evil wrapped in skin?"

"Yeah, that's him. Told him not to get in your way, just shadow y'all. Likes you to call him 'Cheesy.' "

"Might be better to call him an ambulance," I said dully.

"So, I take it you've met?"

"In a manner of speaking. I'm pretty sure I just killed him."

CHAPTER THIRTEEN

After Daddy quit calling us a pack of idiots and stopped shouting that we didn't need protection from anyone but ourselves, I hung up, pulled the wallet out of the man's back pocket, and rifled through it until I found a driver's license. Sure enough, it read: ROQUEFORT, ROBERT EARL. I found a badge case in the other pocket that held professional private investigator credentials. Then I thumbed through his wallet looking for health insurance coverage.

I shouted for Teensy's assistance. Blued by the cold, my useless sister pressed her cheek against the screen door to get a better look, but she wouldn't come inside.

I dropped to my knees and got right in his face. Then I inched away. We'd come to the part that evokes blood-curdling screams from moviegoers at horror flicks—the part where the villain you think is dead suddenly comes back to life and grabs you.

"Hello?" The moment of truth arrived. I waved my hand in front of the only eye I could see at that angle and watched his eyeball roll up past his eyelid like a murky blue marble. By this time, Teensy had reentered the kitchen and she took the phone, trailed by our shivering, blue-lipped houseguests.

"Mr. Cheesy?" I poked his shoulder. "Can you hear me?"

"You're saying his name's Cheesy . . . or he's a cheesy kind of guy?" Teensy asked.

"Just call an ambulance."

"What do I say?"

134

"Fine. Give me the phone. I have to do everything around here."

I actually considered it my good fortune when Daddy arrived within the hour, drove up the circular drive, and parked in front of the front door. He keyed his way inside and found us in the kitchen with Cheesy. Beneath the brim of a serious gray Stetson, his normally handsome face twisted into a grotesque mask of disgust when he caught a whiff of burned eggs and nearly gagged.

"Teensy did it," I said.

Daddy shot me a wicked glare. "Idiot."

"I don't know why you're blaming me for the way Teensy turned out. I wanted to trade her for a pony when I was six and you put the kibosh on that deal. You ask me, you're to blame. I did my part."

Daddy studied the bodyguard, then took a pulse. "Did either of you heroines call an ambulance?"

"About an hour ago," I said.

He leaned in and checked out the groove down the center of the man's head, as well as the crescent-shaped bruise above the man's ear. "Looks like you really made an impression on him."

Ba dum tisssss. He actually said this with a straight face.

"Yeah. I think the moment I parted his hair down the middle really brought us together."

"Frying pan?"

I did a little head bob. "Cast iron skillet."

"Not bad." He nodded in approval. Then he shouted, "Only he works for us—idiot!"

Teensy said, "Ha-ha, Daddy called you an idiot."

Daddy and I barked out simultaneous "shut-ups" and then returned our attention to Cheesy.

"I don't suppose he'll be much good to you now," Daddy grumbled.

"Want me to fix you breakfast, Daddy?" Teensy said sweetly.

I intervened. "Your cooking stinks." Then I laughed. Daddy didn't need a case of ptomaine.

"Oh, yeah," she retorted, "well I've cooked a lot more breakfasts than you, smarty pants, so what skill set do *you* bring to the table?"

"I've criticized a lot of bad food—most of it yours—so . . . professional food critic."

"Daddy's the tiebreaker," Teensy said. "So . . . want me to fix you breakfast, Daddy?"

"No. The last time I ate your cooking, it made me constipated. I ended up on the commode trying to expel what felt like a newborn wrapped in barbed wire."

Venice and Dawn hooted.

I wanted to laugh, too, but the ambulance people were taking their time about getting around on icy roads, and we needed to tend to Mr. Cheesy before he slipped into a coma—if he hadn't already.

Daddy said, "I picked up burritos. They're on the front seat. Teensy, go get them. And don't break your neck. You dimwits need to spread rock salt on the porch."

When she returned, he'd miscounted and there were only enough burritos for three people. I learned this when Teensy distributed the contents of the sack among the girls. Teensy already had the tin foil pulled back on one of the burritos, and it smelled pretty good.

I said, "Give me part of that."

"No. I don't share food."

I said, "I can tell that." She must've figured I might lunge for it because she grabbed a fork from the silverware drawer and held it aloft, thereby ensuring if I got anywhere close to her, I'd get shanked.

Daddy looked at me. "Get me a glass of ice water, Dainty."

"Would you rather have hot coffee? Because I can put on a pot."

He set his jaw. His jaw muscles flexed a couple of times before he spoke in a calm, controlled voice. "No, Dainty, the ice water is for Mr. Roquefort."

"Oh," I said, but I was more interested in how he planned to get Cheesy to drink when the man was clearly knocked out. But I filled up a glass with ice water from the refrigerator's automatic dispenser and took it over to him while everyone else enjoyed their breakfast burritos.

Instead of trying to get Cheesy to take a sip, Daddy tossed the ice water in his face. The porcine man's eyelids cracked open. Stubby brown eyelashes fluttered. Ricocheting eyeballs focused.

Daddy said, "Hey, Roquefort, how-ya feeling, buddy?"

"Oh, hey-there, Mr. Prescott." He touched his scalp. "Doin' pretty good. Pret-ty good."

"I see you met my oldest daughter, Dainty."

Daddy, starched and pressed in a pinpoint oxford shirt and blue jeans that could've stood on their own, was still squatting next to Cheesy. With the brim of his Stetson pulled low enough to cast a shadow across his face, he assessed the damage to his contract employee. *I can only assume.*

"Packs a pretty good wallop," Cheesy said, gingerly touching the area of scalp where I'd parted his thinning brown hair with the skillet.

"Yeah, well, she's an idiot." He thumbed at Teensy. "That other idiot standing guard over the 'fridge is my daughter, Teensy."

Cheesy said, "You remember us talking about hazardous duty pay?" Daddy nodded, and Cheesy continued his thought. "Well, it's going to cost you double-time, not time-and-a-half."

Daddy nodded again. I thought it was awfully nice of him to

pay Mr. Cheesy hazardous duty pay just to watch the four of us, until he looked over at me and mouthed, "It's coming out of your trust fund."

Cheesy said something inaudible to me, but Daddy heard and leaned in closer.

Seeing our father distracted, Teensy seized the moment. "Daddy, can we have a cat?"

"Sure," he said reflexively, and resumed his conversation with Mr. Cheesy without even realizing what he agreed to.

"Score." Teensy raised her closed fist to "fist-bump" me like stupid high school locker room shenanigans. Apparently, she'd figured out if she asked Daddy a question while he was either dead-asleep or preoccupied, he'd most likely answer yes. Incidentally, it looks like we're getting a cat.

I shook my head in disgust. "You're even stupider than I thought."

"Hey—I scored us a cat, didn't I?"

This could hardly be viewed as a victory. The last time we owned a cat it scratched me so badly, people kept asking me if I was a cutter. The high school counselor even called me in to discuss my "issues" when several anonymous students reported scars on my arms. She didn't believe me when I told her I didn't cut myself. Nor did she believe I had a crazed cat that viewed me as its personal scratching post.

On the other hand, Avery Marshall's stepdaughter had turned twenty-one, wasn't a ward of the state, and, because she'd pretty much never had a real date, we could give her our cat to help her start her own inevitable collection.

"Clean this place up," I said nastily, circling my hand through the air in front of me like a witch whipping up a spell.

"I'll get to it," Teensy said in her blasé, couldn't-care-less manner.

"Yeah, well, you have a bad habit of not doing the dishes

when it's your turn, and not following through when you say you will. What the fork is wrong with you?"

Venice laughed. Not just a little chuckle, but one of those resounding maniacal cackles, like those people who get discharged from the nuthouse too early. But Venice wasn't the only one who'd become slap-happy. With bad men hunting us like we were Bambi's mother on the opening day of deer season, being iced in had made us all feel like we were about to crack up.

The quiet conversation between Daddy and Cheesy ended. Daddy helped the man to his feet and steadied him against the door frame.

When he was sure Cheesy could walk, he said, "Y'all are on your own for now. I'm taking this man to the hospital." Then, good will degenerated into a rant. "Damned ambulance drivers shirking their duties . . . can't even get to an emergency call. Jeez. Snowfall turns to ice, and people think they can't drive without chains on their tires."

He helped Cheesy out to the pickup. Just when we thought he'd driven away, Daddy walked back inside. "Teensy—" the stern look on his face made me glad he hadn't singled me out "—quit texting me crap."

Teensy pulled her infamous, innocent *What, who me?* act so he got down to specifics.

"You've clearly attained a new level of drunkenness. You texted nude pictures of yourself to friends and family—including me. Then you replied to your own message by telling yourself to fuck off and saying you aren't gay. Pull it together, will ya?"

Through my laughter, I did a little knee-swat.

He shot me a glare designed to liquefy metal. "Don't push your luck. You're no better."

Then he explained that, in my OCD-quest to make sure I'd

locked the house up tighter than Dick's hatband, I'd inadvertently unbolted the front door when I tried to lock it for the last time, which was how he and Cheesy walked into Gran's house in the first place.

Teensy let out one of her obnoxious, donkey-bray laughs and fell across the kitchen counter in a fit of deep guffaws. She did this at my expense while the girls smiled without humor.

Then Daddy's next comment cast a pall over the entire room. "Be very careful if you return to the Rivercrest house. Coyotes are moving in. They're starving, so they're out looking for food. There's a huge bloody spot next to the house, so I'm pretty sure they got one of the neighbor's dogs."

I realized I'd been holding my breath the entire time he'd been talking. I let it out slowly and took another deep breath while I formulated my thoughts. "Coyote?"

"Could be a panther. There was a report of a panther near Lake Worth a while back."

"Panther?" I darted a quick glance at Venice and Dawn, who seemed totally on board that I'd turned into a parrot.

"All I'm saying is *be careful*. These nocturnal predators are desperate. They're not waiting until dark to come out and wreak havoc."

Damned right, I mused, as the four of us exchanged eye-encrypted thoughts and head-bobbed in unison.

By way of a polite departure, Daddy touched the brim of his cowboy hat while simultaneously uttering, "Ladies, have a nice day."

Discussing life-shattering events over the phone is frowned on in the Prescott household. A Prescott delivers bad news in person. Not that a face-to-face delivery of the unthinkable softens the blow, but at least the person is available for a hug and a *There, there.* In the calamity, asking Daddy whether he knew about Gran had completely slipped my mind.

I sprinted through the house and caught him at the front door. "I need to talk to you about Gran."

"What's done is done." He looked me dead in the eye. "Accept it. Life goes on."

Then my father practically created a vapor trail tearing across the yard, leaving me slack-jawed and thunderstruck by his callousness.

CHAPTER FOURTEEN

After Daddy left, I went back to the kitchen and zeroed in on Dawn's appalling clothing. Ladies of The Rubanbleu dressed in muted, yet elegant, colors such as rich shades of cream, taupe, and brown. What Dawn had on was less of a "Nailed it!" and more of an epic fail.

Until she ran for the back door, I hadn't had a chance to fully take in her appearance. When I asked her to come out from behind the table, I experienced a hand-to-mouth moment. "Oh, dear Lord, what're you wearing?"

"I got it out of Teensy's closet."

"When Teensy wore those things, she didn't put them all together, or even at the same time. You shouldn't wear that. It's tacky."

"A little clothes-minded, are we?" she snapped.

Teensy's immaturity broke through with a vengeance; she laughed until she snorted.

Dawn defended her "look." "It's not tacky. It's neon. And it makes a statement."

In an unusual departure from what had become her continuous and awkward silence over the past few days, Venice weighed in. "It makes a statement, all right, such as you patronize strip bars, or you're a hype, or you have a gambling addiction—"

"Or you have bad taste." I punctuated Venice's list of concerns with a nod.

Out of the blue, Teensy said, "I think Daddy has a gambling addiction."

"What?" My response came out louder than I'd intended, and caused me to put Dawn's fashion *faux pas* on the back burner. "Why would you say that?"

"Because he has lots of twenty-dollar bills in his wallet."

"Well, Gran kept a lot of one-dollar bills in her purse, and that didn't make her a stripper." My sister's an ass.

"I need clean clothes." Dawn whipped around to face me. "And stop being mean. Avery paid you. You *have* to deal with me. So . . . *ha.*"

Dawn's smart mouth earned her the title of "World-class ass." I wanted to beat her senseless, but it isn't against the law to be an ass. If it were, authorities would have to erect a concertina-wire fence around the entire state of Texas and inform everyone they were in custody.

"What's wrong with you? I'm supposed to be teaching you good manners." Even though I'd resorted to complete honesty, she burst into derisive laughter and asked if I was running for the empty spot vacated by Mother Teresa. I took a new approach with her. "Are you supposed to be on medication?"

"What of it?" Dawn defensively braced her arms across her chest and shouted, "Stop reading my mind!"

"You think I can read your mind?" I'd taken on a client who'd, at first, seemed to be fairly normal: two arms, two legs, two nostrils, two ears . . . two personalities.

"You know you're doing it. And if you don't stop pretending you're not doing it, I'll slit your throat in your sleep."

Tiny hairs on the back of my neck stood up. I took a step away from her, increasing the distance between us.

Across the room, Teensy's eyes widened.

Venice stiffened, then breathed out, "Dear Lord in heaven," in such a way that it sounded like an invocation.

Paranoia had fast become the norm for each of us. But with the advent of a new kind of danger, I started to think Avery's stepdaughter might murder me. Threatening one's mentor was an illogical leap for a prospective debutante who professed to want to be just like me, but Dawn had definitely gotten weirder since we'd been forced to stick together. In lieu of pity, I felt a nervous sympathy for her. I don't think she wanted that from any of us. She had a track record for putting up with people's cruelty and she'd learned to take it in stride. Who's to say she wouldn't eventually crack?

I eyeballed the nearest exit. "I'm pretty sure you need to get back on your meds."

"Screw you."

"That's venomous, Dawn."

"Yeah, it's almost as bad as when that white-trash girl you avoided like the plague in high school officially became your stepmother."

One thing about dealing with people with diminished social filters, you at least get the truth. Or their perception of the truth. Stricken, I cut my eyes to Teensy, who'd flattened herself against the pantry door with her mouth agape.

Vicious words triggered my ferocity. Without warning, I jumped Dawn. But only in my head, because I couldn't imagine the day getting any worse than it already had gotten, and didn't like to think about having to repay Avery all that money if I lost my temper and punched his stepdaughter.

I'm not a judgmental person, but you're probably going to hell, Dawn.

The ride on Dawn's bipolar-coaster made me dizzy. No question, she needed her points adjusted and a tune-up at the county psychiatric hospital. Excusing myself from the drama, I lost no time finding Chopper Deke's *Get Out of Hell Free* card and phoned the devil himself to ask a favor.

Would've been nice if he'd paused the porn I could clearly hear in the background.

He greeted me with a roguish inflection. "To what do I owe the pleasure?"

"I need you to come get us. We have to get Dawn to the county hospital for a psychiatric evaluation. She's off her meds, and I'm pretty sure she's planning to kill me in my sleep."

Based on the time showing on the grandfather clock in Gran's rotunda, I knew Chopper Deke still had to fly Traffic Monitor Joey around the Metroplex to deliver the station's morning traffic report. Still, I wanted to make sure he could work a trip to the nuthouse into his schedule.

When I returned to the kitchen, I found Teensy hovering over the toaster oven, where she'd taken the jackal approach and ripped open a box of frozen cherry strudels to crisp. She hadn't wasted one precious second trying to digest what Dawn's problem might be, or figure out how to handle it. Instead, she resorted to cooking. As I fully entered the room, she caught sight of me and contorted her face into an ugly expression— which I believed to be a sad commentary on my recent behavior until she cut her eyes toward the breakfast nook.

I took stock of our houseguests.

Apparently Teensy had gotten a dose of Dawn's craziness, too. We shared eye-encrypted looks that signaled we needed to disenfranchise ourselves from this lunatic as soon as possible. But we didn't need to be telepathic to know that things were about to get worse. If we waited much longer, we might all end up in the county hospital's psyche ward.

Once I made up my mind that Dawn had to leave, a sense of peace came over me. Tucking her away in the mental hospital was the right thing to do, and would actually keep her safer than letting her stay here with us. After all, the psychiatric ward had better security, and being confined to a locked ward would make it next to impossible for murderous men to gain access to her.

While waiting for Chopper Deke to show up, I suggested we adjourn to the sun porch to watch a movie. We had a couple of subscription DVDs Teensy and I hadn't watched, and it seemed like a good way to kill time. I told them they could bring their toaster strudel and juice with them.

Teensy balked. "Gran has a rule that we don't eat anywhere but the kitchen."

I reminded her that Gran wasn't here, and that according to the terms of her Last Will and Testament, the house belonged to Daddy. And Daddy didn't give a hoot what went on as long as we didn't badger him with our problems—problems that apparently included hiding out from hit men.

Tears puddled at the rims of her eyes. I could've cried and wailed too, but I kept my composure as she maintained hers.

I slid a movie into the DVD slot and pressed the power button. The movie company logo came on-screen, a lion roared, and the opening credits scrolled up the big-screen television. I occupied the large leather recliner that Daddy paid the furniture store to deliver to Gran's over Thanksgiving, which she agreed to let him keep on the sun porch, but only on condition that he increase his semimonthly visits to once a week. When picking out the chair, Daddy went white-trash, motorized, all the way. I could see why Gran considered it an abomination next to her eighteenth-century treasures. I never expected to fall asleep in such a monstrosity, but the black leather felt buttery soft to the touch and, like my first tryst with Bruckman, it just happened.

When I woke up to the musical soundtrack at the end of the movie, the credits were rolling and the girls had cleared out. From the sunroom, I wandered into the adjoining den, and from there, into the kitchen to have a word with Venice. Not finding her in any of those places, I heard the thinnest hint of voices overhead and climbed the stairs to the second story.

The door to Teensy's bedroom was ajar and when I walked past, I saw her standing in front of the mirror scrutinizing her clothing.

"I can't believe I got so fat over the winter." Teensy pinched her skin through the fabric.

Dawn's head reared back. "You're not that fat."

I had to get in on this, so I stepped inside the room.

Venice, seated in the corner with a magazine on her lap and a faraway expression on her face, suddenly became animated and shot me a fat-encrypted look.

She said, "People are always more critical about how they look than others around them are."

Teensy gave her reflection a slow headshake. "I don't think so."

Venice opened the magazine, which, judging by its cover, was a wellness guide. I couldn't see Teensy buying anything that might improve her health unless it came covered in chocolate, so I figured Gran must've bought it and left it lying around in the scant hope she'd flip through it.

"I think I've diagnosed the problem." Venice glanced at the magazine a few seconds and then slapped it closed. "Clearly, according to this body mass index chart, you're too short."

Dawn gave Teensy the visual up-and-down. "You're too hard on yourself."

Teensy continued to stare at her reflection, pulling at the sleeves on her sweater and readjusting the neckline. "You've never seen me naked."

"Not that you know of," Dawn said.

I rolled my eyes and walked out. Avery's stepdaughter had definitely worked my last nerve raw. I wandered up the next flight of stairs to change out of my bedclothes and to contemplate our next move.

In the privacy of my room, I called the number Ranger Dusty Hill had given me. Until the Texas Ranger could connect the dots and solve the case, it looked like we'd be stuck with Dawn. The call routed to voicemail so I left another message for him to call me. Even though I hadn't seen any news reports of dead men being discovered in exclusive Fort Worth neighborhoods, I felt he ought to know. Without a body, I'd underestimated the capacity of these men to destroy evidence and make us think this had never happened at all. Because of this recent turn of events, I believed them to be even more sophisticated and deadly in their villainy—like those clean-up crews made up of CIA operatives in old espionage movies.

There's often a criminal component underlying a person's behavior. I figured I was about to be introduced to mine in about two-point-three-six seconds if I didn't get away from Avery's stepdaughter because I wanted to throw a chair at her. It's what Jesus would've done.

I quickly dressed in a pair of yoga pants and a pinpoint oxford shirt with a cashmere sweater pulled over it. Then I went down to my sister's room and sat beside a gold-leafed Italian accent table with a thick glass on top. While Teensy primped in the mirror, I placed the Glock on the table and covered it with a doily. Staring at my reflection in the glass tabletop, my pale blond hair, blue eyes, and flawless skin were a testament to my mother's incredible beauty. When I looked over at Teensy, with her straw-colored hair, full lips, and huge haunting blue eyes, it seemed uncanny how closely we favored each other.

When the girls dispersed to other parts of the house, I pulled Teensy aside and informed her that Chopper Deke would arrive in a few hours. It wasn't my intention to openly deceive her—as far back as I could remember, I'd never misled her by omission except when it came to hiding chocolate—but under the "loose lips sink ships" category, I didn't want to take the chance that she'd get so angry at Dawn that she'd mouth off: *We've decided you're crazy and voted you off the island.*

I rounded up all three girls. "We'll be leaving soon."

"Where are we going?" Venice asked.

"We need disposable phones." True, but not the reason for leaving. "Teensy, take Dawn and Venice downstairs. Watch TV. Bake a cake. Pop popcorn. But whatever you do, *do not* leave this house and *do not* open the door to anyone. Understand?" I delivered this with confidence and I meant business.

"Where will you be?" Teensy wanted to know.

"Taking care of business." Might not be the answer they were looking for, but it'd have to do.

While Teensy played hostess, I picked up the Glock and slipped down the hall to Gran's room. Pure exhaustion had kept me from thinking straight—like those POWs in internment camps; or mentally ill people suffering from sleep deprivation; or debutantes in hiding who were afraid to close their eyes in case monsters slipped up from behind and killed them. On one hand, I was thrilled that Teensy, Dawn, and Venice looked to me as the strong one. The protective one. The one who'd throw herself in harm's way so they could escape. In the back of my mind, I always thought I'd sacrifice myself for a loved one. But a nagging doubt persisted—when the time came, would I abandon them like a coward and run for my life? So far, I considered that I might actually be brave. And fantasized that if I'd been in the military, I would've received the Silver Star for selflessly saving my troops. Which called for an acceptance speech, which I would have to work on during whatever time I had left.

Whenever the weather dipped into the teens, my bedroom in the attic turned cold and drafty, even with portable electric heaters. But Gran's was quiet and toasty . . . the perfect place to grab a power nap before Chopper Deke arrived.

Once inside, I toggled the bolt and rested the Glock on the nightstand. I took off my shoes. Then I slipped off my yoga pants, slid off my cashmere sweater, shrugged out of my shirt, neatly folded my clothes and placed them on the cushion of the down-filled chair next to the bed.

I had no idea that Gran had purchased a thermonuclear, atomic-powered electric blanket and put it on the bed. She'd never mentioned it to me. I dialed the controls down to the lowest setting, climbed between the sheets, and fell right off to sleep. I guess "Low" meant "Incinerate" because, sometime during my nap, I woke up smelling fried meat cooking. By the time I cleared the sheets, I noticed my legs looked like Slim Jim beef sticks with midget beef jerky feet on the ends. My toenails had practically fallen off, and looked like tiny Pringle's Potato Chips stuck to the ends of my toes. Unless the cold snap pushed us into the Ice Age, I figured I'd sleep on the couch in front of the fireplace until the next thaw.

According to the clock on the nightstand, an hour had passed since I locked myself in Gran's bedroom. I quickly redressed, made the bed, and grabbed one of the purses out of her closet to carry the Glock in.

The intercom buzzed and I answered it before Teensy could intervene. Sure enough, Chopper Deke waited at the mouth of Gran's gate. I pushed a button and then ran to the window. The wrought iron gate groaned open and he pulled onto the driveway.

After trotting downstairs, I whiffed the air and followed the scent of popcorn until I found the girls in the den watching TV. The den had a smaller television, but on a cold day, the ambience of a blazing gas fireplace with its carved marble surround more than made up for the TV's size.

"Come on." I motioned them toward the front door. "We have to go."

Venice asked, "Are we leaving for good?"

Before I could say anything, Dawn broke in with what was fast becoming an accusatory sullenness that drove me even closer to slapping the fire out of her. "I don't know why we just can't check into a hotel. They have room service, you know."

I accepted the challenge with a patronizing smile. "Are you going to pay for it?"

"If I have to." Said nastily. "Or it can come out of the retainer Avery paid you." Once again, she lorded my unfortunate business deal with Avery over me.

Teensy came into the room without me seeing her. She made her presence known with her big idea. "We could go to Tandy Westlake's house."

Tandy Westlake was a friend of mine. And Venice's. And Salem's, although my tentacles penetrated the Westlake family far deeper than either of theirs did. We'd gone through school together since kindergarten, but people tend to avoid getting involved in trouble they're not already covered up in. Still, I believed Tandy's mother would let us stay there. After all, Venice had made her wedding dress.

"I don't want to involve anyone else we know. It wouldn't be fair."

"Yes, but Mrs. Westlake's house is a nightmare," Teensy said. "You *know* that. There's probably even a panic room, or walls that seem to be part of their library, but they open up into a different part of the house. We could live there like Anne Frank."

"Ya think? Keep in mind, Anne Frank didn't make it."

But Teensy was right. The Westlake house was the ultimate carnival funhouse. It had thirteen staircases, and just when you thought the one you were descending was about to spit you out into the right part of the house, you ended up someplace completely foreign. But the entire back of the house had floor-to-ceiling windows that faced the golf course. The view enraptured Mrs. Westlake so completely that she refused to let her designer put up window coverings that had been ordered and paid for.

So . . . no thanks, don't want to live in a fishbowl.

CHAPTER FIFTEEN

Guilt gnawed at me for coaxing Dawn into Chopper Deke's SUV by telling her we were going to buy disposable phones, and to consider it an adventure. Again, I reminded myself that taking her to the hospital to get her medication refilled would be the best remedy possible. Because she acted skittish, I suspected she might be plotting ways to kill me. Well, not really, but people who didn't act fidgety and restless had actually tried to kill me in recent months, so my feelings weren't all that illogical, and it didn't take much of a leap to figure it could happen again.

Chopper Deke stopped at one of those mega-discount stores, the kind that, under normal circumstances, the four of us wouldn't be caught dead in—mostly because of the bizarre clothing worn by their customers. The longer we watched the extra-terrestrials going in and out, the more I realized Dawn could've shopped there unnoticed. Since I scolded her earlier for poor clothing choices, she'd darkened her eyes and lips with black eyeliner until she looked like a Kiss roadie.

I first noticed Chopper Deke exit the store when people in the parking lot moved aside to give him room, because, let's face it, he's a scary-looking dude. He arrived at the SUV with a bag of disposable phones that came with prepaid minutes. As we'd discussed, he paid cash to keep from leaving a paper trail, and as soon as he handed them out, we sat in the parking lot and activated each one. We wasted no time calling the people we loved.

Except Dawn. I almost felt a twinge of sadness. But after spending the past week with her, I mostly felt sorry for all of the people she could've called who had to deal with her on a daily basis.

I used my disposable phone to contact Jim Bruckman. When he answered, I opened with a doozie. "I wanted to talk to you before you saw it on the news."

"I'm in a meeting."

"Can I talk and you just listen?"

"I'm in a meeting with the Chief."

I caught myself nodding. "I'll try back later."

"Call you when I'm done." He thumbed off the phone before I could give him the new number.

I placed my second call to Salem. As soon as I heard her voice, my words came out in a breathless rush. "Listen carefully. Can't talk long. Are you okay?" She told me she was fine and that her parents warned her not to talk to me since they blamed me for almost getting her killed.

I occasionally wonder what it would've been like *not* to have had a privileged upbringing. I've generally found that others endured far fewer murder attempts, so I didn't waste time trying to disabuse Salem and her parents of the notion. I spoke fast and hoped she'd follow my instructions.

"Pay attention. When we're done, turn off your phone. Chopper Deke thinks they're tracking us through the GPS. Buy a disposable phone, but don't pay for it with a credit card. Do you have something to write with?" I gave her a few seconds to find a pen before reciting my new telephone number. "We have to talk, Salem. Call me when you get the new phone."

I disconnected and took a deep breath.

Chopper Deke kept glancing at the rearview mirror. "You

have to go to the police."

"I just did. The police can't help me." And by that, I meant Bruckman was useless to me. I twisted in the front passenger seat to see what he was looking at.

"Don't do that," he snapped.

Heart pounding, I faced forward and eavesdropped on the one-sided phone conversation Teensy was having with what sounded like a boyfriend of sorts—news to me. Based on the exchanges coming from her half of the dialogue, I accepted that whoever she had on the line was chronologically twelve, intellectually twenty, and emotionally maybe fifteen or sixteen. Which would make him perfect for her. Based on my interpretation of what I'd overheard, she'd just confronted him for two-timing her.

Her voice rose in pitch. "What do you mean you're not cheating *on* me, you're cheating *with* me? You're married?"

"Who're you talking to?" I said in a voice much calmer than I would've expected.

She thumbed on the mute button. "It's Jake. From State Farm."

"Hang up the phone." Nobody was more surprised than I was when Teensy actually did what I said. I turned my attention to Venice. "Everything okay?" She didn't answer, so I turned to Dawn. "Are you doing okay?"

"Why don't you go deep-throat a cactus and leave me the hell alone?"

Not only was her suggestion unimaginatively rude, I wondered if Chopper Deke—who has a reputation as a world-class letch—might be trying to get a visual on her suggestion.

Everyone riding inside the SUV had to feel the vehicle surge ahead when Chopper Deke unexpectedly floored the accelerator. It was so abrupt and jarring that I had the disturbing feeling we were being followed. We didn't need to be telepathic to know that our outing had gone terribly wrong.

"What's going on?" I asked.

Chopper Deke kept frowning at the rearview mirror. "Not a thing, toots."

"You keep checking the mirror. It's nerve-wracking."

He wove in and out of traffic, exceeding the speed limit by at least fifteen miles per hour. He stayed in the right-hand lane for almost a mile. Then he put on his blinker a few hundred feet from the off-ramp. He dropped his speed until the car behind him had to slow to keep from rear-ending us. He took the turn, but at the last second, he floored the accelerator and whipped back into the lane. By this time, a caravan of accelerating vehicles forced the driver to take the off-ramp.

"Who was that?"

"I dunno. But they're not following us anymore."

It was almost as if we were auditioning for bit parts in *A Beautiful Mind*. I had no idea if we were being followed by sinister operatives, or if Chopper Deke had become as delusional as the rest of us. Either way, he scared the hell out of the girls, who—thank heavens—had the good sense to keep quiet.

Except for Dawn, who couldn't seem to stop babbling. I viewed this as a symptom of her manic state, but found it difficult to make sense of the sentences she strung together without concentrating.

". . . and they all thought they were the same, but they weren't because everyone's unique. But unique means one-of-a-kind, right? So how can that be? I don't know. Everybody stop talking. You're making my head hurt." She massaged her temples through the silence before picking up where she left off. "I've decided to kill Avery."

I sat up straight. Not wanting to get my hopes up, my eyes darted to Teensy, then to Venice, and over at Chopper Deke, who sat behind the wheel like a fearsome, sociopathic sponge, soaking up the ambience of a protégé. None of us made a single comment, but I thought the ladies of The Rubanbleu might agree that Dawn would be doing a public service if she followed through with her threat. After all, everyone knew of the great debutante ball seating debacle of 1973, when Avery showed up with his mistress and sat at the same table with his soon-to-be-ex-wife, Bitsy.

I liked Bitsy much better than Avery. So sue me. When the Marshalls got their divorce, Bitsy's friends in The Rubanbleu told her if she needed anything to call them. Avery's friends told him to call the voluptuous blond stripper from the previous weekend to see if he could get laid again.

Just thinking about it made me dizzy.

Almost a half hour later, we pulled up to Fort Worth's county hospital. When Chopper Deke got out of the SUV and opened the door for Dawn to step out, her reaction turned to one of bewilderment and betrayal.

"Why're we here?" Wild-eyed, she glanced around for a panicky review of her options.

Chopper Deke said, "Let's go." He had a formidable voice with a resonant timbre that made him sound like what I imagined the executioner sounded like after hanging up from the governor, but just before injecting the lethal cocktail into a death row inmate's drip line.

Dawn came along without incident and we took the elevator to the tenth floor, where the psychiatric emergency unit processed-in patients who were being screened for admission. I volunteered to fill out the paperwork, but beyond Dawn's name and age, I got little cooperation. I filled in the blanks as best I could, but when I got to the reason for bringing her to the psyche ER, all I could think of to write in the blank was: *She's nucking futs.*

I turned in the paperwork to an African American lady of

indeterminate age who was conducting intake behind the protective glass.

"Please hurry," I said in a ventriloquist voice so Dawn wouldn't catch on. The longer Avery's stepdaughter hung out with me, the more she developed a sense of humor that fell into the dark-to-black-to-sick range. Which made me realize, when this ordeal was over, I probably wouldn't get paid a bonus. "Really. I'm not kidding. Hurry."

"Girl, you see all these other people in the waiting room?" She waved her pencil through the air like a tiny wand.

I detected a tinge of incredulity in her tone and could tell by the frown deepening between her eyebrows, and the glossy red lips that had thinned into a crimson string, that this woman loved her job. I also divined from her sunny disposition that the hospital's affirmative-action push might've hit a snag. It takes a special person to work with doctors every day, knowing you'll get bitched-out by a bunch of freaking lunatics—and that doesn't even include the patients.

I glanced around at what lay behind me, and every muscle in my neck tightened. "Please. She needs to be on medication. It's gotten worse the last few days. I don't know when she'll twist off again."

"Girl, they all gonna twist off."

I figured the only reason the admissions lady stayed calm was because she had a thick piece of Plexiglass between her and these unmedicated bipolars and schizophrenics. I had the presence of mind to glance over my shoulder in case one of the patients waiting to be evaluated crept up behind me.

"She threatened to kill me," I hissed.

"Girl, what in her wee, hamster-trap of a brain made her think she could get away with that?"

I wasn't totally convinced that Dawn could pull off a murder as long as I stayed on my toes and didn't fall asleep, but I was absolutely certain at the time she threatened to kill me that she wanted me dead. Now that we'd arrived at the hospital, I couldn't imagine things getting any worse. Add "lack of imagination" to my growing list of epic fails.

Dawn clearly was having a bad day and had been rude from the get-go, but things went to total hell when she unleashed a string of expletives, ending with, "Which one of you asshats stole my purse?"

Dawn didn't have a purse with her. None of us had brought one in.

The contours of Dawn's face hardened. Her eyes looked as dead as a shark's. I watched in horror as a new—possibly more sinister—personality slipped into Dawn's body while the personality I'd previously thought of as *Dawn-off-her-meds* won free airline tickets and jetted off to Maui. The current persona occupying Dawn's body appeared to be far more competent— and therefore, more dangerous—than Dawn-off-her-meds. Organized, rather than disorganized, like a serial killer. While a roomful of people looked on, aghast, this new and unexpected personality skippered Dawn's central control station.

First, the new and improved Dawn announced to the room at large that she intended to try out for one of those singing competitions in order to jump-start her music career. If things weren't bad enough, Teensy goaded her into singing a song for everyone in the room so we could play like we were judges and vote on how well she did.

Because we wouldn't want to complicate matters, Teensy, you psycho.

Teensy has always fancied herself as a music critic. Once, when we were young, I had to put her to bed. Usually, our mother would sing her a lullaby, so I did, too. After finishing the song about an ant and a rubber tree plant, my sister looked me dead in the eye and said, "This is the reason I tell people we're

159

not related." And that's when I said, "You're right. We're not. You're adopted."

When Dawn finished belting out an off-key rendition of "All By Myself," Teensy burst into contemptuous laughter and told her to stay in school. That's when Dawn announced to everyone in the room that she was a lesbian and that she'd slept with Venice, Teensy, and me.

My family lives in a ground-zero of intolerance for the LGBT community. Relying on the "innocence cries out" theory, I yelled as loud as I could, without regard to the mentally ill people who'd dozed off in the waiting room, "Oh, no, you did *not.*"

Dawn looked like she wanted to kill me. Crazed eyes were shooting blue daggers from all directions. "Remember what I said about Avery in the car? You're next."

I got the intake lady's attention. "You don't by chance have a screwdriver I could borrow, do you?"

"Girl, whatchoo want with a screwdriver?"

"Well, this was my ingenious idea; therefore, I must have a screw loose."

Based on the intake lady's intense scrutiny, I was pretty sure she based her impression of us on "the acorn doesn't fall far from the tree" theory, and thought we must all be related to Dawn—one dysfunctional family of psychos. She told me to go sit down, and as soon as I occupied the only vacant chair left in the room, which happened to be almost directly across from Dawn, the woman in the chair to my right screamed, "Jesus, God, just kill me now."

I immediately got up and moved closer to the employee behind the Plexiglass. This apparently touched a nerve, because, finally, the intake lady called Dawn's name.

The staff buzzed her in through an electronically controlled door. Beyond our view, Dawn shouted new and even more colorful obscenities. I heard "cockbite" and "douche-idiot" at least three times while I stood, in shock, imagining how that might go over if she pulled the same stunt when she took her bow before the ladies of The Rubanbleu. I looked over at Chopper Deke, who'd been standing next to the elevator in case she tried to bolt.

The jaws of the elevator slid back, and he inclined his head toward the open door. "Ready?"

Teensy jumped in first. Venice followed and punched the floor-selector button.

We heard the hard crash of a fall that suggested Dawn had knocked over hospital furniture in a sudden bid for freedom. Or maybe the techs put her in a "take-down" to get her under control. Thinking I should go back and make sure Dawn was okay, I hesitated at the mouth of the elevator. The doors started to close.

Sensing my dilemma, Chopper Deke grabbed my arm and yanked me aboard. Offering up words of wisdom, he said, "Don't try to make sense out of *crazy* unless you want to become crazy."

Again, I reminded myself on the ride down to the ground floor that Dawn would be safe in a locked unit, and that no one could get to her while Ranger Hill figured out why those mass murderers continued to pursue us with the vengeance of a Biblical punishment. I only hoped the four of us who were still running around out in the free world were stronger than their efforts to destroy us. To me, the worst thing that could happen wasn't becoming their next victim. The worst thing would be if they killed someone I loved—Venice, Teensy, Salem, Daddy. And although Dawn's premier role in the grand scheme of things seemed to be little more than getting in the way, I cared enough to get her the help she needed.

That's why Dawn went from being the life of the party, to not being at the party at all.

★ ★ ★ ★ ★

Chopper Deke tried to deter us from returning to my grandmother's estate, but it was the safest place I knew of, so the three of us cast eye-encrypted votes before I ultimately vetoed his idea.

As he made the final turn to Gran's house, sirens shrilled and horns blared long before I actually saw fire trucks roaring up behind us. Chopper Deke pulled over into the right lane and waited for them to pass. When they'd cleared the SUV, he pulled back onto the roadway and continued on the route to Gran's. Lost in thought, I sat in the front passenger seat and questioned whether I'd done right by Dawn. The four of us—Dawn, Teensy, Venice, and I—possessed way more intelligence than these murderous men, but we weren't nearly as cunning. And we had fewer street creds.

About the time I'd reconciled the decision to drop Dawn off at the psyche ward, I came out of my stupor when Teensy shouted, "Look!" I followed the direction of her pointed finger. Peering into the distance, I saw flames shooting out of Gran's bedroom window.

Fire trucks that had careened past us were now at the mouth of the formidable wrought iron gate. I urged Chopper Deke to speed up so I could jump out and open the gate before they rammed it. If they disabled it, we couldn't stay at Gran's mansion because the gate would no longer keep the fortress impenetrable.

Despite firemen waving us back, Chopper Deke gunned the engine. He floored it so hard I feared he'd run them down, but at the last second, he skidded to a stop, propelling the rear of the SUV into a 180-degree spin. I bailed out and ran toward the gate. A firefighter intercepted me halfway.

Words rushed out in a torrent. "I have the electronic key. Let me through."

I ran past him with the key card held aloft. When I reached the sensor, I swiped the card and the gate groaned open. But instead of hanging back while the fire trucks drove in, I dashed toward the house.

Masochistic curiosity couldn't hold me back. A sick feeling refused to let up. My OCD and blossoming paranoia had forced me to check the locks five times or more; and to pull all the window coverings before twilight; and to make sure all of the lights were extinguished to keep us from becoming targets. But it didn't prepare me for the invisible piranhas shredding my gut or the devastation I'd find inside Gran's house.

No one knew I'd been the last person inside Gran's bedroom, and now the room was in flames: the matched set of Chippendale chairs that Gran bought at auction; irreplaceable period pieces from the 1700s, like the Philadelphia chair that she used at her vanity; and an antique slipper-footed table in near-mint condition. I wanted to throw up. I was responsible for the fire.

I forgot to turn off the thermonuclear-charged electric blanket.

Ignoring the din of "stop" commands, I continued up to the house. I slipped on a patch of ice near the base of the front steps, but managed to Marine-crawl until I reached the front door. I seemed to have teleported myself to my feet from sheer thought. By the time I keyed my way inside, I had little recall for how I got from the gate to the inside of the marble rotunda. My most memorable event entailed sprinting through the acrid, gauzy layer of smoke toward the sweeping staircase.

Suddenly, I was floating, running in place with my legs churning air.

A brawny male had grabbed me from behind. He placed me in a bear hug in order to pull me from the grand staircase. I slipped into survival mode. Thinking this was an intruder who'd managed to sneak onto the grounds and conceal himself, I simultaneously kneed him in the groin, delivered an elbow to the ribs, and smacked the back of my head into his jawbone. The next thing I knew, I was summarily hauled back outside and deposited on the front steps with a frightful scolding and the threat of jail.

All I could think was *Gran's going to kill me.*

That, and the notion that the FD might condemn Gran's house. If they did, then where would we go?

CHAPTER SIXTEEN

By the time FD put out the fire, Teensy, Venice, and I were warming our hands against the vents in Chopper Deke's SUV.

Staring into the distance, Teensy put a finger to her lips. "Wonder how it started?"

Venice nodded. "It's what? A hundred-year-old historical home?" She said this with a quiet sense of nobility, as if a tiny member of British Parliament rested just inside her ear canal, feeding her lines.

"It's a perfectly preserved historical mansion," I said with a sniff.

Chopper Deke weighed in. "Probably faulty wiring."

Teensy and Venice nodded their heads like those bobblehead Chihuahuas with springs in their necks, common to the back dashboards of lowriders. Apparently they revered Chopper Deke and bought into his theory on how Gran's room caught fire, but I knew better.

"That's pretty amazing," Teensy said.

I nodded pensively, determined to keep up a normal conversational tone in an effort to deflect any attention that might be directed toward me. I also realized if I didn't immediately change the subject—my personal favorite has always been *"Look—that lady has on the same dress as you"*—people would start asking the inevitable, such as whether I knew anything about how the fire started, or outright accuse me of leaving Gran's electric blanket on.

"What do we do now, Dainty?" Teensy said this weakly and somewhat apologetically.

I stared out at the horizon, as if a response to her question could be found there.

And what I came up with was Rubanbleu inappropriate. "I have no frickin' idea."

A few hours later, after one of the firefighters pulled the charred remains of Gran's electric blanket out of the room and held it inches from my face, saying, "Here's the culprit," the FD allowed us to return to the house to remove whatever belongings we needed for the night.

Chopper Deke said, "You can come home with me."

Teensy, who stood behind him, peered past his shoulder and gave me a "thumbs-up," coupled with an enthusiastic head bob.

I declined. "That's okay. We'll just stay here."

Part of my motivation to remain in Gran's house had to do with assessing the damage. The other part was so I could take a load of her clothes to the resale shop to get enough cash to hire restoration professionals to come in and clean up the damage as quickly as possible.

Preferably before Daddy found out.

Chopper Deke interrupted my reverie. "Le Jardin de Loire is providing free rooms to the homeless through New Year's Eve." I noted his blank reaction to our predicament and didn't like to think he'd lie to me.

I fantasized about being in a king-sized bed with freshly laundered linens and a door with a double-locking dead bolt and safety latch. The idea of a long, hot shower thrilled me. Actually, not true. I dreamed of room service. Room service thrilled me. With dry-cleaning services. And cable television and movies, and a microwave for theater-buttered popcorn. Selfish curiosity beguiled me.

For now, this could be the perfect solution to our problem.

We definitely fit the homeless criteria, and we'd be relatively safe in the midst of so many "real" homeless people. The killers wouldn't dream of finding two debutantes and a couture dress designer in a hotel filled with bag ladies and hobos.

"Take us there." Teensy and Venice looked at me like I'd sprouted horns and grown a goatee. "I'll pack a few things and we can be on our way."

"Yeah, like chocolate chip cookies," Teensy blurted out, "and a box of those snack cakes with the squiggly white curlicues on top."

But I was thinking more on the order of bringing a suitcase filled with Gran's Chanel suits, Ferragamo shoes, and Escada ensembles. After I sorted through Gran's closet and packed her things, I hauled the Louis Vuitton out to Chopper Deke's SUV.

He stared through jaundice eyes. "Louis Vuitton? Really? Let me get this straight—you're going to try to pass yourselves off as part of the homeless problem, and you're carrying Louis Vuitton?"

"What am I supposed to pack stuff in?"

"Doesn't your grandmother have a set of old alligator luggage stored in the attic? You know—the kind with scuffed corners and brittle decals stuck on the sides?"

I dragged the suitcase-on-wheels back into the house and hauled it, bouncing, up each step until I reached Gran's sanctuary. In ruins, the room offered an eerie glimpse into a stately mansion without humans. Charred walls inspired a sense of loss like I'd never felt before. Feeling sad for myself and the havoc I'd wreaked, I repacked Gran's treasures. This time, I came out of Gran's charred room dragging two king-sized pillowcases that I'd stuffed with her things and knotted, prepared to drag them to the landing and roll them down the stairs.

Halfway down the stairs, I heard a noise that made my stomach clench. With my heart thudding, I reached the last step. A long shadow, from which I couldn't discern the owner, grayed the marble. It wasn't a firefighter—of that, I was certain. The shadowy outline had no helmet or other gear one might associate with firemen. Staving off a panic attack, I tried to make myself invisible by pressing my back against the wall while gauging how long it'd take me to fly out the front door.

Suddenly, I made a break for it, running like the devil was breathing down the back of my neck.

I heard a shout behind me. "Diva . . . like, *what the fuck?* Did you do this? This is your handiwork?"

I kept running.

My internal sensor had equipped me with a seven-second lag time, and it didn't kick in until I reached the front door. I stopped dead in my tracks.

Only one person ever had the nerve to call me that.

"What. The. Hell?" was all I managed to bite out before I turned. "Amanda?"

A small, dark-skinned woman of indeterminate age, with chiseled features and a complexion so black that it seemed to have a purple tint, stared at me through reptilian eyes. Her hair didn't look anything like the cascading platinum wig she wore the first time we met, and her garish clothing had been replaced with stylish apparel. I'm only five feet four inches and 110 pounds, but I towered over her like the jolly green giant, which I guess was to be expected, since Amanda's a pygmy.

She glared at me, and I felt the need to defend myself, *because, in case you hadn't noticed, Amanda, my grandmother's house caught fire, you crazy trespasser. And who gave you permission to wear my pink silk pajamas?*

The last time I saw Amanda Vásquez, with her gap-toothed grin and over-modulated cadence of a drag queen, she was waving good-bye in the rearview mirror of her crappy, circa seventies Chevy Vega with gray primer. El Paso bound, she had a court hearing to pay off her restitution in full, as a condition of her probation. Authorities believed she'd stolen a Bichon from a family in one of El Paso's poorest colonias. The owners filed a police report accusing her of pulling up in front of their ramshackle house in a taxi and committing a criminal trespass into their backyard with the intent to steal their expensive dog.

I knew better. Amanda returned to that cab with a matted, malnourished dog with protruding ribs that were visible through the caked-on mud. She'd rescued that animal from an abusive family, but the judge didn't believe her. I knew enough to make the distinction between theft and a rescue, because I was with her when it happened. But I was long gone when it came time to testify. I blamed Jim Bruckman for putting me on the last plane out of El Paso. He believed Amanda had almost gotten me killed down in Mexico, but the truth was that she probably saved my life more times than I cared to count.

My mouth dropped open. I peppered her with rapid-fire questions. "What're you doing here? Are you the one who called the fire department? How'd you get inside Gran's house?"

"Same way you did." Her broad, flat nose flared. Her speech patterns had an interesting kind of rhythm to them, with an upward intonation at the end of each sentence that made her statements seem more like questions. "Gran gave me a key."

"Stop calling her Gran. She's not your grandmother."

"She told me I could call her that."

When they first met, Gran loathed Amanda. But shortly before Christmas, she'd taken Amanda shopping at Harkman Beemis. There she introduced Amanda to her friends as her personal elf. Under no circumstances can an educated person mistake a pygmy for an elf. Nevertheless, there'd been speculation that Gran was getting a little senile, because ladies of The Rubanbleu would *nevah-evah* be seen at Harkman Beemis or anywhere else with a pygmy. Not even a pygmy goat.

I was about to lambast Amanda for having a key to Gran's house, especially when Gran had taken my key away from me days ago, so I demanded that she hand it over. She shrugged and left the room. About the time she returned, dressed in her own clothes, Teensy be-bopped in to see what was taking so long.

She squealed "Mandy!" at the top of her lungs, which made me want to drive an ice pick through my ears, because, for God's sake, the pygmy's name is Amanda, not Mandy. Her real name isn't even Amanda Vásquez. To be exact, I'm not even sure what her real name is.

Teensy jumped up and down like a float bobbing in the water. "Mandy's here, Mandy's here. *Squeeeeeee!*"

You'd have thought the ice cream truck crashed through our living room and spilled its inventory. Amanda slapped Gran's house key in my hand and I passed it over to Teensy. Now we each had our own key. As firemen trekked in and out, I realized Amanda had no way to get through the big wrought iron gate, so how'd she get onto the grounds? Because of my blossoming paranoia over the past week, I demanded an explanation.

"Gran gave me a key to the side gate." This time, Amanda spoke in exclamation marks.

"Give it to me."

She huffed out her displeasure and left the room for the second time. In a few minutes, she returned with the gate key.

"Don't make me turn you upside down and shake keys out of your pocket," I said.

"Hey, I can't help it if Gran likes me better than you."

The remark stung, probably because it had a ring of truth to it. In less than a few weeks, Amanda had gone from being reviled by Gran, to juicing a couple of keys to the estate out of her that she didn't even trust her own granddaughters to carry around—which made perfectly good sense, in retrospect, since one of her granddaughters had become an accomplished arsonist and tried to burn her house down. That would be me.

Amanda said something and I missed it.

"What?"

"Where's Gran?" Dark eyes pinned me.

I cut my gaze to Teensy, who'd fixed her eyes on me. "Gran's dead."

Amanda's mouth went slack. Usually calm and controlled to the point of aggravation, she suddenly dropped to the floor in a sobbing, wailing heap. Which was far more emotion than I'd displayed. I looked to Teensy for help—fat chance—and when I looked back at Amanda, I found her doubled-over, rocking back and forth, keening uncontrollably. I didn't even recognize the noises as human.

Watching Amanda fall apart put a damper on things, making Gran's charred bedroom seem positively uplifting by comparison. I mean, you go through the day thinking how great it'd be to have a chili dog and—holy cow—you suddenly remember Gran's ship sank, and that she and Old Man Spencer are presumed dead.

"So let me get this straight," Amanda said after the firefighters cleared out and we threw the stuffed pillowcases with Gran's things in them into the back of the SUV, "assassins are chasing you?"

The three of us nodded in unison. I locked the house and we piled into the vehicle. Once we buckled ourselves in, Chopper Deke pulled out onto the street and headed in the direction of the freeway.

Amanda digested the chronology of events, starting with the lodge and ending with Gran's burned-out bedroom. "So, now you're trying to get me killed, too? Why didn't you tell me before this crazy guy drove us away?"

"Hey, now." Chopper Deke's eyes flickered to the rearview mirror.

Secretly thrilled that we'd left Dawn at the psyche ward—after all, as a potential debutante of The Rubanbleu, Dawn would've outright rejected Amanda—I quickly introduced Amanda to Chopper Deke and Venice. Venice, who wasn't a Rubanbleu debutante, was studying Amanda with intensity, probably designing salesman samples in her head in case she was ever called upon to outfit a tribe of pygmies. When she asked Amanda what part of Africa her family hailed from, they got into an esoteric discussion of what to see and do while on the continent. I felt like Teensy and I had been pushed out of the conversation.

Oh, wait—we had been.

Along our route, I began to fear for Amanda. With Dawn gone, our numbers had shrunk to three, but now climbed back up to four. If Amanda tied up with us, they'd kill her, too, whoever "they" were.

Chopper Deke seemed to read my mind. "Last chance."

"Last chance for what?" We chimed in as a group.

"To reconsider. You can still come to my house." He shifted his calculating gaze over to Amanda. "I don't know about you." Then he looked back at me. "You'll be safe there."

I inwardly scoffed at the idea. Chopper Deke probably lived in a pig sty, with dirty clothes strewn everywhere and half-empty bags of cheese puffs littering the house. I imagined he slept on a cotton mattress with old ticking and had a ham radio set and an old tube TV in his living room. Taking advantage of Le Jardin de Loire's generosity seemed like a no-brainer.

Since Amanda didn't know where we were going, I filled her in.

"I'd rather stay at Gran's," she sulked. "Gran's house is better. What's a little smoke? Just keep the door closed. I live across the border from Mexico and inhale toxic fumes on a daily basis. Get used to it."

"Toats be-goats," Teensy said, punctuating the idea with a nod.

"What?" Amanda reared her head back like she'd observed Teensy speaking in tongues. "What'd you say?" She gave Teensy a blank stare.

"I was just agreeing with you," Teensy said.

"What'd you say?

"Toats be-goats. Toats." When Amanda still didn't understand Teensy's special language, Teensy said, "Toats—totally? Be-goats, because it rhymes?"

"What is wrong with you? Speak English." Amanda jarred us with her next question. "When's the service?"

"Service?" I'd been lost in thought, wondering if the hotel people had a way to determine whether we were actually home-less, or just pretending to be homeless so we could stay there for free.

"Gran's service. The memorial service for Gran," Amanda shouted. "Don't you even care about your grandmother, diva?" She snorted in contempt. "Because she cared about *you*." She shifted her eyes to Teensy. "And you, *selfish*."

"We care, Amanda. We were raised to not make a scene."

So back off already and stop judging us.

And Teensy was all, "Yeah, Mandy. Exactly." And I wanted to hit my head against the windshield for twenty minutes. Either that, or knock Teensy to the floor and yell, "Debutante down. Cleanup on aisle five."

Before Chopper Deke let us out beneath Le Jardin de Loire's portico, he reached over and tousled my hair. "Can't go inside the hotel having everyone think you're privileged."

It might've been the dead of winter, but at the hotel, we walked past a man in a suit, who I figured worked there. He was talking to a bearded, fat, naked guy stretched out on a chaise lounge by the pool with his junk on display. The image got branded into my retinas, and I can never un-see this, ever.

At the front desk, I saw a huge bowl stacked high with apples in various shades of reds and greens. Five-star hotels always have fruit for the guests, so I reached for one.

The lady behind the counter said, "Snow White did that. It killed her."

I figured her sister worked intake at the county hospital psyche ward. And that loving one's job ran in the family. I grudgingly put the apple back.

Then I found out we had randomly assigned roommates. Out of a thousand homeless people taking Le Jardin de Loire up on their offer of a free hotel room, I just happened to get assigned to a girl who threatened to kill me in junior high. I begged the lady to keep all four of us together. She begged me to go to the back of the line and zip it.

At the end of the line, I looked down at Amanda. "What about Dainty says I want to room with people I don't know?"

"I don't know. What about Amanda says I want to share a bed with people who're trying to get me killed?"

"Shhh. Lower your voice."

"Don't shush me. You cannot shush me. I'm telling Gran on you." And just like that, her face wilted and big, fat tears splashed over her dark chocolate cheeks. "It's like it's not even real, what happened to Gran." Her voice choked on *Gran*.

The check-in line continued to shrink. We were three people away from being waited on when the woman who sent me to the back of the line went on break and a nice-looking black man took over. Men are usually putty in my hands—except for those who were trying to kill us.

I flashed a hundred-watt smile. "We're together."

CHAPTER SEVENTEEN

The hotel people put us on the third floor, and when we keyed open the door to our beautiful room, we found a connecting suite with the door locked. To make sure no boogieman stood behind the door leading into the adjacent suite, I opened the connecting door on our side and gave the door to the next room a gentle push. It didn't budge. Satisfied, I toggled the bolt on our side.

Teensy wasted no time hogging the bathroom. I heard her singing in the shower and grimaced.

"I have a whole new appreciation for Teensy's singing. I appreciate when Teensy doesn't sing," Amanda deadpanned.

You can say that again.

Our spacious room had two queen-sized beds, and I noticed Amanda had pushed my things aside and put her junk on the side of the bed that I claimed. While she waited for Teensy to towel off and relinquish the bathroom, I reclaimed my space.

For good measure, I yelled, "Teensy—there are others who'd like to freshen up."

"Hold your horses."

"Your train's about to run out of track, Teensy. Quit being a selfish ho."

"Bet you're glad Dawn isn't here," she retorted. "It's very un-Rubanbleu of a debutante to resort to name-calling, and we wouldn't want to teach Dawn bad manners, now, would we?"

"I've had my fill of you, Teensy."

To kill time, I pulled out a novel I'd snagged from Gran's stack of unread books and waited for my sister to flounce out of the bathroom. The mystery turned into a great read, and ticked all the boxes on my list of book requirements. As a matter of fact, I laughed so hard in a couple of places that it qualified as an abdominal workout.

Raucous laughter interrupted my concentration.

Bookmarking my place, I set the novel aside and followed the first sounds of merriment that I'd heard from our group in several days. I found Venice and Amanda yukking it up in the living room.

"What's so funny?"

"Amanda just cracked herself up. She saw a hole in her sock and said, 'Darn it.' " Venice let out what I considered to be an unhealthy cackle.

I gave them a heavy eye roll.

After encouraging them to make their food selections from the menu, I called for room service and placed their respective orders for beef and chicken dinners. Since my clothes had already loosened over the past week—probably a combination of fear and the lack of food to kick-start my metabolism—I stuck with a salad.

"Got your pen ready to write?" I prompted the person taking the food orders. "I want the chef's salad, but not the one with the fried chicken in it. I want the one with ham and boiled eggs and tomatoes. And I do want chicken in it but not if it's fried. I want grilled chicken. But if you don't have grilled chicken, you can put fried chicken in it, but peel off the breading. As for the lettuce, I don't want arugula or field greens or anything like that—only butter lettuce and maybe a little radicchio, but just enough to give it color. Wait. Never mind. Skip the radicchio. Make it all butter lettuce. And I want honey mustard dressing on the side, and I'll need three little ramekins full of it. Oh, and absolutely no onions. And I don't want cucumbers either."

"She's doing it again," Amanda announced to the others.

"She always does that," Teensy said.

I fanned my hand at her in an attempt to get her to muffle her voice—and got a rude awakening from the other end of the line. "What do you mean you have a special menu and it's limited to beef or chicken?" I cut my eyes to the three lemmings sitting on the sofa, as the female on the other end of the line described my food choices. "But I don't want beef or chicken." Long pause. "What do you mean it's the homeless menu. You have a special menu for the homeless? Well, I'm sorry, I just don't think I can accept that. Look, I really want a chef's salad. Please-please-please? I'm not picky."

Amanda talked smack about me in the background. "Not picky? Ha."

"I don't think I've ever seen her order anything the way it appears on the menu." Venice.

"That goes without saying. When we were in Mexico," Amanda said, "she wanted Mexican hot chocolate. But with those little marshmallows, not the big ones. And could they take the cinnamon out of the hot chocolate? Hell, that's what Mexican hot chocolate is—just order hot chocolate and deal with it if you don't want the cinnamon, right? Aiiiiiieeeeee," Amanda gave her south 'o the border battle cry of disgust, "Dainty's such a diva."

I'd become distracted by their mockery and asked the girl taking my order to read it back to me. She never mentioned cutting the onions, so I reminded her. "No onions. Cut the onions. Absolutely no onions. Okay? Say it: 'No onions.' " After she grudgingly repeated it back to me, I said, "I'm not kidding. If there's so much as one onion in that salad, you'll have an ambulance out in front of your hotel and that'd be bad for business."

For the record, I'm not allergic to onions, I just hate them.

After she hung up on me, I nudged my way onto the couch between Amanda and Venice, while Teensy picked out a mind-numbingly stupid movie for us to watch. About fifteen minutes into it, the Rottweiler in my stomach growled.

"Watching a movie isn't the same without popcorn." Venice, who'd been unusually quiet until Amanda joined our group, fixed her gaze on the little refrigerator—the one the hotel stocked with guest refreshments for a fee. "Do you think we should see what's in there, Dainty?"

Before I could answer, a strong knock at the door caused us all to jump to our feet.

"Wait. We have to make sure it's the hotel people." I saw no need to stop exercising caution just because we were at a five-star hotel. I looked through the little peephole enough to see a young man about my age, wearing black pants, a black vest, and a white shirt, holding a large food tray. The oval plastic name tag read *Raul,* and I assumed that must be his name. I opened the door until the slack played out of the safety bolt. While eyeing him from head to toe, the smell of beef, chicken, and ham wafted up my nostrils.

The smell of food convinced me Raul was harmless.

I closed the door and immediately slid the safety bar off. When I opened it again, I stuck my head out and looked the entire length of the hall. Raul had arrived alone.

"Okay, come on in."

When I turned around, Amanda had assumed a little pygmy martial arts stance. I wasn't sure if she planned to use those deadly little hands to cut Raul in half—or to cut her sandwich. Raul just smiled and told us to have a nice day. I guess he'd been told not to expect tips, because, after all, we were supposed to be homeless, but I called out for him to wait and ran to get a couple of dollars from my purse to tip on the cheap.

After hanging out the *Do Not Disturb* sign, we went back to eating our food and watching the worst movie ever made . . . well, they watched it while I picked through my chef's salad to make sure the cook hadn't dropped an onion in the bowl for spite.

The girls had already finished eating, and I was only half-through when an unexpected visitor pounded on the door. It sounded like a brazen cop knock, not a polite, *Sorry to disturb you but we forgot to leave your complimentary chocolate-covered strawberries* knock.

"Room service," a male voice called out.

We stayed deathly quiet. We had no idea how long the caller had lingered outside our door, listening to us talk past the blaring TV. It could've been long enough for him to know we were inside.

Distress pinched Venice's lips.

My Pollyanna-ish sister whispered, "Open it. Maybe they screwed up and doubled our order."

"They didn't screw up." My heart raced. My stomach knotted.

Since we'd been assigned to a room on the third floor, my mind ran through a panicky review of escape options. In Mexico, I'd fashioned a rope out of bed sheets and thrown it over a second-floor balcony, in case I had to take flight. I'd done so knowing I'd probably break an ankle when I hit the ground, but I was willing to take the chance if cutthroats burst into my room. Third floor, though? I was pretty sure going over the third-floor balcony would accomplish what those men hadn't been able to do.

"Maybe they're delivering food to the wrong room." Teensy tried again. "We should take it. I'm still hungry."

"It's not for us. Be quiet."

Amanda slipped up beside me. "I have a bad feeling. Don't open it."

The color drained from Venice's face. White as a ghost, she moved toward the balcony. I motioned for her to steer clear of the lanai. I'd come to embrace the benefit of having curtains; who knew who might be watching from the ground?

The second knock sounded much louder than the first. Again, we heard "Room service," in a louder, angrier voice. I crept to the door and carefully reengaged the security bolt. Then I peered through the peephole.

A man dressed in black stood in front of the door. He held a food tray, but I could tell from the disarranged cloches, as well as evidence that the food on these plates had been eaten, that he carried it as a prop. At first, I thought he might be an employee sent to pick up empty trays. Then I saw the black knit cap stretched tightly on top of his head—a cap that could easily be pulled over his eyes. Another man in similar clothing stood behind him. He had his back to me, but I could still make out the outline of a ski cap on his head. I motioned the girls farther back into the room and urged them toward the door leading into the adjacent suite.

"It's them," I mouthed without sound.

"But . . . how?" Venice asked, just before her eyelids fluttered and her knees buckled. Teensy and Amanda caught her in mid-collapse as I hurried over. I opened the connecting door and lightly tapped at the entrance to the next suite. When nobody answered, I sent Amanda to the nightstand for the complimentary pen and notepad. Upon her return, I wrote *Please help us,* and slipped the message under the door.

Softly and steadily, I knuckle-rapped like I was tapping out Morse code. I looked over at Venice and experienced a new level of fright coming from her eyes that froze me in midtap.

On the other side of the door to the adjacent suite, rustling sounds and shuffling feet filled me with hope. But nothing sent a sense of reassurance through me like the snap of the toggle lock opening.

The connecting door swung open.

A tall man with olive skin and a long salt-and-pepper beard pierced us with his murky stare. He'd dressed in one of the monogrammed hotel robes and held an unlit tobacco pipe in his hand. Just beyond his shoulder, and slightly to his left, a middle-aged woman with dark hair strained back from her face waited to see what we wanted. She looked like she'd dressed from the rag bin, and nothing she had on matched.

I spoke in a whisper. "Please let us in. A man's trying to get into our room."

Our suitemate appeared to be in his sixties. Experience and rural cunning probably made him eye each of us up and down— especially Amanda. When I shifted my gaze to her, Amanda scowled back at him.

"Want me to beat him up?" the man asked in a three-pack-a-day voice.

"Oh, God, no," I said. "We just need to use your phone to call security. And please don't open your door. I'm pretty sure he has a gun."

"What does he have to do with you?"

I shrugged. "What does anybody have to do with anything?"

The racket in the hall persisted. Our tormentor gave the door handle a loud shake, then hammered the door with his fist. My heartbeat quickened.

Our suitemate invited us in. To the woman, he said, "Let the ladies use the phone, Ria."

When he opened the connecting door enough for all of us to file in, I made a beeline for the telephone. Over the sounds of a TV sitcom volumed down low, I contacted the front desk. A man answered, and my words tumbled out in a winded rush.

"Please help us. We're in Three-Oh-Two. A man's impersonating a hotel employee and he's trying to get into our room. Please send security."

"What does he look like?"

"Black clothes and a black ski mask on top of his head. He has one of your food trays and he said it's room service, but we already got our food a long time ago."

"We'll send someone up."

"Not some*one*. Send several security officers. I believe this man is dangerous, and there's another man with him. Also dressed in black, with a ski mask. I have good reason to believe they have guns."

After I hung up, I looked at the couple over their intent regard. Part of me wanted to explain. The other part contemplated what to do if the men in the hall managed to gain access to our room.

The lady introduced herself. "I'm Ria." She shifted her eyes. "This is Gustav."

Intent on listening to the noises in the hall, I barely caught their names. Incorporating more people into our doom-filled situation didn't make me feel any safer. I'd seen what those horrible men had done to the people at the lodge and didn't want to see what else they could do.

Then Ria averted my attention from the rattling door. "I'd like to tell your fortunes."

Do what?

She lined us up side-by-side and, facing us, took a seat at the foot of the bed. First, she invited Amanda to stand in front of her. "Just as I thought." She cocked an eyebrow and her facial expression turned mysterious. "All of your troubles are behind you."

Amanda scowled. "You got that right, lady. Doesn't take a clairvoyant to figure that out."

Ria's next comment took the sass out of Amanda. "I know your secret. Now step back."

I, too, knew Amanda's secret, having made the jaw-dropping discovery through the reflection of a cracked mirror on my side of the bed in Hotel Malamuerte, down in the pulsing black heart of Ciudad Juárez. I'd never uttered a peep about Amanda's private life to anyone, especially my blabbermouth sister and my hyper-critical grandmother. After she saved my life, I concluded that Amanda's mysterious secret was hers, and hers alone, to tell.

Amanda got back in line.

Ria motioned for Venice to approach. "People are after you. You have something they want." She glanced over at Teensy. "You—you're interfering with the frequency. Move away."

Teensy struck her *Who, me?* pose, and finger-pointed at herself like she'd been unfairly accused.

"You're a hot mess." Ria flicked her fingers to shoo my sister away. "Step out on the balcony."

Strong male voices filtered in from the hall. The food tray crashed to the floor with an awful clatter. Sounds of a struggle ensued, followed by the squawk of a hand-held radio. A stampede of footsteps, and the banging of a stairwell door being shouldered open, raised my comfort level—they were gone. Hotel security might actually apprehend and identify these men.

Ria said something, and I missed it.

When I turned my attention from the connecting door, she beckoned me closer. "Come."

"I'm not sure I want to know my future."

"Nonsense." Dark eyes glittered. "You will have a wonderful, happy, and healthy life."

"Really?" Until that moment, I couldn't envision anything but doom and despair and a chronic black cloud following me around. I knew it was silly, and I didn't buy into the whole fortune-telling idea, but a sense of relief washed over me and I let down my guard.

A half hour later, a knuckle-rap on the door to our room ended our conversations with Gustav and Ria. I heard, "Hotel security," and broke away, reentering our room through the connecting door. My hope for "a wonderful, happy, and healthy life" tanked when I overheard Gustav say to Ria, "Why'd you tell her that? Her future is dark."

Followed by Ria's comment, "It won't hurt to let her think happy thoughts, since the unthinkable is about to happen. What, Gustav? You wanted me to tell her she's going to die?"

CHAPTER EIGHTEEN

After the hotel security guards returned for more information, we learned the assassins got away during the chase. To our chagrin, one of them fired on the security guards. Fortunately, the shot missed. Unfortunately, it blew out a window in the hotel lobby, and Dallas PD had been called.

Smears of red, white, and blue emergency lights strobed in the parking lot below. We watched from the safety of our room, awed, as each beacon swept across our lanai. I felt incredibly lucky we weren't asked to leave, but at this stage of the investigation, hotel representatives acted horrified and apologetic that random bad guys would try to harm their guests. They even offered to let us keep the robes as a gift. They had yet to figure out that we were the ones who'd visited this calamity on their hotel.

Hotel personnel lingered nearby as police interviewed us. Then the inevitable happened. The cops wanted our names for their report. As soon as I provided mine, the hotel manager interrupted.

"You're Dainty Prescott? Of the Fort Worth Prescotts?" Then recognition dawned. "Wait a minute—aren't you on TV?" He snapped his fingers a couple of times to jog his memory. "You're not homeless. Why're you freeloading? We have real people who need our help. Is this a publicity stunt? Are you doing this for ratings?" He glanced around. "Are we being videoed?"

We asked to be relocated to a different room. They seemed

thrilled to relocate us to a different room—just not one in this particular hotel. Because we weren't actually homeless by their definition, we were instructed to leave within the hour. Which instantly made us homeless. Ironic.

After the hotel people left, I called Chopper Deke to come get us.

"And take us where?" Amanda snapped as my message cycled to voicemail.

"Back to Gran's. We can get her car and drive to the TV station. It's a fortress."

Venice and Teensy agreed. We certainly couldn't wait around for those men to come back. Neither could we leave until Chopper Deke arrived or we took a cab to the station.

Amanda said, "I think we should have a private memorial service for Gran."

Teensy perked up. "When?"

"Right now. Let's just say the spirit has moved me to comment about Gran. Each person says what Gran meant to them, and then we finish with a little prayer."

Knowing we faced forcible eviction, Teensy ramrodded the show. "Why don't you start, Amanda, since it was your idea. You must have something you want to say about Gran."

"Remember when she thought I'd steal her stuff? She watched me like a hawk while I polished the sterling silver." Amanda said this with a smile, but tears beaded at the rims of her eyes. "And what about the time she took me to Harkman Beemis and told all her friends I was an elf?"

Venice looked like she was itching to say something so Teensy gave her the go-ahead.

Venice cast her gaze to the floor. "I remember how infuriated she got when I painted the trompe l'oeil fireplace in your bedroom, Dainty. She bitched us out because of the paint fumes and scolded me for defacing her attic. Later, after she came up to inspect my work, she complimented me on my artistic talent. That meant a lot to me."

Amanda squirmed excitedly, raising her hand and waving it around. "I thought of something else. Remember when Gran asked you to set the table and you didn't do it fast enough, and she threatened to 'twerk' in front of your friends?"

"Thanks for sharing," I said nastily, "because it wouldn't embarrass me unless everyone knew."

Teensy was chomping at the bit to talk. "She always bought me pretty clothes at Harkman Beemis, and made me pledge not to tell Dainty."

"Yeah?" I said with snappish irritation. "Well, I have memories, too. Like when I went down to Mexico to drag our wicked stepmother back so she could stand trial, only to have Gran and Daddy conspire to sell my Porsche. I loved that car."

"You can't blame them," Teensy said. "They figured you'd be killed, with that bounty on your head, and they wanted to sell it before it got tied up in probate since you didn't leave a will."

"Who the hell my age has a will? I don't own anything."

"Well, you owned a Porsche until they sold it."

Heat climbed my neck. Then it radiated across my face.

Then Teensy made it worse. "Remember that time Gran saw Bruckman for the second time ever, and said, 'You're an idiot for dating my granddaughter'?"

"When did she say that?"

"Oh, right. That wasn't Gran. That was Daddy."

"When did Daddy say that?"

Venice came out of her stupor. "Remember when we were in high school, Dainty, but we didn't have our driver's licenses yet, so she agreed to take us to the mall? And then you had to ask her not to meditate while driving, remember that?"

This so-called private memorial service for my grandmother turned into a real a-ha moment for me. Ready to drop the hammer on my temper, I said, "Let's wrap this up."

Amanda said, "Remember when Gran took Teensy to a psychiatrist after she came back from Mexico all fucked up? And after Teensy unloaded all of her problems, the shrink told Gran that she picks up a new client about every five years who's completely beyond her ability to treat. And Gran said, 'I guess that makes Teensy your five-year epic fail.' Remember?" Amanda fell into a fit of raucous laughter.

Teensy bristled. "Hey—that's mean."

"Uh . . . yes. Yes, it is." Amanda eyed her knowingly. "Gran was mean. I mean, we loved her, and everything, but she was mean."

"And spiteful." Obviously Venice felt well enough to contribute.

"And hateful," Teensy added, now that Amanda had lured her over to the dark side.

"Remember when she shot the man who carjacked us the night we came back from Mexico?" Amanda filled Venice in. "You never heard such nightmarish screams coming from the back seat. And then she yelled at Dainty for calling 9-1-1 and trying to get them to send an ambulance for the guy she plugged." She took a deep inhale. "Man, I wish my grandmother'd had a permit to carry a gun. White people have all the luck."

"I mean it. We're done here. Let's kill this switch." I sliced the air between us to show that I was fed up, and we were through. "Memorial service, over."

Forty-five minutes later, we gathered our meager belongings and waited for our ride in front of the hotel. The hotel people eyed us with cold scrutiny when a cab pulled up and we climbed inside.

Once the cab driver dropped us off at the TV station, I found places for Venice and Amanda to crash. Our photographers often napped in a small room with a couple of couches arranged in the shape of an "L", and the quiet space was far enough away from the hustle and bustle outside of the studio, so I felt they'd be safe there. Chopper Deke's office also had a sofa—a buttery-soft leather beauty that I figured Teensy could crash on, since she and I were about the only people known to man who could handle Chopper Deke if he arrived early and found that his office had been invaded. As for myself, I returned to my little closet next to the break room that Gordon keeps trying to pass off as an office. Even if I was out like a light when the resident early birds arrived, I'd hear the first can of soda pop roll down the chute of the vending machine before anyone came inside my room and discovered *moi*, Dainty Prescott, with sleep crusting my eyes and drool oozing out of the side of my mouth.

I didn't anticipate Gordon reeling through the station like a whirling dervish, hollering at the top of his lungs about "that damned Steve Lennox calling up, iced-in, because he couldn't get a damned flight out of Chicago."

Gordon yelled, "He needs to rent a car, drive to St. Louis, get his ass on a plane, and do the news like I pay him to do."

Figuring I could solve the problem by delivering the morning broadcast in Steve's place, I blinked away grogginess and wiped the corners of my mouth to sounds of Rochelle placating the boss. I glanced at the clock. Not much time. Whenever we were short of on-air talent, Gordon preferred to read the news rather than allow Tig Welder to do it. Why he hadn't already fired Tig, I'll never know, since Tig was a person of interest in a homicide, and yet . . . still here.

I stepped out of my office to the sight of Rochelle in her fiery red twinset, looking like the CEO of hell's complaint department, and Gordon, in his rumpled suit, needing only a piece of straw sticking out of his hair to convince people he'd spent the night in a hayloft. Rheumy-eyed, his nose had the bulbous glow of Rudolph the red-nosed boozer.

"Prescott," he bit out. "What're you doing here? Aren't you on bereavement leave?"

"I can do the news. Let *me* do the news." I cringed, thinking he might pick one of the SMU idiots—*ahem,* interns—over me. They tended to freeze in front of the camera, and, believe me, there's nothing worse than watching one of these slack-jawed, unblinking nitwits sitting, transfixed, behind the anchor desk while the video rolls. In the industry, it's what's known as "dead air." At WBFD, it's what's known as "You're fired."

Gordon said, "Thought you were off the grid."

"I am, but I can help out. You need me."

"Like a hole in the head," Rochelle mumbled.

"In my office." Gordon motioned me to follow him. I found myself sitting on his furry cowhide sofa. "Are you back to work for good?"

I grimaced. "Not really. We came here a few hours ago because the hotel kicked us out."

"Hotel?" His hand went from the blotter to the bottom drawer where I knew he kept a bottle of whiskey. He pulled the bottle out by the neck and held it aloft. I declined with a head-shake. He took out a glass, poured two fingers, and belted it back in one continuous gulp. "The hair of the dog that bit me."

He returned the bottle to the drawer and watched me with intent regard.

"Anyhoo, I'm here and I can sub for Mr. Lennox."

"*Mr.* Lennox," he scoffed. "Mr. Lennox will be lucky if he still has a job when he comes back. Which brings me to you. When are you coming back?"

"I'm here now."

"You need to leave, and take your entourage with you."

"But why? You need someone to do the news and I'm already here."

"You're endangering lives. You really think I want whoever's after you to see that you're doing the damned news, and show up here to pick off my employees like a bunch of low-hanging fruit?"

I had to give that a wee bit of thought. What he said was true. Still, I wanted to prove I could pull it off. "Stay right there. I'll be back in twenty minutes, ready to go on-air. If you say no, then I'll leave."

"And take those idiots with you." He reached for the drawer, and I excused myself before he poured himself another drink.

Since we didn't have anywhere else to go until the consignment shop opened well after the morning broadcast, we needed to stay put. And I could accomplish that by convincing Gordon to let me read the news.

Fifteen minutes later, after I'd gone to wardrobe and found a cascading black wig, I applied my makeup. An extra swipe of mascara darkened my lashes and gave them a luxurious look; my lids, shadowed in the palest hint of ice blue, made my light blue eyes sparkle like six-carat gemstones. After scoring a cool pair of dark rhinestone eyeglasses that had been designed by a famous tattoo artist, I punched out the lenses and centered them on my face. Perfect—made me look smart and trendy. Then I changed clothes.

Dressed in a shock of color, I passed Rochelle's desk to get to Gordon's office without saying a word.

"Oh, this I've gotta see." Smirking, she pushed back from her desk and trailed me in.

I did a little curtsy. "I'm ready for my close-up, Mr. De Mille."

Gordon gave me a dedicated eyeblink. "Who the hell are— wait a minute—Prescott?"

"Yessir."

"No. They'll know you're here as soon as you open your mouth and say your name.

"That's just it, Mr. Pfeiffer—"

"Gordon."

"That's just it, Gordon. Today, I'm not Dainty Prescott. I'm going on-air as Pixy Merriweather."

He did a drunken face scrunch.

Rochelle eyed Gordon up. "You could probably use a bowl of menudo. Think I'll get you an order from that Mexican café down the street."

"I don't need a hangover cure," he growled. "I don't have a hangover."

"Of course you don't," she said in that trademark patronizing way.

After she glided out of the room, Gordon turned his faulty attention back to me. "You're gonna make this station a laughingstock."

"No, sir, I'm not. I'll do the news and you'll love it."

"How'd you come up with that name?"

"It's a family name. Don't worry, everything will be fine."

It was obvious that things were going to get better for me at the station. Once I finished the morning broadcast and signed off with, "Now back to your regular programming," I pulled off my mike, left the anchor desk, and fist-bumped the photographers on the way out of the studio. I hoped this would convince Gordon to let me and my entourage move into the station for the duration.

I found him seated behind his desk with his chair swiveled away from me. With the phone pressed to his ear, he carped about his "useless, money-siphoning staff."

"Pixy Merriweather?" His tone changed for the better. "Yeah, I'm trying her out. What of it?" Long pause. "You watched her?" Short pause. "Think she's any good?" He swiveled his chair around and saw me—or rather, Pixy Merriweather—framed in the doorway. His jaw dropped. "British accent?" He shot me a wicked glare. "Think she's as good as Dainty Prescott? We might keep her around. Gotta go. I'll catch up after lunch. No, I only have time for nine holes." He hung up the phone. "That was Byron."

Byron's Gordon's best friend. He's also a lawyer on retainer for the TV station if a member of the on-air talent gets into a jam. Gordon turned to Byron when he thought his wife had been murdered, which was exactly what he should've done when a dead woman rolled out of the station's broom closet. If Byron liked Pixy Merriweather, that'd carry a lot of clout with Gordon.

When I left his office to wake up the girls, I had to walk past Rochelle's desk again. All of the phone lines were glowing. She'd put every caller on hold except for the one she was talking to.

She said, "No, we don't have a copy of Pixy Merriweather's audition tape. And if we did, I wouldn't send it to you. She works for us"—followed by—"that'll be a cold day in hell."

Sensing I'd made a good impression on our viewers, I walked on a cloud on the way to find Teensy and Venice, but I didn't see Amanda. I sent Teensy to find Chopper Deke to give us a ride to Gran's house, while I searched the station for our pygmy friend. The last place I looked turned out to be Gordon's office. They were playing poker and it looked like Amanda had the winning hand.

I rapped on the door frame. "Sorry to interrupt, but we have to leave."

"Not so fast." Gordon pointed a fat sausage finger at Amanda. "I'm interviewing her."

My jaw dropped open. "For what?"

"Not sure. But I like her and she's a good card player, and

193

she doesn't talk too much, so I just might find her a job here." Which was almost the same thing he said to me when he came up with funds to pay for my externship. And then promptly gave it to my sister, who had absolutely no journalistic credentials whatsoever. Then he gave it back to me after he lectured me about not having any qualifications either. Ironic, since he tailored the job to fit my experience.

I told Amanda not to hold her breath.

To Gordon, I said, "We have to get moving. I need to talk to that Texas Ranger about where the investigation stands. Meantime, I can come back in the morning to do the news as Pixy, if you like."

CHAPTER NINETEEN

The first thing we did when Chopper Deke dropped us off at Gran's house was to pile into her turquoise circa sixties' Cadillac. I got behind the wheel; Teensy settled into the shotgun position. Since we were driving around, open and notorious in a classic car, on the way to the consignment shop, I caught flak from Teensy and Venice.

"We're not being ostentatious. We're hiding in plain sight," I said. "They're looking for a pink Porsche. Besides, we need money for incidentals."

"Like what?" Teensy wasn't really listening; she was back on her phone texting again.

"Like everything. Who're you talking to?"

"If I wanted you to know, I would've announced it."

"You'd better tell me what you're up to, Teensy."

"Fine." She huffed out a big sigh. "I'm texting my boyfriend."

"You don't have a boyfriend."

"Do too. He's a new boyfriend. He loves me."

"What are you telling him?"

"If you must know, I just told him he acted like an animal in bed."

"I can just imagine what he texted you back—he said you acted like a dead animal in bed?"

Venice and Amanda hooted.

Bitter cold took a miserable bite out of what should've been a decent afternoon when dull gray skies opened up to empty skeins of rain and pearl-sized hail on us.

I glanced past the steering wheel to check the gasoline level. A faulty float in the Cadillac's fuel tank made me nervous not knowing whether the tank was full or running on fumes. Stopping to fill the tank made more sense than running out of gas and getting stranded on the highway.

This actually happened to me the previous month.

I still had on the black wig and lens-less black eyeglasses from wardrobe when we pulled up under the metal awning at the gas pumps near Gran's neighborhood.

While Teensy stood by the pump at the ready, I scrambled inside the convenience store to pay for fuel. The cashier was an older man in his fifties, with a pinch of snuff inserted between his bottom lip and gums. A dirty Styrofoam spit cup lay off to his right. The wall-mounted TV above the countertop had been tuned to WBFD-TV, and while the volume had been muted, I knew our programming by heart.

I pretended to be a foreigner and used alternating sentences that were strung together using flawless French, mixed with broken English, spoken in a daring French accent.

"*Bon après-midi, monsieur* . . . good afternoon." I fluttered my hands as I pretended to struggle with the language. "*Ce temps est horrible, no?* . . . what you call a horrible weather day . . ." I waffled back and forth until I frustrated him into finishing my sentences.

The store clerk's attention slewed to the TV and back. "I know you. You're that Pixy girl from the TV."

Playing dumb, I handed over the money to cover the cost of gas. "Who is zees Pixy?"

"Jig's up. It's you." He shook his head knowingly. "I watched you on TV this morning. You still have on the same outfit."

Preferring to think of my clothing as an ensemble, I grudgingly admitted that I was, in fact, "the" Pixy Merriweather, and that I'd grown tired of being recognized in public. The man, whose name was Burt according to the cursive script embroidered above his shirt pocket, offered to pump my gas in exchange for my autograph; and because Teensy and I hate pumping our own gas, especially in the rain, I obliged. He followed me into the downpour, deflecting raindrops with an open newspaper held over his head. Teensy wasted no time jumping back into Gran's car. Since the last thing I wanted to do was stand in the rain and make face-to-face conversation with Pixy Merriweather's biggest fan, and since etiquette dictated that I do just that, I told him I'd look in the car for a scrap of paper to autograph. He shoved the nozzle of the hose into the tank and squeezed the lever. Whirling numbers hummed on the calculator.

I pawed through Gran's glove box—*score!*—and found a small derringer, introducing yet another side of Gran to me. When I came up with a "gimme" calendar from Gran's bank, I ripped off the December page and signed the back of it: "Best wishes, Pixy Merriweather."

Burt pumped gasoline until the last splash triggered the nozzle lever off. Then he clanked the hose back into the nozzle boot. I got out of the car and handed him the autograph.

"Thanks. Please keep watching Channel Eighteen. We love our viewers." I resumed my place behind the wheel and headed for the consignment store with the girls acting as my scouts.

We mostly rode in silence, listening to the hypnotic *Thump-squee, thump-squee, thump-squee* coming from the windshield wipers. When we arrived, I got the pillowcases containing Gran's things out of the trunk while Amanda stood beside me and held a little collapsible umbrella overhead that she found on the floorboard beneath the front passenger seat.

We unloaded Gran's nicest clothes and several pairs of breathtaking Italian shoes. After the shop owner priced and tagged the garments, I printed my phone number and signed the contract. A woman about Gran's size eyed the clothes from afar. As soon as we were under contract, she scooped up the entire lot. Since the four of us really needed money, I hung around while the shopkeeper paid out.

Flush with cash, we piled into the Cadillac and I sped away, traveling the speed limit through the drizzle. Our weather-drenched spirits had gotten the better of us, so I suggested we stop in at a sports bar to see what kind of snacks they served, since we were less likely to have to endure the piping screams of unruly children at Rooster's Pub than at a kid-friendly restaurant.

The afternoon fare turned out to be grilled chicken quesadillas—chicken and jalapeños with Monterrey jack cheese sandwiched between two flour tortillas and grilled on each side until the cheese melted. The quesadillas were cut into wedges and served with guacamole, salsa, and sour cream on the side. We wolfed down our food and ordered more. At first, we sat at the bar and sipped club soda while the bartender brought out tortilla chips and queso to snack on while we waited. He seldom wandered far away and occasionally joined in our conversation by playing a game I like to call *Who do you know that I know?* He should've been looking me in the eye when he spoke to me, though, not making conversation while ogling my breasts. Even Venice remarked on it. When the second order of quesadillas came out, we moved to a corner booth where we weren't likely to be overheard.

I wanted to give Amanda a chance to bail out of our ill-fated group, so I told her that the lodge assassins, as I'd come to think of them, might not be the worst of it all. I'd put off telling her about the murderer I'd snuffed as he attempted to break into the Rivercrest estate, and the fact that I'd almost killed the bodyguard Daddy'd hired to protect us at Gran's. Now that we'd broached a new crossroad, Amanda deserved complete disclosure in order to make an educated decision regarding her future.

When it came right down to it, I could be dead now, or I could be dead later. Keeping Amanda around would be an extreme step toward prolonging my own life, but I knew that being affiliated with us would endanger her life. Bottom line: Without my sister, Amanda, and my best friend, I might as well join them in death.

My disposable phone rang. I fumbled it out of my purse and took the call. It was Salem—sobbing in my ear. I mouthed Salem's name so the girls would know who I was talking to, and pressed the air down in front of me with my free hand to motion them to be quiet. The speaker mounted in the ceiling of Rooster's Pub made it hard enough to hear over the canned music.

"Salem, what's wrong?" I drove my index finger into my other ear to drown out the noise.

Between the music and the vocal rumblings of a group of city utility workers at the bar, I could barely understand her. But I caught snippets of her conversation that included the words "shot at" and "hit" and "father" and "ambulance." I repeated what I thought she said back to her, and, sure enough . . .

Nailed it.

Men in a black SUV peppered Mr. Quincy's Suburban with lead.

The dull edge of misery in Salem's voice grew suddenly sharper as she approached the part of her story where her dad took a direct hit to the shoulder. Her mother accompanied him to the hospital in the ambulance. The dark tinted glass on the black SUV made it impossible for Salem to pinpoint the number of occupants involved, but she knew if the men ever caught her family alone again, they wouldn't hesitate to execute every one of them. Or torture them into disclosing our whereabouts, and then execute them.

I heard her swallow hard as she tried to get her breathing under control. Then the other shoe dropped. Because I didn't think I heard her correctly the first time she said it, I had to listen to her say it all over again: In order to spare her family from tragedy, Salem wanted to join my rag-tag team of survivors.

I caught myself shaking my head. "You absolutely *don't* want to do that." The look I gave the other three wasn't one I would ever want caught on camera, nor photographed for use in any of WBFD's PR campaigns. And since each girl's facial expression looked like a camel having a stroke, I figured they'd heard enough of the conversation to realize that adding Salem back into the mix could bring a new dimension of terror to our situation and escalate our demise. Over the girls' vehement head-shakes, I cast an invisible die.

"Is there any way you can meet us at Gran's in forty-five minutes?" I figured she'd probably be coming from one of the downtown hospitals in Fort Worth, so, in the best of circumstances, it'd take at least thirty minutes on the Tom Landry Highway. Even that guesstimate only worked in the absence of heavy traffic or speed traps, if she exceeded the speed limit by fifteen miles per hour. To make the opportunity even less glamorous than it sounded, I pulled out my hole card. "We'll be staying at Chopper Deke's. I know you think he's a perv and a dirtball, but if anyone can keep us safe, he can. He was a POW in Vietnam, you know."

"Well that kind of indicates he couldn't even keep himself safe, doesn't it?" Salem said.

Even dropping Chopper Deke's name into the equation didn't dissuade her from joining us. I snapped the phone closed and handed our tab over to Teensy to settle the bill. I remembered the warning Chopper Deke had given us about being tracked through our credit cards and shelled out enough cash to pay out. She carried the money to the bar, and the bartender gave her the change—plus a telephone number he wrote on a scrap of paper. While we gathered our things at the table, I did a heavy eye roll.

Then she disappeared in the general direction of the washrooms.

When Teensy didn't reappear in what I considered to be a normal amount of time, I called her cell phone. She didn't answer. My inner survivalist—whatever instinct or sixth sense that had gotten me this far—warned me that each time any of us strayed from our group, we exposed ourselves, our families, and our friends to more danger. So I called her repeatedly and she still didn't answer. I felt years being removed from my life while I waited to hear from her. Five minutes later, I saw her dead in the hedges, savagely brutalized by one of the men from the resort who'd watched us through the front window and waited for one of us to become separated from the rest of the pack. Several more minutes went by before I went to look for her. When I didn't find her in the ladies' room, I returned to the booth in a panic.

"She's gone." I punched out 9-1-1 to get the police, when *guess who texted me?*

"9-1-1, what is your emergency?" said the dispatcher.

"Misdial. Sorry. Won't happen again. I apologize. Please don't file charges against me."

When Teensy returned to the table with her hair damp and her face dotted with moisture, I wanted to slap her silly for making me worry. In fact, only seven minutes went by, but that just reinforced how paranoid I'd become.

"Where in the hell have you been?" I practically spat each word.

"I stepped out the back door to text a friend."

"I came looking for you and couldn't find you."

"Which is exactly why I stepped outside to conduct my private business."

"Who are you texting all these messages to?" My face burned with anger.

"Chill," she said. "I heard a song I liked and added it to my 'Sex Songs' playlist."

I knew she was lying, so I asked which songs she had on her so-called list. When she named a few, I was more disappointed in her mediocre-to-bad taste in music than the fact that she was apparently sexually active enough to need a playlist of songs.

"You almost caused me to have a heart attack," I finished bitterly.

"Quit stalking me."

"I'm not stalking you, pea brain."

I held my hand, palm up, in demand for the change, and then grilled her. "What'd you say to the bartender to make him give you his number? You better quit flirting. We don't need this right now."

By *this*, I meant more drama.

"The number's not for me. It's for you." She grudgingly slapped the paper scrap into my palm.

When I glanced over at the bartender, he winked. I gave a feeble little finger wave as we left the restaurant. Out on the sidewalk, under the cloth awning, I scanned the parking lot for anything that might seem out of place. Rain fell in sheets, obscuring anything farther than thirty feet in front of us.

Any Texas afternoon when the sky is azure-blue-and-gold should've been magical on the drive out of the city. But the gloominess of lead-gray skies cast a pall over our energy. Having not only been raised by overprotective family members who worked hard to shield me from the ugly side of life and educated me in the sterile environment of private schools, I was as green as a gourd at this whole "any weirdo wearing a ski mask is never friendly" thing, and had limited perceptions of how the real world worked. And yet I experienced the unique sensation that casting any bad thought out into the universe, especially dwelling on the probability of savage brutality and violence, would cause it to happen.

Inside the car, I defended myself by putting everyone on notice that it wasn't my goal to call attention to us. I didn't want the bartender to even remember that we'd been there at all, and I never planned to patronize Rooster's Pub again—even though the quesadillas were some of the best I'd ever eaten.

My accusatory sister looked me dead in the eye. "Hey, pot—this is kettle."

"What do you mean by that?"

"Everywhere you go you call attention to yourself."

"How can you say that? I wasn't doing anything I don't usually do."

"You didn't throw his number away, though, did you? Just sayin'." She gave me an aristocratic sniff of absurdity and turned her head to the window.

In the back seat of Gran's Cadillac, Amanda snickered.

Venice said, "It's true, Dainty. You're Fort Worth Barbie. You're pretty and blond and you're a fashion plate. It's only natural for people to notice you. And you don't have a ring on your finger."

I admit it. That last little dig hurt. The engagement ring I thought Bruckman would give me for Christmas turned out to be an eighteen-karat gold "friendship" ring. True, it was made in Italy, and the engravings were beautiful, but it wasn't what I expected, and yes, it disappointed me. I loved Jim Bruckman and knew he loved me enough to marry me. He just hadn't come to grips with marriage. Yet.

Steering Gran's Caddy out of the parking lot, I did a quick

head-swivel. As I merged into the flow of traffic, Amanda launched into the pygmy rendition of Beyoncé's hit song, "Single Ladies." She did a little car dance while waving her hands and pointing to her naked ring finger. I inwardly winced.

With tightly controlled emotion, I met several pairs of eyes in the rearview mirror. "I wasn't trying to flirt. I have a boyfriend."

Teensy cackled. "Yeah? When's the last time you heard from him?"

"Back off, Teensy. I wouldn't be talking if I were you."

Amanda guffawed and slapped her thigh. "Riding around in a big-ass Caddy with the white folks, I sure do like being part of this dysfunctional family."

I glanced in the rearview mirror and shot her a *You're not family* look.

"I'm family," she snapped. "Family isn't who you're related to by blood. It's who you choose to be with."

"So you're choosing to be with us," I challenged her.

"Or die trying." She punctuated this with a curt head nod.

I'd had about enough of this rag-tag outfit, so I decided to let Venice off the hook, too. My eyes flickered to the rearview mirror again. "Vinizzia, you want to be on your own?"

"No."

"Why not?" I challenged her, too.

"I don't like guns and you do. So you can arm yourself to the teeth and I'll hide behind you."

"You're almost a foot taller."

"I'll take my chances," Venice said airily.

"Oh, *puh-leeze*. Kumbaya." Exasperated, Teensy folded her arms across her chest. "This isn't a love fest. Except for Dainty, who only loves herself."

If only she knew how much the three of them meant to me . . .

I decided not to tell her.

Rain continued to pelt the windshield, graying everything ahead of us. By the time we hit the freeway, the tires droned against the asphalt ribbon of highway leading back to Gran's house.

The uneasy feeling I'd tried to stifle at Rooster's Pub grew stronger.

Several blocks back, a dark-colored car swerved around another vehicle and cut in behind us. My heart quickened. We'd entered one of the many small suburbs of Big D. Suddenly I no longer knew whose jurisdiction I'd driven into, nor the location of that town's police department. I gripped the wheel, deliriously wishful for anything to prevent the onset of uncontrollable trembling.

The relieved sigh I heaved when the car behind us entered the left-turn lane and waited for the light to change made Venice sit up straight. As BFFs for years, we could almost read each other's minds.

"What is it? What'd you see?" She whipped her head around and tried to look out the back windshield where visibility was practically zero.

"Nothing." I said this with a chipper lilt.

"Honestly, Dainty." She huffed and sank into the seat back. "You're so dramatic."

We arrived at Gran's unscathed. But the sight of Salem's billowy red hair falling flat the second she stepped out of her vehicle flooded me with anxiety. Her mother already blamed me for what happened at the lodge, so I couldn't let Salem park her car on the street, because . . . who drives around in a conspicuous hot pink Smart Car? Somebody who doesn't want to blend in, that's who. I rolled the window halfway down. Bullets of rain ricocheted off the door as I waved her back into her vehicle.

"Follow me."

The gate to Gran's estate yawned open. We drove to the back

of the house to the detached garage, which once served as a carriage house for my late grandfather's parents at the turn of the twentieth century. I left Gran's car running while I opened the collapsible umbrella Amanda found under the seat and got out long enough to urge Salem to hide her car inside.

"We need to go," I insisted. "Right now."

"I'm coming," she said shakily. Distress thinned her lips.

"No, really. Now."

"I'm coming, I'm coming," she snapped.

"Something's not right." I kept cutting my eyes back to the main street, past the cul-de-sac where Gran's house sat. I don't know what I expected to see, but like art appreciation, I'd know it when I saw it.

Venice's door swung open. By activating a button on my key fob, I powered the garage door closed. I heard it slowly roll down behind us as we made a mad dash for the Cadillac. Once I landed behind the wheel and Salem jumped into the back seat next to Venice, I wrenched the gear shift into drive and we were rolling down the circular driveway again. Nobody spoke; they simply stared at me.

The urgency to leave the property grew stronger.

I caught Salem's gaze in the rearview mirror. We exchanged smiles, and, for a few seconds, I felt good about our ability to stay secreted away. We were almost in the home stretch. Once we made it to Chopper Deke's, things would change for the better. Chopper Deke would keep us safe. Nobody would find us unless we wanted to be found.

Rolling my eyes to indicate Amanda in the back seat, I made introductions. "Salem, Amanda. Amanda, Salem."

As the iron gate closed behind us in the thunderstorm-dimmed light, skeletal trees receded in the rearview mirror. For a grand and majestic mansion that had always warmed my heart at every visit, Gran's estate took on the mystery and danger of a haunted house.

I don't know if I hyperventilated, but I had trouble catching my breath and breathing in air. What I did know was that it felt like I had an elephant sitting on my chest. For this time of year, what usually made an enchanting winter-scape composed of varying shades of blue and gray shadows, the view of this exclusive neighborhood had turned creepy.

"Back there"—Salem thumbed over her shoulder—"you said something's not right. What's not right, Dainty?"

Operating on a theory of "the less said the better," I battled the urge to address everyone in Gran's car. I was certainly thinking uncharitable thoughts, like, "Let this be a lesson. Salem recontacted us. And by contacting us, she gave these men a chance to get a new lead on her—and on us." I didn't answer her.

Halfway down the street, my heart *thunked.* In the distance, on a cross-street, a black SUV idled in the left turn lane, waiting for the light that led to Gran's street to change. I knew this neighborhood. Nobody owned a black SUV. And in the past year that I'd lived with my grandmother, I'd never seen any visitors with a black SUV park in front of neighboring homes. I immediately slammed on the brakes and extinguished the headlights.

Jostling my passengers, I reversed gears and floored the accelerator, backing up in the driving rain until I came even with Old Man Spencer's estate. Tires spun as I pulled into his driveway, just as the traffic light changed and the black SUV made the turn down Gran's street.

Instead of stepping on the brakes, I downshifted to slow the Cadillac to a crawl. When the driveway ran out, I engaged the emergency brake rather than tap the brake pedal. Otherwise, the taillights would've come on and the people in the SUV would've noticed us.

"Everybody down, everybody down," I howled. The girls hit the floorboards. I instinctively grappled at the glove box for the derringer I'd seen while rummaging for paper at the gas pumps.

"What the hell, Dainty?" Teensy.

"Quiet. Nobody move."

Hard splatters of rain drummed against the roof and sluiced down the front and back windshields.

I heard Salem sniffle in the back seat. Guilt twisted her upwardly corkscrewing voice. "Dainty, call the police."

"They'll never get here in time."

"This is it." Venice's voice sounded more lifeless than ever.

Unwavering in my faith, I knew I'd done the best I could under the circumstances. "If you need something to calm yourself, then pray. Just . . . nobody panic."

I raised my head enough to peer out the back windshield. With the rain pouring down and the windows fogging up, I couldn't see past the trunk and hoped no one from the street could see us hiding inside Gran's car.

Then Teensy, who'd curled up on the floorboard and was rocking back and forth, whimpered like an injured puppy. Her eyes went glassy. I'd seen this exact same behavior several months ago, when Gran, Teensy, Amanda, and I got carjacked on the way home from the airport.

Windmill palms lining Old Man Spencer's driveway thrashed in the breeze, their fluted fronds already brown and dried from the cold snap. What tugged at my heart was the old codger's love for these trees and how he always had them wrapped in burlap before the first hard freeze gridlocked the city. But Old Man Spencer hadn't called in the lawn people because Old Man Spencer was dead. Drowned, along with my grandmother, in the Gulf of Mexico.

I felt myself yielding to the crushing clutch of sadness.

The wait seemed eternal. I grabbed Teensy by the wrist and

stared at the dial on her watch; in fact, only minutes had gone by. I'd seen the full range of the assassins' cruelty and didn't like to think how this might end with one little derringer-toting seventh-generation Texan and four members of her posse whose only talent seemed to be Olympic-worthy screaming.

Envisioning men in black brandishing survival knives while creeping stealthily up to the car, I opened my purse, pulled out a powder compact with a mirror, and balanced it on the dashboard where I could see headlights on Gran's street or people approaching the car. The worst part of the wait was wondering if the last seconds of my life were ticking away.

CHAPTER TWENTY

Ten minutes after we rolled onto Old Man Spencer's driveway, the gold wash of headlight beacons illuminated the mist. I heard the faint sound of an engine cruise past as the black SUV faded down the street.

"Nobody move yet, but I think they just passed us by." After another five minutes ticked away, I raised my head enough to peer over the seat. Nothing. "Let's go."

I didn't activate the headlights until we reached the end of the street.

Then Teensy came up with a plan. During her psychotic break on the floorboard, she apparently had an epiphany and decided we should take refuge at our church because, "It's a sanctuary. You're not supposed to be able to attack people in church. It's sacred ground."

Feeling pleased that nobody had tried to kill us in the last thirty minutes, I leveled my blue gaze at her. "Have you lost your mind?" Apparently, she was too young to remember when a gunman entered Fort Worth's Wedgwood Baptist Church in the middle of a prayer rally and murdered seven people and wounded seven others. "It's not Mission San José. It's not the Abbey. It's not the freaking Alamo. I'm sticking with Chopper Deke's plan, and so are you."

"You think you're so smart," she said, all cocky and self-assured.

"Let me remind you—we're still alive." What I really wanted

to say was, *If you think you can do better, then have at it.* But I knew better than to take my marching orders from a brain-damaged debutante who probably couldn't pass a field sobriety test if she drank alcohol-free wine and swallowed a whole pack of breath mints.

More than ever, I wanted to contact Bruckman for help—and if not for help, then for advice. But I hesitated because involving anyone else could make them a target, and I knew I couldn't live with myself if anything bad happened to the love of my life.

I drove to the TV station hoping Gordon could use me—or, rather, Pixy Merriweather—for the six-and-ten broadcasts. I knew if I didn't show up to work each day, he'd probably fire me. He'd have to. On the way over, Teensy whined that she was freezing to death, so the rest of us had to travel in a car with the heater set to "inferno," just so we didn't have to listen to her.

When we arrived, I noticed our weathergirl, Misty Knight, hadn't parked in her reserved space, so I wheeled Gran's behemoth Cadillac into it. The girls bailed out and scampered to the building's entrance and waited as I locked the car and caught up with them. Once I keyed us in, I headed to Gordon's office.

Again, to get to Gordon, I had to pass Rochelle's desk. She was in the process of cracking open a fortune cookie and handed me the paper fortune as I walked past. It read: *You will do great things.* I actually got excited, my self-esteem had plummeted just that low.

"He's not here," she said, "but he told me to call you and tell you to do the news tonight."

"I never got a call from you."

"Could that be because you never bothered to give me your new phone number? By the way, I invented a new word game and I'd love to have your input. You know how doctors and hospitals ask you to rate your pain on a scale of one-to-ten? I want to come up with words instead of numbers, so let's say number one is 'Meh' and number ten is 'Get me the fucking painkillers or I'll kill you.' We need terms for numbers two through nine."

I blinked. "Are you kidding me?"

She picked up her pen. "That's good. We can make that one number two."

"I'm not participating in your game; that was my actual response to playing your game."

"Since you want to be that way about it, my response to you is number six."

"What's number six?"

"Because you have a sucky attitude, I'm not going to tell you. And by the way, callers keep asking where you got those stupid glasses."

"You know they came from wardrobe."

"Well, make something up so I can get them off my ass. They're clogging up the phone lines."

After I went to wardrobe and tried on clothes until the room looked like a war zone, I finally put a new outfit together and finished the six o'clock news broadcast. I didn't realize how famished I was until I rejoined the girls in my office and we ordered pizza. Then I took a much-needed nap until it was time to return to wardrobe, redress, and do the ten o'clock broadcast. When I woke up and lifted my head from the desktop, I blinked in my surroundings. Teensy was missing.

"Where's my sister?"

Salem said, "She got a phone call and left. We tried to talk her out of it."

"Why didn't you wake me up?"

Venice said, "She's probably somewhere in the building."

Shaking so bad that my friends probably thought I was having a seizure, I glared at Amanda. "This is your fault. You should've stopped her."

"Don't look at me. She's a grown-up. I'm pretty sure she stopped taking orders from people a long time ago."

Teensy walked in. I'd seen that look before, like she'd just had the greatest sex of her life.

"Where have you been?"

"What if I told you Tig Welder let me borrow his computer?"

Immediately, I got an ugly visual of the senior investigative reporter's porcelain veneers and his penetrating anthracite eyes. If you've ever seen a rattlesnake on a hot rock at eye level, that's what dealing with Tig Welder meant to me. That, and I didn't believe Teensy.

"What'd you need to look up so bad that you'd risk causing me to stroke out?"

"I wanted to see if my boyfriend signed up for one of those online 'cheater' dating sites. Think of it as one of those 'Do you like piña coladas?' deals where you end up meeting your own girlfriend."

"And did you find him?" I gave her a blank look, because—again—I didn't believe her.

"No, I did not." She flounced across the hallway to the ladies' room.

When I finished the ten o'clock broadcast, Rochelle met me coming out of the studio and handed me a message she'd written on a pink message sheet.

"Chopper Deke left y'all directions." Berry-stained lips turned into a polite smirk. "Are you dating him?"

"That's not funny, Rochelle." I walked away before I made a snide comment that could come back to haunt me. Rochelle had lots of clout at the station; one misstep could get you fired.

Back in my office, I reviewed Chopper Deke's directions, which called for me to pull into a truck stop outside of Weatherford, Texas. When I mentioned that we were to stash Gran's car in the back of the truck stop between a couple of eighteen-wheelers and wait for Chopper Deke to come get us, the girls all agreed he was paranoid. I knew different; he was our best chance out of this.

Before leaving the TV station, I called the hospital to inquire about Dawn.

With professional detachment, I identified myself to the nurse so she could check Dawn's chart to verify I had permission to receive information that was protected by the medical privacy act. Instead of switching me to the day room so I could speak to Dawn myself, the woman reamed me out because the doctors had been trying to contact me. Unsuccessfully, I might add. Apparently, they wanted me to report for a so-called "family" meeting to discuss how Dawn's obsession with one of the techs on the ward had crossed over into illegality. According to the nurse, if I'd come in the following day, the treatment team might consider releasing her into my custody.

Really? They thought I'd be chomping at the bit to do that? Seriously, the woman must be a drooling, wingnut imbecile.

Clearly, the hospital people thought we were related. This triggered an ugly visual of Dawn, wearing a paper hospital gown, telling the treatment team how she and Dainty Prescott, of WBFD-TV fame, were cousins. Or sisters, God forbid.

"Dawn needs people to help her, not ignore her. A truly caring sister would rally around her," the nurse said, seizing the opportunity to dress me down. The herpes-infected whore.

I wanted to smack both her and Dawn hard, but I reminded myself I don't look good in stripes.

"Since Dawn gave your name as a source for collateral information," said the nurse, "I'd like to ask a couple of questions."

"Like what?" I took a deep breath and held it.

"She believes men are chasing y'all."

Not knowing if I should even comment, I downplayed my answer. "Dawn told you that?"

"I'm afraid so. We often have patients who think they're being followed, or that government operatives are after them—usually the FBI or CIA. Or aliens. Or their delusions take on a religious bent, such as they claim to see God, or be God, or they're having God's baby."

"I see." *I couldn't possibly see.*

"She thinks you're very brave. That you saved your friends. And that she helped by . . . wait—let me read this from her chart . . . 'she helped karate-chop killers into submission at a resort.' So . . . are people after y'all?"

It was one of those *Damned if you do, damned if you don't* questions.

Nausea got the better of me—and fear. My nerves were shot, and inside, I was a mess. But Dawn thought I was brave. Instead of answering, I redirected the conversation. "Before I meet with the doctors, I want to talk to Dawn."

After leaving the number for my disposable cell phone with the nurse and a request for Dawn to contact me, I hung up.

Inhaling sharply, I formulated the best way to carry out our itinerary. On the way out of the station, I said good-bye to Rochelle while wondering if this would be the last time I'd ever see her. I gave her a long look and, just for a fleeting second, I felt a tug of affection for her. After all, running hell's complaint department required a lot of work.

My entourage piled into Gran's car. Following Chopper Deke's directions to the letter, I headed west on I-30. Once we'd left Fort Worth and crossed into rural Parker County, we encountered relatively few cars on the road. Without street lamps to light the way, the headlights on Gran's Cadillac cut through a pitch-black part of the county that pushed us deeper into despair and dread. If we ran into trouble, there'd be no one to help us.

I pressed my foot against the accelerator. An inch of rainwater probably covered the road. I didn't worry about the car hydroplaning, though, since I was hydroplaning on my own sweat.

A big rig roared past, hurling a waterfall across the wipers and temporarily obliterating our view out the windshield. Against my better judgment, I eased up on the accelerator to let the Peterbilt overtake us more quickly. Part of me wanted to pull over until the lashing rain passed; the other part of me felt an urgency to keep moving.

Each time a car passed us, rain smeared the glass so thoroughly that I considered pulling off the road. But that would've been the start of every slasher film ever made, and we were already scared enough without wondering what would come looming up out of the gully while we fogged up the windows with our panicked breathing. Occasionally, pockets of light from a few small settlements would pop up out of the abyss, but the glow quickly diffused and the gloom of night swallowed us up again. We swept past a car parked on the shoulder of the highway. No hazard lights blinking. No signs of life inside. No police tag slapped on the back windshield to show they'd checked out the abandoned vehicle.

A shiver went up my spine. In my mind, I saw a dead body in the trunk. The girl looked exactly like me, and I knew those men had snuffed out her life in a case of mistaken identity. I gave a violent headshake to vanquish the image. Whatever my passengers thought about me, they kept it to themselves.

Bright lights gained on us, illuminating the inside of our vehicle.

Another eighteen-wheeler roared up from behind. Its running lights came into sharp focus as the semi moved around to pass us. Another sheet of water drenched the Caddy's windshield. This time, I took my foot off the accelerator without hesitation.

We'd turned onto a lonely stretch of highway with only a few distant headlights visible atop the rolling hills. In the daylight, the view of this picturesque and charming countryside would've worked its magic on us—especially Amanda, who resided in a colonia of corrugated metal lean-tos in El Paso. But as the lights from the nearest town played out, all of the comforting landmarks I'd visited as a child got swallowed up behind me, leaving only a void of complete darkness in the rearview mirror.

Raindrops shrank in size until we were enveloped in a continuous tunnel of fog and mist. The *Thump-squee, thump-squee, thump-squee* sound of the windshield wipers that I normally found hypnotic, now cried *Squee-squee-squee,* like the scream of violins that underscored the shower stabbing scene in Hitchcock's classic horror movie, *Psycho.*

About the time I'd convinced myself we'd be fine if we teamed up with Chopper Deke, a primitive section of my brain—the part that cloisters one's survival instinct—forced me to acknowledge that at least four people were dead at the hands of these cut-throats, and others would likely follow. I felt an unexpected compulsion to take the next exit, turn around, and head back to Fort Worth, where I at least had a certain familiarity with powerful people, local haunts, and streets I'd traveled my entire life.

Ahead, on the distant horizon, the neon sign of a truck stop popped into view and lit up the roadside like the Mothership had landed. I exited the highway at the first off-ramp that would take me there. Despite odd characters milling around the gas pumps at the service islands, and those roaming the parking lot on the way to the souvenir shop or convenience store, the diner looked inviting.

Teensy tuned up whining. "I'm hungry. I want to eat. Does

anybody else want to eat?"

"We'll eat when we get to Chopper Deke's," I said, hoping he'd feed us.

"What if he doesn't know how to cook? I didn't come here to starve to death." She looked into the back seat, expectantly, and took a poll. "What about y'all? Am I the only one who's hungry?"

Amanda piped up. "I'm starving."

"You're not starving," I snapped. "You have a tapeworm."

"No, I don't. I have a healthy appetite."

"You call it healthy. I call it a tapeworm eating for four."

Amanda smirked. "Potato, po-tah-toe."

I looked across the seat at Teensy. "Fine. You go inside, pay the clerk, pump the gas, and I'll feed y'all." I stopped under the metal awning of one of the service islands and dug in my purse for cash. Instead of complaining about the rain and badgering me to let her out at the front door so she wouldn't get wet, Teensy sprinted across the parking lot and inside the store with enough money to get the pump unlocked.

The smell of grease and gasoline fumes hung heavy in the mist. I promised myself I wouldn't eat anything fried or sweet, even if they served coconut pie. Teensy had accused me on more than one occasion of having a problem with coconut pie. I don't have a problem with coconut pie. I have a problem without it. The more I thought about food, the more I realized that, at any given time, whatever I ate could be my last meal.

So . . . fried, it is.

I felt conspicuous waiting in Gran's car. The used car dealership next to the truck stop seemed like a much better place to stash a vehicle—even a classic like Gran's. But Chopper Deke had been explicit about hiding the Cadillac between big rigs, so I stuck with the plan and we went inside the diner to wait for him to arrive. A half hour after we'd eaten at the chicken fried steak buffet, I called him.

"We're here."

"About that . . ."

My lungs almost collapsed waiting for the bad news. He wasn't coming to get us. We were on our own. Where would we go now? If we returned to Fort Worth, where would we stay? Was there even enough cash left for a sleazy motel room for the night? I cringed at the thought.

"I had a situation come up so I'm sending Hacksaw to pick you up."

"Hacksaw?" I got a visual of a serial killer and thought, *Why not?* "How will we know him?" But my mind screamed, *Well, he'll be the one with the duct tape and Bowie knife.*

"For one thing, he's ugly. He dresses in biker clothes. Wears a bandana. Has yellow-green eyes. Looks like he could kill you with his little finger. He knows who to look for. He'll find you."

"He'll need to produce some form of ID."

"Probably doesn't have any. I'll give you a code word so you'll know it's him."

"Which is?"

"Got your pen ready to write? Okay, two words. First word: Heywood."

"Spell it."

"Spelled just like it sounds: H-e-y-w-o-o-d. Second word, I'll spell it out. J-a-b-l-o-m-e."

I said, "Let me read it back to you. When your guy comes into the truck stop, I say, 'Heywood Jablome?' "

The girls' jaws dropped open.

Chopper Deke said, "Sure—if that's what tickles your fancy."

It took a few seconds of lag time before I got it. "You're such a douche."

"You're gullible. Grow up." He hung up on me.

Within fifteen minutes after the waitress dropped off the

check and cleared away our dirty dishes, she returned no less than five times to ask if we wanted anything else. I recognized this as a shameless ploy to get us to leave so she could turn over our table to the next customers. After all, this wasn't France, we weren't French, and we didn't rent the table all night. But until Chopper Deke's friend arrived, I wasn't budging.

A big guy sauntered in wearing biker leathers and a blue bandana form-fitted to his head like a 'do-rag. He looked around and we made eye contact.

Strolling past the buffet, he swaggered back to our table and loomed over us. Eyeballing each one of us creeped me out. Intense yellow-green eyes made me feel like prey fending off a jaguar attack.

I swallowed hard. "Mr. Hacksaw?"

He said, "Code word."

I said, "Chopper Deke's a douchebag." Again, the girls' mouths gaped. "Don't look at me that way. He's a total dick."

Hacksaw's mouth split into a grin. He bent at the waist and swung his arm through the air in a swashbuckling, *After you* gesture. "Let's hit the road."

CHAPTER TWENTY-ONE

At the north-central edge of Parker County, the undeveloped countryside—thick with a variety of oak trees and scrub brush—was home to as many raccoons, coyotes, bobcats, and deer as people.

Undulating roads carried commuters away from the town of Weatherford and into isolated, tree-surrounded properties, or small farms, dairies, and ranches. The road to Chopper Deke's seemed as mysterious as Deke Richter himself. It hinted of violence, hostility, and a cover-up for nefarious activity operating away from the probing eyes and eavesdropping ears of small-town America. The farther we strayed from the highway, the darker and thicker the canopy of trees became.

Amanda and I sat in the front seat of Hacksaw's pickup, while Venice, Salem, and Teensy shared the pickup bed with a number of hay bales. I didn't even have to turn around and look at their faces in order to know they were furious with me. In protest, Teensy whined that we could've at least entered into a lively game of *Rock-Paper-Scissors* for our seats, but I wasn't about to sit on a hay bale and let the wind and rain mat my tresses into Rastafarian hair. I chose Amanda to sit up front with me because, for all intents and purposes, she was an innocent bystander and didn't deserve any of this.

From the two-lane blacktop, Hacksaw turned off onto a gravel road, and after that, an unpaved ribbon of caliche rock that he explained the utility agents used as an easement. Wet Johnson grass lapped at the sides of the pickup. On such a cloudy night, with nothing but the filtered moon to guide us over the rocky road, the darkness was as absolute as a tunnel with no light at the end of it.

In the distance, shrouded in fog and mist, a container house surrounded by oak trees rose out of the gloom. The house faced the gravel road we'd turned off of to get to the caliche road. Lamp-lit windows appeared far from inviting, reminding me of a nocturnal predator's glowing eyes, watching us from the trees with calculating precision.

We bounced over a few big stones and rocked to a stop. The slam of the pickup doors carried in the cold night air. As we walked up the footpath to the house, deadfall from the red oaks crunched underfoot. I once stepped out of my car in WBFD's parking lot and crushed a mouse skull underfoot. The dead leaves sounded like that.

Standing next to Hacksaw under Chopper Deke's awning, I lightly touched the leather sleeve on his biker jacket. "Pardon my cynicism, but we're sleeping in box cars?"

"Oh, my bad," he said mockingly, "was I supposed to drop you off at the Ritz instead?"

"Beggars can't be choosers—I get it." I lifted my finger to press the doorbell.

Chopper Deke answered as if he'd heard trespassers outside the door. I suspected he'd been studying us through the peephole before deciding who to let inside. When he yanked open the door, intense blue eyes assessed us through a calculated squint. He wore a wife-beater "T" in midnight blue and dark jeans that looked blue but could've been black. The gun in his hand that looked more like a small cannon was as cold and steely and blue as his eyes.

"Did you park where I told you?"

"Yes, but the car dealership next to the truck stop seemed

like a much better place."

"It isn't. Your car would either end up getting towed, or it'd stick out like a sore thumb, or they'd call the police. If you sandwiched it between two eighteen-wheelers like I told you, it's not likely to be seen unless people know where to look. Plus, I have a friend, Ginger, who takes her smoke breaks in the back of the building. She'll keep an eye on it."

Chopper Deke left us standing at the front door while he walked Hacksaw back to his pickup. When he returned, he gave us the grand tour.

He'd built his home out of shipping cargo containers, those corrugated metal rectangles you see stacked on the backs of train cars, or on freighters. Because Chopper Deke's property was in an unincorporated area of Parker County, he didn't need permits to put his house together. Still, I suspected the plumbing and electrical had been done without licensed workers since he had a reputation for going rogue at the first sign of governmental interference.

At best guess, each container measured around nine or ten feet high and stretched approximately forty feet long and had been welded to a similar container with the same measurements. Cutouts between containers made it possible to access other rooms within the house. He'd purchased nine cargo shipping containers to build his two-story house, with four on the first floor and four on the second. The ninth container was subterranean, with natural foliage to disguise the ground-level escape hatch.

"Here ya go, toots." Chopper Deke handed me a key ring with an electronic key in the shape of a disk about the size of a thumbprint. "You do the honors."

To gain entry, I had to thrust the electronic key near the key pad with the built-in code reader. Once swiped, it chirped, clicked open, and permitted entry.

Above ground, Chopper Deke had a comfortable and modern, if not environmentally green home, where he'd incorporated the latest in sustainable products into the house. The floors were strand-tiger bamboo planks throughout the first level, except for the full bathroom and half bath. Those rooms had heated floor tiles, art glass vessel sinks, and a walk-in shower made of glass panels. One of the bottom floor containers had been turned into a combination garage–workroom–atrium, with a retractable garage door with glass panes. It made for a fabulous view of the county's eastern overlook, but it was also the most exposed part of the house. That's probably why he installed a closed-circuit TV, so he could see if anyone came in uninvited. We angled past a restored Studebaker in a luscious shade of aqua. It might've interested me enough to slide behind the wheel, just to be able to say I'd sat in one, but I checked it out with a wary eye and kept walking. I mainly wanted to see where we'd be sleeping.

We ended up in the kitchen. Remnants of food lay on a plate near the sink. Chopper Deke had been eating supper before we arrived: brisket sandwich on grilled Texas toast, potato salad, and cowboy beans. As he talked, he stood at the edge of the granite countertop, sopping up the remaining liquid from the beans with a hunk of Texas toast. As soon as he finished, he rinsed off the plate and put it in the dishwasher. Everything we'd seen so far had been neat and clean, especially the stainless steel appliances.

Steam rose from a vat of beef stew brewing in the crock pot, and it took all of my reserve and good manners to keep from ripping off the lid and attacking what I believed might be the best meal I'd ever eat with a big spoon. I'd only picked at the diner food—fried okra, instant mashed potatoes, and greasy chicken fried steak—but this . . . this was real food, and just sniffing the air made my mouth water.

When Chopper Deke gave us the tour of the second floor, we learned that he had a beautiful library filled with floor-to-ceiling mahogany bookcases, including fabulous mahogany crown molding and a rolling ladder for accessing books on the higher shelves. I noticed that we owned a lot of the same book titles—especially those I'd banished to the "I will never ever finish this. Like. Ever." category.

After switching off the overhead light, he walked us through additional bedrooms. That's when Teensy and Amanda called dibs on the same room. The one they wanted had a cantilevered balcony that overlooked the front of the property, including the road. Fortunately, they were able to work it out like adults the mature way—by resorting to the use of *Rock-Paper-Scissors.*

Teensy won.

She ripped open the glass doors and stepped out on the deck.

Chopper Deke issued a stern warning. "Don't go out there. Anyone concealed in the woods might see you. I suggest you keep the blinds pulled, too. Wouldn't want any Peeping Toms watching you."

Say what?

Teensy came inside. Against Chopper Deke's wishes, I stepped out onto the balcony.

Exasperated, he snapped, "What'd I just tell you?"

I had good reason for checking out the deck. Curiosity made me gauge the drop-off distance in the event we needed to use the lanai as a means of escape. These murderers seemed almost mystical in their ability to track us down. And while Venice, Teensy, Salem, and maybe even Amanda were willing to stay ostrich-headed, I didn't underestimate the ability of those evil monsters to do us in.

Pale plumes of warm breath vaporized in the chilly air. I turned to the sound of twigs snapping. As I scanned the tract of land, I detected movement in the shadows.

Hand to mouth, I sucked air. "I saw something."

Chopper Deke stepped out onto the balcony. He shifted his gaze, following the trajectory of my pointed finger. "Feral cats. They live in the woods. I rattle a sack of dry food every morning before work and they break from the woods like the Rice University Marching Owl Band."

I belly-laughed. Anyone who'd ever seen a Rice University football game knew what kind of halftime to expect. The MOB was less of a marching band and more of a satirical scatter band where instruments, if any, could be kazoos or didgeridoos.

Chopper Deke gripped my elbow and steered me back inside. "Because this is the most vulnerable part of the house, it's booby-trapped to light up like a football field if an intruder tries to make entry. Alarms go off with all the bells and whistles. Ever heard of a 'flash bang'?" I shook my head. "It's what the SWAT team throws into a room before they charge inside. Stuns the occupants." I nodded. "One's rigged to the door. If it goes off while you're staying here, and you're not stunned shitless, you'll have about forty-five seconds of lead time to get the hell out."

"So let me get this straight. If the booby trap goes off, we have forty-five seconds to . . . what? Get out the back door?"

"No. I'll show you in a bit." He double-locked the lanai and pulled the silhouette shades closed.

I glanced over at the girls to make sure they'd understood the gravity of Chopper Deke's speech. Venice did a little head nod to indicate she got it. Amanda, too. But instead of wide-eyed understanding, Teensy appeared to have slipped into a state of rapture. I'd seen this look before and knew what it meant, and I didn't want any trouble out of her.

I shot her a warning glare. "No."

"No, what? What're you glowering at me for? I didn't do anything." She gave me a patronizing smile, and when she smiled, dimples formed on the sides of her face. But Teensy couldn't fool me with her innocent look—I invented that look, and she stole it from *moi*.

"It's not what you've done, it's what you're planning to do, and the answer is no. I mean it."

Teensy's jaw dropped open and she pointed to herself. "What am I planning?"

"You can*not* have a cat."

"It's not for you to say. That's between me and the cat."

"Fine. Go ahead. Try to tame one. They're all wild. They'll probably rip out your heart and eat it in front of the rest of us."

"Animals love me. It's like I'm their queen."

This was astoundingly true. Animals gravitated to Teensy like a stalker to a victim. I figured by the time we left—assuming we weren't all dead—the Prescott girls would own a cat.

Next stop, the gun room.

Like most Texans, Chopper Deke owned an arsenal of weapons. He showed us how to access his gun collection when he led us to a room with a fake panel that opened into a recessed area that had been so expertly crafted that it couldn't be differentiated from the rest of the room's interior unless one previously knew it was there.

He steered us toward his collection of revolvers because "they're easier to handle" and "require less instruction" for those among us who'd never fired a weapon.

Teensy appeared to be spellbound as she held the little Smith & Wesson Chopper Deke picked out for her. As if she'd been swept away by a romantic memory, a warm pink blush suffused her face. I wouldn't have been stunned to learn she'd killed somebody during her Mexican escape, and decided to conduct my own probe, later, to ask her about it.

Amanda gripped hers like a gangsta, while Venice opted out of our firearms lesson.

Mesmerized by the gun Chopper Deke selected for me, I tuned him out. The snub-nose revolver I held in my hand looked a lot like the retired service revolver Bruckman kept beside his bed.

Then I realized that Chopper Deke was talking and I'd missed what he said.

"Sorry, what was that?"

"These guns don't have serial numbers." In a remarkably hushed voice, he said, "So it's illegal to own them. My father got them during World War II. He was a bomber pilot in the European Theater. I inherited them from him. As far as anyone's concerned, they don't exist. So, bottom line, it'd be bad if they fell into enemy hands."

Message received. *Don't get caught with these guns.*

I watched Venice recoil. She wanted nothing to do with handguns. And while I hadn't always been gung-ho about firearms, I became an instant fan of gun ownership and permits to carry concealed handguns when Gran shot the man who tried to carjack us. I assumed it worked the same way with the death penalty if you weren't a big fan of it before some dirtbag, scumbucket criminal murdered one of your family members. It'd probably make you a convert.

I planned to lobby for Nerissa to get the death penalty. And the mass murderers who were after us, too. In my book, they were all death-row candidates.

"Tomorrow, I'll teach you how to shoot these," said our host as he returned the empty boxes to the gun safe and resecured the hidden room. "We'll have firearms training as soon as I get back from work."

He provided each of us with enough ammunition to load our revolvers, which we did under his intent regard. Then we dispersed to our respective rooms and placed the loaded weapons on the nightstands before meeting him in the hallway and trailing him downstairs. Teensy wanted to watch the big-screen TV and to poke through Chopper Deke's movie collection, but he insisted we follow him into the last room—the one behind what appeared to be a wall of built-in bookcases.

He pulled out a book and felt around the vacant space with his fingertips. Then he took a step back.

Mechanically triggered gears hummed, turning inside the steel barricade and retracting a series of tumblers from the jamb. We stood at the mouth of a steel door that resembled the door on an oversized, fireproof gun safe. Chopper Deke showed me where to swipe the keypad. As soon as I did, the door yawned open and we entered a rectangular space with a landline installed. To me, this was a panic room. But to Chopper Deke, a governmental conspiracy theorist with a strong survivalist mentality, like those militia people in Idaho I'd read about, we'd entered the Armageddon room.

Several fluorescent-tube lights continuously blinked overhead.

Teensy gave us her take on the matter by drawling out the word, "Wow."

Amanda mumbled, "Holy crap."

Venice said, "Whoa. Reality check."

Salem said nothing.

I took in the room in a glance: the two-piece bathroom with a toilet and corner sink; a couple of bedrolls; cases of bottled water stacked to the ceiling; and a couple of cases of MREs. I opened my cell phone to test the signal in case we ended up in this container and needed to call for help, but the amount of metal in the panic room interfered with the reception.

The main chamber consisted of a small living area with an open-concept kitchenette. Electric lights that ran off a generator, in the event the main house lost power, had their own electrical panel. An elaborate exhaust system dispersed any smoke via an underground system of pipes that emptied into the stand of oaks thirty feet or so from the house. The idea behind the design, according to Chopper Deke, was for the ventilation system to dissipate any exhaust from the subterranean container so that—assuming anyone detected it—it could easily be confused with fog.

When I probed further, I saw that Chopper Deke had furnished the stronghold with several overstuffed armchairs that unfolded into twin-sized beds. Off to the side, I noticed that the bedrolls, when upended, had been fitted with wooden trays with elasticized, slip-on bonnets, to form primitive end tables.

He'd fully stocked the safe room with enormous quantities of MREs and other freeze-dried meats and vegetables, as well as canned meats and vegetables. Obviously, one person could've held out for days—but there were five of us, including a pygmy whom I suspected had a tapeworm, not to mention that the absence of windows in the Armageddon room caused me to claw at my throat with the onset of claustrophobia. While the girls nosed around, Chopper Deke pulled me aside.

"Let's take a walk." He jutted his chin toward the door.

He showed me around the perimeter of the house, and when we came to a break in the trees where I could clearly see a small clearing, he pointed to a house in the distance and told me about the nearest neighbors who lived a mile down the road. According to Chopper Deke, they were reclusive people who'd managed to break away from a polygamist cult. If anything happened and we had to escape, he told me not to go there.

At first, it creeped me out knowing we were out in the middle of no-damned-where, where God left his right shoe. For a fleeting instant, I thought how easy it'd be for us to "disappear" or be picked off one at a time. My mind started to go places that gave me the shivers until he stopped at the rear of the house, near a small patio made of Saltillo tiles and stocked with colorful pottery to hold container plants.

"See those?" He pointed out the tiles that formed the patio. "Those are real. See those?" He pointed to specific tiles running along the edge. "Not real."

The way it worked, the fake tiles actually had dirt glued onto them with an epoxy or adhesive to conceal the hinged lid of the panic room's escape hatch.

"Don't use it unless you have to," said Chopper Deke. "It's hell combing the dirt back in place so it looks normal."

"Have you ever used it?"

"I did a dry run to test whether it worked. It does. Let's hope you don't have to use it."

We retraced our steps. He pointed to a chicken coop at the rear of the property and told me we could gather fresh farm eggs for our breakfast if we wanted. The last time I gathered eggs as a young child at my mother's parents' ranch, I reached in and touched a chicken snake. *I can only assume.* I like yard eggs, but that cured me for life from actually gathering them.

So, no thanks.

When we returned to the kitchen, Teensy, who I'm starting to think of as more of a pillow and less of a person, was sitting on a bar stool at the peninsula. Across the table, Venice and Amanda engaged in murmured conversations, with Amanda doing most of the talking. Chopper Deke spooned vanilla bean ice cream into dessert bowls and we ate our fill. After he stacked the dirty dishes in the dishwasher, the four girls followed him into the den to watch a movie.

Completely exhausted and crabby from sleep deprivation, I retired to my room. As long as we had Chopper Deke downstairs and guns within arm's reach, I felt relatively safe.

As I ascended the stairs, I heard Teensy chattering about her favorite TV show. I glanced back for one last look and saw Chopper Deke gently sandwich her face between his palms.

"You're so pretty," he said. "Why must you ruin it with words?"

Alone in my room, my thoughts free-associated.

Since Salem and her family had come under fire, I felt a strange compulsion to call the psyche ward to check on Dawn. Without her ID code, the hospital wouldn't give out any information, nor would they confirm or deny whether they'd admitted such a person. So I dug in my purse until I found the ID number I'd been given in case I needed to call her.

I stabbed out the number to the nurse's station and asked for the on-duty nurse who treated Dawn. Instead of being switched to the charge nurse, I was put on hold. Listening to canned music over the phone while I waited for the nurse to come on the line was like having to listen to strains of "Toque a De-güello," the Mexican death song from *Rio Bravo*.

During my wait, Teensy and Venice popped in to say goodnight. I did the finger-to-lip thing to show I had an ongoing conversation. Then—*surprise*—my phone beeped with an incoming call. When I switched over, Dawn herself came on the line.

She said, "Are you with the other girls?" I told her I was, and she said, "Put me on speaker."

"Hold on." I muted the call. "It's Dawn." The girls' cow-to-slaughterhouse faces showed their distaste. "Okay, we can hear you now."

"Hey, bitches," she said with mock cheer. "The doctors said I could leave if I had a place to go. Dainty, pick me up."

Our mouths fell open. This was exactly what I didn't need—for Dawn to join my mounting list of problems. Amanda walked in and everyone in the room fell silent, probably because they were busy thinking, *Yeah, that'd totally be a great way to start a new day*. I gave the phone a dedicated eyeblink, because, like, yeah—springing a certifiable whack-a-doo from the nuthouse wouldn't complicate matters at all, now, would it? Nosirree.

Teensy said, "Those men tried to kill us last night."

Instead of high-fiving her for discouraging Dawn from rejoining our group, I just hit the mute button on the phone and dropped my head into my hands.

Then Dawn said something that made me jerk my head up and un-mute the speaker.

"Well, one of them tried to kill me, too. Thanks for putting me in here, by the way. You think you're safe, but if one of them pulls some shit and acts crazy, guess what? Yep, that's right. The cops bring them in and they get thrown in the same ward as me."

We exchanged horrified looks.

I must've misheard. *Did she just say . . . ? Oh, my Lord.* "What happened?"

"I told you, bitches, they found me."

Chills crawled across my skin. "What do you mean *they found you*?"

"What the hell language do I need to speak in order to get the message across?" she snarled. "I already told you. One of them got himself thrown in here. He came into my room after 'lights out' and tried to kill me."

To anyone who didn't know the back story, including her treating physicians, Avery's stepdaughter might sound delusional. But not to us.

"We need details." The words caught in my throat.

"Fine. The nurse brought me my Trazadone to help me sleep. And I *cheeked* it because I don't need it. I sleep just fine. And it's a damned good thing I didn't swallow their damned pills because I'd be dead. I hadn't dozed off for five minutes when that"—she spewed out a litany of profane descriptions to label the man who entered her room—"sneaked into my room and tried to strangle me."

Good manners dictated that I ask if she'd been harmed.

"I lost a fingernail prying his hands off my neck, and I hurt my hand defending myself."

My head spun with ugly visuals. "Where is he now?"

"They transferred Moby Dickwad to the medical unit. So I'm ready to get out of here, and I expect you to pick me up first thing in the morning, Dainty. Do *not* disappoint me."

Over the vehement headshakes of the others, I weighed our options. Dawn had achieved a new level of crazy, but that certainly didn't diminish her value. Back at the lodge, while the rest of us hid in the woods, Dawn went for help. She didn't judge me when I killed that fiend at the Rivercrest estate. And, by her disabling another of those monsters, we'd pared their numbers down from four to two.

"I'll come get you, but you have to promise me certain things."

"Haven't I been through enough? What the hell do you want from me?"

"Stay on your medication. And stop cursing. Profanity isn't Rubanbleu-appropriate behavior."

She left the conversation by describing—profanely, I might add—exactly what The Rubanbleu could go do to itself.

After the girls retired to their respective rooms, I considered the ramifications of my decision. It was one thing for our group to successfully fight off an outside enemy; it was quite another to fight off the symptoms of an unpredictable enemy you couldn't see.

In time, I drifted off to sleep. Around two in the morning, I was awakened by a subtle shift in the air. I opened my eyes to see a human form standing beside the queen-sized bed.

I came fully awake, simultaneously sucking air and raising my arms in self-defense to shield my face against the blows I expected to come raining down on me. The shadowy silhouette turned out to be Venice, clutching a pillow and dragging a blanket behind her like a bridal train.

"You scared me to death."

"I'm afraid, Dainty. Can I climb in bed with you?"

"Bet you wish you'd taken one of Chopper Deke's guns, huh?"

She shook her head. "I'd probably shoot myself by accident. But I trust *you* with a gun."

I made room for her, moving from the middle of the bed to the side closest to the window. Once we both settled in with the covers drawn up around our necks, Venice breathed easier and eventually drifted off into deep slumber.

Unable to sleep, I moved to the overstuffed bedroom chair and sat, slumped but alert, listening for sounds of intruders. Nothing relieved the tap-tap-tapping of the rain except for the occasional thin, wispy snore from Venice. It was such a mundane thing, and yet I experienced one of those prosaic moments that brought a smile to my face. I caught myself nodding stupidly, like a bobble-head doll, and secretly wanted to check each girl's room but was afraid they'd hear a noise, wake up, and reflexively shoot me dead in my tracks.

Especially Teensy.

CHAPTER TWENTY-TWO

Staying overnight at Chopper Deke's house exceeded my expectations so completely that I had to reexamine my first impression of him. Despite the pack of coyotes that howled all night and the complementing rooster that crowed at dawn, his unconventional home held all the allure of a four-star hotel. Apparently, the coyote–rooster duet happened every morning.

Resisting the urge to awaken Venice, I dressed quickly and went downstairs to investigate the smell of bacon and coffee.

At first, it looked like it'd just be me and Chopper Deke at the breakfast table. I wanted to come clean with him about picking up Dawn at the psyche ward later in the day. In Vietnam, after he rode his helicopter to the bottom of a three-canopy jungle, he became a POW at the Hotel Saigon for a year after the Viet Cong captured him. He wasted away until he hit 117 pounds, surviving off rodents he pulled into his cage, putrefied rice, and dirty water. Still, he survived, and I figured we could all profit from his unique military and survival experience. And because he almost went crazy, he could help with Dawn.

But I didn't get the chance to speak to him alone, because around the time he blotted the grease off the bacon and set the plateful of crispy strips in the middle of the kitchen peninsula, Amanda bounded down the stairs like a zombie packing heavy munitions. I'd long suspected that her tapeworm had a bacon fetish, and her sudden and dramatic appearance shored up my suspicion.

"Coffee," she gasped.

Chopper Deke plucked a mug from the cabinet and made a thumb gesture at the brewing pot. Amanda and I poured our cups almost full and topped them off with heavy cream.

While the others slept in, the three of us ate crispy bacon, egg-and-cheddar omelets with spinach and mushrooms, and toasted English muffins with butter and strawberry preserves. As Chopper Deke went to get ready for work, he insisted I occupy a chair in his room so we could talk. Distracted by our host's bedroom, it was hard to keep my train of thought as I took in the décor. Paneled in marble and mirrors, the master bedroom looked like I imagined a brothel would look. The only feature lacking to complete the impression was red carpet, big pink satin pillows on the bed, and a brass pole mounted in the center of the room for the occasional guest's striptease.

When he sat on the edge of his bed and laced up his boots, I wasn't the least bit fooled by his nonchalance. Those men weren't playing a cat-and-mouse game to torture us—they wanted to exterminate us like they would an infestation of cockroaches . . . human beings were just that insignificant to them. Chopper Deke knew the gravity of our predicament, and I sensed he feared for his own safety by bringing us out here, as much as he feared for ours.

He finished tying his shoelaces and glanced around, distracted. Then he grabbed a leather-bound notebook off a bachelor's chest, along with his keys.

I checked the time. "Aren't you going to be late?"

"No. We're flying."

Flying?

"I have a small airstrip and a Cessna in a hanger at the back of the property. You're going with me. And wipe that look off your face. If there'd been room for you and your black leprechaun, you would've gotten into my helicopter down in Mexico when I flew your sister and her friends out, so quit acting like you're afraid to fly with me."

"Amanda's a pygmy."

"Whatever. We're flying to Dallas, and, just like I do every morning, I'm meeting Joey at the airport where we keep the chopper so we can knock out the morning drive-time report. I keep a Jeep at the airport, so while I'm flying Joey around, listening to him scream bloody murder because he thinks we're going to crash, you drive my Jeep to the station and see if the boss needs anything. And since one of the blow-dries will probably call in sick, Gordon will need you to fill in, so once you're done, take the Jeep into Fort Worth and pick up that wingnut friend—"

"Dawn's not my friend; she's my project."

"—of yours and bring her back to the airport. I'll fly us back to the house, and we'll have a firearms lesson so you don't shoot yourself in the foot. After that, you can sit around all afternoon and sing campfire songs, for all I care. Got it?"

With only minutes to spare, I scampered back to the group and relayed the plan. Then I put on my Pixy Merriweather garb and off we flew.

Gordon let me do the morning show because, once again, Steve Lennox claimed he was still in Chicago, snowed in. Gordon didn't believe him, of course, and set about making phone calls to Byron to see if the station could terminate Lennox's contract.

Turned out he couldn't. As I sat in Gordon's office waiting for Chopper Deke to call, Gordon said, "Looks like Lennox is asshole buddies with one of our big sponsors. So I can't fire the bastard or we'll lose their business. I'm too old for this shit." Then he clapped his hand over his mouth in mock embarrassment for cursing in my presence, although I knew he wasn't the least bit sorry and would do it again, probably within the next few minutes. "Here's a lesson for you, Prescott. You never want to work for somebody who doesn't want you working for them. I've had it up to here with Lennox." He measured above his head to show how fed up he was with the morning anchor. "Hide and watch. He'll be looking for a new job within the month."

I wasn't so sure. I had yet to reconcile why Tig Welder still worked at WBFD, when everyone at the station thought he'd committed murder, plus he'd popped up on the PD's radar as a person of interest. To be sure, Mr. Welder was one of the oddest newsmen I'd ever met. I kept telling myself that it's not against the law to be odd, or to do odd things, but it piques the attention of homicide detectives when a person acts odd less than a hundred feet from where a body lies. I figured if the cops ever arrested him, I'd get called to testify in that case, too. After all, as the owner-proprietor of the Debutante Detective Agency, I took surveillance photos of him letting that lady into his house—that's right, the same woman who ended up dead in WBFD's broom closet a month or so back.

Thoughts turned to Nerissa, awaiting trial in the county jail.

Since Chopper Deke was still in the air, scaring the dickens out of Traffic Monitor Joey, I left the studio, took the Jeep, and headed into Fort Worth. My eyes constantly flickered to the rearview mirror as I checked for black SUVs, but the ones I saw were driven by soccer moms with kids strapped into car seats.

The Tarrant County Jail loomed in the distance. Instead of driving straight to the hospital psyche ward, I detoured. Rather than stay ostrich-headed, I planned to confront my wicked stepmother.

Normally, I wouldn't have been allowed to see her since I wasn't on her visitation list. But my celebrity status scored points with the jail lieutenant, so he sent a jailer up to ask Nerissa if she'd see me. The jailer returned to take me upstairs, and after I secured my purse in a metal locker, we took the elevator.

The Tarrant County Jail, a towering brick-and-mortar building, not only houses inmates, it also traps a variety of human odors. The jailer escorted me to a level normally reserved for lawyers and seated me in an individual compartment with telephone receivers on each side of the Plexiglass screen that separated the attorneys from the inmates. The space even had a small metal built-in where lawyers could write on their legal pads.

Suspecting that Nerissa would bear only a faint resemblance to the mug shot taken the day deputies transported her from El Paso back to Fort Worth, I waited for a guard on the other side of the cell block to escort Daddy's soon-to-be ex-wife to my compartment. In El Paso, even wearing stripes, she appeared healthy and almost radiant, considering she'd been dragged across the Mexican border and back into Texas by Amanda and me. And why wouldn't she look like the cover girl for one of those health and fitness magazines? She'd been eating well and exercising regularly in that Mexican banker's Olympic-sized pool while she hid out from the authorities, never thinking Amanda and I would come calling.

Knock, knock. Time to pay your debt to society.

The clank of restraints jarred me from my trance. Nerissa padded into the attorney conference area, taking little Geisha steps from the leg irons chaining her ankles together. Her processed blond hair had grown out several inches and she looked more cheap and hooker-esque than ever. Besides eating too many starches, her sallow complexion, and the puffy skin under her eyes, made her look unhealthy.

She wore prison khakis, socks, and rubber flip-flops, and had her hands restrained at the wrists by a belly chain wrapped around her waist. The jailer on my side explained that precautionary measures were being taken since Nerissa had tried to escape a few days earlier. The only thing missing to complete the loser-look was bubble gum and a teardrop tattoo next to her eye.

A Cheshire grin spread across her face. The smile I returned wasn't because I was happy to see her. *Au contraire.* I smiled because I was happy to see her in such awful shape.

Swear to God, I don't know what my father ever saw in you.

Be nice, Dainty. You won't get answers if you're hateful.

Oh, look, I'm having a dialogue with myself—just like Dawn.

I picked up the phone receiver on my side and waited for the guard to unhook one handcuff on the belly chain so she could slide onto the metal stool and use the phone on her side.

"I'm kind of digging the black hair," she said. "Think mine would look good that way?"

I'd made a grievous tactical error. I'd gone incognito as Pixy Merriweather for the viewing audience so that those men wouldn't find me as blue-eyed-blond Dainty Prescott. By appearing in the long dark wig, I'd outed myself. Now her goons would be searching for a brunette.

"I thought I'd try a new look," I said easily, and got in a dig about her roots. "And you're already halfway there."

"You're almost in time for lunch. Maybe you can get one of the screws to let you try the cuisine. Today, it's green baloney and stale bread sandwiches. Oh, wait—this is jail. We get green baloney and stale bread sandwiches every day."

If she wanted me to feel sorry for her, I didn't. She landed in jail for murdering my mother, yet I fought the urge to berate her. I'd come here to save my life. And Teensy's. And I didn't want to dry up the conversation before it got started.

Suddenly businesslike, Nerissa said, "Why'd you come here?"

"Call them off."

Calculating eyes thinned into slits. "Call who off?"

"You know who. *Them.*"

"I don't know what you're talking about."

"Are they relatives of yours? Cousins?"

She continued to deny any knowledge of the four men who were trying to kill us, and I didn't feed her any information about the mass murders. Clearly, I'd reached a dead end, and was starting to feel like maybe Nerissa wasn't the impetus behind the men who wanted us dead. But she'd paired that innocent expression with words calculated to throw us off before, like *Of course I love your father, Dainty, I'm not marrying him for his money.*

The jailer gave me the *Let's go* thumb gesture, and I hung up the receiver. The watch commander may have made me lock up my purse before entering, but he didn't get my camera phone. While the jailer turned his back to key off the elevator, I readied the camera and raised it like I was taking a selfie.

I mouthed, "Smile," and caught her in midscowl. I clicked the picture and texted it to Daddy.

Around eleven o'clock, I arrived at the hospital's psychiatric unit and checked in with the receptionist at the front desk. After a quick phone call, the lady told me a nurse would be down to escort me upstairs. I took a seat in one of the vinyl-upholstered chairs lining the sage green wall, wondering why they didn't just give me directions. It would soon be made clear.

While flipping through my list of contacts on my disposable phone, I gave the lobby an eye scan. The place had an inviting feel, not the "Cuckoo's Nest" vibe I'd imagined. An aquarium of colorful fish brightened one side of the room, while the foliage of lush container plants gleamed in a different corner. I didn't see a wall clock, but there were big canvases of people I presumed were doctors because of their lab coats, and plaques from a local magazine for the annual award-winning physicians.

I dialed Avery Marshall. We exchanged mindless pleasantries before I tackled the situation head-on. "Were you aware Dawn's been in the psychiatric lock-up the past few days?"

"Yes. She only called me about a hundred times. I had to get her telephone privileges suspended."

"You knew she had psychiatric problems?" This almost left me speechless. Why would he pawn her off on me if she had mental problems? I wasn't equipped to deal with that.

Avery's anger flared. "Look, she's your problem now. Deal with it."

"*Deal* with it? I'm not a doctor. She should be getting long-term treatment if she's that bad off."

"She's not that bad off. Just . . . take her for a few more days and teach her as much as you can about etiquette and grooming and whatnot, and we'll call it even."

The *click* of his hang-up call echoed all the way down my ear canal. I wished I'd never done business with Avery—but hey, lesson learned. I resolved never to do business with him in the future.

If I had a future.

The question as to why I couldn't roam the place answered itself when the nurse who came to get me led me past a series of doors with automatic locks as we moved between floors, including the elevator. Adjacent to these locked areas were posted signs that read: Escape Precaution.

When the elevator doors slid open on the second floor, a cinder-block wall of colorful handprints with patients' first names beneath each one greeted me. Doctors, dressed in white smocks with their names embroidered in the area where a pocket should've been, milled around in the halls. The nurse took me to a conference room, and I pulled up a chair around a small table. A three-ring binder with Dawn's name printed on the spine lay in the center.

From my seat, I could see through the glass partition into another windowed area with safety filament that looked a lot like chicken coop wire sandwiched between the glass. My view into the psyche ward conjured up old memories of sleepless nights from reading horror stories. When Dawn's doctors joined me, they used words like "dissociative personality disorder" and "non-compliance with medication" as well as other medical terms that made my head spin. My disposable phone purred in the middle of our meeting and when I glanced down to silence it, Chopper Deke's name appeared on the digital display.

"So, bottom line," I said in a rush, "can I take her out of here now?"

A Middle-Eastern man whom I assumed to be the spokesman for the treatment team spoke in stilted English. "Yes. We're putting her on furlough. But she must stay on her medication and she must return for outpatient treatment, or we will file an order of protective custody. That means the sheriff will pick her up and bring her back. Do you understand?"

Dawn, check. Meetings, check. Crazy person on board, check.

"By the way"—I tried to sound casual but my heart beat so hard that I thought they might hear it—"Dawn mentioned another patient came into her room and attacked her while she slept. Can you tell me about that?"

The head doc stiffened against his seat back. "From time to time, patients are intrusive and walk into rooms without invitation. We discourage men and women from fraternizing in each other's rooms by redirecting them, but, on occasion, a patient slips by. Your friend was not harmed."

I'd risen to my feet and was digging in my purse for the keys to the Jeep. "So, did you transfer the patient to a different wing so he wouldn't bother her anymore?"

"In a manner of speaking. That man is in the medical unit now."

"I certainly hope he's not contagious." We had enough problems without having to deal with the flu, or TB, or multiresistant staph on top of what we already had on our plate.

"He was not contagious. He was healthy until Dawn karatechopped him in the neck and jammed his nose practically up into his brain."

What?

He nodded. "They had to operate on his crushed larynx and reset his nose. Mental patients can be quite strong when they are out of control. Bring her back at the first sign of medication non-compliance or behavioral change."

Thanks, and have a super-sparkly day.

As I waited downstairs by the receptionist's desk, a nurse escorted Dawn to the front door. She wore the same psychedelic mismatched get-up she'd been wearing the evening we brought her in to the psychiatric ER. Only now, she carried a brown paper bag with her name written on it, and I assumed that this bag contained her disposable cell phone and whatever other incidentals she'd brought into the hospital.

"Hi, Dainty." Dawn spoke softly, with contrition, and seemed gracious and mood-appropriate for a person who'd just gotten her way.

We had a brief conversation while standing in the lobby, but once we were seat-belted into the Jeep and I pulled away from the curb and merged into heavy traffic, the old obnoxious Dawn revealed herself.

"Sayonara, cockbites." She flipped the hospital a stiff middle finger. "Now what?"

I explained that we were meeting Chopper Deke in Dallas so he could fly us back to his house. She wanted me to describe the accommodations. I told her it was on par with a four-star hotel. Once she digested this information, she raised her voice at me because I didn't get her out of the hospital quickly enough

245

to suit her. Fed up, I curbed the Jeep and slammed on the brakes.

Borrowing from Chopper Deke's playbook, I gave her an *I mean business* look. "What'd I tell you?"

"To be nice and not cuss."

"We're in the dogfight of our lives, Dawn, and if you can't behave yourself, then none of us want to be around you. This is your only warning. Do you understand? I can take you back there, same as the first time." I stared at her profile and watched her bottom lip slightly protrude.

"No, thank you. I would prefer not to go back."

The drive back to Dallas was uneventful—just the way I liked it. We rode in relative silence, and the few attempts at conversation were brief and done with an economy of words.

I checked the gas tank out of habit. We had plenty, so I declined to stop at a convenience store for chips when Dawn mentioned she was as "hungry as a horse."

At the airport, Chopper Deke had already done the preflight on the Cessna and waited beside the airplane.

That's when Dawn announced, "Flying makes me sick."

Chopper Deke said, "No, it doesn't. People do *not* get sick in my bird. If you're going to puke, do it now."

After she buckled herself into the back seat, he handed her a barf bag as a precaution. A short time later, we lifted off, and once we were airborne, the urban blight of Dallas started to look more and more like tiny Monopoly houses. As we made our way across two counties, the countryside reminded me of a patchwork quilt of yellows, tans, and various shades of green. Despite my efforts to get a visual on Chopper Deke's container home once our altitude dropped, I still couldn't see it from the air. Nor the hangar. As scattered showers dotted the Cessna's Plexiglas windshield and dimpled the stock tanks below, I barely located the strip of runway.

Once Chopper Deke made the descent, we got a good look at his container home in the stark light of day. The exterior had been painted camouflage. A little green, a splash of brown, a spritz of olive, a dash of tan, a shock of black. It reminded me of the Army jeeps at Carswell Joint Reserve Base on the west side of Fort Worth. And it also explained why the house was virtually impossible to see from the air. Or the road. My comfort level instantly rose.

We'd no sooner trudged to the house when our host showed Dawn around while I found Teensy, Salem, and Venice in the den, glued to the big-screen TV. Amanda was there too, slumped in a chair, but she'd fallen asleep and was snoring like a sea lion. As soon as I entered the room, Amanda jerked awake.

"I didn't steal your man—he wanted to be with me. Oh. Hi, diva." She wiped her eyes and smiled her gap-toothed, sheepish grin.

"Did you see me do the morning news?"

All eyes moved to me in a collective shift.

Amanda said, "Yes, diva, we watched you. We took a poll and decided we like you better as Pixy Merriweather."

"I'll be anybody they want me to be as long as I get a paycheck." Expecting Chopper Deke to have his refrigerator stocked with groceries like those college kids crave—lunch meat and soda pop—I walked over to the icebox and opened the door. "Anybody else hungry?"

"We already ate," said Amanda.

I looked at her knowingly.

Before I could raid the refrigerator, Chopper Deke staggered into the room in a fit of laughter. Dawn clung to his arm like a hyena trying to take her prey to the ground.

"What's so funny?" I asked.

"Wouldn't you like to know?" said Dawn.

Chopper Deke's face changed. "Everybody get your firearms

and bring them back downstairs. Your first lesson's today."

He took time to warm up several pounds of barbecued brisket and link sausage, along with a container of cowboy beans and homemade potato salad. I'm not much of a barbecue aficionado, but when I caught a whiff of perfectly cooked meat, I pulled a stool up to the peninsula and waited for Dawn and Chopper Deke to join me. A tall glass of sweet tea refreshed me.

A half hour later, after we'd eaten and the dirty dishes were tucked into the dishwasher, Chopper Deke walked us past the hen house and out to the rear of the property, carrying a bag slung over his shoulder. To teach us the fundamentals of basic marksmanship, he led us down a dirt road filled with ruts and weeds, with the glare of the afternoon sun in our path. In a small, but open clearing, we watched as he lined up various sizes of tin cans along the top of a cinder-block fire pit. Then he outfitted us with our choice of belt holsters, ammo, and shoulder holsters. He even had a thigh holster and an ankle holster in his little bag of tricks. I could tell Amanda felt pretty badass once she got suited up.

With our pistols loaded and pointed at the ground, Chopper Deke showed us the Weaver stance, the textbook FBI position he wanted us to fire in. When we mastered the Weaver stance, he demonstrated how to load our weapons. Finally, he had us holster our pistols while he drew a line in the dirt with a stick. Then he told us to stay behind the line and pronounced us ready to fire.

I heard Amanda shriek at the far end of the line. "Stop doing that, Dawn. That's how I shot my uncle Mbuge."

Chopper Deke stalked down to where Amanda and Dawn were standing and lectured them for not taking the lesson seriously. "People pay a lot of money for this kind of training. I'm giving it to you free. The least you can do is pay attention."

Whatever Dawn had done, Chopper Deke got the situation

under control. Then he lectured the whole group on responsibility—or the lack of it—and how we were each accountable for learning to take care of ourselves in a life-or-death situation, but we were also our brother's keeper. Satisfied that we'd heard him, he handed out earplugs.

Like a drill sergeant, he yelled, "Ready on the right," and then looked to the right. "Ready on the left." While he watched to ensure we followed his instructions, my mind hearkened back to a chant we called out while learning to count off steps in my prep school's marching band:

"Left, right. left, right; I left my wife with forty-nine kids,

"In a starving condition and thought it was right; left, right. left, right . . ."

Chopper Deke came up behind me, barking orders. "Fire one shot."

Bullets pinged off tin cans. A few completely missed the targets. Bullet-scored cinder blocks went *pock-ping* when one member of our group aimed too low.

The first time I fired my pistol, images of cartel victims falling to the floor of the Chihuahua desert, their blood soaking into the cracked dirt, filled my head. I'd seen so much death that day. The mind is a funny thing—not funny "ha-ha" but funny "strange"—and each time I fired the revolver, my mind tricked me into thinking I smelled the metallic odor of blood instead of gunpowder.

My eyes blistered with tears.

Most memories fade over time or disappear altogether, but my memories of that horrible afternoon on the outskirts of Ciudad Juárez six weeks ago were as fresh as they were moments after the massacre happened. For weeks afterward, my irrational fear was that the men who had killed all those women—women whose only crime had been to search the desert for their lost relatives—would sneak across the border into Texas and kill me, too. And once I put that out into the universe by thinking it, men actually were trying to kill me, my sister, and my friends. Not the cartel, but worse.

While Chopper Deke praised us—especially Dawn, who seemed to have a knack for hitting the target every time she fired her weapon—he swaggered over and stood next to me. I pretended to have dust in my eyes, but when I raised the back of my hand to smash my tears into oblivion, he cupped his palm against my cheek.

"You can do this. You're a lot stronger than you think you are."

I nodded. He was right. Once we were armed and had mastered the basics of shooting, we'd be less vulnerable than we had been.

We shot fifty rounds apiece and, as we progressed, he brought out a stop watch to time us. Why? Because, according to him, in a real firefight, we wouldn't have the luxury of taking our own sweet time. We moved closer to the targets; we moved farther away from the targets. At the end of our first lesson, Chopper Deke showed us how to clean our firearms.

Walking back to the house at twilight, I sniffed the air. The only semblance of a lush lawn had been planted next to the house, and now that the rain had abruptly dried up, the yard had the smell of freshly mowed grass suffused with mold. I was pleased that nobody tried to kill us, especially Dawn, whom I didn't trust without a firearm, much less with one.

Nobody could know where we were, but my OCD and blossoming paranoia would force me to close all of the window treatments at the advent of twilight. By dark, I made sure everyone had turned off the upstairs lights to keep us from becoming targets and turned off their phones so the GPS features wouldn't give away our position. This turned out to be a double-edged sword. If we needed to call for help, we couldn't.

But hey—it wasn't as if we knew how to give directions to our location, right?

If we needed the sheriff, the best I could do to help the dispatcher send units to Chopper Deke's house would be to tell that person to have deputies turn off the Interstate near the truck stop and take a road through town, and then turn off on another road, and then onto an unpaved road, and on and on.

So—bottom line—if we were attacked and couldn't make it to the panic room in time, we'd be screwed.

CHAPTER TWENTY-THREE

Before Chopper Deke went to bed, he warned us "not to go outside for any reason" once he alarmed the house. Unless the house was on fire. Or we smelled a gas leak.

Wide awake, while part of my entourage slept soundly in their rooms, and the other part made their beds on the living room floor because they'd totally immersed themselves in my "safety in numbers" theory, I lay in bed and tried to think of all of the good things that had happened to me over the years—things I should be thankful for. But try as I might to derail negative thoughts, especially those having to do with my early demise, I dwelled on those monstrous men.

Real monsters assimilate into society by pretending they're compassionate, sympathetic, and empathetic human beings like everyone else. The crocodile tears they shed fool others within their social and professional networks, but their civilized demeanor is merely a cover-up for the impending terror they intend to inflict. The moment you figure them out, their eyes change, their faces harden, and they behave like attack animals. Call them sociopaths. Or psychopaths. Or sadists. Even terrorists. Call them anything but normal.

With my thoughts free-associating, I'd originally operated under the assumption that the massacre at the lodge had been committed by hit men to get rid of Teensy and me so we couldn't testify in Nerissa's upcoming murder trial, and that our friends, the lodge owners, and their staff were collateral damage. But now I had to consider that the men hunting us had nothing to do with Nerissa—nor Teensy and me—but had everything to do with a secret in one of my friends' backgrounds.

While deeply pondering this last possibility, I reviewed the fact that we hadn't all remained together since that fateful night at the lodge; regardless, the men continued to pursue each of us. From the moment we left west Texas and returned to Fort Worth, Venice had been with us. So had Dawn. It was Salem who'd refused to stick together until they targeted her family. Those men had plenty of opportunity to go after her, separate and apart from us, but they didn't . . . not until four out of the original five of us were all together . . . with our disposable phones. On some level, I wondered if they eventually went after Salem because they needed to get a lead on our whereabouts. And talking to me on her smartphone led them right to us . . . and to Gran's house.

That alone shored up my willingness to eliminate Nerissa as the mastermind behind these attacks, since she knew our routines well enough to know where to find us. Plus, she seemed genuinely bewildered when I told her to call off the dogs.

Convinced that this tragedy had nothing to do with Salem, my mind spun with possibilities. It had nothing to do with Amanda, either. Amanda wasn't at the lodge. She'd only stumbled into this mess when she showed up, unannounced, at Gran's house. So if these killings had nothing to do with Teensy, Salem, Amanda, and me, then that left Venice and Dawn.

The first opportunity I got in the morning, I planned to delve into the matter. I rolled over to face the window in case someone scaled the side of Chopper Deke's house. Then I rolled back over, thinking I'd have a heart attack if I woke up and saw crocodilian eyes peering over the window sill and hot breath steaming up the glass. Instead of leaving the gun on the night-stand, I slipped it under my pillow. But the horrible visual quickly caused me to reject the bed and head for the nearest overstuffed chair where I could see both the window and the door if awakened in the middle of the night. I took the gun with me and rested it in my lap with a fluffy, lightweight throw covering my legs.

When I finally closed my eyes, the image of Jim Bruckman sprang up behind my eyelids. I decided to jump-start my dream by orchestrating the initial content. So in my head, Bruckman was taking me out to dinner in my new dress from Harkman Beemis—the one I saw at their trunk show but couldn't afford because Daddy refused to give me the money. But, in my fantasy, I had on this same dress, and Bruckman wasn't annoyed with me for being an independent Texas woman. In fact, he was quite proud and even opened my car door for me. Whereupon he reverted to the police officer he is by putting his hand over my head and shoving me inside.

Screech. Starting over.

On my imaginary dream date we were not going to dinner; we were in a Tiki hut in Bali and . . . .

I felt myself drifting off. It was going to be a good night's sleep.

Hoof beats on the stairs had no place in my dream, but I attempted to incorporate them into it anyway. My dream moved to the racetrack, and I wore one of those big southern belle hats and a beautiful mushroom-colored dress with cream piping. The starting pistol had gone off, and the horses were halfway around the track. I held the winning ticket on the Trifecta—

"I won, I won, I won."

—when my bedroom door suddenly banged open and the racetrack went *poof* and I was back in Daintyland, hiding out from murderous men.

Having slumped into the overstuffed chair, I sat bolt-upright. Every hair on the back of my neck stood up like needles.

Venice barged in calling my name. "Come quick. Something's wrong with Dawn."

"What's wrong?"

"No. You have to see this for yourself."

Because of the urgency in Venice's tone, I thought, *Oh, crap, what's she done now?* I tramped purposefully down the stairs in my underwear, with nothing to wrap around me but the fluffy coverlet, muttering curses I didn't think anyone would hear.

Dawn sat yoga-style on the floor with her legs crossed in front of her. Amanda had propped herself against the arm of one of Chopper Deke's recliners, a safe distance away. I didn't hear Amanda's unintelligible comment, but whatever came out of her mouth caused Dawn to react with an eerie calmness that seemed unnatural.

Dawn spoke in a soft, controlled baby-voice that I'd never heard her use before. "Chopper Deke was not in my room."

"I didn't say it was Chopper Deke," Amanda insisted. "I said I heard you talking to a man. Who is he? Did you let him inside?"

"I wasn't talking to a man." Dawn delivered her denial with the petulance of a child.

"I heard you, Dawn. I heard a man's voice. You were arguing with him."

The thought of Dawn letting a man into Chopper Deke's house chilled me to the core. I walked over and stood directly in front of her, clutching my thin blanket around me. "What about it, Dawn? Is this true? Did you bring a man into this house?"

"Dainty, I would never do anything like that. Chopper Deke said not to open the doors after he set the alarm."

"Maybe you let this man inside before the alarm was set? Is that what happened?"

"Dainty, I would never do anything to upset you or the others."

I studied her face for signs of deception. Noting her blank reaction in the face of our grave predicament, I didn't like to think about her lying to me. "Dawn, you have to stop upsetting the others. If you keep this up, you can't stay here."

My lecture, and the sternness in my voice, caused a reaction—and not in a good way. What came out of her mouth was anything but childlike.

"What are you saying—that I'd have to go back to that awful place?" Her voice spiraled up from Buddhist-like calmness to the kind of shriek you'd expect to come from inside an insane asylum at the advent of electroshock therapy. "That hospital? I'm not crazy."

Abruptly, her eyes glazed over. The lively blue color descended into the murkiness of shark-infested waters. It was like staring into a peephole, backlit by a bright glow, and watching the radiance obscured as the occupant of the home stepped up and blocked out the light.

Dawn's voice unexpectedly changed. The contours of her face hardened. Suddenly, we were confronted with a male personality who raged against us in a deep and angry voice. "Dawn would *never* do anything like that. Stop accusing her."

The air went stale around me. Goose bumps popped up on my forearms. An icy cold shiver went up my spine at the same time my stomach flipped.

Venice burst into tears and dashed up the stairs to take cover. The door slammed shut and we all heard the lock toggled. I figured our resident pacifist would end up in Teensy's room and then we'd really have problems. I'm squeamish and don't like to hear all of the gory details, but my sister just soaks that bizarre stuff up like a chamois cloth. By the time Venice got Teensy stirred up, my unbalanced sister would probably come down with her gun locked and loaded.

Dead air all but swallowed me up.

Lightheaded, I dealt with the problem head-on. "Who are you?"

"I'm Boris. And you'd better stop fucking with Dawn or I'll make you wish you were stillborn."

Chills crawled up my spine. I locked my knees together to still the tremble in my legs. "Like . . . what would you do to somebody who tried to hurt Dawn?"

Catlike, Boris jumped to his feet and assumed a karate position. He sliced the air between us with such swiftness that the wisp of a breeze caressed my cheek. "I'd crush his windpipe—and jam his nose up into his brain."

He gave an upward thrust with the heel of his palm to indicate how he'd take a person out. Call it crazy, but my mind cast back to *The Karate Kid* and all my mind could process was, *"Sweep the leg, sweep the leg."*

I slid into one of Chopper Deke's motorized recliners, positioning myself directly in front of "the aspiring debutante formerly known as Dawn." Enraptured by masochistic curiosity, I made good eye contact and softened my voice. "Where's Dawn, Boris?"

"She's hiding. Dawn's afraid."

I detected movement on the staircase. Sure enough, Teensy didn't stay out of the loop for long because Venice turned into the town crier and brought them all running. They lined up on the steps like barn owls on a pecan tree branch and presided over the room. For a second, I thought Teensy had brought her phone to call for an ambulance to take Dawn away, but no, she brought it along to video the debacle.

"She's afraid?" I parroted. "What's Dawn afraid of?"

"Dawn's afraid of these bitches. And she's afraid of you."

I slowly shook my head. "Dawn doesn't need to be afraid of us. We want to help Dawn. She's our friend." While those were the actual words that came out of my mouth, the tiny voice inside my head screamed, *For the love of God, one of you lily-livered fashionistas wake up Chopper Deke.*

Amanda seemed to read my mind. She rose from her nesting place on the arm of Chopper Deke's oversized, motorized recliner and moved nonchalantly behind me. As soon as she cleared the last chair in the room, she disappeared in a blur.

Only one problem—I couldn't seem to take my eye off the gun Amanda left on the end table.

Boris shouted, "What'd Dawn ever do to you? She just wanted to be friends."

"And we *are* friends." The calmness in my voice surprised me, especially since my heart tried to beat a hole in my rib cage trying to get out. "We're going to make Dawn look and feel better about herself. To get her ready to make her debut into society. It's very important to her, you know?"

"Yes." His chin hit his chest. "Nobody wants to go out with her. Men."

"Well . . . she's a lesbian. Lesbians don't want to date men."

His head snapped upright. "Dawn's a lesbian?" He seemed truly shocked. "She never told me."

"Kinda wish she hadn't told me."

"She's not ugly. She has a beautiful spirit." As abruptly as this softer, gentler side of Boris emerged, it died out. His voice escalated to *voce fuerzo* mode. "But you stuck-up fashionistas—with your fancy clothes and your maxed-out credit cards—can't even begin to see it, because you have less candlepower than the yapping bitch of a dog Dawn carries around in her little tote bag trying to pretend she's one of those Beverly Hills sluts the tabloids write about."

Common sense dictated that I turn Boris into a friend. A caring, non-threatening friend.

"May I ask you a personal question, Boris? When did you meet Dawn?"

"Long time ago." Cerulean eyes went glacier cold.

"You came to help her?" Suddenly, revelations from the psyche doctor fell into place. Dawn had been diagnosed with dissociative identity disorder—multiple personalities. Since I hadn't yet upset Boris, I probed further. "What happened to Dawn? Can you tell me? It would help."

"It's not your business. Dawn doesn't want people to know. That's why I'm here."

"You rescued her from something terrible, didn't you? I'm proud of you, Boris. You've done a great job. You're *doing* a great job. And we're going to help." I would've said anything at that point to keep him away from that gun. And I did. "We're going to turn Dawn into the most beautiful debutante at this year's ball, mark my words. There's just one problem."

"Problem? What kind of problem?"

"You'll kind of have to stay out of the picture. It's strictly girl stuff. Think you can do that?"

"Why should I?"

"We don't want to make her self-conscious. It's kind of a . . . process. So will you promise to stay away and let us turn Dawn into Cinderella?"

Boris took his sweet time deciding. Then he nodded.

A horrible thought occurred to me. "Wait—one more thing." If the Boris-personality was the one who karate-chopped that fake mental patient . . . "How do I summon you if we need you?"

"Summon me? I'm not an evil spirit. You don't need a Ouija board. Are you retarded?"

"Calm down, Boris. I misspoke. I apologize." *Well, that's a lie. I do not apologize.* "How shall I contact you if we need you?"

My inner voice screamed, *Beetlejuice, Beetlejuice, Beetlejuice.*

"I'll find you."

"Are there more of you people helping Dawn?" I filed this

question under the "Good to know" category. Recent events reminded me that we should be clear about what we were dealing with in case a Las Vegas showgirl popped up in church without warning. Or glided onstage at the debutante ball wearing troweled-on makeup and performed the Texas Dip, only to rise from her bow and burst into a drag-queen rendition of Lady Gaga's "Bad Romance."

Without warning, the aspiring debutante formerly known as Dawn suddenly began to speak in tongues. At least I thought she was speaking in tongues until Chopper Deke appeared and communicated with her by speaking in tongues himself. Or it could've been Chinese. He'd fought in Vietnam; maybe they were speaking Vietnamese. Regardless, they understood each other in a *Close Encounters of the Third Kind* sort of way. I heard musical notes in my head that I knew weren't actually there and figured I might've gone off the deep end myself.

They both laughed—the knee slapping, belly laughing, roll on the floor guffawing of two people sharing an inside joke. They probably wanted me to leave the room so they could talk about me.

I cut my eyes to the girls, still perched on the stairs, waiting for a sign or a movement that would either send them running up to lock their doors or bring them down to gawk. In the next few seconds, we began the process of learning how incredibly difficult it is to be around someone who's bat-shit crazy (*ahem* . . . Dawn), and someone who's perpetually curious and makes bad choices, and who's sort of high strung, but in an "At least I still know what complementary colors of clothing go together" kind of way (*cough* . . . that'd be me).

Chopper Deke glanced over at me, wrapped in my flimsy coverlet. Pulling the blanket tighter, I could only imagine what lewd thoughts swirled in his head.

"I see you haven't met Kim Ho," he said. At the same time

he made introductions, he coolly plucked the handgun off the end table and shoved it into his waistband. "Say, hi, toots."

"Hi." To Chopper Deke I said, "Boy or girl?"

"Definitely one or the other. What the hell does it matter?"

The whole time Chopper Deke and I discussed the appearance of Kim Ho, Dawn's beautiful blue eyes didn't cloud or darken—they merely stared at us in disbelief. And why wouldn't she be confused?

Because she didn't speak the language.

Before he went back to bed, Chopper Deke called the girls down from the staircase and suggested we each lock our rooms since we now had guns, and because Dawn's imaginary friends were unpredictable. A suggestion we were only too happy to take.

While everyone else went back upstairs and toggled their locks closed, I tried to make conversation with Dawn's personalities. An hour later, I was still trying to communicate with Kim Ho, saying, "Dawn? You know Dawn? Kim Ho, tell Dawn, 'Come out,' " until I accepted the fact that yelling wouldn't make her understand the language any better.

Finally, I left Dawn or Boris or Kim Ho or Little-Bo-Dawn in the den, holding the remote control to the big-screen TV, and schlepped upstairs. As I started to lock myself in my room, Teensy's door cracked open a sliver. As she looked the length of the hallway, a black cat darted out.

"Teensy. What do you think you're doing?"

"Heading for the bathroom."

"Did a cat just come out of your room?" For sure, there were enough feral kittens outside to make a crazy cat-lady starter kit.

She shrugged. "I don't know. Did you see a cat?"

"Do you even remember our cat? He figured out how to grab onto the ceiling fan blades, build momentum, and launch himself into the chandelier. Even when cats are having fun,

261

they'll find a way to ruin your life. Now find it and put it outside."

"Chopper Deke said not to open the door."

"Then you can throw him off the balcony."

"I'm pretty sure that's the same thing as opening the door."

"Fine. I hope Chopper Deke catches you with a feral cat in the house."

"You're not going to tell him, are you?"

I suddenly remembered my silence could be bought. "Not if you go downstairs and watch Dawn all night so the rest of us can get a decent night's sleep."

After I locked myself inside my room, I called Daddy on my disposable phone. I wanted to talk about Avery, and to find out if he knew of anything drastic that'd happened to Dawn to make her spawn multiple personalities. And to see if he'd been contacted by the police about the man I killed. And I hoped he'd volunteer information if Gran's body, and the remains of Old Man Spencer, had been recovered.

I started the conversation with, "So what's going on?"

"I may need bypass surgery. That's the thing about this town. You love it more than any other place in the world, you make it your home, and it tries to kill you."

"What're you talking about?"

"Brisket. Cowtown has too many damned barbecue joints. And the sauces on the meat all taste different. So right about the time you think you have a favorite, a new place opens up and that's your favorite."

"Wait a second. Let's get back to bypass surgery."

"Yeah, I was pretty nervous about it from the get-go, but the surgeon kept saying things like 'death' and 'fatalities' and 'high risk' and 'never wake up' throughout our discussion. He told me to prepare for the worst and hope for the best. So now I'm thinking of changing doctors since hope isn't a very accurate diagnostic tool. Want to meet for dinner tomorrow night? A new barbecue joint opened up at the Stockyards. The barbecued ribs are like candy on a bone. They're so good they'll blow back your hair and make your tongue slap your brain. We can catch up then."

"Sure." My self-esteem rose. "Does Teensy have to come, too?"

"Especially don't bring her. You know, your sister's only alive because of a defective condom."

"For real?"

"No. Not for real. Your mother and I had a very satisfying encounter that could be heard over the baby monitor in your room that we neglected to turn off while your maternal grandparents were in town staying with us. They never did like me. Anyway, I have something important to tell you, but it needs to be done face-to-face, not over a wireless phone."

"Really?" He probably meant to tell me Gran's body washed ashore, poor thing. Waxing nostalgic, my fragile underpinnings needed shoring up, so I asked him if I made him proud, and then listed my accomplishments, ending with, "And I never did drugs, hardly ever drank alcohol, and don't have psychological problems."

"Yeah? Well, I guess that just makes you boring."

I never got around to asking him about Avery, or whether he knew any details about Dawn's childhood because the next thing out of his mouth broke my heart.

"Forgot to tell you . . . I found a buyer for the house."

CHAPTER TWENTY-FOUR

Early the next morning, Daddy called to say he couldn't take me to the restaurant he'd promised to take me to because his friend broke his arm and he had to take him to the hospital. A female voice in the background said, "She'll never buy that."

I didn't buy it since I couldn't imagine why it'd take all morning to set a broken arm. Worse, to add to my list of things to do, I had to figure out a way to torpedo the sale of our childhood home.

The container house seemed eerily quiet, and when I walked downstairs, the green diode on the security alarm made me realize it'd been disarmed. I found Chopper Deke outside, next to the house, digging a hole in the flower bed.

"Good morning, Deke. What are you doing?"

"Digging your sister's grave. She brought in one of the barn cats last night. I found it walking on the kitchen countertop and had to disinfect everything with bleach."

"Teensy loves animals."

"Well the cat rendered an opinion of your sister by clawing the furniture and spraying her bed." He gave me a flinty-eyed look. "And she named my chickens, which I don't appreciate. I heard her talking to them. She called them Shania, Kelly Clarkson, Carrie Underwood, Paula Deen, and Ruta Lee. She named the rooster Bob Seeger. I told her not to name them because they'd eventually end up in the oven. Then we got into a lively discussion about how you don't cook animals you've named, so my own hens are now off limits to me, according to your sister."

"Typical Teensy," I said. "Daddy's hunting dog, Barbie, used to play dead just so she'd leave him alone."

"Your father had a hunting dog named Barbie?" I nodded and he said, "And Barbie was a male?"

"My mother didn't want Daddy to get another dog so they compromised, and Teensy and I got to name him. We named him Barbie."

"I can't imagine how it must've been for your old man living in a houseful of females."

"Now that Teensy's recent obsession has taken a step further into the ridiculous, you should probably know that I heard her discussing our predicament to the cat. Unless it was Dawn talking to the cat. What'd you think about last night—with Dawn, I mean?"

"Pretty sick. I saw guys in 'Nam that age who just snapped."

"Yeah, well, until this is over, I'm stuck with her. So what I came out here to tell you is that I need to stop by my grandmother's house for clothes. We're all looking pretty raggedy wearing the same outfits, so I thought I'd pick up a few things. Will you take me there?"

"Take yourself. You can borrow the Jeep. But don't dawdle. It's probably not smart to go there at all, but I can't see you shopping for clothes at a discount store."

Chopper Deke had made a little compost heap near the flower bed that consisted mostly of eggshells and fruit peels. He finished spreading it around the shrubs and rose to his feet. A bucket of chicken feed lay off to one side and he carried it out to the hen house. I waited for him to return after scattering the feed and saw that he'd brought back at least a dozen eggs.

"I can't let her have a gun," he said out of the blue. "And the rest of you better keep yours away from her. That chick's pretty messed up. One of these days, when she can't figure out how to cope with life"—he formed his thumb and forefinger into a gun and stuck it under his chin—*"Gun. Mouth. Bang."*

"Do you really think she'd hurt herself?"

"Either that, or one of you. Whoever's causing the most problems. Probably your sister. Or you. I've seen this kind of thing before. In 'Nam. Young men who witnessed their buddies slaughtered and went off the deep end from all the carnage . . ."

"Should we take her back to the hospital? I mean—that man tried to strangle her."

"And Boris took care of him."

"Yeah. About Boris . . ." I let out a slow, deep breath. "Where do you think he came from?"

Chopper Deke gave me a wary headshake. "God only knows. I've read about stuff like this . . . abused children splitting off into different personalities in order to protect themselves. Maybe Dawn couldn't take care of herself around, oh, say"—piercing blue eyes nailed me—"*a child molester.* So Boris appeared in her place. Or Kim Ho, the prostitute."

"Kim Ho's a prostitute?"

"That's what she said. Offered to do me for sixty bucks."

"I don't want to hear any more." To illustrate the point, I plugged each ear with an index finger.

I trailed him through the house and into the kitchen. He pulled a frying pan from the cabinet, placed it on the stove, and turned on the burner. Momentarily, he cut several pats off a fresh stick of butter and tossed them into the pan. As the butter sizzled, he took a loaf of bread from the pantry and pan-fried a couple of slices in the skillet.

"I'm not doing bacon," he said. "If I do, those girls will come out of their room like jackals."

We talked over coffee, fried eggs, and toast, and decided we'd fly in to the airport even though we had enough time to drive. Once Chopper Deke flew Traffic Monitor Joey out for the morning traffic report, and after I presented the morning drive-time news broadcast, I'd take the Jeep to Gran's.

Then he dropped a bombshell. "I want to buy your grandmother's car. I'll pay you two grand."

That didn't seem like enough money, even for a fifty-year-old classic, but Teensy and I needed cash and I couldn't imagine Daddy wanting anything to do with an old car; and Gran's Cadillac had always irritated the living daylights out of me from the time children finger-pointed at it on those inevitable days when she had to drive me to school in it.

"Five thousand, and it's yours."

Chopper Deke grinned. "Sweet."

Feeling guilty about disrupting Chopper Deke's life by taking over his house, I said, "I know my friends and I are a lot of extra work, but we'll be out of your hair soon enough. I promise."

"I know." He looked at me slitty-eyed.

"What do you mean by that?"

"I'm saying you probably already used up seven of your nine lives."

"You don't think I'll live through this?"

"Look, toots, I like you or I wouldn't have let you and your pussy posse commandeer my digs. But the truth is, no. You've been lucky so far, but I don't expect your luck to hold out. That, and you just don't have the necessary survival skills to go up against professionals."

"But you taught us how to use guns."

"It takes a lot more than guns to stay alive. Y'all need boot camp."

"Then give us boot camp."

"Too late. Boot camp should've started a year ago. Now you're operating on auto-pilot and your fuel tank's almost empty." Chopper Deke often put things into perspective using

267

aeronautical metaphors.

"I'm a quick study. We all are."

He let out a derisive grunt. "You're a damned debutante. Y'all think like a bunch of debutantes."

My chin corrugated. "I want to live." Tears beaded along the rims of my eyes. I double-dog-dared myself not to cry. "And I'm not just a debutante. I'm a Daughter of the Republic of Texas. I'm a seventh-generation Texan, and my ancestors fought at the Alamo." My chest swelled. "They stepped over the line when Colonel William Barrett Travis drew a line in the dirt with his sword. What do you say to that?"

"It's a start."

In an ideal world, I would've flown to the TV station in the Cessna with Chopper Deke, but Dawn woke up and wanted to go, too, so we agreed to take her and her imaginary friends with us. Then Venice wanted to come along. She'd left her bag of textiles behind the day we abandoned Gran's house, and she needed to retrieve it in order to do her design work. Dawn just wanted to tag along to ruin my life.

Before going on-air as Pixy Merriweather, subbing-in for Dainty Prescott, I pulled Venice aside and had a little talk with her.

"I don't know how long we'll be stuck with Dawn, but it'd sure make things easier if you'd take an interest in her. Teach her how to do makeup. Fix her hair. Maybe keep her out of my hair."

"I don't like her."

"Nobody does. But I think something bad happened to her a long time ago, and I'm pretty sure that's why she split off into different personalities. The only personality I want to see today is Dawn. Not Boris. Not the Vietnamese ho. Not anybody else. So would you please help me out here?"

Venice grudgingly agreed. While I reported the news, she and

Dawn went to wardrobe and tried on clothing donated by our sponsors, and experimented with makeup. When I walked in on them an hour or so later, Venice was applying eye shadow to Dawn's lids, and they were both giggling like schoolgirls. They swiveled their heads when they heard me come in.

I considered Dawn's well-tweezed eyebrows an improvement. They certainly looked better than the time I let Amanda wax my brows and got to look super-surprised until they grew out. "Dawn, you look so pretty. Venice, you did a great job."

"It wasn't me," Venice said. "She's kind of a natural beauty."

Dawn blushed. "Really?"

"Really," we both said in unison.

Midmorning, I chalked up the beginning of the day as a success and gave them the option of going to Gran's with me. Secretly, I hoped one of them would come along, but the one I wanted to accompany me was Venice. The one who agreed to go with me was Dawn.

We made small talk on the drive over until my phone chimed with a message. I fumbled in my purse and dug out my phone, only to find that the message came from Teensy, and was *not* meant for *moi*.

Reminder to Teensy: *If you're going to be sexting on your phone, at least have the common decency to dial the correct phone number.*

On the heels of that thought, I formulated a second aide-mémoire to Teensy: *Just because the thought automatically pops into your brain doesn't mean it has to jump-start your tongue. Even toasters have settings before the bread has time to brown.*

I snapped the phone shut and made a mental checklist for when we arrived at Gran's.

Venice told me I'd find her textile bag in Teensy's room, which was also where I figured we'd select clothes for Dawn and the others since we were all roughly the same size.

At the big iron gate, I stopped to check the brick mailbox.

Circulars and bank statements had started piling up, and I
made a mental note to have Gran's neighborhood post office
hold the mail for a week. While waiting for the gate to swing
open, I rifled through junk mail, magazines, letters, bills, and a
package. She'd clearly ordered this prior to the cruise so I ripped
it open.

Surprise. A dildo.

My grandmother had ordered a sex toy. How fortuitous that
it arrived in a timely fashion, just a few days after we held her
memorial service at Le Jardin de Loire. I quickly shoved it back
into the box so Dawn wouldn't see. Assuming she did see, at
least she had the good manners to pretend not to notice, so I
figured she'd learned the art of discretion during the short time
we'd been shotgun married to each other.

Not wanting to spend more time than I had to inside Gran's
house; and knowing Dawn had a tendency to be easily side-
tracked, I suggested she stay in the Jeep and wait for me.

"You don't trust me."

"I trust you fine," I said. But I was thinking, *Not fine.* "I just
don't want to spend a lot of time here so if you'll wait in the
Jeep, I'll run in and pack what we need."

She reluctantly agreed, and I gathered the mail together, took
it inside the house, and set it on the marble-topped console
near the front door, next to *The Watchtower* issues Gran found
twist-tied to the gate. To be sure, Gran didn't like the Jehovah's
Witnesses, but she kept *The Watchtower* pamphlets in a little
stack to give to the Mormons in case they slipped in.

As soon as I walked inside, the hair stood up on the back of
my neck. I distinctly recalled setting the security alarm after the
fire in Gran's bedroom. Now, the tiny light bar glowed green, as
if it had never been set at all.

I proceeded cautiously through an eerily quiet house.

When I went for the first landline, the one near the baby

grand in the rotunda, it was dead.

I rationalized this away by telling myself that the storm had probably knocked out the power lines. I didn't think phone lines relied on electricity, but convincing myself that they did made me feel better. Then realization dawned. The alarm panel had a green bar on it, so that worked. And I could see the faint glow of a lamp through several rooms. This, I justified by reminding myself that Amanda had come from that part of the house during the fire.

She'd probably left it on. I'd extinguish it on the way out.

Upstairs, I went through Teensy's closet like a marauding vandal, pulling out clothing that I thought would look good on each of my friends, and picked out the smallest things in my sister's wardrobe for Amanda. I hurriedly stuffed these items in a sturdy cloth carry-on, including Venice's textile bag, which I found next to the nightstand. I also came across Teensy's old Walkman and put in new batteries. Upon closer examination, I saw that she'd swiped one of my favorite CDs and stuck it in the CD player, so I hooked it onto my waistband and nestled the ear fobs into my ears. Listening to music and head-bobbing to my favorite track, I shut Teensy's door and stepped out onto the landing.

From my position at the top of the stairs, I paused to get my footing before taking my first step.

A shadow fell across the opening off the marble rotunda where I'd seen the light on.

I froze in my tracks and yanked out the earbuds. Tinny strains of music filtered out. My heart drummed in my chest as my mind tried to talk myself out of what I'd seen. I carefully set the bag of clothes down beside me before shutting off the CD player.

Then a second shadow swept across the doorway.

My heart beat so loudly, I could actually hear it hammering between my ears. Then a *très, très* bad thing happened. My mind unexpectedly played a trick on me. In the most fleeting of seconds, I thought I heard my dead grandmother's warbly, bird-like voice insisting that she'd been on a cruise and didn't know anyone named Venice Hanover, nor where to find her.

I didn't know whether to scream with joy or stroke out from terror.

Since Gran was dead, I even considered I might actually be dead. If so, I had no recollection of it happening. I finally talked myself off the ledge by convincing myself that I hallucinated this. Then I took Chopper Deke's advice: *Don't try to make sense out of crazy unless you want to become crazy yourself.*

The sound of flesh striking flesh made me wince.

Definitely not a hallucination.

My grandmother's painful cry and the hard crash of her fall suggested she'd hit her head against the library table that had once belonged to my grandfather.

I found myself in the grip of a revulsion so deep that it petri-fied me.

Somehow, I gathered the strength to rip myself from the clutches of fear and creep down to the far end of the hall, to Gran's burned-out bedroom. I covertly opened the door and stepped inside. Acrid smoke from charred wood burned my eyes. I opened the drawer to the nightstand, but the gun had been removed. Despite searching places I thought my grand-mother might've stashed a pistol, I found nothing.

I emerged from the room with great stealth and looked the distance of the hallway before creeping back to the landing. Descending several steps, I peered deeper into the parlor off of the rotunda and glimpsed Gran from the knees down. Dressed in the taupe-colored knit dress that I'd often seen her wear to the country club for midweek bridge games, she had matching Ferragamos on her feet and a Ferragamo handbag in her lap. Leather gloves from the same neutral color palette were folded over the metal purse frame. She sat in a silent daze, in one of the eighteenth-century Philadelphia chairs that she refused to let anyone else sit in, and offered no resistance.

With my hand lightly grazing the mahogany bannister, I took several more steps in the scant hope that I could make it to the front door and out to the Jeep. I hadn't informed Chopper Deke that I'd taken to carrying his unregistered pistol in my purse during the few times we left his property. I neglected to tell him because I didn't think he'd approve since none of us had concealed handgun licenses, or as we Texans liked to call it, a "permit to carry."

In the next few steps, my grandmother would notice me and I wondered if she'd betray me with a glance when I came into view. I stepped down onto the next tread. By now, she could see my feet if she looked past the entrance to the parlor and into the rotunda.

So far, so good.

I took another step. She could probably see my knees.

I descended another step. Five to go. If I made a mad dash, I'd make too much noise. I could probably leap the steps if I had to, but I couldn't outrun the bullet that would surely follow.

My eyes flickered to the front door. For no good reason, my mind played another trick on me. I could've sworn I'd seen the latch turn. As the door gently swung open enough to cast a sweep of light across the marble floor, I watched, helplessly rooted in place. Dread filled my soul.

God help me, it's Dawn.

Dawn saw me on the stairs. When I made good eye contact with her, I put my finger to my lips. She nodded understanding. Motioning her to go back to the Jeep, I held up my fingers, *Nine, one, one.* Like a game of charades, I molded my hand into a telephone and held it, briefly, up to my ear.

My entire body wilted as she stayed put and carefully closed the door behind her. Such a move wasn't exactly a strong mental-wellness benchmark. Obviously, Dawn was younger and hadn't considered how much it hurt to be shot, so she shrugged off the danger. This was the only reason I could come up with on short notice to explain her bad judgment. Well that, and her mental illness.

At the exact same time the door closed, I was thinking, *Oh, dear Lord, let this be the onset of a delusion from schizophrenia.* I might have to ramrod this debacle all by myself.

I took another step to get a better view.

Part of me wanted to bitch-slap Dawn into oblivion. She'd had the perfect chance to save us by running back to the Jeep and calling the police, and she didn't take it. Now we'd all probably die.

I took another step. If I shifted my weight, the tread might creak. With no lights on in the rotunda, the glow from the parlor lamp would throw my shadow behind me, where they couldn't readily see it.

In the end, it wasn't my grandmother who betrayed me, but the weight of my body on the next tread. The wrenching sound beneath my foot was enough for my grandmother's head to snap up in recognition—and for the gunman to notice and turn around.

The only words that I managed to choke out were not meant for my grandmother, but, rather, for the man in black with a deep groove across his forehead who held her at gunpoint.

"You're alive."

CHAPTER TWENTY-FIVE

The man holding my grandmother at gunpoint had the kind of face you screamed at when it jumped out at you in horror flicks; or when it emerged unexpectedly when the curtain ripped back while you showered; or when in the throes of a dengue-induced fever; or when a form you didn't notice as you first entered the alley suddenly stepped out of the shadows and into your path after it was too late to run in the other direction. He had a wide, square face, murky caiman eyes of an indeterminate color—the kind governed by the shade of clothing worn nearest them—ruthless lips, thick caveman-like bone structure protruding above bushy eyebrows, and a deep groove across his forehead that required many staples to close it. The only thing missing to complete the Frankenstein look were a couple of bolts sticking out of the sides of his neck and a tattered, ill-fitting tweed jacket to pull his whole outfit together.

We had instant recognition because we'd met when I left my calling card across his face.

My voice went flat. "How'd you get here?"

My suspicion that the lodge men somehow managed to attach a transponder to Gran's car or my Porsche was short-lived. The assumption was that Gran had called my cell phone—not the disposable one—without knowing that the lodge men were after me, and that was her undoing.

The man whose head I grooved raised his voice to me. "Get down here."

I borrowed a line from Melville's *Bartelby the Scrivener*. "I would prefer not to."

"Perhaps you'd rather I killed your grandmother?"

My gaze flickered to Gran. Delft blue eyes weren't shrouded by fear; they merely held me, spellbound in their grip, as if she were trying to communicate with me without words. The spell quickly lifted when Gran closed her eyes. I studied the parchment folds of her eyelids in the room's pale glow, and after a long silence, she opened eyes as clear and glittery as glacier ice.

I sensed things were about to get worse. Sure enough, they did.

A second gunman stepped out of the shadows and stood closer to Gran.

"Since you put it that way . . ." Looking over at my grandmother, I gave her a heartfelt apology. "Hi, Gran. I'm so sorry," as I slunk down the rest of the stairs, across the rotunda, and closer to the doorway. Off to the side, beyond the men's view, Dawn's well-tweezed brows furrowed in undisguised panic. Then her face grew taut. She held up her hand like a traffic cop and mouthed "Stop," when I came within a few feet from the entry to the parlor. For reasons unbeknownst to me, I froze.

Gran kept a Doré candelabra with eight candleholders in the rotunda, and featured it atop the eighteenth-century console that held *The Watchtower* pamphlets. The candelabra served two purposes: one, its beauty; two, in case of a power failure, Gran could light the area.

Confused, I glimpsed Dawn lighting one of the candles out of the corner of my eye. As the man threatened me with his gun, she raised the burning candle to the fire alarm. All out of stall tactics, I had no choice but to take another step. I even tried to make myself vomit to disgust him, and to buy time.

The fire alarm went off.

Instead of moving into the room with Gran, I screamed,

"Fire!" at the top of my lungs.

That's when Frankenstein stepped out of the doorway. His hand shot out and grabbed me by the arm.

That's also when Dawn dented his face in with the burning candelabra.

Wrenching free from his grasp, I dismissed the gunshot I thought I'd heard, but not the splintering antique table next to where my grandmother stood.

Taking a backward step, I ignored my grandmother's harpy shrieks, berating the "clumsy oaf" for breaking "a gift from my husband on our wedding day," punctuated by profanity I'd never heard her use before. All the while, I watched Boris beat the living daylights out of Frankenstein.

First, Boris karate-chopped his arm. The gun clunked to the floor and went into a slide. In a mad scramble, I followed it under the baby grand. My sweat-dampened fingers missed the first time I grappled for it. By the time I retrieved it, Boris had karate-chopped Frankenstein's windpipe. When the monster clutched his throat and wheezed for breath, Boris kneed him in the testicles. Finally, Boris delivered the *coup de gras,* violently shoving the heel of his hand against Frankenstein's nose, driving it up into his skull.

The frightening *pop* of cartilage and the *crack* of broken bones echoed through the room. The whole encounter needed speech balloons—that graphic convention used in comic strips for readers to understand what the character was thinking or feeling. The first speech bubble attributed to Frankenstein could've read: *"WTF?"*

Standing near the stairs with Frankenstein's crosshatched Glock in my grip, I looked into the parlor and saw the second gunman, face-down, on the floor. But like every horror movie you've ever seen, he suddenly rose like a pop-up target.

The next gunshot traveled through the second gunman, then

through the rotunda, and blew out the hundred-year-old beveled mirror in the next room. My grandmother had risen from her antique chair, taken aim, and capped him again as he dropped to his knees. As I briefly noted that she did *not* use the Weaver stance, as taught to me by Chopper Deke, she fired again.

The third gunshot exploded with a heavy crack, louder and sharper than the first two and every bit as devastating, as if the devil from hell had lifted the entire pink granite stone known to Texans as Enchanted Rock and smashed it against the world's largest glass tabletop. The Baccarat chandelier hanging in the center of the rotunda's ceiling shuddered above the blast.

The fourth round blew Frankenstein back against the curved staircase. He bounced off the spindles and collapsed onto the floor. When he raised his bloody head, my grandmother shot him again. Blood pooled beside him, like red paint, inching closer to where I stood.

Frankenstein begged my grandmother not to shoot him anymore. Entranced, Dawn and I watched and waited for the outcome.

My grandmother, a gentle woman of good breeding and impeccable manners, has never been a pushover. "Get out of my house, you son of a bitch."

Possibly, I'd heard her use a curse word before, although she'd once conceded that she'd let out a string of profanity giving birth to my father. Cursing was so un-Rubanbleu and not permitted in the Prescott family. And yet . . .

I rather liked this new side to my grandmother.

Frankenstein took labored breaths. "Can't . . . move. Need . . . ambulance."

"Should've thought about that before you came in here trying to hurt my granddaughter and me." She cut her eyes to Dawn. "And her friend, you son of a bitch."

"Don't . . . let me . . . die . . . please." Sprawled out on the floor, he remained motionless, but Gran still kept a two-handed grip on her Smith as she drew closer.

Keeping the gun pointed at his head, Gran glided into the room with the grace of royalty. "Dainty, check him for weapons." She motioned with the gun as if it were an extension of her own finger.

I took a step toward him. His ice-pick glare narrowed. His lips thinned into an ugly gash.

Seeing this, Gran said, "Do not think for one second I won't kill you if you so much as flinch. There's over an acre of land to this estate, and the ground's moist from the rain and snow. My granddaughter and her friend can dig a hole, and nobody will ever know what happened to either of you. Understand, son of a bitch?"

"Please . . . help me. I . . . beg you."

"Like I begged the two of you not to hurt me? You were going to murder me. And my granddaughter." Her gun hand never wavered. "And her friends. Perhaps I should show you the same courtesy?"

"Please . . . ma'am. Mercy . . . have mercy . . . on me."

"He cut the telephone lines," I said. "Want me to get my cell phone and call the police?"

"No," she said casually, as if I'd asked whether she wanted another cherry cordial from the box. "I want you to make sure he doesn't have any more weapons on him."

Then she shot me a look of utter disappointment. Or maybe shock. It was hard to tell. Gran's a hard person to rattle.

"And after that, I want you to take his arms"—she said this to Dawn, and then swiveled her head back to me—"and I want you to take his feet, and I want y'all to drag him outside where he can bleed on the snow instead of staining my marble floor . . . if that's all right with you, you son of a bitch."

Then she looked over at the other gunman. The gunman who

wasn't moving, not even to breathe.

"Well, hell," she said, "that other son of a bitch ruined my Persian rug. We'll just see about that."

CHAPTER TWENTY-SIX

Gran announced that she'd take care of the mess and shooed us out of the rotunda. I two-stepped around the gore on the marble floor and raced toward the kitchen with Dawn in my wake. Then Gran chastised me for not being a proper hostess and offering Dawn so much as a simple lunch of tomato basil soup and a ham sandwich. Really? Tomato basil soup? Was she kidding? Why not just throw a Vlad the Impaler theme party?

I doubted either of us happened to be in a mood to eat, so sue me.

Normally, my grandmother would've called in the help to clean up the mess. But ever since the economic downturn, the maid's and gardener's schedules dwindled from six days a week to three. And this wasn't Lydia's day to work. Which turned out to be a blessing, since I kept thinking about that old "two can keep a secret if one of them is dead" adage, and reluctantly conceded that there were already three of us.

Gran kept trying to engage Dawn in conversation while I silently begged Dawn to keep her trap shut. Or, Boris to keep *his* mouth shut. I really didn't know who Gran and I stood next to at that moment, because Dawn's face seemed to be undergoing a conversion—and not in a good way. Pretending to be normal must be draining for her.

Gran noticed me massaging my aching wrist and insisted that I go to one of those doc-in-a-box clinics to have it X-rayed. If nothing else, getting out of her house would clear my head and give me time to think about our next move, so I was only too happy to leave. Boris came with me.

I wanted to call Bruckman, so I rummaged through my purse until I touched the phone. I figured he'd be behind his desk, mainlining an IV of coffee through his vein.

When he came on the line, he was all business. "Major crimes, Detective Bruckman."

"Hey, gorgeous and talented. I'm checking in to see how things are going." I left off the last part of my sentence, the "with us" part.

"Pixy Merriweather? Really, Dainty? Do you really think people won't know it's you?"

"It's worked so far."

"Proving, once again, that Channel Eighteen viewers are gullible halfwits."

"So if you know about Pixy Merriweather, then you watched the show."

"Yes. No. No, I did *not* watch your morning broadcast."

"*A-ha.* Then how do you know I was on TV this morning?"

"I'm not going there, Dainty. Did you file a police report?"

"About that . . . I didn't file one because that Texas Ranger's handling the case."

"If somebody did something to you in this county, this county has jurisdiction, not your Texas Ranger friend." He greased that last word with a sneer. I may not have seen it, but I certainly sensed it coming across the air waves. "Dainty," he said through a sigh, "you frustrate the hell out of me. I have to go. I have a meeting. File the report."

"I'll do it after I talk to—"

He cut me off in the middle of my sentence. "Remember, you're only my current girlfriend. File the damned report."

The phone went dead in my hand.

I looked over at Boris. He said, "Men. Can't live with 'em . . ."

Finishing his sentence, I simultaneously chimed in. "Can't live without 'em."

Then he said, "Got any money? I'm hungry."

"How can you even think about food?"

Boris said, "A man's still gotta eat."

I spotted a fast-food place up ahead and pulled into the drive-through. We inched up to the squawk box and I ordered a diet drink for myself and Boris ordered a combo. That's when I changed my order and added a sandwich. After I paid at the window, I handed Boris the grease-stained sack meant for him. Before we left the parking lot, he ripped into his meal with the intensity of a wild animal. While waiting at the mouth of the fast-food exit, I reached into the sack meant for me and pulled out my snack. Seeing I had time to take a bite out of my machine-formed rib sandwich before merging into traffic, I folded back the paper wrap and chowed down.

I took one bite out of my compressed pork sandwich and pitched the rest out the window, to a dog seated next to a bus bench. Only after the dog pulled the old lady off the bench did I realize I'd thrown my meal at a service canine—specifically, a seeing-eye dog.

"Bet the old lady didn't see that coming," Boris deadpanned.

"Do you think she's hurt?"

"Have no idea."

I curbed the Jeep and wrenched it into park. Leaving Boris in the Jeep with the engine running, I ran over to the old lady and helped her up off the sidewalk and eased her back onto the bench. Offering profuse apologies, I dusted off her dress. Over vehement protests, she told me to get away from her. The bus pulled up. When I asked if she'd let me help her up the bus steps, she dripped acid assuring me that I'd helped enough.

Humiliated, I climbed back into the Jeep. People in nearby cars, waiting for the traffic signal to change, turned and watched intently. I'd never had so many enraged faces staring at me before. In shame, I glanced away, only to make eye contact with two more horrified commuters.

My chance encounter with the blind lady made me feel guilty and filled me with shame. I got stuck at a red light for ten minutes on a deserted stretch of road near a construction zone and used the time to replay the events over and over in my mind, before I realized that not only was I looking at the wrong light, but the light I kept thinking was broken was actually a stop sign.

I glanced over at Boris. "Thanks for what you did."

His eyes were as narrow as coin slots. "There's a place for me in Dawn's life—just so you know. I've known her a lot longer than you have."

"I don't mean to appear ungrateful. You saved our lives back there, and I'll always be beholden to you. But you have to go now."

"Why?"

"Because the police will come. It's better if Dawn can truthfully say she knows nothing about what happened. Don't you see? All she'll remember is waiting for me out in the Jeep."

We entered a virtually empty lobby at the doc-in-a-box, so I stood at the counter and filled out the paperwork at my leisure. Then, the only other person in the waiting room, a man wearing a jaunty red wool beret and leaning on a carved wooden cane, approached the counter, pulled me aside, and described to me in graphic detail how his nuts swelled after his vasectomy.

Harsh truths should be sugar-coated.

I refluffed my hair and, with professional detachment, told the receptionist in no uncertain terms that I absolutely had to be seen next, no matter what. She told me, in no uncertain terms, that I absolutely had to wait my turn, no matter what. The syphilitic whore.

"Well, I never." I said with a sniff of unsuitability and finished filling out the paperwork under her accusatory watch. Fortunately, a nurse stuck her head out an interior door and called my name.

I handed Boris a tattered magazine to amuse himself while the doc-in-a-box treated me. "There's an article about one of the Kardashians in there that you might find interesting."

"What's a Kardashian?"

"It's a form of succubus."

Back in one of the treatment rooms, they gave me pain medication. It made me loopy, but then the painkiller wore off and I thought how nice it'd be if the nurse would escort Boris out of the room so I could rest. Then I realized Boris was waiting for me out in the lobby, and I wished my mother could somehow come back to Teensy and me. And then I promised myself I wouldn't let what Nerissa did to our family make me bitter. And then I tried to capture the spider monkeys as they bounced off the walls and knocked over the instrument tray.

I knew better than to drive myself back to Gran's house, so I reluctantly turned the wheel over to Boris and dozed. I didn't realize he'd gone away until we returned to my grandmother's estate and Dawn shook me awake.

"What's going on, Dainty?"

"What?" Still groggy, it took a few seconds to realize I might actually be sitting next to the real Dawn—not Boris or Kim Ho. I came out of my stupor and looked around, focusing on my surroundings in the event the fourth man popped up from behind Gran's marble David statue. Everything came rushing back to me as the sense that something was out of place gradually registered in my mind. I sat, perplexed, wondering why Gran's estate looked idyllic and breathtaking when I'd fully expected to see strobing red and blue emergency beacons flashing from the visibars of police cars. And there seemed to be a serious absence of yellow Day-Glo crime-scene tape.

"What am I doing?" Dawn glanced around too, until her gaze rested on her hands—hands still gripping the steering wheel. "Am I driving? How'd that happen? Chopper Deke told me I couldn't drive any of his vehicles, and if I did, he threatened to prosecute me to the fullest extent of the law."

"You're not driving. You're sitting behind the wheel."

"Good." She heaved a relieved sigh. "Because the last thing I want is to piss off Chopper Deke."

"Make him angry," I corrected her. "The last thing you want to do is make him angry. When you're a debutante, you're always in training. Always."

"Sorry."

Dawn started to annoy me again. Not so much that I wanted to feed her to the neighbor's dog, but enough to make me analyze why I preferred Boris's company to hers.

Twisting in my seat to face her, I changed the subject. "I want you to stay put while I go inside."

"But I want to come with you. I can carry stuff."

I felt like roadkill and could've used her help, but I said, "No," and leveled with her. *Sort of.* So sue me. Being around people with more than one identity was new to me. Dawn had at least two strong personalities rattling around inside of her, and each one told me a different story. And neither of them communicated with each other to get their stories straight.

I reasoned with her. "I'd rather you wait for me out here. I found out my grandmother's actually alive." Dawn mimed an expression that fell somewhere between happy and awestruck. "Gran's been through an awful tragedy, so I'd like to speak to her alone. Please?"

"Sure," she meekly obliged. "Go ahead. I'll be right here."

"One more thing"—because I was starting to realize that no matter what happened, there would always be "one more thing" as long as Dawn stuck around—"if you see any of those men, lay on the horn. I mean honk for dear life."

She'd placed her dove-white hands around the steering wheel at the ten and two positions. When she dropped them into her lap, I noticed that her knuckles were swollen and bloody, like the work-roughened hands of a cotton picker. She followed the trajectory of my gaze and saw the crimson streaks, too.

"Oh, no. I'm hurt. How'd that happen?" She held up her hands to inspect the damage.

"You don't remember?" I asked as a test.

She shook her head.

"Don't rub it. And don't get blood on your clothes." I told her this not because blood's hard to get out of fabric, but because I realized by doing so, the police might seize her clothing and tag it as evidence when they, most certainly, came to arrest us all. Then I thought, *That's what you're worried about? You're not worried that one of those men might have AIDS?* "I'll bring antiseptic and gauze. We'll get you fixed up good as new. But you probably need a tetanus shot."

"You're so sweet, Dainty. You're such a good person. And, no, I'm not getting a shot."

But I was thinking, *Holy cow, life with Dawn just keeps getting creepier and creepier.*

I anticipated that, at some point, Gran would come out to the Jeep to thank Dawn for her part in saving our lives, and I figured it'd be wise to nip that conversation in the bud before it ever took place.

"You know, Dawn, my grandmother's not as sharp as she used to be. She often gets confused." Dawn did a little head bob, and I went on. "So if she should talk about things that, oh, say, don't make sense, just go along with it, please?

"Sure. It's the least I can do for you helping me get ready for the ball." Dawn stared off into the distance as if she'd seen a ghost. Her face went pale and her lips, paler. Her voice dropped to an eerie softness. "I thought he'd die when I switched his medication. I knew he was allergic and I thought it'd kill him. But, no, the ambulance came and got him and he got better and came back home."

Plot twist.

Did she just say what I think she said?

The confession Dawn made was jaw-dropping. Was this the "Dawn" from high school, or a younger elementary school version of Dawn, or even another personality I had yet to meet? I seemed to have lost the capacity for revulsion. Was she referring to Avery, or someone else? I studied her with the intensity of a scientist pouring highly volatile solutions into beakers.

She sighed deeply. Then she made direct eye contact and I saw that her eyes were clear and focused. I continued to stare in disbelief.

Fresh from her altered state, she reared back her head and said, "What?" as if she'd caught me boring a hole through her with my eyes. Which I had been.

My heart raced. "What?"

"What? I asked you first. Why're you looking at me that way?"

"Did I really hear you say what I *think* you just said?"

"What'd I say? I already told you I'd play along with your nutty grandmother."

"Is that all?"

"*You* tell *me*."

"Can I ask you a question?" Too tired to worry about being rebuked, I asked, "Where'd you learn to speak Vietnamese?"

She leveled her sapphire gaze at me. "I don't speak Vietnamese. Whatever gave you that idea?"

"Do you know any Vietnamese people?"

She did a one-shoulder shrug. "I used to have a Vietnamese nanny."

This tidbit of information, when dropped into the proper puzzle place, made sense as to how the Kim Ho personality knew the language.

"Do you know a lady—or man—named Kim Ho?"

"No. Why're you asking me these questions? Is that someone from high school?" She gave a slow head shake. "Because I don't remember a whole lot about high school."

"Never mind. Look, just sit tight. I'll be back with antiseptic for your cuts."

She glanced down at her hands, still stymied as to how they got that way. I got out of the Jeep, dreading what horror I'd find inside Gran's house. I steeled my nerves, fully expecting to be called on to help clean up the bloodbath.

The moment I entered through the front door and stepped into the rotunda, the strong odor of bleach burned my nostrils and made my eyes water. What I saw had all the spookiness of watching a horror movie in reverse: Blood that had pooled beneath Frankenstein's body had disappeared, and the marble floor now sparkled. The parlor hardwoods gleamed as if a magic wand had been waved over them, and everything vile about the morning's experience went *poof.*

The only residue of what happened in this mansion could be felt in the lingering memory of that traumatic event. I'd be lucky if Boris and I—and maybe even Gran—didn't end up in the county psyche ward, diagnosed with post-traumatic stress disorder.

My eyes itched so badly from the odor of caustic solutions that'd been used in the room that I wanted to claw them out of my head. In the deafening silence, I called out for Gran.

Nothing.

Having gotten all the clothes and Venice's textile bag loaded into the Jeep, it looked like the only thing left to do was to sit in our wind tunnel and listen to the white noise that had taken over the downstairs since the fire.

I called out for Gran again. She'd gone upstairs, presumably to her bedroom to change clothes, because she no longer had on the taupe dress when I noticed her staring down at me from the top of the landing. Sporting a jaunty track suit and athletic shoes that looked like they needed to go straight into the washing machine, she saw me in the middle of the rotunda—*the very spic and span, spotless rotunda*—and descended the stairs with her hand lightly grazing the bannister.

From the time I was a small child until I went away to college, memories of Gran, elegant and self-assured as she glided down the sweeping staircase without ever glancing down at the steps to check her footing, filled my head. No longer confident of an old person's balance, her eyes flickered to each tread, then looked back up, before she stepped down onto it.

Fearful and uneasy, I glanced around. The bloody mess had been thoroughly cleaned, but I couldn't help but speculate how the blood spatter pattern might look under the purple glow of a UV lamp. In my mind, I had it worked out that the smear would coat the wall like a poor reproduction of Van Gogh's "Starry Night." Even the shattered glass in the dining room had been vacuumed up. Aside from the killers, the only things missing from the house were the Persian rug in the parlor and the antique birdcage piecrust table my grandfather gave Gran as a wedding present. I assumed she'd taken the beautiful tilt-top table to the back porch with the expectation that it could be repaired. As for the Persian rug, I assumed she'd wrapped the bodies in it.

Seeing no one else in the house with us, I returned my attention to my grandmother. "Where are those men?"

"I have a better question." She pinned me with her stare.

"Where are all my clothes?"

"Your clothes," I said dully.

"Yes. My clothes."

"We sold them at a consignment boutique."

I didn't think it was possible for her voice to spiral up another octave, but it did. I considered that her shrieks probably sounded like Pterodactyls from the Jurassic period of the Mesozoic era. It seemed a crying shame that my camera phone wasn't fully charged so I could video this and send it to Bruckman in the coming days; maybe show him what he missed while he went bow hunting at the deer lease with his buddies, filled his buck tag, drank beer, and grilled steaks around a campfire. Then I realized I'd zoned-out and blocked out part of my grandmother's rampage, so I tuned back in. Really, this was the only way I could stand to be around her for long periods of time. Either that or take up binge drinking.

"I spent a lifetime collecting those clothes. I have Chanel suits that were made for me *by the woman herself.* And my shoes—where are they? I've been collecting Ferragamos since college, and now they're gone. Irreplaceable. What the damned hell happened to my belongings, Dainty?"

Taking a deep breath, I delivered the answer in a hyperventilating rush. "We sold them."

She raised her hands to the air while seemingly questioning the ceiling. "Why would you dimwits do that?"

I leveled with her. "Remember when I went to Mexico and you sold my Porsche and gave my clothes to Teensy because I had a two-million-dollar bounty on my head? And you didn't think I'd make it back alive; and you didn't want to have to go through the hassle of probate court, to get the court's permission to sell my car?" This was a perfect example of how sarcasm worked in our family; I paused long enough to let my words soak in. "Well, Gran, there you have it. We thought you drowned at sea. We even held a memorial service for you."

"You have a lot of explaining to do, starting with my bed-room."

"I'll be happy to talk to you about your bedroom. But first, where are those men?"

"I wouldn't worry about it."

"You wouldn't worry about it?"

"No, I wouldn't if I were you. And I wouldn't talk it up, either." She oiled her next sentence with a sneer. "Everything's fine, and we just need to let sleeping dogs lie."

I'd become drunk on confusion and whatever medication they'd given me at the doc-in-a-box, so a bit of lag time passed before my mind caught up. "No, wait. You have to tell me."

"Fine." Which was Gran's way of saying *not so fine*. "Here's what happened. I told them to leave and showed them the door."

"You told them to leave?"

"Yes. And they did."

No matter how I tried to process this information, it still registered "tilt" on the murder pinball machine. "They just left?" I mentally dusted away the cobwebs in my brain, and when her explanation was no clearer, I shook my head with the vigor of a wet dog.

"Fine. It wasn't quite that simple." She huffed out a defeated sigh. "While they were lying on the floor, I made a phone call to a hit man I know."

"You know a hit man?" My blue-haired, blueblood grand-mother—a doyenne of The Rubanbleu—knew a hit man? I did another wet-dog headshake. "Seriously, you know a hit man?"

"Actually, I know several."

"I don't want to hear anymore."

"Yes, you do. If you didn't, you wouldn't have asked. First, I took their IDs off them. Then I called a hit man and told him I'd pay a million dollars if he'd kill them both for me. After the hit man negotiated the price up to two million, I told those men to get out of my house and never come back. And they left."

I don't know why it made me suddenly want to climb the walls knowing that WBFD-TV and the rest of the local stations might end up covering this incident as "breaking news." It didn't bother me before. But now I had wild images of injured psychopaths riding around in taxis, looking for hospitals, and in the end, the injuries they sustained would be traced back to this house.

Nail, meet coffin.

"How'd they leave?"

"Leaking like sieves."

"No, Gran, what method of transportation did they take?" Under my breath, I muttered, *Please, God, don't let it be a taxi.*

"Mr. Spencer let them off a few blocks from the hospital."

"Old Man Spencer's alive?"

"Why yes, dear. Did you sell his belongings, too?"

CHAPTER TWENTY-SEVEN

While searching the medicine cabinet for antiseptic and gauze, I did a mental head count. If one of the killers had been admitted to the medical floor at the county hospital, and two others were admitted to a hospital in Dallas, that just left one to worry about. Which meant Gran couldn't safely stay here.

Having contacted a cleaning crew to improve on what she'd already done in the rotunda and the parlor, and having contacted a restoration specialist to start reconstruction in her bedroom, my blue-haired grandmother trailed me out to the Jeep. I wasn't able to convince her that the electric blanket caught fire so I pulled out a copy of the fire department's report from my purse and gave it to her.

"See?" I pointed out the proper paragraph. "It says that the homeowner—that's you, Gran—likely left the electric blanket on low after leaving on vacation, and that's why your room burned. Sorry."

"Sounds fishy to me."

"Call the fire chief. You should definitely get to the bottom of this." *Definitely not.* "I've given this a lot of thought, and I think you should check into a spa for a week. After what you've been through, you deserve the royal treatment. And while you're gone, get Lydia to come in while a paint crew repaints the rotunda."

"I don't want the rotunda repainted."

"Oh, I think you do." I sent her an eye-encrypted look that

telepathically suggested she get the painters to use several coats of a good brand of combination-primer-and-stain-blocker, especially on the "Starry Night" section of wall.

Then Gran turned to Dawn. "Thank you, dear, for saving our lives today."

"What?"

I shot Dawn a wicked glare. And since Gran had her back to me, I reminded Dawn of our earlier conversation by twirling my index finger around my ear in the universal "crazy" motion.

Dawn nodded understanding. "It was nothing, Mrs. Prescott."

Then Gran said, "You really should sue the plastic surgeon who did your nose job."

My mouth dropped open.

Dawn said, "Beg your pardon? This is the nose I was born with."

"Oh. Really? Well . . . carry on." Gran gave the air a little wrist-flick and headed back to the house. She stopped at the base of the steps leading up to the front door and turned. "You look ridiculous in that black wig, Dainty. I know what I'm talking about."

My eyes bulged. Projecting my voice, I called out to her. "It's a persona. For TV. I'm Pixy Merriweather."

"I know. I saw you do the morning broadcast earlier, and I'm telling you, that hair looks ridiculous."

Dawn muttered, "You should listen to your grandmother. Old people are allowed to tell the truth."

Since the TV station had social media pages for each member of on-air talent, and since Rochelle had hastily compiled a presence for Pixy Merriweather, I intended to turn to the experts to see what they had to say—which, of course, was everyone following the TV station on social media.

So . . . *ha.*

The last thing I said to Gran before she closed the front door was, "I'm really glad you're alive."

The last thing she said back to me was, "Sarcasm doesn't suit you, Dainty."

On the drive over to the airplane hangar where Chopper Deke tied down his Cessna, Dawn cleaned her cut hands and wrapped them in gauze. I suggested that we not talk to Chopper Deke about what happened at my grandmother's earlier. I did this for two reasons: First, I wanted to be sure I wasn't talking to Boris; second, I wanted to be sure I was actually talking to Dawn.

"What—so your grandmother's kind of batshit?" She said this in a *meh* sort of way. "Big deal."

"No, eliminate batshit. It sounds crude, and you're going to be a debutante. Restated, my grandmother's a bit unconventional. You might even say eccentric."

"Face it. Eccentric is the word you use when you're talking about filthy-rich people who're crazier than a rat in a drainpipe."

We were bottlenecked in traffic when my cell phone went off. While Chopper Deke groused about us getting to the airport before bad weather moved in again, the driver behind us tapped his horn to motivate us into noticing that the light on the traffic signal had turned green. While we played inch-worm with the traffic bottleneck, my thoughts free-associated.

On occasion, I do my best thinking in my car with the music off, especially out on the open road. The drive back to WBFD turned out to be one of those times. I've found that when the mind can sort out the day's problems, I can usually come up with a solution.

In my head, I replayed the catastrophe in Gran's house. What didn't add up was hearing Gran tell the gunmen that she didn't know Venice Hanover. She's known Venice and her family since the two of us were in elementary school. I assumed she denied knowing Venice to protect her. The bigger question, however, was why Venice was specifically mentioned by name.

Another piece of the puzzle dropped into place.

Whatever had gone on had nothing to do with Teensy and me, and everything to do with Venice. And I intended to get to the bottom of things when we returned to Chopper Deke's house.

With three of the killers crossed off the list, I called Ranger Hill to let him know where he'd likely find those men.

Once we returned to Chopper Deke's, I encountered Teensy standing on the back porch. She had a little painter's mask in her hand and was about to slip it on. I knew she had pollen allergies so I wasn't surprised when she seated the mask over her nose and mouth.

"Don't be alarmed, I'm not going to rob anybody." She grabbed a broom propped against the side of the house.

"I'd be more alarmed if you actually swept something."

I noticed food scraps and an overturned bowl and deduced that she was trying to get rid of the evidence before Chopper Deke discovered she was putting food out to draw the rest of the feral cats up to the house.

This cemented my belief that Teensy'd moved one step closer to the crazy cat lady people read about.

"Good news, bad news," I said. "Which do you want to hear first?"

She stopped sweeping and got a stranglehold on the broom handle. "Gimme the good news."

"Gran's alive."

"Really?" Her voice shot up; blue eyes misted. "You better not be kidding, Dainty. Gran's alive?"

I nodded.

"What's the bad news?"

"Gran's alive."

"It's a miracle. And Old Man Spencer?" She fixed her expectant gaze on me.

"Alive. Enjoy the moment while you can. You're about to catch all kinds of hell now that we sold her clothes and her car."

"At least I didn't sell her car." She braced her arms across her chest. "You did."

"In for a penny, in for a pound. I'm just saying get ready."

I left her to clean up while I went in search of Venice. From the back porch, I entered the atrium, and from there, I went to the den. Since I didn't find her glued to the television, I checked the kitchen. I found her upstairs, curled into a fetal position on top of her bedspread. Twisted in sleep, her mouth emitted a thin snore.

"We need to talk." Dropping her textile bag at the foot of the bed, I took perverse delight in watching Venice's eyes pop open. I planted a fist on one hip and took a bracing breath. "You made me feel guilty, blaming me because those men came after us. And I just took it because I thought Nerissa was behind it since she doesn't want us to testify at her trial."

Stunned into silence, Venice stared, wide-eyed.

"So what do you have to say for yourself?" I demanded.

"I don't know what you're talking about. Why're you being so mean?"

Salem popped her head in the doorway for about two seconds. "Yeah, Dainty, why're you being so mean to her?"

"Stay out of it, Salem. I'm warning you." I returned my attention—and my venom—to my best friend. "You have everything to do with this, and now you're going to tell me exactly what happened twenty-four hours before you left Africa, until you got into Mr. Quincy's Suburban with us. Out with it."

"Nothing happened."

"Something happened," I insisted. "And we're going over it with a fine-toothed comb until we figure out the reason those men are trying to kill us."

We started with her last day in Africa, with me grilling her about the people she interacted with. Next, we covered more ground, discussing her wait at the airport.

"Did you see anyone suspicious?"

"I'm pretty sure I'm the one who looked suspicious to them, not the other way around. I mean—look at me—a white girl in a sea of black faces."

"Did anything happen at the airport?"

"No, not really."

"What's that supposed to mean? What happened at the airport?"

Venice insisted nothing happened. I insisted that she go over how she spent her time, step-by-step.

"Fine," she said, which I interpreted to mean *Not so fine.* "I picked up my boarding pass and I waited. My plane arrived at the gate and I got on it. I flew home. There—are you happy?"

Interrogating my best friend made me anything but happy. "Did you go through Customs?"

"Yes."

"What'd you have with you?"

"My purse, my textile bag"—her eyes cut to the tote at the foot of the bed—"and a couple of little gifts I brought back for you and Salem." Her chin tightened.

I could tell she was about to burst into tears, and I'd had my fill of crying females. For one thing, crying females don't help in a crisis. And we'd definitely moved into crisis mode.

"Did the Customs people go through your things?"

"No, they just asked me what was in the packages."

"They didn't make you open them, or declare anything?"

She shook her head. "It's fabric. Why would anyone care about cloth?"

"Let's get back to the airport. What'd you do while you were there? Did you leave your bag or your purse unattended?"

"Of course not." Clearly offended, Venice jutted her chin while simultaneously tossing her hair back over her shoulder.

I was about to launch into the next question when her expression suddenly changed. Seeing her positively shrink in size and demeanor, I confronted her. "What? You remembered something. What'd you remember?"

"Nothing. It was nothing." She shook her head. The tension in her face relaxed, but the fear never left her eyes.

"Tell me."

Salem returned in protest. "Come on, Dainty, leave her alone."

Without a word, I sauntered over to the door and shut it in her face. Then I toggled the lock. "What happened at the airport, Venice? What happened when you left your bag unattended?"

"I didn't leave it unattended," she insisted. "It's just . . . I had to use the ladies' room, and I'd been sitting there for hours talking to this really nice man because the plane was delayed."

"Out of all of the people in the terminal, did you seek him out to sit by?"

"No, he sat next to me. Then he struck up a conversation . . . turns out we had a lot in common."

"You trusted him to watch your stuff while you went to the ladies' room?"

"Not my purse. But the textile bag was bulky and weighed too much to be lugging it around—as you've discovered—and I didn't want to haul it into the bathroom with me. Germs, you know . . . setting it on the floor. So I asked him to watch it for me while I went into the bathroom and he did. And then I got home and went through Customs, and that was it."

But I had a creepy feeling that wasn't it at all. My heart pounded. My stomach roiled.

"Dump the bag onto the bed."

"Dainty, what's wrong with you? Do you think I'm lying? Nothing happened." With each protest, Venice's voice became louder and her words more urgent.

"Just do it, please?"

Grudgingly, she complied with the request. Then I told her to shake out each textile, one by one, and refold it.

"You think I smuggled contraband?" Exasperated, she shook out the first piece of fabric, a colorful tribal configuration in what appeared to be cotton. "Honestly, Dainty, I often wonder why I even like you."

I wanted to cry at her hurtful words. Then like a drill sergeant, I barked orders. "Do the next one."

She shook out three or four more pieces of cloth and refolded them. But the next piece of fabric in her stack of dry goods made my heart skip a few beats.

We both saw the folded piece of paper at the same time. When she looked up expectantly, I knew she didn't know what it was, or that it had even been there.

"It's not mine." She blinked several times, as if that would make it go away.

"What is it?"

"I don't know. I just told you it isn't mine."

"You were that guy's mule."

"Mule?"

"You know what a mule is. It's a gullible person who couriers illegal contraband into the country. You were that guy's mule. Now, open it."

She shook her head, eyeing it as if we were staring into the reptilian eyes of a Gaboon viper. "*You* open it."

Salem rattled the door handle—at least I assumed it was Salem—since, by process of elimination, she was the only other one who had a dog in the fight.

"Go away," Venice and I yelled in unison.

I carefully lifted the paper from the stack of dry goods. It'd been folded numerous times until it formed a thick packet. While cautiously unfolding it, I felt hard lumps and already knew what was inside before I ever opened the last pleat.

As I revealed the contents, Venice's eyes nearly popped out of her head like champagne corks—not because of what we were seeing, but because of how many there were.

"Oh. My. God," she said, almost breathless. "I didn't know. He must've put them there." Then she broke down into sobs. "I'm so sorry, Dainty. It's because of me . . . all of this."

Salem pounded on the door. "Open up."

"I accused you when it was me who caused the deaths of those people."

Without a word, I crossed the room and untoggled the bolt. When the door swung open, I saw that Salem had brought along a posse composed of Amanda, Dawn, and Teensy.

Amanda barged in, as I knew she would. "What is it? What's got us all on the run?"

Venice and I answered simultaneously.

"Diamonds."

Chapter Twenty-Eight

Late afternoon, as the sunset turned the horizon bright red, I felt a significant disturbance in The Force. It started when Chopper Deke came out of the shower, freshly washed and well dressed, and announced that he was driving over to see his girlfriend for a few hours.

Girlfriend? Who knew?

But that actually made sense as to why he didn't have a crippling case of carpal tunnel with all of the estrogen swirling through his house.

I followed him into the garage to get an idea when he'd return. He jumped into the SUV and invited me to join him.

"No thanks, I'm not going to visit your paramour. I don't want to befriend her because I'd eventually end up on her subpoena list of reputation witnesses, and I'd rather not be called to testify." I winked to show I didn't mean it. I figured he wanted to show me off, maybe make her think he could get a young girl interested in him, and I wanted no part of that.

"I'm taking your grandmother's car, toots." He held out his palm in demand for the keys. "I need you to drive this one back after I pick it up from the truck stop."

"About that . . . turns out Gran's not dead."

"What?" Eyes bulging, he quickly recovered. "Well, that's a crying shame. Not that your grandmother's alive, toots, but that you can't sell me her car."

I hadn't previously paid much attention to the video equipment mounted in the upper left-hand corner of the garage, but I wasn't the least bit surprised to see a pretty sophisticated system. With surveillance all the way around the property, Chopper Deke could tell if anyone strayed onto the grounds, or waited to bushwhack him. The word that sprang to mind was "overkill" but in our case, his neurosis worked to our advantage.

Chopper Deke left in his vehicle. Having forgotten to ask when he'd return, I went back inside.

The shift in The Force continued when Teensy took it upon herself to cook dinner and singed her eyebrows. Well, more like, burned them off. The odor of burning hair blanketed the kitchen, proving, once again, that Teensy's not a good cook. Bad, bad cook. Then she emptied pizza onto the kitchen floor when she took it out of the oven. *Really, Teensy, when a store-bought pizza says "Caution, hot after cooking," what it really means is that you should take it out of the cardboard box before baking it, and that scalding hot cheese will run down your hand.*

At our house, it's *de rigueur* when Teensy cooks and the fire alarm goes off, that means dinner's ready.

Instead of kicking back in one of the matching recliners with my feet up on the footrest, I felt the sudden urgency to vacate the house and take in the fresh air, so I invited Dawn to go for a walk around the perimeter of Chopper Deke's property. The walk would give us a bit of one-on-one time when I could give her pointers on the expectations of The Rubanbleu doyennes. But first, we needed to clear up a rumor that'd been circulating around the country club for years.

"I don't want to pry." *Untrue.* "But I have to ask you a personal question. Word around the country club is that you showed up at your ex-boyfriend's wedding, uninvited, wearing a wedding dress."

"Never happened," Dawn said. "I've never even had a boyfriend, much less an ex-boyfriend."

"Then we need to do damage control. I was thinking in terms of a PR campaign to rehabilitate your reputation, starting with your name. Is Dawn short for Dawna or Dawnette?"

"Just plain Dawn."

I'd hoped her given name was a variation we could improve upon. "Dawn's a beautiful name."

"It's not glamorous like Dainty," she said.

"Ha. If my grandfather hadn't paid Daddy two hundred dollars, my name would be Bratty Spice."

She laughed in dulcet tones, like a mallet struck against a series of bars on a xylophone. I liked that I'd made her laugh. I suspected Dawn didn't have a lot of laughter in her life.

"My grandfather said they could name me anything they wanted, but if they didn't call me Dainty, he'd cut them out of his will. What about a middle name? Do you have one?"

"Patrice."

We walked to the high point of Chopper Deke's property, which overlooked neighboring farms, including the place he claimed belonged to cultists. I gazed beyond his land, into the distance, where fields of dead grass looked like bolts of burlap unfurling. Denuded trees resembled a cemetery of moldy hands jutting up from the ground, with a thousand gnarled gray fingers grasping at the air. Fence posts stuck up from the ground like strings of birthday candles atop Methuselah's cake. On the horizon, the tangerine sun dipped below the thick of trees. Gray clouds hung from the sky as thick and opaque as steel wool pads. Under ordinary circumstances, I wouldn't have taken this walk—too creepy—but knowing Boris could appear at any time gave me the courage to venture out.

"I think you should go by Patrice." I mustered a smile of encouragement. "No more chance that anyone can call you 'Candida.' " The nickname just slipped out; I instantly regretted reminding her of it.

The breeze caught a lock of Dawn's hair. She pushed it back into place and eyed me through a measured squint. "You knew about that?"

"Everyone did." Embarrassed for her, I sighed. "It was wrong of those boys to treat you that way. But we're older now. Besides, those idiots are probably doing time in the pen."

Dawn blew out a deep breath. "Guys like that just need to donate their belongings to charity and run onto the tollway blindfolded."

This time, I laughed.

I'd been laboring under the misapprehension that everyone I knew had enjoyed high school—at least those like me who were crowned Homecoming Queen and got to be cheerleaders; or the captain of the football team and quarterback; or class president and drum majorette; or those whose memories didn't develop black holes from the PTSD school gave you from being bullied. High school was the baseline by which you could measure future disappointments. Football hero one day? Fifty-year-old tub of lard managing a greasy spoon the next. Or the fifty-year-old version of Barbie after three kids, forty-thousand miles of stretch marks, leathery skin from too many hours on the tanning bed, and a whiskey voice resulting from a three-pack-a-day nicotine habit. Better still, when a victim awakened in the wee hours of the morning to find herself in the middle of a deadly home invasion, she could say, "Well, at least I didn't have to attend prep school with those Prescott sisters." And I could always look back and say, "At least I didn't have to wear a hand-me-down prom dress."

"At least you didn't get nominated for one of the unofficial polls, like *Person Most Likely to End Up on Death Row*," I murmured helpfully, while patting Dawn's arm in a consoling manner, which she probably interpreted as me flirting with her.

Dawn caught me off guard. "Would you like to catch a movie

with me sometime?"

I shook my head. "I've already seen it."

"But I didn't say what we'd go see."

"I've seen that one, too." I checked my snootiness; the hurt in her eyes was palpable. "I'm kidding, Dawn. *Patrice*. Sure, we can catch a movie. Might be fun."

She fist-bumped me. This small act of camaraderie represented a moment in time that would become branded in my mind, and probably haunt me for the rest of my life. But I also considered the possibility that knowing Dawn— *Patrice*—might change my life in a positive way.

My mind cast back to an incident in the school cafeteria, back when students in Dawn's grade whose mothers were in The Rubanbleu took turns eating lunch with her. Because Dawn was a legacy of The Rubanbleu, the mothers insisted that their children make a seating arrangement so Avery's stepdaughter didn't have to sit by herself. To be fair, they set it up on a rotation basis because nobody liked Dawn, and they didn't want any part of it. What stuck out in my mind was the day a fight broke out because one of them tried to skip her turn. For the lonely and emotionally fragile girl with a damaged soul, public humiliation was every bit as devastating as an actual physical blow.

If I'd known back in high school what I knew while we took our walk, I'd have been the bully—and I would've bullied those other kids in Dawn's class into treating her better.

Momma always said that I had a kind spirit. And that I should use my popularity to do good things and help others. I should've done more to help Dawn. To help Patrice.

Dawn sheared my trance. "It's stupid for me to make my debut into society."

"Think of it as a rite of passage."

"For what?" she scoffed. "To meet rich Westsiders, get married, and live happily ever after?"

"Well, sure."

Dawn halted in her tracks. She grabbed my arm and held me in her azure gaze. "I'm not interested in getting fixed up with a bunch of guys. Okay?"

"You sure?" She nodded so I pressed the issue. "Why do you suppose you turned out this way?"

"Why do you suppose you like chocolate? Would you stop eating it if you were told you had to switch to butterscotch?"

I looked at the tips of my shoes. "No." Then I lifted my gaze, not relishing the inevitable. "You realize if you don't make your debut, you'll have to explain it to Avery."

She huffed out a resigned sigh, walked around me, dropped onto a primitive stool next to a hydrant, and abruptly came unhinged. "Screw Avery. I hate Avery. I wish he were dead."

She stared off into the distance, and I knew in an instant that I'd just lost Dawn.

Every muscle in my body tightened. I'd met this personality before, when she confessed she'd tampered with someone's medication—possibly Avery's.

We were losing daylight and had stopped near the chicken coop, and I wondered if she'd taken her daily dosage of prescription medication. If she hadn't, I didn't want to be alone with her out in the dark.

Helpless, I appealed to her sense of fair play. "What am I supposed to do with this, Dawn?"

In that unguarded moment, she burst into tears and buried her face in her hands. When she looked up, her cheeks were bright pink and blotchy and the bloodshot whites of her eyes made her blue irises look electric and neon. It was enough of a reaction for me to suspect that her mother and biological father had met in a mental ward, where they were both being hospitalized.

I tried again. "Avery seems like a nice enough guy."

"He is."

"I thought you hated him."

"Why would you think that?"

"Because you said, 'I hate him.' "

"He buys me things." Ice-flecked irises gleamed stubbornly.

A creepy feeling overtook me. "Have we met before?"

"Once. I don't think we were properly introduced." She extended her hand for me to shake it. "I'm Angela."

"I'm going to throw up." Not true, but my declaration amounted to a super-great subject-changer because it created such a jarring image that Angela-Dawn stopped crying.

As I attempted to delve into Dawn's new persona, Boris unexpectedly returned.

"Don't listen to Angela. She's a chronic liar. And quit harassing Dawn."

After denying that I'd intended to harass Dawn, I demanded to know what'd happened to her that'd caused such hatred toward Avery.

"I'd worry less about Avery and more about Kim Ho. If I ever get my hands on that bitch, I'll kill her."

My jaw went slack. "Dawn needs professional help. She needs a good doctor to help her sort out what's going on with her." Then again, after extensive work with a therapist, she'd probably be more likely to get struck by lightning than to be able to maintain a stable relationship.

Before Boris could respond, I stopped him with an upheld hand . . . and listened.

Voices. Footfalls.

Boris assumed a defensive stance.

Suddenly, Teensy burst into view, her straw-colored hair wild, her eyes wide. "We have to talk."

"You scared the living daylights out of me."

"Please, Dainty, it's important." She looked at Dawn, who'd abruptly returned in Boris's place. "I need you to excuse yourself, Dawn. I have to talk to my sister. It's urgent."

Dawn took a deep breath and seemed to reorient herself to the hen house. It must be maddening to have Boris and the others slip in and out of her life, leaving her in a fugue state with gaps in her memory and a serious lack of continuity whenever they took over.

Teensy said, "What're you two doing out here, anyway?"

Dawn said, "She was giving me advice on how to act for the next ten months, before the Rubanbleu ball."

Teensy threaded her fingers through her hair and swept it back from her face. "Well, for one thing, definitely whatever you do, do *not*, under any circumstances, be yourself." Then she snapped her fingers as if she'd remembered an important detail. "And you'll need a good photograph—one that doesn't look anything like you."

"Shut up, Teensy. That was rude." With put-on sweetness, I asked Dawn to excuse us and told her I'd see her back at the house.

Dawn flounced off in a huff.

"Whether you know it or not, Teensy, I was making progress with her."

Teensy gave the air a quick flick of the wrist. "I couldn't care less. I'm in trouble, and you've got to help me get out of it."

"What're you talking about?"

"I did something stupid."

"I'm shocked." Hand to mouth, I reacted with mock horror. It would've been more surprising if she announced she'd made a smart decision. Or an altruistic one. "How stupid?"

Her breath turned to vapor when she spoke. "Bewilderingly stupid."

"What've you done?" I omitted the "now" part of my sentence.

"I slept with the Ranger."

"What?" It wasn't that I didn't hear her; it was my way of giving her a chance to change what she told me. If I'd said, "Say what?" instead, she would've known it was time to run. The cringe-worthy disclosure made my heart drop to my feet. "You'd better be talking about a baseball player from the Texas Rangers ball club, Teensy."

"I slept with Dusty . . . Ranger Hill."

"Have you lost your mind?" I yelled in the face of her confession. "How is that even possible?" Then, like the impending car wreck you can't seem to tear your eyes away from, I listened in abject horror as she described their trysts. Nothing about her admission carried anything remotely close to a patina of respectability. And while it's true that I'm always finding out new stuff about my sister, it's that lately, none of it happens to be the result of good judgment. "When? When did you do this?"

"That morning. After we went to the police station for questioning. And don't judge me. I didn't set out to do that. It just happened."

"It just *happened?* Like how does that just *happen?*" My voice corkscrewed upward until I was pretty sure only dogs could hear it. "Spontaneous combustion just happens. The Big Bang just happens. Sex with a Ranger takes forethought. Did you shave your legs?"

"What kind of question is that?"

"Well, did you?"

"Yes."

"*Ha.* You planned it. Why else would you shave your legs? *The fuck, Teensy?*"

Sheepish, she swallowed hard. "It wasn't just that one time, Dainty."

"Oh, hell, no." Now she should run. Clearly, Teensy was a lot craftier than I gave her credit for. I demanded that my sister explain herself. About the only excuses she didn't use were *The dog ate my homework, and the elephant stepped on my science project.*

To my shock and amazement, she confessed to sending the Ranger what can only be described as inappropriate emails, which proved that she shouldn't be allowed to use email when she's plastered. And then he came to Fort Worth—to the house we'd grown up in—and they'd been sexting ever since. By the time she finished telling me about their tawdry sexcapades, I couldn't think of a time I'd been more infuriated—not with her, but with myself. She couldn't have known that, because of my tanking relationship with Bruckman, it actually offended me that he'd chosen to pursue her rather than me.

"Why are you telling me this now?"

"Because he's acting all weird and stuff."

"If a guy you're involved with starts acting weird, there's probably a good reason. Like he has a wife and three kids."

She absorbed my words. "You think he's married?" Her voice crescendoed.

"How would I know? What I do know is that you have no business messing with this man."

"But he loves me."

"Loves you? He doesn't even know you."

"You're just saying that to be mean."

I hated the waver in Teensy's voice because it usually brought about the inevitable crying jag.

"All I'm saying is that it's an unrealistic relationship." I broke it down for her. "Logistics, Teensy. You live in Fort Worth. He lives in west Texas. It's never going to work because he doesn't have a penis that's four-hundred-eleven miles long." Waiting for that to soak in, I thought of another "con" to add to the list of pros and cons. "He has an established career. What're you planning to do—move there?"

Teensy sniffled. Then her chin quivered. Blond brows, recently penciled on, slammed together. Then she burst into tears. "I confronted him for cheating on me. He said, 'Technically, I'm cheating *with* you, not *on* you.' "

"That's a nice way of telling you that he's either married or has a girlfriend. You need to banish this non-relationship to the *'I will never, ever, ever talk to him again. Like. Ever,'* category."

"Never?" she said, testing the word.

This might've gone on another ten minutes if we hadn't lost the last of the sun. Shadows played tricks on me when I scanned the woods. Trees took on the shapes of people, animated by the evening breeze. I sensed a presence behind me and carefully repositioned myself where I could see without drawing attention to myself.

Then a twig snapped. I could've sworn I saw one of those bad men receding farther into the stand of oaks. Instead of slipping into denial, I couldn't make that vision go away.

I did see the man.

He'd retreated into the tree line with such fluidity and gracefulness that my first impression was, *Such a finely tuned classical ballet move—almost like a* glissade—*what school of dance did he train at?* Followed by *Screeeeeeeeech!* Reality check: *Oh, dear God, they're here.* He was over six feet tall, with a neck like a life-sized bronze statue and a torso built like a concrete bridge abutment.

Frosty puffs of breath escaped my thunderstruck, slack-jawed mouth.

The men from the lodge were bonded together in murder forever, but they weren't untouchable. Between Dawn, Gran, and me, we'd winnowed their numbers from four down to one. We could do it again if we had to.

Terrified, I needed to shut Teensy up. She was still gushing over the Ranger's sexual prowess when I grabbed her by the scruff of her jacket and yanked her inches from my face. Jagged pain knifed through my injured wrist.

"Listen carefully," I said under my breath. "Don't turn around. I saw one of the men. Do you have your gun?"

Frowning in the hurling confusion, she shook her head no. Her face drained of color. Her breathing became quick and shallow.

"We're going to walk ten steps toward the house. When we get down to five, I want you to laugh like I just told you a joke. But if I tell you to run, you run like your life depends on it. Understand?"

She nodded. Under the rising frosted moon, she took on the appearance of a ghostly specter.

I took a few steps backward and smiled. "If we make it to the house, head for the panic room."

Yes, she mouthed without sound.

"Let's go. Ten steps." I positioned myself at an angle where I could keep an eye on the trees. My heart beat so fast I could actually hear it thundering between my ears. "Ten . . . nine . . . eight . . ."

I might as well have given instructions to a brick wall. At the five-count, Teensy bolted for the house, leaving me to fend for myself. Her blood-curdling screams filled the night, but Deke's place was miles from any of the neighbors'.

The first drops of rain fell on my face. Then the skies opened up and rain poured down in sheets.

All I had to do was make it inside the back door and dead-bolt the lock behind me.

CHAPTER TWENTY-NINE

Teensy and I plunged through the heavy metal door within seconds of each other. With my heart beating so hard that it masked other noises, I double-bolted the lock and darted toward the alarm panel. The system had a panic button and I intended to press the same series of numbers Chopper Deke showed me on our first day. I didn't have to remember them because he directed me to start on Number Three and go straight down the keypad if we ever needed to tap out the emergency code. As soon as I pressed *Three*, the alarm panel brightened with options. I pressed *Six* and *Nine* and ended with the police option.

Nothing happened.

Reality soaked in. All of the lights in the house were off, including the ambient light the TV would've cast over the room. I wondered if the girls had even heard Teensy's and my desperate reentry into the house as I pitched into the den screaming, "Everybody into the panic room," and saw the frozen faces of my friends.

Except Amanda.

The collective reaction of the others felt like a kick in the gut. Over their ghastly expressions, I actually noticed Teensy's feral barn cat snuggling against Dawn, glaring resentfully and trying to wither us with his accusatory stare. When nobody moved, I shrilled, "This isn't a drill. They're here."

As for Amanda, I found her sacked out in one of Chopper Deke's motorized recliners, snoring like a sixty-year-old bald guy with sleep apnea. Urging sleep upon Amanda had never been a difficult sell. This was no exception.

I barked out her name. She sat, bolt-upright, and said, "I didn't do it; it wasn't me," while glancing around disoriented.

I restated the problem. "They're here. Everybody into the panic room."

I grabbed my purse from where I'd dropped it near the hearth and fumbled through it until I felt the gun at the bottom. As I raced for the panic room, I saw the gun in my hand, even though I didn't recall having yanked it from my handbag. Amanda fell in behind me, using spinning-windmill hand motions to urge the others to follow.

Downy hairs on my arms stood straight up. "Power's off?"

"About five minutes." Amanda punctuated her comment with a nod. She reached under her jacket to make sure that her shoulder holster was snug and her pistol, ready to use.

Then the lights flickered on. As we scrambled for our lives, Teensy took the stairs in twos.

"Teensy, come back," I shrieked. "It's too late. Come back."

She disappeared at the top of the steps. I heard her cell phone ring as I pulled the book out of the bookcase. We'd be fine, I told myself. After all, the panic room operated off of a generator. If the power had been cut, the generator would immediately kick on. And maybe the alarm code went through, too. After all, it had a back-up battery. Then again, I didn't know this for certain. After all, I'm not smarter than everyone else, I'm just more stubborn.

My fingers fluttered against the shelf, touching all around the vacant space left by the book, until I found the button. As soon as I pressed it, the bookcase peeled back. Mechanically triggered gears hummed. We stood at the mouth of the steel door waiting. Too late, a skin-crawling realization snared me in its grip. I didn't have the little electronic disk to swipe the keypad.

"Nobody move." I rushed back into the den and grabbed the strap to my purse. That's when I saw Teensy at the top of the stairs.

She called down to me in a sing-song voice. "False alarm, it's Ranger Hill. He's coming here any minute. He needs to talk to us—all of us." In the light of the frosted moon, shining through the upstairs window and bathing her in its icy blue glow, I'd never before seen her face radiate with such love.

Movement outside the house drew my attention to the windows flanking the front door. I flattened myself up against the nearest wall as the crown of Dusty Hill's white western hat bobbed across the length of the glass casement. He'd assumed a crouched position, and ape-walked below the highly placed windowpane.

"I'll get the door." Teensy scampered down the steps, gripping the Smith in her gun hand.

Normally, I would've been all for letting a Texas Ranger into the house—until horrific thoughts flashed through my mind in rapid succession. It took all of two seconds for them to pass, but what struck me as odd was how the Ranger knew to come here. I presumed Teensy had given him directions and that he'd made the trip to see her. I wanted to believe that more than anything . . . until I saw a much bigger man following on the Ranger's boot heels. The man crept, hunched over, and while I couldn't see his face, I noted he'd dressed in black clothing.

Any affinity I'd built up for Ranger Hill turned to dread.

Every fiber of my being said, *Trust your gut.*

And I did.

"It's a trap," I screamed, motioning her down the stairs with a whirling hand once I knew Ranger Hill was in cahoots with those men. "Don't open the door." And then, "Hurry, Teensy. Hurry!"

With more ballerina's grace than I'd ever exhibited at any

recital I'd starred in, I whirled in the direction of the panic room and bolted as if the imaginary breath of a dragon, crisping the back of my neck, would turn me into charcoal. Sensing that we only had a few minutes left to live, I rushed toward safety, grappling through my bag for the key card.

A hundred thoughts cycled through my mind—none of them good. Thoughts like, *How'd they get the jump on us?* And, *How do we survive this?* And, because those men probably had the kind of rap sheets that were measured in pounds rather than pages, *They're killing machines, we don't stand a chance.*

Cursing Dusty Hill under my breath for setting a trap that would likely set off a bloody chain of events, I made it to the steel door and swiped the keypad with the electronic disk Chopper Deke had entrusted to me. Once the electronic pad read the data, the door gaped open.

Jockeying for position, we plunged through the opening and into the rectangular space—Venice and her textile bag; Salem, buffered by Amanda; and one terrified Dawn, whose eccentricities took on an even more disturbing bent.

Fluorescent lights flickered overhead in the crowded space.

"Teensy, please," I insisted.

I recognized the distinctive cop knock, followed by the persistent jamming of a finger against the doorbell.

Next came a sickening thud.

The house fell deafeningly quiet. Then, for a few agonizing seconds, every corner of Chopper Deke's container home produced noises.

As the first kick rattled the door, my sister stood at the top of the stairs, inert and dumbfounded. Instead of the winning pageant smile she'd been sporting for Dusty Hill, her eyebrows shot up into peaks. An unholy combination of terror and betrayal melted the joy on her face. She settled her carefully lined eyes on me and her lower lip protruded slightly. It broke my heart watching her come to grips with the man's duplicity. Dusty Hill had not come here out of love, or even a physical desire to be with my sister.

He and his confederates wanted to kill us.

No wonder the investigation hadn't gone anywhere. It wasn't supposed to.

Until the steel door almost completely closed Teensy off from view, I didn't fully appreciate that my cheeks were wet and my nose, running. Seconds before the door sealed itself, I cried out again.

"Outside. Escape hatch."

At the last second, I made a snap decision, lunging for the opening in order to be with my sister, but Amanda yanked me back inside. I could do nothing more for Teensy. Now my responsibility lay with my friends in Chopper Deke's panic room.

Mechanical gears turned again as the door sealed us off from the outside world, and the bookcase eased back into place. Instead of feeling safe, I felt like we'd been buried alive in a mausoleum.

In the pale blue light, with the buzz of the flickering fluorescent tubes, I went for the landline to call 9-1-1.

Dead.

Then I tried my disposable phone.

No service.

"Can anyone get a signal?"

Those who had their disposable phones with them tried to activate them. One by one, they shook their heads in disappointment.

Venice said, "I can't get a signal either. But I dialed 9-1-1 as soon as you told us to get in the panic room."

I looked over hopefully. "Anyone answer?"

"A lady."

"What'd you say?"

"I told her they were trying to kill us. And to hurry."

CHAPTER THIRTY

Beyond the panic room, one of the men spoke in a low-density muffled voice. I couldn't make out his words, but it really didn't matter once they gained entry into the house. I said a short prayer for my sister's safety and asked that she be given nine lives, even if it meant taking one of mine away.

Then I prayed for Chopper Deke since we had no way to warn him . . .

I shuddered to think of the carnage about to play out while the rest of us were safe behind the steel door. Recalling a phrase Daddy often used, *God protects dogs and stupid people,* I figured, *Well, at least Teensy has that going for her.* One never knew how events would play out under pressure. Teensy might just turn out to be the superstar in the family constellation.

Muscling my way past my friends, I pressed my ear to the door. Muted rumblings told me the men were probably just on the other side of our wall. I felt like a rabbit surrounded by pit vipers; one look at Amanda told me she did, too.

In the den, the voices and footsteps dampened to nothingness.

I whispered, "I'm going for help."

"Bull," Amanda said softly but firmly. "Nobody leaves."

The probability of losing my friends, or my sister, stretched my nerves tighter than a stringed instrument. I tried to think like Chopper Deke. "Teensy's up there. And Chopper Deke will be walking into an ambush. I can't let that happen."

"I'll go. This is my fault."

All eyes collectively shifted to Venice. Her voice trembled with fear.

"You're not going," I insisted. "You don't even know how to fire a gun."

Amanda said, "So what's the plan?"

I glanced over at Dawn, hoping to see Boris so I could take him with me. But, no, it was Dawn I was looking at, pitiful, frightened Dawn, sitting all by herself in the corner, sucking her thumb; and oh, how I wanted to kick myself for sending Boris packing. We exchanged smiles—hers, trusting; mine, not so much.

The way I had it worked out in my head: I'd leave through the escape hatch, take cover in the stand of red oaks, and work my way along the tree line until I got far enough away from the house to travel the road. Once I got a signal on my phone, I'd call 9-1-1. Then I'd call Chopper Deke to warn him off. I'd take the road to the highway and run toward the nearest town like my life depended on it, until I could flag down a big rig, or a car, or even a rider on horseback.

And I'd call for an ambulance . . . because I had the most ghastly feeling that one or more of us would be shot dead within the hour.

Sleep deprivation brought on by nightmares of Mexico had kept me from exercising good judgment over the past few months. In those dreams, unknown subjects in Ciudad Juárez hunted me. But now I was operating on my home turf, and I'd picked up a few street creds along the way. Before I lost my nerve, I revealed my plan to the group. As usual, they thought I'd lost my ever-loving mind.

I typed a quick text message to Bruckman on my disposable phone and got it ready to send. Once I went through the escape hatch and saw that the phone had a signal, I'd send it. The message was simple, a four-word text that contained Chopper Deke's address, and should put everything into perspective using an economy of words.

It read: *Dirty Ranger. Send help.*

CHAPTER THIRTY-ONE

One thing I hadn't taken into account was whether the escape hatch could be opened at all. With a hinge rusty from the elements, it could conceivably sound like Voodoo priestess Marie Leveau's coffin groaning open. That'd bring Ranger Hill and his fellow assassin running. A pale, sliver-sized glow from an outside security lamp suggested that the escape hatch wasn't airtight as it should've been.

I was almost ready to leave when the next sound I heard from outside the panic room was an exclamation of surprise, followed by thundering footsteps. As Amanda pulled a couple of sturdy plastic milk cartons beneath the escape hatch and stacked them on top of each other, I almost lost my nerve. Since Venice was the tallest, she climbed on top and freed the bolt. It gave off the same unforgettable sound as a shotgun being ratcheted back, and I instinctively knew that if one of these men were standing anywhere nearby, they would've heard it.

The next sounds coming from inside the house turned my heart into a block of ice—gunshots—followed by what sounded like return gunfire.

Plenty of people managed to go an entire lifetime without getting shot at. Which made me figure that people who weren't dodging bullets had such good luck because Teensy and I were catching the brunt of it lately.

It dawned on me that Venice couldn't be the reason we were in this jam, because I saw no connection between Ranger Hill and those men if this horrible mess centered around diamonds from Africa. But out in west Texas, we were near the Mexican border; because of the cartel, Mexico's commerce was drugs. We'd simply been at the wrong place at the wrong time, and got caught up in a drug war where maybe the owners of the resort, or their son, got in over their heads.

Or not. I didn't have time to figure out how Ranger Hill fit into the scenario other than accepting the fact that a man I'd trusted turned out to be bad news.

In desperation, I looked at Amanda, the eldest of our group— late thirties—and the one among us who should've had the most common sense. She'd helped Teensy and me before, down in Mexico, and I trusted her to do it again.

I touched her arm. "Listen to me. Teensy has her own distinctive knock." I tapped it out for her on the wall opposite the big steel door. "Here, I'll do it again." All eyes focused on me. "Once I go out this door, you lock it and don't open it for anyone unless you hear Teensy's knock. Got it?"

Amanda said, "Got it," while the others bravely nodded.

I heard more shots coming from inside the house. Behind cinder-block walls that buffered the panic room, they sounded like a cap pistol. We all knew better.

Time to go.

Amanda grabbed my arm. "Here, take my jacket."

She shrugged out of it and helped me work my arms into the sleeves. Then she buttoned me up. I could tell she wanted to cry because we found ourselves at the epicenter of such a lost cause, but she hugged me instead and said, "*Vaya con Dios,* diva." It meant "Go with God" in Spanish. I knew this because Daddy once made me sit through an old western with him when I was little so he could drool over one of those actresses that looked a lot like Angie Dickinson, while I stuffed my face with buttered popcorn and just wanted to die.

"Amanda." I knew she'd probably give me guff and would consider my cautionary words unpopular, especially since she loved to eat and was surrounded by several weeks' worth of canned food and MREs. "After I leave, turn out the lights and don't turn them on again unless you have to."

"How are we supposed to see in the dark?"

"Amanda," I said testily, "I have an idea that you, of all people, can find a way to open these boxes and prepare one meal without benefit of light."

She gave me a slow blink.

"Just turn them off and leave them off." Pointing to the sliver along the hatch where the seal had eroded, I said, "If those men are outside and you have the light on, it could lead them right to you."

But my real concern—the part I omitted—was that I feared that if those men discovered the breach outside the panic room, they might pour gasoline down the opening and set fire to it. Or worse, if there could be anything worse than that. And then my mind went haywire and spun other atrocities, like shooting fish in a barrel, and I finally decided that when this was all over, assuming I lived to tell about it, I should probably make an appointment with a counselor to find out how *moi*, Dainty Prescott, privileged Westsider and debutante, whose background included accomplishments such as years of ballet training, art appreciation, a love of dogs, high-fashion clothing and Italian shoes, modeling, and, most recently, broadcast journalist extraordinaire, could've developed a mind that was even remotely capable of imagining such gruesome scenarios.

I glanced over at Dawn but couldn't get a read on her. She still sat, alone, in the far corner of the room, only this time, she'd wrapped her arms around her knees and was rocking herself. At first I thought she was talking baby talk, but as I made out a few of the words, I realized she was quietly singing herself a lullaby. Venice sat in the other corner, clinging to her textile bag. Salem huddled next to her looking as spooked as I'd ever seen her, with the thousand-yard stare of a combat veteran.

I took a long, last look at my friends, and a deep breath for courage.

The next time a barrage of gunfire opened up, so did the escape hatch. Since I didn't have the luxury of peeking out to see who might be standing around outside, my getaway became a do-or-die moment. Then everything happened in rapid succession. I hoisted myself through the opening with splats of rain pelting my head and promptly face-planted. Blood whooshed between my ears. Hearing the men rampage through the house, I got up off all fours, feeling the freezing cold air envelope me. Moist leaves, suffused with mold, clung to my chin. Slippery deadfall, as silky and smooth as coffin crepe, stuck to my shoes. Shaken, I staggered toward the trees as the lid to the panic room sealed off the people I loved from view.

CHAPTER THIRTY-TWO

My first instinct was to melt into my surroundings until I was no longer visible. I crept through the trees, away from Chopper Deke's container house, and prayed that my sister had the presence of mind to hide in a place where she wouldn't be found. Spongy leaves, marinating in decay beneath my feet, didn't bother me half as much as the nocturnal animals around me that I couldn't see or smell. I knew they were there, though, because of the occasional sets of opalescent eyes reflected in the security lights at the perimeter of the container house.

For a few seconds, I studied the house in an effort to vector the location of anyone who'd stepped outside with the intent to kill me. With the shades lowered on the second-story windows, and the downstairs casements uncovered like a slack-jawed lazy giant, the container house appeared to be as asleep as a GI fresh from a grueling reconnaissance mission.

I heard a twig snap, followed by the slapping of feet against puddles of water. After a sudden wave of nausea passed, I held my breath, expecting to see Ranger Hill and his henchman come around the corner with guns blazing. I had no place to run where I wouldn't make noise. Mind-numbing fear gripped my throat. They had no reason to come looking for me out here, but my mind was stuck on high alert and it swirled with a variety of horrific ways to die.

Teensy.

Wild-eyed and breathless, she sprinted around the front of

the house with wet hair plastered to her face. Instinct made me want to call out to her, but the driving rain came down so hard that it obliterated other sounds around me. I pulled out the gun and waited to see who came after her, hoping I wouldn't have to fire on them and give away my position.

Teensy barreled toward me. I knew she didn't see me tucked away deep within the oaks. Ploughing me under would catch her by surprise, and I couldn't take the chance that she might scream.

I crouched.

And waited.

With my heart hammering, she burst through the scrub brush and into the trees. I tackled her, slapping my free hand over her mouth. Like any good surprise in any decent action movie, I moved my lips near her ear.

"Don't scream. It's me."

The security globe, which had been mounted against the telephone pole, illuminated the grounds closest to the panic room as well as the den. In the ambient blue light, I cautioned Teensy to be quiet before releasing my hand.

"Dainty." She blinked. "How'd you get away?"

"Escape hatch. But the others are still down there. I'm going for help."

"No, I think we should stay here until help comes."

Then a *très, très* terrible thing happened. Teensy's phone shrilled.

Did anyone besides me ever get so angry that they saw gold spots fragmenting their vision? When dealing with Teensy, having your inner fury unleashed could be considered an occupational hazard. Strings of whispered expletives such as the ones that hissed out of my mouth came with the territory.

"Mute the ringer, Teensy."

My sister had a way of ratcheting up the discomfort, but she did as I instructed without giving me any lip. This reminded me to send the message to Bruckman. Then I dialed 9-1-1.

The voice of a calm, capable dispatcher came on the line, instantly buoying my confidence and extinguishing my sense of hopelessness. "9-1-1, what is your emergency?"

"Home invasion. Two men are trying to kill us. We need help."

"What is your location?"

I looked at Teensy, who looked back helplessly. I gave the farm-to-market road Chopper Deke lived off of, but there were so many little houses dotting the countryside, and all the roads looked so much alike, that I couldn't be much more specific. I recited the physical address of his house and hoped for the best. Then I positioned myself where I could watch the back of the container home.

"What is your name?"

"Dainty Prescott."

Short pause. "Wait—*the* Dainty Prescott? From WBFD-TV?"

"Yes. Please hurry."

"Do you know these people?"

"Not really."

"What does that mean? Sounds like you know them."

"One of them looks like a guy I know. The other doesn't."

"These men—what are they wearing?"

"One's dressed in black. He's a big man. The other guy—" I hesitated to tell the dispatcher Ranger Hill's name, or even his occupation. I'd come to mistrust law enforcement and worried that she'd either think I made a prank call or that I was the villain in this scenario and Ranger Hill was in their jurisdiction trying to arrest me. "The other one has on a light gray western-style or cowboy-type hat, so light it's almost white, a light-colored shirt, and he's pretty big, too."

My eyes flickered to Teensy. She looked possessed. Eyes, shockingly catlike, barely blinked. I looked back toward the house and saw what she saw.

Not one, but two men, dressed in black, had rounded the back corner. My eyes did a double-take. While their flashlight beacons panned the tree line, I cyphered in my head. The two home invaders Gran shot were either hospitalized or dead. Which meant the other criminal—the one who'd finagled his way into the psychiatric ward and tried to strangle Dawn—must have been discharged from the hospital and rejoined his one remaining confederate.

Unless there were more of them. I shook that thought from my head like a duster on a cobweb. Under no circumstances did I want to toss that possibility out into the universe.

The dispatcher kept asking questions. I managed to whisper, "Can't talk. They're here."

She cautioned me not to hang up. Since she'd become my umbilical cord to safety, I only hoped that atmospheric conditions didn't cause our connection to fail. For a while, I let her do the talking. She asked if the men were still there; they were. Then she asked if I could talk; I couldn't. Each time she asked a question, I spoke in almost a whisper and hoped she could hear me over the driving rain.

Then, for no good reason, the men sloshed back around the house and disappeared from view.

"Let's go, Teensy." When she didn't move, I grabbed her wrist, painfully, and tugged. That jolted her back to reality. "As soon as we get a little farther from the house, we can take the road. But for now, we need to move within the trees."

"I don't like it. And I'm cold."

Any feeling in my fingers had left ten minutes before they turned to icicles. "It'll be over soon, Teensy. You can look back on this part and brag about how brave you were." I squeezed her hands in mine, surprised at the warmth they gave my palms.

"Please, Dainty. I don't want to go."

She'd started getting that possessed look on her face again, and I felt my control over her slipping away. I remembered I had the dispatcher on the line and told her we were headed for the highway that ran past Chopper Deke's house. Then I pitched into a sticky gossamer web and faced down the Godzilla of all spiders. Blind panic caused me to stagger out of the trees. Teensy followed, and we scrambled for our lives.

I climbed up a small berm next to the long drive. Before reaching the top, I spilled onto the muddy bank and fell on my injured wrist with such force that I thought I'd black out from the impact. Blades of dead grass zoomed into sharp focus. Night life moved behind us in the shadows. A scary reptile or amphibian that I wanted no part of slithered past my ear. Without complaint, I picked myself up and sprinted to catch up with Teensy.

An unfamiliar odor filled my nostrils. No matter how fast I ran, it kept pace with me. Then my conscious mind enlightened me—*the stench was mine*. This was what the overwhelming stink of pure fear smelled like.

Carnal panic seeped from every pore. I found myself grasping at silky threads of logic to invent reasons why we'd survive.

I put the disposable phone to my ear. "Are you still there?"

"Yes—I'm not leaving you, Miss Prescott. What's going on?"

"We're almost to the road, I think." *Wishful thinking.* "It'd be super-great if you could have a deputy meet us. It's cold and we're wet, and I think we might be freezing to death."

"You said 'we.' Who's with you?"

"My sister, Teensy. Please hurry." All out of breath and tired from running, my lungs burned with each inhale. "Oh no, there's a dark-colored SUV up ahead. I can't talk. They may've left someone with the vehicle."

"Can you get me the license plate?"

I darted off the roadway and pulled Teensy with me. She

seemed surprised until I said, "We don't know who all came here."

"This is like frickin' *Hotel California*—you can check out, but you can't leave. I'm telling you, Dainty, we'll never make it out of here," Teensy argued. Even in the dark, I could see her eyes flicking knives at me. "Look—there's a car coming down the highway."

I caught myself nodding during the imaginary conversation playing out inside my head—the conversation I should've been having with the dispatcher. Then I said it for real.

"I need you to call my friend to warn him off. He'll be coming back soon. If I give you his number, can you call him, or have another dispatcher call him?" I was so cold I couldn't stop trembling or stammering, or keep my teeth from chattering. While I thought hypothermia had set in, she probably thought I was "special" and needed a fundraiser. My stuttering became so bad that the poor dispatcher had to supply my own words.

"Who's your friend, and what's his number?"

"Deke. Deke Richter." Then I recited his phone number.

"I'm sorry, did you say Deke Richter?"

"Yes. Do you know him?"

"We all know him. Why didn't you say it was his house? He's pro-law enforcement. Always donates to the Sheriff's posse. Even throws an annual barbecue. Are you his girlfriend?"

"Oh, *gawd* no. We work together at the TV station. Please— send everyone on duty."

Hidden in the trees, I couldn't make out any silhouettes in the vehicle. I didn't consciously decide to walk up beside it for a closer look, but when I stared through the driver's window, I realized I'd done just that. Once I was pretty sure nobody occupied the SUV, I moved to the rear of the vehicle and recited the license plate to the dispatcher.

Before heading to the highway, I found a large rock off to the side of the road that looked about the size of an ostrich egg and weighed about as much as a brick. In an effort to cut two heads off the same snake, I picked it up and struck it against the valve stem until I heard the telltale *psst* of escaping air. Then I walked around the hood and struck the valve stem on the front passenger tire. That ought to do it.

I made eye contact with Teensy. "Let's go."

About a quarter of a mile up the road, we arrived at a white pickup. Pushing Teensy back toward the trees, I said, "Can you see anyone inside?"

"That's Dusty's truck."

I couldn't begin to figure out why he'd parked down the road from the SUV, unless he arrived after the lodge men. With the phone at my side, I walked until the thin, tinny voice of the dispatcher filtered up to my ear.

I stopped in the middle of the road. "What'd you just say?"

"We reached Mr. Richter."

"Did he say he was bringing help?"

When the dispatcher reveled that Chopper Deke told her he wasn't bringing help, it didn't particularly frighten me. Knowing Chopper Deke, he'd round up a few of his cronies without notifying the Sheriff's Department. If he told deputies that he was bringing reinforcements, they would've warned him not to and ordered him to let deputies handle the matter themselves.

And that might prove too late.

A message brightened my cell phone display, notifying me that I had less than ten percent battery left. I thumbed the "dismiss" option and told the dispatcher I'd call her back on my sister's phone.

Teensy grudgingly handed it over and I immediately called Chopper Deke. He answered on the second ring.

"Stay put, toots, I'm ten minutes away. Don't go back to the house."

"We need help. The girls are in the panic room. Teensy and I are almost at the highway. Don't come by yourself—I counted at least three of them. And I think the Ranger's a dirty cop."

He didn't say anything. I pulled Teensy's phone away from my ear to see if it showed a low battery message, too. But I didn't get a message. The phone had already shut down on its own.

CHAPTER THIRTY-THREE

While my insides spasmed, Teensy shivered and her teeth chattered like maracas. I considered that hypothermia might've already set in and reached over to wipe the rain off her arms and face.

Any semblance of Teensy's altruism disintegrated into a plaintive wail. "You should go on without me. You're way more resilient than me, Dainty. I'll just hold you back."

"No. Prescotts don't give up. We're not quitters. We're getting out of this together."

My clothes were in tatters. For some insane reason, my thoughts turned to Venice and her ability to design clothing. She should probably forget the African fabrics in her textile bag and concentrate on thermal home invasion wear. There probably wasn't a market, yet, for such forward-thinking apparel, but it made good sense. It could be patterned after a ski or scuba suit, and would need plenty of pockets that could run down the side of each leg. There'd be a place for a first-aid kit, and maybe a Taser. A survival knife and a gun holster. And predator repellent and a snakebite kit. And a couple of those nutrition bars and a place to strap on a bottle of water. The home invasion wear could be sold in a line of ultimate sporting goods stores; that way, when you found yourself out in a freezing drizzle, you'd be warm and toasty and ready to take on bad guys.

We were almost at the highway when Teensy slowed to a stop.

"Why would he trick me?" She shuddered, staring at the tree line as if the answer to her question could be found there.

I massaged her arms and hands. "When you figure out how men are, let me know."

Whipcrack voices pierced the night. I turned and stared in disbelief. Behind us, the creamy wash of flashlight beacons panned the road. The men were fast approaching their vehicles, and I wanted us to be far away when they discovered what I'd done.

An exclamation of alarm rent the air. My vandalism had been discovered. Snappish and vexed, their fury carried on the breeze.

Without warning, the one thing I'd hoped to avoid happened.

We'd been enveloped in almost complete darkness, and I'd grown comfortable with the absence of light. I reassured myself that if I couldn't see them, they couldn't see me, which more or less evened the playing field. Except that they were professional killers. Then layers of gauzy cloud cover peeled back, revealing a pale blue sliver of moonlight.

Few cars traveled the highway. I'd expected to see more, but because of the inclement weather, I figured the truckers had abandoned their rigs and were spending the evening in the warmth and comfort of the truck stop miles down the road.

Out of nowhere, the sudden roar of an engine crescendoed down the highway. It simultaneously petrified and thrilled me. I sensed we could literally be seconds away from rescue and grabbed Teensy's hand. We trotted toward the farm-to-market road as headlights topped the hill. Gauzy air hung in the headlights.

I stood in the center of the road, waving my arms to flag down the driver. The car slowed. Caught in the golden wash of headlights, I knew I'd be visible to those horrible men and it terrified me.

The car pulled up even with me. I ducked down and tapped

on the driver's window. The wizened face of an old Mexican stared up at me.

"Please help us. My sister and I—"

I didn't get the chance to finish my plea. The first bullet pinged into the asphalt. A second round ricocheted off the back bumper and grooved the blacktop. The old man floored the accelerator, leaving us in the middle of the road.

We ran as fast as we could, which was like saying we ran like zombies. Gunshots whistled all around, motivating us to pick up the pace. An engine fired up, and I figured we were probably done for.

A new set of headlights topped the hill. Knowing we wouldn't likely be seen by those men until we got caught in the headlights of the oncoming car, I took the chance and dashed out into the middle of the road.

My heart thudded so hard I could count the number of beats pounding my ears.

Chopper Deke.

The men opened fire when he pulled up even with me. Killing the headlights, he powered down the window.

"What the hell?" He took me in, in a glance. The door locks snapped open. "Get in."

As I yanked open the door, a roar unlike anything I'd ever heard grew stronger and louder.

At least thirty bikers topped the hill like the angry wrath of God.

Teensy jostled me aside and sprang into the back seat. "I don't want to die."

"Nothing to fear." Chopper Deke pulled his eyes from mine long enough to look in the rearview mirror. "That's the sound you want to hear."

My foot slipped on the running board the first time I tried to hoist myself up inside the SUV. Once again, just for fun, my name really is Dainty, and I really do seem to have more accidents than, oh, say, someone named Karen or Lorrie or Maggi. On my second try, I got traction and propelled myself into the back seat. The door locks snapped shut. Even though we were returning to the house, I breathed a small sigh of relief.

"Who are they?" I asked, looking through the back windshield. "Are those Bandidos?"

"Worse. They're friends of mine. Vietnam vets. They're here to help. Ever hear of tunnel rats?"

Daddy had a friend in the oil field who'd been a tunnel rat in Vietnam. The way he told it, his friend, while small in stature, was big in courage to willingly crawl through small tunnels, flushing out Viet Cong. Daddy also said it'd made his friend go nuts.

Chopper Deke met my eyes in the rearview mirror. "Nobody comes into my house without permission. Nobody. Lock and load, ladies . . . lock and load. We're about to kick some ninja ass."

CHAPTER THIRTY-FOUR

There's nothing—and I mean absolutely *nothing*—like watching the fiery red dots of laser sites targeting the kill zones of two bad guys. Think concentrated measles that will kill you if you so much as flinch.

Chopper Deke pitched a handful of zip ties at the killers and issued orders for one of them to bind the other's hands behind him. The remaining man was ordered to bind his own hands in front. I knew how these men operated and didn't put it past them to carry multi-gadget survival tools hidden inside their clothing. When they'd both been suitably restrained for the moment, Chopper Deke and I made our approach. As soon as we came within inches, red dots shifted from the torsos of these men to their heads. Only then did Chopper Deke hand me zip ties and tell me to bind their ankles. At the same time, he cut the zip tie of the man who'd bound himself in front, and rebound the man's hands behind him.

"Anything else, toots?"

I found it empowering, the way he made me feel like I was in charge. Halfway to hyperventilating, I said, "Make them drop their pants."

He fixed me in a calculated stare.

"Don't look at me that way. They can probably still kill us. We need to go through their pockets, and I don't want to be anywhere near their junk when I rifle through their clothes."

He nodded. "Rampage," he called out, and a hulking biker

lumbered up. "Hacksaw," he called out again, and the menacing dude who'd given us a ride strode up, too. "Cut their pants off. Then do their shirts."

The next thing I knew, there were two less laser beams aimed at the assassins' heads, and two scary-looking Vietnam vets slicing clothes off with serrated survival knives they pulled from their steel-toed boots.

Chopper Deke said, "Try not to slip, Rampage. Remember that baritone you turned into a soprano?"

Rampage gave a derisive grunt.

Never in a million years would I have thought the Fort Worth Police SWAT team would roll in from the next county, accompanied by none other than Jim Bruckman. Talk about teamwork . . .

Then, Bruckman sauntered over. I didn't know whether to slap him or kiss him. It'd been a long time. He looked at me, his brow furrowed, as if I'd turned into a veritable disaster right before his eyes.

He said, "You have a problem."

"We all have problems."

"No, we don't. But you do. Seek help."

And that's why, when this was all over, I planned to follow his suggestion and work on my tan, buy new clothes, maybe take a little trip, go on an adventure where nobody's chasing me or trying to kill me, and try to conquer my obsession with Harkman Beemis.

I said, "You're just jealous because, compared to mine, your life's boring."

"Boring? My life? Believe me, there's a lot to be said for having an uneventful day."

I fixed him with a long stare. "I've missed you, too, Jim." Then I smiled.

He tried not to smile, but his eyes crinkled at the corners.

He'd moved from the "Bruckman" phase back to the "Jim" phase, and we both knew that we'd returned to a good starting-over point in our relationship.

Without warning, he pulled me in for a quick squeeze and lovingly whispered, "If you ever do anything like this again, I'll kill you in your sleep." Which, right or wrong, led me to believe I might get to go undercover with him again—which is my euphemism for "under *the* cover"—and that sounded pretty spectacular.

The rest would have to wait.

Even though these men were under the control of law enforcement, I knew we still weren't safe since Teensy's cringe-worthy embarrassment, the currently unindicted Ranger Dusty Hill—soon to be ex-Ranger—was still somewhere back at the house, running around un-arrested.

As soon as the first Deputy Sheriff of Parker County arrived, half of the bikers rode up to the house behind us while the other half stood by until the sheriff put the mass murderers in the cage of the patrol vehicle.

We found Dusty Hill in the driving rain, knocked out cold on the porch next to the kicked-in door. He had a big goose egg the size of my fist on the back of his head. As he roused from his stupor, he made noises that sounded like he'd swallowed a mouthful of cotton.

Ever the drama queen, Teensy tuned up like a howler monkey. "See, Dainty, he didn't have anything to do with this."

For this, I was thankful. Because to a Texan, Rangers represent the last bastion of honor and fearlessness, and I didn't want their reputation tarnished. Everyone needs a legend to believe in.

While Teensy tended to her paramour, Chopper Deke and a couple of uniforms from the SO cleared the house. While Chopper Deke sent the cops to the kitchen to help themselves to food and drink, he and I met at the panic room.

"Had to get rid of them," he said, eyeballing the cops raiding his fridge. "Can't be too careful."

As soon as the door to the panic room opened, I found myself dealing with three out of four howler-monkey-like children. The fourth was still curled up in the corner with a blanket thrown over her. Fast asleep, with her thumb in her mouth, anchored in place by a finger hooked over her nose, Avery's stepdaughter looked as peaceful as I'd ever seen her.

Not wanting to be confronted with Boris pulverizing me as he came out of a deep sleep, I carefully shook Dawn awake while softly calling her name.

She blinked a couple of times and pulled out her thumb. With plenty of suction behind it, the thumb came out with a *pop*. Then a disruption in identity took place and her face changed. The young child faded away, and Dawn returned.

"What? Dainty? You haven't left yet?"

"I left. Now I'm back. Get up. Everything's okay."

"I don't understand. When did you leave?"

"A few hours ago."

"Seriously?" She gave a quick headshake. "I must've dozed off."

"Yeah. Let's get you on your feet."

"What's on the agenda?"

"I'm going to work in a few hours, and you're going home."

Panic stricken, she clutched my injured wrist. I winced in pain and she let go. "Please, Dainty. I don't want to go home."

"Fine. We'll get you a hotel room."

"I don't want to go there, either. I want to stay with you. And you're not through teaching me how to be a debutante."

I gently gripped her shoulders. "We're through. You don't have to make your debut if you don't want to."

"What am I supposed to do the night of the ball? Not show up?"

"No, that would be rude. You're going to tell Avery you're not doing it. It's part of being a grown-up, Dawn. Take responsibility."

She wilted at my lecture.

"Look, I'm going to teach you the Texas Dip. That's all that's left, other than refining your manners, and that's an ongoing process. You'll learn the debutante bow, and practice it every day until it's freaking flawless; and if you change your mind at the last minute and decide to debut, then you'll already know how to do it and it'll be perfect. *You'll* be perfect."

"I don't want Avery to present me," she said with the sulky whine of a three-year-old.

"Then pick a different person. Who would you like to present you?"

"Her name is Sally," she said, with her eyes downcast to the floor.

Oh, Jeez.

"Dawn," I said sharply, "it's a traditional debutante ball. You *cannot* have your girlfriend present you. Or be your escort."

"It's either that, or the gardener."

Oh, Jeez.

"What color is the gardener?"

"The gardener is black."

"Oh, Jeez. This is a hundred-year-old tradition, Dawn. You'll be slapping every Rubanbleu member in the face by deviating from protocol."

"Well, maybe they need to be shaken up every now and again."

What was it with the Marshall family? I could almost hear the updated version of a Marshall family "shake-up" making future rounds:

"Did you hear about the latest Rubanbleu scandal?"

"Say it isn't true."

"Oh, girl, not only is it true, it's legendary. That snooty Avery Marshall's crazy stepdaughter, Dawn Patrice, had her lesbian lover present her at the ball . . ."

And no matter how beautiful the makeover, or how gorgeous the dress, or how Dawn scored a perfect ten with her debutante bow, the story of her debut would undoubtedly end with *"and then this big fight broke out, and the police had to be called, and that Dainty Prescott knew all the time that Dawn Patrice was a lesbian—a lesbian, of all things—and she groomed her to make her bow at The Rubanbleu ball anyway."*

"That Dainty Prescott has always stirred up trouble . . . remember the time she . . ."

Fill in the blank.

And while I cringed at the thought of how the debacle would ultimately be retold, I had to admit that whoever did the gossiping would have to concede that Dawn was the prettiest deb who made the best bow, and that I'd done my job.

In the other room, my sister could be heard caterwauling like she needed to be put on suicide watch—all of this over Dusty Hill. With Chopper Deke's help, they'd dragged him inside the house and out of the rain, and, from deep within the den, Teensy tended to his injury, while asking nurse-type questions calculated to orient him to time and place: "How many fingers am I holding up?" And, "What day of the week is it?" And, "What's your birthdate?" Which is when I knew she'd gone on a fishing expedition and was probably already baking him a virtual cake in her head—*Good luck with that one, Ranger Hill; hope you can cook.*

Then, Teensy, who'd studied to become a nurse, apparently figured out that Dusty Hill wouldn't be dying anytime soon from the knot on his head. And when that happened, she reverted to her nurse persona.

"When you're on a ventilator, with six drips running, then you're sick. Otherwise, don't complain to me about your *whittle boo-boo.*"

I thought, *Poor, poor Ranger Hill, I hope you're paying attention . . .*

CHAPTER THIRTY-FIVE

Once things settled down and the men in black were hauled off to jail, I called Gran. Sure, it was late, but I needed to make certain she was all right. She invited us to lunch the following day, and I accepted for us. All of us. We arranged to meet at the Rivercrest house, where she said she would have an important announcement to make.

I figured the big announcement had to do with her and Old Man Spencer, and I hoped she wouldn't tell us they were getting married because that'd mean I'd have to deal with two elderly people. Just contemplating the possibility caused me to have another flashback about a recent and unpleasant encounter with Old Man Spencer. A few weeks before the cruise, he asked me to drive him to his doctor's appointment. To keep a dangerous driver off the road, I said I would. As previously agreed on, I arrived at the Spencer estate around seven-thirty the next morning, only to find he had no idea who I was. Although his memory might've been faulty, his aim was not. He stood on the veranda and pelted me with eggs until I fled the property. Later that same day, he called Gran, ranting that he'd missed his doctor's appointment and blamed it on me for not giving him a ride.

Gran and Old Man Spencer probably shouldn't be allowed to get married. Or go out in public unsupervised. Or talk on the phone. Or even make eye contact with each other.

After I hung up from Gran, I called Gordon to let him know

we were safe and that I'd be back at work in the morning. In that no-nonsense, *je ne sais quois* voice, he told me we had a problem. I figured it had to do with getting rid of the Pixy Merriweather personality without actually killing her off, but I was wrong. Turned out he thought I should know that Rochelle wanted him to fire me now that she's dating Daddy—*Say what?*—because she doesn't want things at work to be awkward if the relationship sours.

If I'd learned anything from working with misfits, oddballs, loners, and cranks, it was that even mercurial employees have their jobs because somebody in a power position wants them working there. So I reassured Gordon that things would never be awkward on my part. Since I'd only scratched the surface of Rochelle's inner craziness, I figured if things didn't work out between her and Daddy, she'd probably commit some vengeful atrocity that would cry out for a lengthy prison sentence. Either way, Gordon had nothing to worry about. He told me to take the next couple of days off and spend it with my family since I'd been through so much trauma with my grandmother's ship sinking and assassins trying to kill me, which sounded like code to suggest that since I was probably in the throes of developing a case of PTSD, I should hang out with undiagnosed mental patients.

Then I pulled Venice aside. "As long as you have those diamonds, those men will never leave you alone. And by *you*, I mean *us*. So what's your plan for the diamonds?"

She sighed. "Chopper Deke should take me up in the plane so I can throw them out."

"Total waste. After all we've been through you should at least put them to good use."

"What would *you* do with them?"

I did a one-shoulder shrug. "If it were up to me, I'd donate them to a children's cancer hospital. They always need money for research and state-of-the-art equipment." Whomever the beneficiary, she should ensure that those men or their lawyers wouldn't come after them.

I left her to reflect. The choice was hers. The only diamond I wanted anything do with was the one Bruckman might one day slip on my ring finger.

As for staying the night at Chopper Deke's, I decided to return to the Rivercrest estate since my two best friends ratcheted up the tension by refusing to speak to each other. Apparently, while safely ensconced in the panic room, Salem and Venice compared notes about their latest boyfriends, who happened to be smart, successful, funny, and good-looking. They also drove the same type of car. Went to the same university. Worked at the same place. Had the same name.

On that note, I said good-bye to each of them, separately, rather than watch them strut around eyeing each other like a couple of gunslingers. Next, I returned my firearm to Chopper Deke. Then I asked Bruckman for a ride back to the truck stop where I'd left Gran's Cadillac.

Amanda and Dawn insisted on coming along. Teensy wanted to stay with Ranger Hill. So the four of us said *au revoir* to Chopper Deke and set out to pick up the Cadillac.

Once we were on the highway, Bruckman turned on the stereo. Hank, Sr., was singing about being in love with a beautiful girl, and Bruckman sang along. I liked it when he sang. He had a good voice. I just wished he'd tune the stereo to one of the pop or rock stations. Even oldies would've been fine.

As Bruckman belted out the chorus, I said, "So that's what's the matter with you? You're in love with a beautiful gal?"

He stopped singing. "Yes. That's what's the matter with me. Does that bother you?"

"What? That you're in love with a beautiful gal?"

"Yeah."

"Of course not. Why should that bother me?"

"I'm relieved you're not mad." Bruckman said. "Because I thought you might find that upsetting."

Amanda cackled. Dawn experienced a bit of lag time, but then she laughed, too.

When we arrived at the truck stop and everyone climbed out of Bruckman's vehicle, I pulled him aside and mentioned an article I'd read because it reminded me of our relationship. The gist of the article was about meeting one person who's unlike any other, someone you can talk to for hours and never get bored, and that you can confide in and they won't judge you because they're your soul mate. The moral of the story was that we shouldn't ever let them go.

Bruckman said, "I agree with that statement."

"So you believe in soul mates, too?"

"Sure. So in the meantime, what do you say we stay together until ours come along?" Then he kissed me hard while the others pretended not to watch and we went our separate ways.

I drove Amanda and Dawn back to Fort Worth and we rode in relative silence. Each of us needed to process what'd happened in our own way, and I just naturally assumed that they were sorting out the events the same way I did. But within minutes, the droning of the tires along the pavement worked its hypnotic effect on my passengers and, before long, Amanda and Dawn fell asleep.

When I rounded the last corner, the headlight beacons panned across the lawn of the Rivercrest estate, illuminating the *For Sale* sign still planted firmly in the ground. Because of the late hour, I let Dawn stay over, installing her in the guest bedroom while Amanda and I took over Teensy's room.

In the middle of the night, I woke up thirsty, and padded, barefooted, into the kitchen. When I flipped on the light, I found Daddy, drunk and stark naked, arguing with the convection oven. Which was as horrible as it sounded until Rochelle LeDuc glided in naked, too.

"Oh, hell no." I may not have said that aloud because I'm well bred and belong to The Rubanbleu, but the sentiment was totally there. Reflexively, I lifted my hands like Jack popping out of the box, which also contributed to the Jack-in-the-box effect. *Poof.*

Train, meet wreck.

"Nice to see you." With my eyes downcast, I discreetly avoided eye contact. Or any other kind of contact.

"I can't tell you what a treat it is to see you at this hour," Rochelle said, oozing sarcasm behind the diabolical smile. Then she helped herself to a bottled water from the refrigerator before steering Daddy back to the master bedroom.

"Au revoir," I said. Which translated to: *I'll need intensive therapy after this, and will probably be locked up in the psyche ward so long that the concealed handgun permit I'm planning to apply for will expire.* Saying it in French didn't make what I'd just seen any less disgusting.

No matter how hard I tried, I could never, ever, ever un-see this. Like, ever.

I blinked back my shock. Apparently, I couldn't even enjoy the transient pleasure of a simple beverage without being bitch-slapped into retreating without it. I headed back to Teensy's bedroom expecting to spend weeks trying to repress the memory.

On my way down the hall, I peeked into the guest room to look in on Dawn. Instead of finding her in the throes of a deep, peaceful sleep, she lay on her side with her eyes wide open.

Boris, not Dawn, greeted me. *"Entrez-vous?"* he said with a grin.

It'd become easier to recognize Boris, but my increasing familiarity with Dawn's personalities made his appearance no less jarring. "Anything wrong?"

"Just listening to the sounds of the house. Who are those other people?"

"Daddy and his flavor of the month. You should try to catch up on sleep."

"I have a bad feeling." Boris threw back the covers and sat up. Dawn had dressed in one of the nightgowns I'd lent her from Teensy's chest of drawers, but appearing as Boris, she looked less waif-like and more imposing. Like a drag queen.

"I saw Angela earlier," I said. "Each time I see Angela, I get a bad feeling nothing good is about to happen. I'm glad I haven't had to deal with Kim Ho, though, since I don't speak Vietnamese."

"Kim *Who*?" Boris gave a derisive snort. "You won't be seeing that bitch anymore." He did a quick knuckle-crack. "I took care of her for good."

I didn't even want to know how one virtual enforcer personality "took care of" another virtual morally bankrupt personality without killing the core personality, but I assumed it entailed a significant amount of violence, and I'd had my fill of that. And here I thought the only thing scarier than psycho, overbearing, insane men dressed in black were psycho, overbearing, insane personalities who bounced around inside the head of a budding socialite.

Boris reached over to the nightstand and turned on the stereo. He tuned the knob to free jazz, which, in my opinion, sounds like a construction crew assembling a metal shanty for giant, angry hornets.

"Try to sleep." I backed out slowly. When I reached Teensy's bedroom, I toggled the lock.

While Amanda snored like a lumberjack in a sawmill, pangs of longing for Bruckman ate away at me. I sent him a text saying that I couldn't wait to be with him again and that if he'd let me come over after the Prescott family announcement, that I'd dress up like a naked lady. He sent me a text back asking if I could dress up like a lady who was making dinner instead.

I smiled. Bruckman's so hot for me. Really.

Exhaustion finally defeated me. For the first time in days, I slept like a chunk of granite.

CHAPTER THIRTY-SIX

Daylight broke with a brilliant red sunrise, and the smell of bacon frying. Rochelle was in the kitchen, looking respectable while whipping up a breakfast of bacon, scrambled eggs, and toast. While she finished cooking, I poured orange juice and set the table. It felt great not having to eat on the fly and it felt even better having anyone but Teensy whip up a meal. Surprisingly, Rochelle turned out to be a good cook.

Midmorning, I encouraged Dawn to call Avery to pick her up. As a family, we Prescotts needed time to bond again, and having extra people around just made it harder. Amanda didn't factor in to the bonding issue because she'd carved out a place for herself weeks ago. She already knew we were kind of eccentric and not only accepted it but embraced it.

Grudgingly, Dawn called her stepfather and within the hour, we said our good-byes on the front steps. On her trudge to Avery's car, she stopped, midway, and gave me a sobering backward look that reminded me of an old dog being led off to the euthanasia chamber. I resisted the urge to call her back.

A while later, Teensy and Ranger Hill showed up to the Rivercrest estate, hand-in-hand. Instead of carrying a purse, she held a cat carrier by its handle. Upon closer inspection, I recognized the glaring chartreuse eyes of the black barn cat from Chopper Deke's house. When they stepped inside the house and closed the door behind them, she released the spring hinge on the pet door and let the cat out. As soon as I saw it dressed in a little vest and Canadian Mountie hat, it occurred to me that one of us ought to check Teensy's breath.

Note to self: That cat's outfit doesn't match. Self to note: Shut the hell up.

She said, "I asked Chopper Deke if he had a scratching post and he said, 'Yeah, two recliners.' I think he was just trying to act mad because Benny clawed the leather, but that was funny, what he said, right? You don't really think he's upset with me, do you?"

I blinked. "You've cat to be kidding." Sometimes I just crack myself up.

While Teensy oriented her new pet to the Rivercrest estate, I pulled Dusty Hill aside. In the middle of a meaningful conversation, I heard Teensy introducing the animal to the sock monkey in her bedroom. Then I heard breakage.

"I can't believe you're dating my sister."

Sheepish, he shrugged.

I got right to the point. "So why her instead of me?"

"Funny story," he said, with his green eyes downcast to his boot tips, "I thought I was asking you out, but it turned out to be her." He gave another noncommittal shrug.

"I knew it," I said, more to myself than to him. So . . . *ha.*

The smell of smoke wafted into the house and when I didn't find Daddy inside, I wandered onto the patio to the outdoor kitchen. I heard a faraway feminine laugh and immediately wished I'd stayed inside. Daddy decided that since we were having a heat wave in the middle of winter, that he's entitled to have "naked barbecue" events in the backyard. I found this out because I walked in on the living nightmare of his and Rochelle LeDuc's naked middle-aged bodies.

He opened the lid on the barbecue pit and stuck the two-pronged fork into the high end on the brisket. Once he flipped it over, he closed the lid and fiddled with the aperture to release less smoke.

"Gran will be here soon. I think she's bringing Old Man Spencer, Daddy, so you have one job—not to set her off on one of her easily provoked rants."

Daddy said, "Can't promise anything."

Sadly, now that Rochelle had invaded my private life, there seemed to be no getting away from her as she flashed one of her evil grins and said, "Won't that be fun?"

With a heavy eye roll, I returned to Teensy's room and flopped onto the bed. Amanda was taking a shower, and I didn't want any part of accidentally getting a sneak peek at that, so I closed my eyes and thought of Bruckman. With my arm dangling over the side of the bed, I planned the lavish wedding that he knew nothing about. I'd happily come to the part where my bridesmaids were walking down the aisle when I felt something sniff my hand. I simultaneously sat, bolt-upright, stifled a shriek, and stared into the toxic green eyes of Teensy's black cat.

Amanda stepped out of the bathroom wrapped in a towel. She and the cat made eye contact. Amanda hissed and Teensy's cat took off.

She said, "Your sister's a psycho."

"Of course she is. If I distilled what I've learned from her since we've been spending more time together, it'd be this: One, Teensy's a psycho; two, under no circumstances do you close your eyes when told to do so; and, three, a smack in the face hurts. Remember, you heard it here first."

About the time Amanda went on a rant about my sister, the house phone rang. And, since Amanda was in closer proximity to the landline, she picked up the receiver. "Prescott residence." She locked gazes with me. "It's for you."

With professional detachment, I answered the call with an

elegant "Hello."

Salem's mother came on the line. Mrs. Quincy apologized for accusing me of being responsible for the whole lodge fiasco and for saying that what happened to Salem was my fault. Then she invited me to dinner the following week and promised to bake lasagna and whip up tiramisu. I cheerfully accepted her apology and committed to the date because she bakes tasty lasagna. The yeast-infected whore.

After I hung up, Teensy locked her cat in what used to be my room and things calmed down. Freshly showered and wearing nice clothes, Daddy and Rochelle joined us in the living room. While Daddy quizzed Ranger Hill with intrusive questions about his life and his job, I silently begged Teensy to keep her mouth shut. But no. Teensy got everyone all stirred up by informing us that she'd gotten a job working in forensics at the police department.

I snorted. "Of course you did. And I've decided to become a rodeo clown-astronaut," in the most patronizing of ways, because no way was that going to happen. I also felt certain that the romance between my sister and Dusty Hill would soon blow over, since Teensy had a surefire way to get rid of guys by confessing her love for them, and then mentioning she stalked the last guy who tried to reject her.

Daddy said, "Teensy, you're an idiot." Her mouth gaped, and I barked out a laugh. Then he turned on me. "You're an idiot, too." Last, he turned on Ranger Hill. "But I reckon you're the biggest idiot of all for not defending my idiot daughter."

If having my daddy call you an idiot didn't just choke your goat, I don't know what would.

I said, "I want to invite Bruckman to join us for lunch."

"Well, that's a great idea," Daddy said, "because what we need around here is more testosterone."

When Gran showed up with Old Man Spencer in tow, I

would've bet my paycheck that her announcement had to do with marrying him. Or getting engaged. My frustration was temporarily sidelined when Gran and I walked into the living room wearing the same outfit.

I'm becoming my grandmother.

Lydia, Gran's maid and cook, accompanied them. Starched and pressed in her simple blue buttoned-down dress, she was as old as Gran, with hands that were strong and slightly misshapen, marked by years of manual labor. But she had a steel-trap mind and every bone in her body was fiercely loyal to the Prescotts. Gran quickly dispatched her to the kitchen with several sacks of groceries in hand, and it wasn't long before we heard water running, utensils clanging, and meat sizzling in the skillet.

I looked Gran over. "You got a new haircut."

"That's not all that's new." She lifted up the skirt of her dress a few inches above the knee. Where pantyhose or silk stockings should've been, Gran wore a leg holster with her S&W .38 in it.

"You got a leg holster? Why?"

"I won't ever get caught off-guard again."

She dropped the hem of her skirt over the holster. The she took off her wrap, hung it in the hall closet, and patted her heavily shellacked hair. "So do you like it?"

"Your hairdo?" I tried to follow along even though my head was still spinning over what kind of imbecile in his right mind would sell my grandmother a leg holster. "It makes you look like Nanette Fabray."

"Nanette Fabray," she exclaimed as she took Mr. Spencer's overcoat and draped it over a hanger next to hers, "why, she's in her nineties."

"Hey, there's nothing wrong with trying to look younger," Teensy said from her place on the sofa, nestled beneath Dusty Hill's arm. Gran snatched the remote control from Teensy's hand and volumed up the sound of the reality show that Teensy recorded the day we left for the lodge.

Gran eyed the television with cold scrutiny. Then she dug around in her purse. "You should be ashamed. I don't care to watch low-class smut like this."

"I could tell you were offended when you put on your graduated bifocals," Teensy said.

I introduced my grandmother to Rochelle. "She works at the TV station, which is like saying she works in hell's complaint department." Figuring they deserved each other, I left them to get to know each other, hoping they wouldn't forge an unholy alliance and gang up on me. How would I know they'd bond over handguns? Next, they'd be having lunch, and . . . *What on earth made me introduce those two harpies?*

When we finally gathered around the table and sat down to lunch, Gran demanded that my father say grace over Lydia's restaurant-quality food. After our collective "amens" she took control of the conversation, starting with how long I'd remain single.

Then she moved on to a new topic. "I have something to say."

She peered out from behind a stub of gray eyelashes and regarded me with a healthy degree of censure. I figured this might be where she put two-and-two together about the faulty electric blanket, but she simply turned to Daddy and stunned Teensy and me into silence.

"Beau, take down that *For Sale* sign. I'm buying your house and deeding it over to the girls."

Say what?

Teensy and I exchanged dumbfounded expressions. I could use a good house, so this definitely piqued my interest.

"Well, I can't very well allow your grown children to continue living with me, now, can I? So I'll write you a check and we can draw up the deed in the girls' names at the title company tomorrow."

I expected Daddy to pitch a fit, but he'd already dug into his braised beef tips and didn't show signs of stopping until they were gone. "Fine by me." His eyes cut to me, and switched to Teensy, and then back to me. "Have fun paying the taxes." He went back to his braised beef tips and risotto.

I looked up expectantly. "Maybe you could help us the first year?"

He stopped chewing. Swallowed. Took a gulp of iced tea. "By all means. Should've thought of that myself. Excuse me."

He disappeared from the table. A few minutes later, he reentered the dining room with two envelopes, one with my name on it and one with Teensy's. "There's fifteen thousand dollars in each one."

Property tax money.

Elated, I almost floated up out of my chair. I ripped open the envelope and shook out the contents while Teensy simultaneously slit hers open with a fingernail. In mine, I found $14,950.00 in Monopoly money. My own father shorted me fifty dollars in fake money.

Teensy said, "Is this supposed to be funny?"

"It is to me." Daddy resumed his place at the head of the table.

Feeling uneasy, I shifted my gaze to Dusty Hill, who looked about as comfortable as a guilty man in a police lineup.

"So, Dusty . . . when will we see you again?" And by "we" I meant my sister, since I expected him to unceremoniously dump her as soon as he hit the Interstate.

Teensy piped up. "He's getting a transfer here." She gave him a loving gaze and then forked a bite of avocado salad into her mouth.

"She's right, I've asked for a transfer to the Metroplex." Dusty shifted his attention to Daddy. "I'd like to see more of your daughter, Mr. Prescott."

"I'm sure you've seen plenty already," Daddy said, with a biscuit hovering halfway to his lips.

Every family has a crepe-hanger. I used to think it was Gran, gracing us with her presence so that she could kill our dreams with condescension. But lately, I realized Daddy was the family ghoul. While everyone else tried to enjoy the lovely lunch, Daddy dabbed his mouth with a napkin and announced, "I'm not giving either of you girls away."

"Aw, that's so sweet." I thought he might be waxing nostalgic about our childhood and how cute we were as children, remembering the times he took us to interesting places and paid for music, voice, and dance lessons so we'd grow up to be well-rounded debutantes. I turned to Teensy. "Daddy doesn't want to give us away when we get married. He wants to keep us for himself."

Daddy said, "I'm not giving you away because you already gave yourselves away."

He'd just wandered into "Don't go there" territory, and I figured he meant that we'd either dragged in early that morning, or didn't come home at all, so therefore, we must've slept with our boyfriends. *Really, Daddy, it's not like we were wallowing on a mattress in a crack house.*

"I wouldn't pull at that thread," I said in a warning tone that threatened him to back off, *or we can compare how long it took for you to fall in bed with Nerissa before you married her.*

Amanda had been relatively quiet, putting her time to good use by helping herself to seconds and chuckling as each of us came under fire.

"I've always had an interest in forensics," Teensy said. "I just thought nursing might be a better fit at the time." This, coming from a twenty-one-year-old who believed that when you bake sweets, all the sugars and calories are released into the oven so you can't gain weight from them. My sister's a moron.

"Why didn't you express this so-called interest before now?" Gran asked.

"I figured I'd catch a bunch of flak from you people. But Dusty thinks it's a great idea, don't you, Dusty?"

Way to throw your boyfriend under the bus, moron.

Turned out she was right to be afraid to tell us. Gran screamed at her, pointing out that she was too smart to waste her high-dollar education on police work, and accused her of being mentally unstable. For her final cannon salvo, she suggested Teensy had put on a few pounds.

On one hand, it didn't surprise me that Teensy, a year shy of a nursing degree, decided on a career in law enforcement. She thought too many people were lawless, including herself, and that people got away with murder, including Nerissa.

Dusty, who'd caught hell from Daddy earlier for not defending Teensy, rallied to her defense. "I support her decision. You can make a good career in law enforcement."

The entire table fell silent. Then we collectively burst into derisive laughter while Daddy stuck his index finger in the air and swirled it around, indicating that Teensy should get on with her story.

For no good reason, the hair on the back of my neck stood up. A sense of peril gripped me. I tried to pass it off as an irrational fear because nobody else at the table seemed to notice anything wrong. But the clink of silverware, the running water, the clanging of pans as they were put into the dishwasher had all come to a halt, and I heard no sounds coming from inside the kitchen. While lively conversation buzzed around the table, eerie stillness crawled in my mind.

Trust your gut.

My mind harkened back to what Boris had said in the wee

hours of the morning—about how he was *"just listening to the sounds of the house"*—when I poked my head into the guest bedroom and found him lying in the dark with eyes wide open.

"Please excuse me." Placing my napkin near my plate, I pushed back from the table and headed for the kitchen.

The swinging door that sealed off the kitchen from the dining room during parties and dinners such as this one had been closed at the start of our meal. When I pushed it open and walked on through, the door sucked shut behind me. At first, I didn't see Lydia. Then my heart caught in my throat. She lay, face down, on the floor with her legs splayed. A blossoming red stain spread beneath her blue dress like spilled paint.

Sucking air, I rushed to her side. When I dropped to my knees and felt for a pulse, a man stepped out from the pantry. Tiger eyes narrowed into the shrewd glint of a predator. Lips thinned into an angry crimson thread. In one hand, he held a bloody survival knife. In the other, he brandished a gun.

He addressed me with only one word, but it was enough to send a lance of fear through my heart.

"Diamonds."

CHAPTER THIRTY-SEVEN

"Don't speak." The man in black eyed me with a stone-cold stare. "If you say one word to alert the others, I'll carve your face up. Understand?"

I nodded, continuing to probe Lydia's neck for signs of life. If she had a pulse, I couldn't feel it.

"She needs a doctor," I mouthed without a sound.

"Where's your friend? The one with the bag?"

"I don't know.

His fingers whitened against the pistol grips. "Think again. I can kill them all." He wagged the gun at the swinging door to indicate wiping out my entire family.

Tiny hairs on my arms stood up like needles in a pin cushion. "I swear I don't know."

"Get up."

"Please—she needs help." My chin corrugated. Lydia never hurt anyone. Cowering helplessly caused me to become more than slightly unhinged. "I'm begging you."

"Get up."

The second time he said it, I had to suppress my gag reflex. When I didn't move fast enough, he stuck his gun in his waist band, yanked me up by my arm, and held the knife to my throat.

Gran called out from the other room. "Dainty, are you on the phone? You'd better not be in there texting your boyfriend. You need to return to the table. This is just plain rude."

I wanted to horse-kick him in the knee, but the man held me

off-balance. I recognized him as one of the two men from Gran's house—not Frankenstein, but the man who broke Gran's two-hundred-year-old antique table. He forced me at knifepoint toward the swinging door.

Gran projected her voice. "Dainty, do I have to come in there and get you?"

The central heat shuddered on, forcing a blast of warm air through the overhead vent.

Melodic and taunting, the man said, "Tell her you're coming out."

Badly shaken, I called out to my family. "Be right there."

The door swung open. Animated conversation died out and I was treated to the stricken faces of my family, a dement, and a Ranger, caught off-guard. Reactions occurred in quick order.

Daddy came halfway out of his chair. "What the hell do you think you're doing?"

Rochelle's fingers whitened around the handle of her steak knife.

Ranger Hill set his jaw in a murderous bent.

Amanda's mouth gaped. She dove for the floor in a fluid move similar to a fireman's *Stop, drop, and roll* drill.

Gran's hand disappeared under the tablecloth. Her eyes thinned into slits. "I know you." She brought her napkin up from her lap and slapped it onto the tablecloth. "You broke my wedding table."

Infuriated, she pushed back from her plate. Glittery blue eyes narrowed into an ice-pick glare, faltering only for a second when her gaze flickered to me, and back to the man who'd hurt Lydia. With a flash of her eyes, she communicated her sleight-of-hand with the napkin to me, telepathically urging me to hit the floor. Dusty reached out a hand and placed it on her arm as if to calm her. I read his movements, too, and knew what I had to do. Knife-be-damned, I back-kicked the man's knee and dropped to the floor.

Orange fireballs rocked the house from three different directions.

The man in black sank to the floor like a cartoon character sliding down the wall. Despite his body armor, he leaked like a sieve.

I scrambled to the telephone and dialed 9-1-1, not for the man in black, but for Lydia. When Gran heard me, she placed her gun on the table and hurried to the kitchen.

Except for when my grandfather died, I don't remember ever witnessing my grandmother cry. She'd always been the strong one. Seeing our faithful Lydia on the floor, with Gran cradling her head in her lap, broke everyone's heart.

CHAPTER THIRTY-EIGHT

After the ambulance left with Lydia and Gran, police processed the crime scene before personnel from the medical examiner's office took the man in black away in a body bag. It bothered me to have police officers traipsing through the house while detectives interviewed those of us who were left. Dusty had already notified his superior that he'd been involved in a shooting; Old Man Spencer sat quietly at the table with his own gun lying next to his dinner plate; and Daddy went outside to pull up the *For Sale* sign.

From my place on the sofa, I noticed a chip in the molding around the swinging door and figured Old Man Spencer had been responsible for the stray shot. I surmised this because I'd seen Gran shoot and I knew she could hit what she aimed at. But Dusty carried the biggest firearm so I figured ballistics experts would determine that the well-placed shot that killed the intruder came from the Ranger's gun.

Daddy came inside, dusting off his hands, and I asked to speak to him, privately, in the den. After I pulled the door to, closing off everyone else from view, he looked me dead in the eye and said, "What?"

My mind cried, *Why can't you see how much we love you?* but I couldn't choke out the words. Instead, I flung myself at him and gave him a tight hug. For a few long uncomfortable seconds, he went rigid.

"Is this about money?" he said. He was so off base that I

couldn't even formulate a response, so I clung to him even tighter. He said, "All right, that's enough," and tried to push me away. I hung on.

Surprisingly, his body wilted and he returned my hug—if you can call a hug putting his arms around me and patting my shoulder in a dead-fish-washed-ashore kind of way.

"No, Daddy, hug me like you used to. Hug me the way you did when Momma was still alive."

I hung on tight. We must've stayed that way for a minute or more, but I never let go because his hug might have to last me for the rest of my life. Dishrag-limp arms unexpectedly took on the strength of a python. His body trembled as he squeezed the breath out of me.

"What'd I do wrong, Daddy, to make you hate me so much?"

All of a sudden, his body shook so hard that it frightened me. He let out an uncontrollable sob. Next thing I knew, he lifted me up on tiptoes and buried his face in my neck. Hot tears streamed down my skin and dampened my hair. When he finally relaxed, he sighed so hard that it sounded like his body deflated.

"I find it hard to look at you most days—you look so much like Pixy. I can't apologize enough for bringing Nerissa in to help care for your mama, but you girls were off at college and I needed help. How could I have known that venomous bitch would kill to take her place?"

He couldn't even make eye contact with me, and choked out the words with his lips pressed against my ear. But his epiphany didn't make me let him off the hook, or say, *It's okay, don't cry, it'll be all right*, the way he used to do when I skinned my knee or took a fall. Because my mother's death wasn't all right, things would never be normal again, and on a primitive level, Teensy and I blamed him for what happened. But I also realized I'd probably always be there for him, no matter how many foolish choices in women he made.

As quickly as he hugged me, he regained his composure. "Don't tell your sister. Fear's the only way to control her." Then he left me standing, alone, and struck out to find Rochelle.

Hours turned into a half-day. I sent Gran a text message asking her to wish Lydia "Good luck" for me, only the autocorrect wrote, "Good-bye." When Gran didn't return my calls, I knew she was peeved, so I phoned the hospital for news. Their only update confirmed that Lydia was still in surgery.

Knowing that the fourth man was still running around, unarrested, I placed calls to the Parker County Sheriff's Office to confirm that the two men they had in custody hadn't escaped and were being held without bond. I saw no use in calling the Dallas hospital closest to Gran's house to inquire about Frankenstein, because I didn't have a name for him, and I didn't think asking whether they'd treated a guy wearing black with multiple gunshot wounds would get the response I was looking for.

Note to self: Next time this happens, go through the man's wallet and check ID.

Self to note: So, you anticipate these shootings will become a habit?

I glanced around the living room. Daddy and Rochelle were conspicuously absent, so I parted the curtains and looked out the window. Sure enough, the ENG van, or Electronic News Gathering van, from WBFD had set up in front of our estate and Rochelle was outside giving an interview. I suspected she'd called the station in order to ensure WBFD-TV got the big scoop for the day and wondered how this would go over with Daddy once we settled in to watch the evening news. To her credit, she wore clothes.

Finally, law enforcement officials vacated the Rivercrest house, leaving nothing but a few business cards and a couple of bloody floors to clean up. While I found the bloody dining room floor repugnant, something inside me snapped when I looked in the kitchen where Lydia's blood had pooled. Nothing I could say or do would change what happened. No amount of rubber gloves and bleach in the world could make me clean up the unspeakable horror that remained on the kitchen floor.

Choked with grief, I broke things. After I composed myself, I contacted a specialist who cleaned up crime scenes. When I found Daddy and asked him for the money to pay for the job, he said, "It's not my house anymore. Good luck with that." Then he offered to lend me a stack of Monopoly money. Fortunately, we were able to barter. He wrote a check to pay for the cleanup, and I agreed to give him pointers on how to dump Rochelle without getting killed in the process.

Late in the day, as moths fluttered beneath the amber glow of the porch light, Dusty left Teensy with a tender good-bye kiss. After he pulled his pickup out of the drive, headed in the direction of the Interstate, all she could talk about was Dusty-this and Dusty-that. Then she sent him a text—lewd, no doubt—and the phone chimed with a return message. Teensy jumped up and screamed with excitement.

Then her eyes bugged and she made a face scrunch. "What the hell?"

"What is it?" She handed over her cell phone so I could read the text from Dusty.

The message read: "I think we should move in." Followed by, "Typo. Move on."

I figured we'd have to put Teensy on suicide watch for the next few days, but I really couldn't blame him for not wanting to spend any more time around our family. Just because I accepted the fact that we'll one day be attending family reunions in a mental hospital didn't mean potential mates had.

CHAPTER THIRTY-NINE

A week later, instead of behaving like a tranquilized wolverine, Teensy got out of bed, dressed in an exquisitely tailored suit, and set out for her new job in the forensics lab. I still couldn't believe the PD hired her. They obviously didn't contact me when they did her background investigation, or I would've told them she couldn't even use a hair dryer without electrocuting herself, much less become qualified to operate an electrostatic lifting device and other expensive equipment.

As far as life at the TV station went, Gordon concocted a story about Pixy Merriweather that he hoped would pacify viewers. Apparently, Pixy would be sorely missed at WBFD-TV now that she'd returned to London to take a lucrative broadcasting job, but Channel Eighteen viewers were assured that they'd be seeing more of Dainty Prescott in the future, which sounded a lot like job security for *moi.*

Rochelle stopped seeing Daddy a few days after the shooting, leading me to believe the Prescotts were too conflict-habituated even for her.

Things at work continued to be weird with Chopper Deke, since he kept letting me know that I owed him "big time" for saving our collective skin—and skin was *not* the word he used. Finally, he confronted me in the foyer of WBFD and told me what I could do to repay the debt.

Recalling what happened after his daredevil rescue getting Teensy back from Mexico, I went on the offensive. "I'm not kissing you, so forget it. And unless you take Monopoly money, I can't pay you."

"Let me see you naked."

"Out of the question." I flounced off and ate lunch in my office with the door closed.

The next time I ran into him in the hallway, he said, "I ate a breath mint. French kiss me for one minute."

"No."

"Turn around and let me squeeze your ass."

"Hell, no."

"Hug me."

"No. I don't want you grinding yourself against me." Then I remembered how he'd wanted to take me to meet his girlfriend, so I asked him why.

"She gets a little cocky thinking she's the only woman in my life. I figured if she saw me with you, she'd try harder."

"Or get jealous and kill me." Then it occurred to me that Chopper Deke wanted my celebrity more than he wanted me, so I came up with a payoff I could live with and offered to cook dinner-for-two at the Rivercrest estate, with a promise to wait on them hand and foot.

When he agreed and we shook on it, I walked away stunned. At this juncture, I figured if I could press Aspen Wicklow, the darling of nighttime news, into service, I wouldn't have to be alone with Chopper Deke and his lady friend, and she'd get two celebrities for the price of one.

Dusty Hill kept refusing Teensy's calls, partly because of the ongoing investigation during which authorities determined he'd fired the fatal bullet that killed the man in black, and partly because Teensy had reverted to the hostile, passive-aggressive Teensy, and not the sweet and loving side she'd previously shown him. Back to her lonely, bitchy self, she transferred her anger to me and started leaving sticky notes on food in the refrigerator and the pantry.

I came across one stuck to a carton of juice that read: *I spit in the OJ so it's mine. Just sayin'.*

I took a laundry marker and wrote over her note: *I spit in it, too. Is it still yours?*

When I found a threatening sticky note stuck to a box of brownie mix, I tacked my own over hers that read: *Teensy, you psycho, don't bother scrawling hostile, passive-aggressive comments on the food. It only makes you look bitter. And fat. And you better stop laughing when I eat cereal. Or crackers. Or anything else. Like you're trying to make me nervous. Or make me think you poisoned my food.*

The next time I opened the refrigerator, I found a sticky note tacked to mine: *I'm going to poison your food, Dainty. You figure out what.*

I resumed having regular lunch dates with Salem and Venice, but not with both of them together. They still weren't speaking, even though they dumped their shared boyfriend via text messages.

As for Lydia, the hospital discharged her to my grandmother's care. She'd been staying at Gran's estate ever since. Now, my grandmother waited on Lydia instead of the other way around. Since Amanda resumed her pizza delivery job and was staying at my grandmother's estate too, I imagined Gran was eating more comfort food and a lot less country club cuisine.

I remained blissfully unaware as to whether Gran and Old Man Spencer were still dating. I didn't think so. Gran finally concluded that he only wanted to hang out with her because she could still drive at night, plus, it turned her off knowing that he couldn't hit the side of a barn with his lousy aim.

As for Dawn, she called to ask me if I'd meet her when she told Avery that she didn't want to make her debut later in the year. She said she'd been in therapy and actually sounded much healthier than the last time we'd seen each other.

We met at a French-inspired café located within walking distance of the TV station. Since Gordon insists that the on-air talent wear gem-tone colors because he thinks they photograph better, I changed out of the bright red suit one of our sponsors donated to wardrobe and resumed my day wearing Rubanbleu-approved clothing. By that, I mean camel-colored slacks in tropical wool gabardine, a cream-colored duppioni silk blouse, and a matching camel-hair coat. I chose the high neckline because it covered the cat scratches on my décolleté. Teensy's psychotic cat woke me up—not by kneading my chest—but by pouncing on the laser pointer Daddy shined on my cleavage.

After I gave the barista my order, I took my morning latté and waited for Dawn at a bistro table near the front door. I chose it because of the newspaper that'd been left on the tabletop, since I wanted to see if the local paper carried anything about Nerissa's trial or an update on the men from the lodge. It didn't, and for that, I felt grateful.

Then Dawn walked in. I took her in, in a glance: beige slacks, an ivory shirt, and a cappuccino colored wool overcoat—all Rubanbleu approved. With her sandy blond hair made into a halo by the morning sun slanting through the windows, she greeted me in the traditional European way, with a *mwah, mwah* of kisses to each cheek that never actually grazed my skin. Then she shed her coat and sat across from me.

Even though I'm broke, I offered to treat Dawn to a latté. Knowing that I'm a penniless heiress with a trust fund that had so many locks on it you could penetrate the gold Bullion Depository at Fort Knox easier than I could get to my money, Dawn showed good breeding by politely declining.

I studied her new look. An extra swipe of mascara had darkened her lashes and a good haircut framed her pale face. With the proper amount of makeup and eye shadow, her piercing blue eyes had never been more mesmerizing, and I felt obliged to meet her gaze if for no other reason than to search for extra personalities.

"How's Teensy?" she said in a polite way that actually made it seem like she truly cared. "Is she still seeing that Texas Ranger?"

"No, but she finally swore off drinking after she and her friends went dancing the other night."

"Aw, she drank so much it made her sick?" Dawn affected a frowny-face.

"No, a really creepy guy in the corner kept ogling the girls on the dance floor all evening. When Teensy complained and pointed the guy out to the bouncer, the leering man turned out to be a coat rack."

Dawn laughed. "How's Venice? It was nice of her to fix my dress. I don't think I really showed her the appreciation she deserved."

"Why, Dawn—*Patrice*—you're actually becoming a delightful person," I said with mock surprise. "As for Venice, I got to listen to her gripe about how early she has to get up tomorrow to board the red-eye to Colorado. She's going skiing. Then I got to listen to her complain about how tiring skiing is."

"Whatever happened to all those diamonds?"

"She sold them and sent the money back to Africa so the kids she worked with at the orphanage could have a water reclamation system and bathrooms built."

"Do you think that'll keep those men at bay?"

"It's a start."

The overhead bell jingled. Our eyes slewed to the door. Avery had walked in and was scanning the breakfast crowd for our faces. Seeing us, he waved and sauntered over to join us.

What started as innocuous chit-chat soon fragmented into years of anger and betrayal. When Dawn insisted that she wouldn't participate as a debutante in The Rubanbleu ball, Avery's face hardened.

He stiffened in his chair and steepled his fingers. "Oh, you're doing it, Dawn."

"The only way I'll make my debut is if my girlfriend escorts me."

Her announcement took a few seconds to soak in. Avery's face changed again, and this time, pure rage set in. It occurred to me that the only reason Dawn wanted me there was to ensure she came away unscathed and unharmed. I expected Boris to pop out any minute but he stayed under the radar, making me wonder if he'd gone for good after having been successfully integrated into Dawn's core personality. The thumbsucking child also failed to emerge, as Dawn held her own.

Then Avery turned his wrath on me. "Did you know about this?"

"About what?" I resorted to my practiced look of innocence.

"Don't play dumb with me."

I did a one-shoulder shrug.

"I want my money back."

"I did exactly what you asked me to do, Avery. I groomed Dawn for the ball. It wasn't conditional on whether she actually attended. And let me just tell you that I earned every cent. Look at her." I directed him with a sweep of the hand. "She's beautiful and articulate; her manners are impeccable, and she passed the Dainty Prescott test with flying colors. You should be proud."

By the time they left the coffee shop—and they didn't leave together because Avery stormed out in the middle of our conversation—I still couldn't predict whether Dawn would make her debut into society. What I did know was that, even though I hadn't originally planned to attend The Rubanbleu ball in the fall because it had disaster written all over it, I instantly knew that I wouldn't dream of missing what might become the Marshall debacle of the twenty-first century. And if it all went to hell, well, like stepfather like stepdaughter.

As for me, I shrugged into my camel-hair overcoat and glanced around the room for any sign of Frankenstein and the other men. I knew I'd be looking over my shoulder for a long time, but I wouldn't let them stop me. I had a job to do: read the news, become a success, and get the attention of people in a major market who could help me get my own talk show.

The overhead bell jingled and a throng of customers piled in from out of the cold. While I stood at the door and waited for them to pass, a look of recognition sparked in one man's eyes.

"Hey, aren't you Dainty Prescott from TV?"

"Guilty."

"Oh, man, I love you. Hey, everybody, it's Dainty Prescott. Can I get your autograph?"

He thrust his folded newspaper at me and I scrawled out my name using his pen. Then I flashed him and everyone else in the room a beauty pageant smile, because we at WBFD love our viewers. Since I'm perpetually on the hot seat, and because favorable call-ins to the station are what make Gordon view me as more than just a celebutante, I acted like my usual charming self.

Then I made it out the door and started my walk back to the station with the sirens of ambulances and emergency vehicles screaming all around me. I picked up my pace. It looked like we might have breaking news and I wanted to be on hand to deliver it.

And the best part was, this time breaking news had nothing to do with me.

ABOUT THE AUTHOR

Sixth-generation Texan **Laurie Moore** received her B.A. from the University of Texas at Austin and entered a career in law enforcement in 1979. In 1992, she moved to Fort Worth and earned a degree from Texas Wesleyan University School of Law in 1995. She is currently in private practice in "Cowtown" and lives with her husband, a rude Welsh corgi, and a Zen Welsh corgi. After celebrating almost thirty-four years as a licensed, commissioned peace officer, she recently retired from law enforcement.

Laurie is the author of *Getting Mama Out of Hell, Deb on Air—Live at Five, Wanted Deb or Alive, Deb on Arrival—Live at Five, Couple Gunned Down—News at Ten, Woman Strangled—News at Ten, Jury Rigged, The Wild Orchid Society, The Lady Godiva Murder, Constable's Wedding, Constable's Apprehension,* and *Constable's Run.* Contact Laurie through her website at www.LaurieMooreMysteries.com.